WHAT JULY KNEW

EMILY KOCH

Harvill *Secker*

LONDON

1 3 5 7 9 10 8 6 4 2

Harvill Secker, an imprint of Vintage,
20 Vauxhall Bridge Road,
London SW1V 2SA

Harvill Secker is part of the Penguin Random House group of companies
whose addresses can be found at global.penguinrandomhouse.com

Penguin
Random House
UK

First published by Harvill Secker in 2023

A CIP catalogue record for this book is available from the British Library

penguin.co.uk/vintage

ISBN 9781787301030 (hardback)
ISNB 9781787301047 (trade paperback)

Typeset in 10.75/15.75pt Scala OT by Jouve (UK), Milton Keynes
Printed and bound in Great Britain by Clays Ltd, Elcograf S.p.A.

The authorised representative in the EEA is Penguin Random House
Ireland, Morrison Chambers, 32 Nassau Street, Dublin D02 YH68

Penguin Random House is committed to a sustainable future
for our business, our readers and our planet. This book is made
from Forest Stewardship Council® certified paper.

MIX
Paper from
responsible sources
FSC® C018179

For Gwen

The bravest are the tenderest;
The loving are the daring.

Bayard Taylor

I

20 July 1995

July Hooper was always hot because she was born in a heat-wave. This rare ribbon of information was handed over by her grandma, who promptly realised she had pulled it loose from the forbidden fabric of conversation that was July's mother, and pinned her lips shut.

Nobody ever talked about Maggie Hooper's life, or the awful way it had ended.

But this rare ribbon could not be woven back into the secrets, re-threaded into the silences, or even fixed into place with an embroidery of deceits. So Yaya cut it free with a sharp change of conversation ('Time we opened the Rich Teas, don't you think?') and July slipped it into her pocket to twist around her fingertips. Many years later, July would wonder how else the day of her arrival had affected her. Was her habit of not telling the truth due to the fact that she was born into a world of lies? Did the violence around her birth destine her to commit an act of it herself?

But she wasn't thinking these things today. Because right now she was only ten. And she didn't know about the lies, or the violence – not yet. In fact, she wasn't ten for another two hours and twelve minutes, but nobody had ever told her the exact moment of her arrival. It was one of the things on the Big List of Questions in her notebook, where her mother's identity was cleverly disguised with celebrities' names in case her father ever flicked through. There were important topics on the list, like the time of day she was born, but also lower-level queries that occurred to her at a rate of about two a day. So 'What time did Princess Di give birth to Prince William?' was sandwiched between 'Was Frank Bruno right- or left-handed?' and 'Did Celine Dion prefer skirts or trousers?'

Right now July Hooper was sitting on the shady edge of the playground, her notebook in her lap, as her long auburn waves were twisted into a tight coil by her best friend, Katie-Faye. 'Did Eric Cantona like mint choc chip ice cream?' July scribbled when Katie-Faye stopped tugging at her hair to glance across the playground and refer to the backs of Sylvie Rose and Helen Knight's heads. Those two girls had identical buns at the napes of their necks, held in place with nets and bobby pins, and encircled with bright yellow scrunchies, which made them resemble a pair of sunflowers, though July wasn't sure any part of Helen Knight deserved comparison with something so friendly and cheering.

'How do they make them look so perfect?' Katie-Faye asked.

'They have good genes. Straight, silky hair.' July dropped her pen and winced as Katie-Faye resumed yanking her own locks into submission. 'And Elnett.' She gagged a little at the thought of the hairspray's overpowering scent. Her stepmother loved it, which was one of many reasons to be suspicious of her. 'Can we stop now?' she asked. 'My feet are in the sun.'

Katie-Faye released July's hair and made space for her to shuffle backwards.

For the past few weeks July had been racing out into the playground straight after lunch to secure their place next to the wall in a coveted strip of shade which diminished as the afternoon bell drew nearer. 'This heat is deafening,' Yaya had said last night on the phone when she called to wish July a happy birthday eve. 'Don't you think?' July had nodded into the mouthpiece while her lips circled around a question. She had no idea what her grandmother meant, but that was not unusual. And whether or not it was deafening, this heat certainly was *something*. Relentless, exhausting, suffocating.

It was the kind of heat that would cause blood to boil in the weeks that followed; the kind of heat that would convert irritation to rage and sadness to madness. But most of the other kids didn't seem to notice its weight pinning them down – especially not the likes of year five's self-designated queens, Sylvie and Helen, who grew more tanned and blonde with every day that carried them closer to the end of term.

'Who are they playing now?' Katie-Faye put her hand over her eyes as she squinted into the sun.

'I can't see.'

Sylvie and Helen were crouching on the other side of the playground where a steady stream of other children had been taking them on at pogs.

'You're kidding,' July said, standing to get a better view. 'It's Darren Emerson.'

Darren had stacked his collection of bottle-top-sized cardboard discs in front of Helen, who was preparing to attack his carefully arranged tower with her metal slammer.

'Have you seen the way she throws it down?' Katie-Faye imitated the motion with a flick of her wrist. 'Maybe that's why she wins so many.'

July lifted her baseball cap and wiped the sweat from her forehead. 'Helen wins so many because she cheats. You realise you're only meant to keep the ones you flip over?'

'That's not how she plays it. She takes an extra—'

'Three. Exactly. Those aren't the rules.'

'But she has the special Three Slammer. So she can have . . . oh.' Katie-Faye stood up too. 'She made that up?'

3

'Why is he playing them again?' July asked. Last week Helen had cheated Darren out of his entire collection. 'He must have bought some more. What a wally.'

'He'll be okay. Mr Silk's keeping an eye on them.'

July scanned the playground. Sure enough, there was the year four teacher, who was known for doling out the harshest punishments in the whole school, twisting his bow tie as he leaned against the main door. He was closely following the unfolding pogs battle.

July looked from Mr Silk to her classmates and back again. Sylvie and Helen were about to get into major trouble. 'I can't let her do this.'

She lifted the hem of her dress and tucked it into her knickers, exposing the backs of her pale and freckled thighs, embossed with the imprint of tarmac.

'Here we go again,' Katie-Faye said, leaning back against the warm bricks of the school building as July stretched her arms above her head to limber up and twisted her pink baseball cap so that it was facing backwards.

She stepped out from the shade and marched across the playground.

July possessed eighteen facts about her mother. They were all she had been able to glean in her ten years – mostly from her Grandpa Tony, because her father found it unbearably painful to talk about his late wife. These facts were a precious collection of ribbons, scraps of thread and shreds of cotton, the odd button and a sequin – each torn from the patchwork quilt of actions and wishes and feelings that, sewn together over a lifetime, had made up her mother. They fitted neatly on to one side of A5 – the List of Mum – which she kept folded and hidden in her pants drawer (her father would never go in there). Number 7 was: Maggie Hooper loved to dance.

The passion was hereditary. As July made her way across the

playground, she began to twist her hands above her head, lunged to one side and launched into one of her painstakingly choreographed routines. At home she rehearsed her moves to the accompaniment of the biggest chart hits of the moment, carefully recorded from the Top 40 on to tape each Sunday afternoon. But that was in her bedroom, or the kitchen if she needed more of a slide underfoot. It was different in the playground. *Better.* As she skipped from left to right, her school mates stopped what they were doing to watch. Girls held their hands over their mouths and pointed at July's exposed knickers. But she kept dancing, spinning round and round. One boy from year six shouted, 'Look at Ginger Nut go!' Still, she kept dancing, flicking her hips from side to side as she imagined strutting down a catwalk. And then Helen and Sylvie turned round.

Helen started laughing, elbowing her best friend. But there was no smile on Sylvie's lips. Her skin flushed a deep red, her eyebrows disappeared up under her blonde fringe, and her mouth hung open.

July stopped a metre away from them and began voguing, staring Sylvie straight in the eye. As she framed her face with her hands to strike her fourth favourite pose, Sylvie jumped to her feet. 'Are you insane?' she hissed. 'Stop it. Stop right now.'

Grabbing July's arm above the elbow, she dragged her away, turning to shout at July's audience over her shoulder. 'Show's over. Stop staring.'

When they made it to the far corner of the playground and were hidden behind the climbing frame, Sylvie pulled July's dress out of her knickers and spun her round so that they were face-to-face. She was surprisingly strong, considering she was so slight, and almost a head shorter than July. 'Why do you do this to me?' Sylvie asked, squeezing her arm. 'Why?'

July sniffed – there was always a whiff of sweets on Sylvie's breath and it was a favourite game of hers to get close enough to work out what she last ate. It was strawberry Millions today. The scent took July back to the happiest moment of her life, when her father had taken her to see *Aladdin* at the Odeon. He hated it, but eight-year-old July had been in awe of the genie who could grant wishes. Daddy had bought her a pick 'n' mix with white chocolate mice and a scoop of strawberry Millions, and she'd eaten the peppercorn-sized pink balls one at a time to savour the treat. The best bit, though, had been when he had let her hold his hand for a whole minute as they made their way through the exiting crowd while the credits rolled.

Sylvie shook her. 'Just because it's your birthday, you can't—'

'Dance?'

'Humiliate me.' Sylvie dug her fingernails into July's skin. It wouldn't be the most painful thing to happen to her that day, July thought briefly as she looked at her birthday badge, pinned to the front of her dress. She always ended up doing something to infuriate her father on her birthday; there would be a new Lesson to learn, she knew that for certain.

'Why did you do the pants thing?' Sylvie went on. 'Why not just dance? That would embarrass me enough, if that was your aim.'

'I had to be sure you'd stop,' July said. 'You're not a bully, Sylv.'

Sylvie let go of July's arm and rested her head against the frame of the monkey bars. 'Not this again.'

'You don't want to do it.' July wiped Sylvie's palm sweat from her skin. 'It's all Helen. You're better than this.'

'Is this about Darren? I hate to break it to you, but she's done it anyway, despite your little show.'

July looked over towards the pogs battleground, where Darren was hanging his head as Helen stacked her winnings. July shrugged. 'But *you* didn't do it.'

'I hate you so much.' Sylvie flattened some flyaway strands of hair to the side of her head. 'Look what you've done. The stress has made me frizzy.'

July was about to dispute that this was her fault when the afternoon bell rang.

As the clock struck twenty-six minutes past two, July turned ten.

If July had known this, she would have said that Miss Glover's classroom was the perfect place to celebrate. This was her favourite place in the world, other than the reading den in her bedroom wardrobe. Here, she knew what was expected of her. She loved the scratched surfaces of the desks, the smell of the board markers and the huge sheets of sugar paper pinned to the walls: they all featured in her top four favourite things about this haven. The fourth was the faded outlines of rectangles that were revealed on the sugar paper when Miss Glover took down an old class project to replace it with a new one – the opposite of the way July's freckles came out in the sun, the way her mother's must have done too. (Number 8 on the List of Mum, via Grandpa Tony: Mum had freckles all over her face and arms. A small cluster next to her left eye formed the shape of the star constellation Cassiopeia.)

As July waited for Miss Glover to finish writing on the whiteboard, she bounced her legs under her desk and fiddled with her badge. It had a big green 10 on it and a little butterfly in the middle of the zero. To July it looked like the butterfly wanted to escape from the confines of its oval-shaped cage, but when she'd made that observation over her bowl of cornflakes this morning, her father had slammed down his coffee and it had spilled a little on to Auntie Shell's newspaper. 'Oh, Mick,' her stepmother had said, blotting the puddle with a tea towel. July thought they were about to have a Level One argument (angry words, no shouting, no broken objects), but then Auntie Shell turned to her instead. 'A little gratitude would be nice, July.'

Miss Glover cleared her throat, and July looked up. Her teacher was fanning herself with an exercise book. On the board she had written in her lovely, looping script, 'Summer Project: Who are you?' Then, underneath, 'Six pages of A4 about a member of your family.'

'Settle down,' Miss Glover said with a huge smile. Miss Glover would be a much better stepmum than Auntie Shell. She wouldn't have bought July a birthday card with a trapped butterfly on its badge. 'And Sylvie Rose, for the thousandth time, stop tipping your chair back, you're going to smash your head open.'

Sylvie giggled from the row of desks behind July.

Miss Glover continued: 'Your summer project is going to be all about one of your relatives. They can be alive or dead, but the idea is to choose someone you know very little about. Imagine you are asking them the question, "Who are you?"' She paused. 'I'd like you to think about whether it's important to know where you come from, to work out who you are yourself.'

As Miss Glover continued to brief them about the project, July made notes in her exercise book, her hot hand making a damp patch where it rested on the lined paper. She wrote the words 'Maggie Hooper' on the page, enclosed them in a heart and then scribbled them out.

'I'd like you all to come up to see me for a quick chat about it,' Miss Glover said. She sat behind her desk, still fanning herself, and crossed her legs. She was so elegant, in a beautiful blue dress which matched her eyes. 'While I do that, the rest of you can read the handout on your desk about researching your family tree.'

July chewed the end of her pencil as Zoe Anderson approached Miss Glover's desk. There were four more people whose surnames came before July's in the alphabet – she didn't have much time to produce a possible subject to impress Miss Glover with. Last year she had come top of the class with her summer project about her favourite hobby (reading), and she wanted to see that look on Miss Glover's face again, when she had said, 'Excellent work, July.' But Mum wasn't helping: all July could see when she closed her eyes to concentrate was her in a long floaty skirt and her red hair at her shoulders. *Someone you know very little about.* No. This month July had made a resolution – to do everything she could to please her father – and besides, there was no way she could find out enough about her mother to fill six pages. Nobody talked about her. Ever. The last time July had asked one of her Big List questions (did Mum like The Beatles?) Daddy had smacked her so hard across the face that her glasses had flown across the room and landed on top of the shepherd's pie Auntie Shell had placed on the table. He didn't Teach Her a Lesson like this every time she asked something, so it was often worth the risk. He never actually replied, but she could occasionally get a sense of the answer from his reaction. Take the time she asked if her mum liked dancing, for instance – he'd nodded without realising, right before he'd sent her to her room.

July strained her ears to hear what Zoe was saying to Miss Glover, hoping for inspiration, but she couldn't make anything out – Ben White had opened the window at Miss Glover's request and the school caretaker was outside their classroom mowing the grass. The droning sound of the motor wasn't helping her think.

Who could she use as her subject? Daddy didn't speak to his parents much these days so he probably wouldn't be happy if she wanted to know more about them. Could she ask Yaya about her first husband, July's grandfather? Or what about . . . she didn't know much about Auntie Shell, but did she count as family? She wasn't really her aunt at all, or her mother.

'Darren? Up you come.' Zoe was returning to her desk and Miss Glover beckoned to Darren Emerson. As the next three people went to speak to her, July fantasised about a prize-winning project all about Maggie Hooper, full of anecdotes and packed with interesting made-up facts, like how her mum spoke seventeen different languages, and how she used to kiss July on each ear every night before she went to sleep because that was their special routine, and how she was a former world champion meringue baker. She imagined Miss Glover's comments and ticks in the margins, in her favoured bright pink marking pen, and one of her yellow heart-shaped sticky notes on the front page revealing July's final mark: '10/10 plus a bonus point for difficult spellings.'

'Miss Glover?' Sylvie shouted over July's shoulder. 'Can we shut the window now? The grass is making my nose itchy.' She sneezed dramatically. It was obviously fake; Sylvie didn't get hay fever. Only Joni Klein and Toby Miller had hay fever in their class, everyone knew that. But Miss Glover waved her hand without looking up and said, 'If you must.'

Sylvie wove her way through the desks to the window. After shutting it, she dropped her pen next to Sarah Lewis's desk, and as she crouched to pick it up, July saw her stretch a hand into Sarah's bag and pull out some pogs.

July's cheeks burned.

'July?' Miss Glover was beaming at her.

She should tell Sarah. She should tell Miss Glover. But she couldn't. She couldn't tell tales on Sylv. Instead, she picked up her exercise book and made her way to the front of the classroom.

'Have a seat.' Miss Glover patted the chair next to her. 'Any thoughts?'

July screwed up her face and shook her head.

Miss Glover lifted the stapler from her desk and spun it in her hands. 'What about your mother?'

'My mother?' July's voice went loud and strange. Everyone in the class stopped talking and looked up.

'I'm sure we would all love to hear what you can find out about her, and it would be a lovely thing for you to do, for yourself.'

'My mother.'

'You could write about what you told me – why she called you July. And why she was sure you were a girl.' (Numbers 5 and 6, passed on by Yaya. Five: her mother had called her July-bear when she was in her belly, because she was due in July, and the name had stuck. Six: a woman had stopped her in the village one day and said her bump looked exactly like her own had, when she was pregnant with her daughter.)

July scribbled over her mother's name in her exercise book so hard that she ripped a hole in the paper, before closing it and pushing it on to her teacher's desk. 'I don't want to do it about my mother.' As soon as the lie skipped off her tongue, Mum was there. Sitting in the corner of the room. Red hair. Flowing green skirt. July could only see her out of the corner of her eye, but she knew she was there, like she was whenever July lied. She knew she would disappear if she tried to look directly at her, so she stared at her hands in her lap instead, enjoying her hazy presence a few metres away. July had started doing this after Darren Emerson told her in year four that dead people hear your lies. He'd said that if you lie too much, they come down to earth as angels, to watch over you and make you feel bad if you fib. 'My mother told me so,' he'd said. The first lie July had told was to Auntie Shell, that same evening, when she'd served spag bol drizzled with ketchup for dinner. 'I don't like spaghetti,' July had said. The row that ensued was standard practice in their house – a Level Two (angry words, shouting, no breakages). But what was not standard practice was the serene figure who had appeared by the window. Darren Emerson was right! But it didn't feel like Mum was cross with her, not like he had suggested. Not that night, or on the hundreds of other times she had lied since. It felt like a secret, one that only July and her mother knew.

'Why ever not?' Miss Glover asked.

July felt two pairs of eyes on her – Miss Glover's and her mum's – and she wanted to say, *Yes. I'll do it.*

She cleared her throat. 'I suppose . . . I could write about the crash? How she died, I mean.'

'The car accident . . .' Miss Glover said softly, frowning a little. 'Yes, that could feature.'

But then July felt her father's familiar hand glancing off her left cheek like a skimmed pebble making its first contact with still water, and her forehead tingled with the possibility of his approving kiss – something she was yet to experience but was certain was within her reach, if she could only be a better daughter. 'No,' she backtracked. 'I can't.' *He wouldn't like it.*

'You can't?' Miss Glover sighed before continuing in a hushed voice, staring at July intently. 'July, I really—'

She didn't get a chance to finish. From the back of the class, Neil Gibson piped up. 'Maybe you'll find out your mum's not dead after all,' he yelled. 'Maybe she's in Spain, on the run from—'

'Mr Gibson!' Miss Glover stood up, pointing with the stapler. 'That is enough!'

I'm used to it, July wanted to tell her teacher, as Miss Glover sat back down. Sometimes the boys said mean things about her mother, coming up with all sorts of dramatic stories. She knew to ignore them, because Maggie Hooper had been hit by a car and killed eight years ago, on July's second birthday. Everyone knew that. She glanced in her mother's direction, hoping to find the courage to speak, but in all the commotion with Neil, she had slipped away.

When she looked back, Miss Glover was flicking through July's exercise book on the desk between them. She looked a little paler than before Neil Gibson's outburst. 'Maybe you'll find out ways in which you are similar to her?' Miss Glover slid the book towards her.

'There is zero resemblance.' July said, repeating the words

her father had spat at her so many times. 'I can't do the project on her. I don't know anything about her.'

Miss Glover lowered her voice again, but this time it felt more like she was sharing a secret than scolding her. 'You could always pad out the six pages with some photos.'

July tucked her thumb into her fist and squeezed. 'I only have one.'

Miss Glover shook her head. 'Well, then, maybe you could—'

'My pogs!' The cry that interrupted the teacher came from Sarah Lewis. 'My Lion King pogs. They're gone.'

Miss Glover dropped the stapler on to her desk. 'Gambling,' she muttered. 'Pure and simple.' Standing, she said, 'Sarah, quieten down, please. Now what seems to be the problem?'

July pulled her thumb out of her fist and exhaled. The interrogation was over. With Miss Glover distracted, she used the opportunity to return to her desk, but not without checking her pocket first. It was still there, a small, heavy disc of metal, warm against her fingertips. Her beloved slammer – a very satisfying trade, even though it had cost her the rest of her collection six months ago. It was white and silver, with red lettering across it, reading, 'Enjoy Diet Coke.' She smoothed her thumb over it as she sat back behind her desk. Number 17 (a rare fact her father had let slip, one afternoon after a few beers): Mum's favourite drink was Diet Coke.

She hid it in her hand to bring it to her lips, then whispered into her closed fist, 'Who are you?'

As she carefully dropped it back into her pocket, her elbow knocked the desk, and her exercise book fell into her lap. A corner of pale yellow paper poked out from between the pages, and July pulled it free. It was one of Miss Glover's heart-shaped sticky notes.

July read the neat pink writing looping across the heart in three lines. *'She didn't die in a car accident.'*

13

Heat rose to her cheeks and she looked around her to check if anyone had seen, but everyone else was engrossed in the pog drama. She stuck the note on to a blank page and reread the message, hunched over her desk. When had Miss Glover put it in her book? Was it even meant for her? Maybe it was a mistake?

But who else could it be for? *She didn't die in a car accident.* Miss Glover had been strangely insistent that July should do the project about her mother. Was this why?

What did Miss Glover know that July didn't?

2

20 July 1995

Sylvie watched July through her sunglasses as she approached their usual meeting spot, just up the road from the school entrance, by the house with the wonky apple tree in its front garden. You couldn't miss her, with her thick white sun cream: she looked like a snowman that someone had adorned with a school uniform, a red wig and a lame pink baseball cap. But, no matter how dorky she looked, if you asked anyone what they thought of Sylvie's stepsister, they'd use a combination of *nice, sweet* and *good-natured.*

If you were to ask Sylvie's classmates or teachers to describe her, they wouldn't opt for any of those words. Sylvie knew this: she knew they thought she was trouble, a bully's backboneless accomplice. And, above all, an attention-seeker who was mostly concerned with how she looked. In year four, after the particularly awful discovery that her father had a new baby daughter, she had tried to cheer herself up by telling a group of friends at Helen's Makeover Sleepover that she was destined to be a film star. Even though she hadn't meant a word, it had instantly become an accepted fact. Helen, July and Sylvie herself talked about her future, dazzling career as if it was a sure thing. Even Miss Glover said things like, 'Another Oscar-worthy performance from Miss Rose,' when she explained why she hadn't managed to do her homework. But truly, she couldn't care less about fame. What Sylvie wanted, more than anything in the world but would never admit to anyone, was a happy family.

But the problem was July. Secretly, Sylvie was quite fond of her stepsister. She was funny and sharp in a way Sylvie wished she could be. She didn't care what other people thought about her, whereas Sylvie spent most of her time wondering who liked her and, if they didn't, why not? And Sylvie had read enough 'Guess Who This Ugly Kid Turned Into!' celebrity features in her magazines to know that when they grew up, July's rusty curls and freckles wouldn't be weird any more – they'd set her apart in a good way. But Sylvie Rose would rather dance with Darren Emerson at a school disco than say anything nice to her stepsister. She was always messing everything up for that perfect family Sylvie coveted – July was slowly stealing her mum's affections, and made her new dad angry all the time.

So, as July got closer to Sylvie, she didn't see a girl who liked her; she saw grumpy Queen Sylv, waiting at the meeting place Her Majesty had decreed in the Stepsister Rules as being an acceptable distance from school to be seen together. Everyone knew they lived together, so this didn't make a lot of sense to July, but she went along with the charade. In school hours she had to pretend they were only classmates.

'Get a move on, November,' Sylvie said, peering over the top of her sunnies. July sighed; she was extremely jealous of her stepsister's ability to wear such glamorous accessories. She had tried, several times, but she could hardly see without her proper glasses. So then she'd attempted doubling them up, with the arms of her purple-rimmed shades and her glasses taped together with plasters from Auntie Shell's first aid box, but that hadn't worked either. It was easier just to go without.

'There'll be birthday cake at home,' Sylvie said. 'And I'm starving.' She swung her rucksack on to her shoulder and strode away from July, hopping off the pavement on to the road. She liked to walk right down the middle, keeping her feet on the white dashed lines. 'So, what's it going to be this year?'

'Chocolate, I think,' July muttered distractedly. She was busy scanning the road for cars as they walked, a few metres apart, her head full of pink handwriting. *She didn't die in a car accident.* But of course she did. Number 2 on her list: her mother died after being hit by a car. July had been there, hadn't she? She had seen her mother die. She remembered it; she had nightmares about it. Her father had never really spoken of it of course, because it was too traumatic for him. But there were things that he *had* said, even so. There was that time when he'd shouted at her after she ran into the road to get her football when it rolled away. 'Don't you remember what happened to your mother?' he'd asked her. And then there was that day when a hit-and-run was on the news, and July had cried, and Shell had asked her, 'Is this because of your mum?' as she gave her a hug. Why would they have said these things if it hadn't happened?

Miss Glover must have made a mistake.

Sylvie interrupted her thoughts. 'Not the cake, dummy. What's your birthday screw-up going to be? Shall I tell him you showed everyone your pants at lunchtime?'

There was something about July's birthday that made her do stupid things – Daddy always said so. She had a list in her notebook so that she could learn to be better: spilled the water at dinner (1994), said she missed her mum (1993), didn't get to the toilet in time (1991). Her seventh birthday was not mentioned because July had rammed that memory into a tightly shut mussel shell at the back of her mind. She needed no reminder of that day's Lesson: never wear lipstick in front of Daddy, even if she was playing dress-up. The scars of the punishment were invisible but still fresh – she jumped whenever someone turned a tap on; she heard her father's words every time she splashed water on her face. 'You're a disgrace,' he'd said. 'What if someone had seen you? What would they think of me?'

July gripped the straps of her rucksack by her chest. 'You wouldn't.'

'Only because I'm still too mortified to think about it.'

July lifted her chin. 'Anyway, this year's going to be different.' She hoped with every one of her thousands of freckles that her words would be proved true. In a few weeks' time, July would think back to this day, and remember saying these words. 'This year's going to be different.' She would ask herself, if she could spin the clock back, would she still want the year to be as different as it had turned out to be?

But Sylvie didn't reply, and this set July's stomach swirling. Sylvie always had a snappy retort ready to toss back at her like a rounders ball urgently needed at second base. They walked on in silence. The village was strangely quiet – the water in the bay behind them was flat and soundless as a huge lake, there were no dogs barking, nobody was drilling holes in walls, no cars were starting. There were no seagulls swooping overhead, calling towards the waves – even they couldn't be doing with the sun's brutal offensive. July wafted her hands by her face to generate a breeze.

The afternoon's stillness was like a pause, as if the very air they breathed was waiting for something.

I can do this, she thought. She would make every effort not to irritate him this time, and she had a plan to help her achieve her goal. Sylvie spent most of her time trying on other people's personalities for size – why couldn't July do the same? She would channel somebody else, a person her father liked. She would be more like Sylvie. That year, so far, her stepsister had emulated several different actresses and popstars – most recently, Rachel from *Friends*, becoming even more obsessed with her clothes than usual and making several disastrous attempts to blow-dry her hair. The only person she didn't copy was her mother, who was the one that she was most like, in July's opinion. But if you tried telling Sylvie that, she'd reach over at breakfast and tip your cereal into your lap, milk and all. July knew from experience.

July had lagged behind, and ran to catch up with Sylvie, who was still tightrope-walking along the middle of the road. 'How can you tell when someone is lying?'

'They stare at the little finger on their right hand.'

'Really? Every time?'

Sylvie threw her head back and laughed. 'I'm joking, dummy. Why do you need to know?'

'Something Miss Glover said.' July kicked a discarded lollipop stick across the pavement.

'What, she lied to you? Was that when she was talking to you about that stupid project?' Sylvie was not a big fan of schoolwork.

'Don't worry, it doesn't matter.'

'I'm going to do mine on my great-grandfather, but make it up. It's not like she can check any of it.' Sylvie was always doing devious things like this and getting away with them; July was always biting her tongue to curb her desire to dob her in to their parents. One of these days she'd get into big trouble, and July would probably have to get her out of it.

July wondered if she could study one of *her* great-grandfathers. What about her father's grandfather Leonard? The one named on that bench along the coast path, where her father made them stop whenever they walked past?

'You should do yours on your mum,' Sylvie said as if reading her mind. 'Like Miss Glover said.'

'Hm.' July bit her lip. Should she tell her about Miss Glover's note? Could she trust her to keep it secret and not go blabbing to their parents? 'Do you think she definitely died in a car crash?'

'Why do you ask that?' Sylvie stopped in the road and turned to face her.

July looked around to check there was nobody else about, then dropped her voice. 'Miss Glover says my mum didn't die in a car crash.'

'No way.' Sylvie's eyes widened. 'What are you going to do?'

'I don't know.'

'You've got to find out what happened to her. All the more reason to do your project on her.' The words rushed out in a flurry of excitement, before Sylvie paused, and added, more slowly, 'There's obviously more to find out.' She shrugged and looked at the ground.

There was something in the way she spoke. Something in the exaggerated nonchalance as she lifted her shoulders. 'You know something,' July said, her fingers itching to grab at a new ribbon. What colour would it be? Yellow? Silver? 'You do, don't you? Tell me.'

Sylvie started walking backwards along the road. 'Why do you suppose Mick never talks about her?' she asked. 'And why does he hate your grandma so much?'

'What do you know?' July studied her stepsister's face, but there was nothing to go on apart from the beginnings of a smile. She wished she could see her eyes behind the tinted lenses of her sunglasses.

'How would *I* know anything?'

She was right. Daddy might prefer Sylvie, but July couldn't see him telling her secrets about her mother, even so. July didn't realise she had contracted every muscle in her body until she released them all in a slump of disappointment and a sigh. For a moment she had thought Sylvie might have been able to take her up to number 19 on her list, or even beyond. She was so close to twenty. Imagine!

Sylvie held her arms out to the side for balance as she edged backwards. 'Don't you think there's some big family scandal he's covering up?'

July was beginning to wish none of this had happened – the note, this conversation. She wanted to yell at her stepsister, to explain that she hadn't meant to get into any of this. That all she wanted to know was what her mother's favourite colour was. Whether she preferred banoffee pie or trifle. What it felt like to hold her hand.

But she couldn't ignore Miss Glover's message. She couldn't ignore the feeling that something wasn't right.

'What kind of scandal?' she asked quietly.

'Like, I don't know. Maybe Neil's right – maybe she never died. Imagine if you found out she was actually in prison –'

'No way. She wasn't that kind of—'

'– or what if she had a whole other family somewhere?' Sylvie put her hands to her face in mock shock, opening her eyes and mouth wide.

'Stop it! Stop saying stuff like that.' July covered her ears with her hands. 'Not funny.'

A blue car appeared on the brow of the hill, hurtling towards them, engine growling.

'Watch out!' July shouted. 'Sylv, get off the road!'

Sylvie spun round but the car braked and turned off into a cul-de-sac. She laughed. 'You've got to stop worrying about me getting run over.'

'You know why I don't like it.' July rubbed the slammer in her pocket. She squeezed her eyes shut as she heard the screech of tyres and the crunch of metal, and tasted blood. If her mother hadn't died in an accident, how on earth could she remember these things?

'It's not going to happen to me, okay?' Sylvie said. 'This is, like, the tiniest village in the whole country.'

It wasn't, but July nodded anyway.

'Although, it would make a good story, wouldn't it? When I'm doing my interview on *Oprah*. How I broke every bone in my body and everyone was sure I wouldn't survive.' She clutched at her chest and faked a sob, before grabbing hold of an imaginary microphone and mouthing 'Thank you' to invisible crowds of adoring fans. 'But it gave me the determination to become the star that I am today.' She spoke as if delivering an awards acceptance speech, then flounced her way further along the white line on the tarmac, blowing exaggerated kisses towards the bungalows on either side of the road.

Was this what Daddy liked about her? Should July attempt to be more dramatic? Should she make more effort with her appearance? She pushed her shoulders back and tried to walk along the pavement with more elegance, but it didn't come naturally to her, as Sylvie always liked to point out: 'I'm, like, a prima ballerina,' she'd say. 'You're more of a baby elephant.' (The truth of this was undeniable. In last year's school play Sylvie was a swan, and July had been cast as a thunder cloud.) Within a couple of steps, July stumbled over her school shoes and fell to her knees.

As she picked herself up off the pavement, Sylvie called out, 'Catch!'

Something hit July on the ear and bounced into the road, narrowly avoiding falling down a drain. She scooped it up. It was a small parcel, held together with a silver hair bobble.

'For she's a jolly good fellow, for she's a jolly good fellow . . .' Sylvie sang as she joined her on the pavement on the corner of their road. 'Open it, then.'

A present, from Sylvie? This was unprecedented. July squeezed the cylinder-shaped package. 'Lip balm?' she asked, her fingers tingling. She pulled apart the wrapping paper, which turned out to be the family tree handout from Miss Glover's lesson. Inside: not a lip balm, but something infinitely better. A stick of perfume. 'Oh my God, oh my God! Is this White Musk? But I thought you said—'

'You were more of a Dewberry girl. Yes. But now that you're ten, like me, maybe you're mature enough to pull it off.'

July removed the cap and twisted the base to push the bar of solid perfume out of the top. It took quite a lot of turns. 'I think they sold you a dud,' she said as a tiny stub of it finally appeared.

'Yeah . . . about that. It's because it's my old one.'

July didn't care that it was a second-hand gift. 'Thanks so much. It's really kind of you.' She smeared the greasy balm across her cheeks like invisible streaks of war paint; she was ready for battle, and just as well. She would need it for this summer, for these sweltering weeks that would forever stay with her.

'What are you doing?' Sylvie grabbed July's hand, her face aghast. 'Why would you do that? You put it on your neck, or your wrists. Jeez.'

'But then I can't smell it *all* the time.' She pulled her hand out of Sylvie's grip and applied some more down her bare arms, inhaling deeply. It smelled of rose bushes and woodland; it smelled of Sylvie. This was really going to help her be more like her stepsister, she thought as they turned into Harmony Close together. 'Thank you,' July repeated, bringing her rucksack round to her hip and dropping the perfume inside. 'I didn't expect you to get me anything.' She sniffed her forearm again and smiled to herself.

'Yeah, well.' Sylvie smoothed her hair back towards her bun. 'You never know when it might be the last . . .' She paused outside number 7 and cocked her head. 'Oh, great. Listen.'

The village silence was punctuated by a steady thudding noise. The swirling in July's stomach began again.

'Sounds like Mick's in a boxing kind of mood,' Sylvie said. 'Always a good sign.' She adjusted her hair once more, then strode off towards their driveway, where July's father's van was parked.

July waited for a moment, staring at their house and listening to her father's fists finding their target, over and over again. She removed her cap and held it between her teeth as she tightened her ponytail. *I must look my best.* Sylvie always looked immaculate.

But then she caught a whiff of the White Musk. What had Sylvie been about to say, before? July took her cap out of her mouth. 'Wait up. Sylvie!' She hurried past number 5's privet hedge. 'What did you mean? The perfume. You said you never know when . . . What did you say?'

But Sylvie either didn't hear, or pretended not to. She walked up the driveway of number 3 Harmony Close, pushed through the door and disappeared inside.

3

20 July 1995

The air was even more sluggish inside. All the doors and windows were open but there was no breeze. 'Hello?' Sylvie called through the hallway, as they removed their school shoes and peeled off their sweaty pop socks. July watched her stepsister carefully, copying exactly what she did: shoes on the rack, socks in a neat pile on the stairs. Rucksack hung on her peg. Tissue from the table under the mirror, blotting her face. Daddy was fastidious about tidiness in the house, and Sylvie was usually the only other member of the family who met his demands for cleanliness and order.

'Sylv?' July whispered, blotting her own sweaty face. The tissue came away smelling of White Musk. 'What did you mean?'

'Nothing,' Sylvie hissed, before stalking off into the kitchen.

July hung back to take a few deep breaths. The thudding noise had stopped, and she could hear her father talking to someone in the back garden. Not just talking – but laughing. That was unusual, on her birthday. *This year will be different*, she repeated to herself in between exhales. This year there would be no need for her fingers to be slammed in the crockery cupboard; her goldfish wouldn't get flushed down the toilet (RIP Dirk); she wouldn't be sent to bed early while Sylvie got to stay up and watch television with their parents. She squeezed her eyes shut. *I can do this.*

'There you are, birthday girl. Good day?'

July opened her eyes to find Auntie Shell standing in front of her. She did her best Sylvie impression and shrugged. (Was that what her father liked about her? The way she treated her mother with such disdain?)

Auntie Shell took a sip of her tea. She said it helped to keep her cool, but that was grown-ups for you – always doing things that didn't make any sense and giving you inadequate explanations. 'That good, hey? How about a present then, to cheer you up?'

'For me?' July grinned, unable to maintain the impression of her stepsister.

Sylvie appeared behind her mum. 'What's she got?' She sounded suspicious; a strop was brewing.

Auntie Shell opened the living room door, and the girls followed her in. The room was dark, the curtains drawn to keep the heat out (another grown-up thing with no decent explanation – keeping the curtains closed made the room hotter, July was convinced, but she still did as her stepmother asked and left the ones in her bedroom drawn whenever she wasn't in there). Auntie Shell put her tea down, crouched by the TV and flicked a switch.

A happy pink glow filled the room, spreading from a glass tube standing next to the settee on the coffee table.

'A lava lamp?' July knelt in front of it, watching the bright orange pool of wax at the bottom and willing it to start sending bubbles into the pink liquid above. She had wanted one ever since Sylvie got hers at Christmas. 'It's amazing, thank you,' she said without taking her eyes off it, not wanting to miss the first sign of movement.

'It'll take ages to warm up,' Sylvie said. July could tell from her tone that she'd crossed her arms and was scowling. 'I'm not sitting here for an hour. When are we doing the cake?'

26

'Not yet. Have an apple if you're hungry.' Auntie Shell was on a mission to make Sylvie eat more fruit, to balance out all the sweets.

Sylvie slammed the door as she left the room, and July turned to look at her stepmother. Her white work blouse was stained pink in the lamplight, her blue skirt tinted purple. It was strange to see her in these colours – Shell only owned clothes that were red, white and blue. 'Very patriotic, your mother,' Daddy had said once. 'Which one?' July had asked. (That night she had scribbled, 'Was John Major patriotic?' into her notebook.) The change of colours made her look like such a different person, in fact, that for a very short moment July considered giving her a hug.

'Your dad helped me choose it.' Auntie Shell said it with softness and a smile, but July knew she was lying.

'I'd better go and see him. Say thank you.'

'Of course,' Auntie Shell said, picking up her mug and following July out of the room. 'Let's see where he's got to.'

Outside, Sylvie was standing in the paddling pool, whose contents glinted in the afternoon light in a bid to attract July's attention, teasing her. The water was her father's ally, not hers, and it knew she would never step foot in it, no matter how hot she was. Her father was leaning on the garden fence, talking to Tim from next door, and he turned to look at July as she walked outside on to the lawn.

'Here she is!' he said. 'My number one girl.'

Auntie Shell lit a cigarette on the patio as July pushed her unease behind a smile for her father and waved at their neighbour. Tim was smaller than her dad – he must have been standing on something to be able to see over the fence. He raised his hand to his forehead in a salute. He always did that – July assumed he had once been a soldier, although he didn't look remotely like one.

27

'Good day at school, Four Eyes?' her father asked.

July nodded, touching her glasses as he used her nickname. Katie-Faye had once asked her if she minded him calling her that, after hearing her dad shout it at her in the playground once when it was time to go home. But July didn't. She liked that she was special enough to him to have a pet name, and she knew that it was just a little joke. And anyway, he only called her that when he was in a good mood, which must mean it was a term of affection.

'I've been showing Timothy here how it's done – how to stop the bag swinging all over the place.' Her father tapped his gloved hands together and nodded towards his punchbag, which hung from the pear tree at the end of their garden. 'You know what I'm talking about, don't you, July?'

'Punch, don't push,' July parroted.

'You don't mean to tell me you've actually been listening?' He grinned at her.

A proper ear-to-ear smile.

This beat the lava lamp. It was even better than the perfume – a smile from her father was the best present she could have hoped for. She didn't care if he was only being nice to her because Tim was there. But as her cheeks flushed with pleasure, she also felt her chest tighten – what if she said something to mess it all up? She glanced at Sylvie for ideas about what to do next. Her stepsister was inspecting her nails. July knew *she* would have had something clever and funny to say in response to her father, but July's mind had gone as clear as the sky above them, so she turned her gaze to the ground. The grass was yellow and crunchy under her feet, curling downwards as if it was scared of the sun that had scorched it.

'And remind me, what were you saying about the numbers?' Tim asked, saving her from having to reply. She looked up to see her father move away from the fence.

'Let me show you again,' he said, getting into position in front of his bag. He loved to get his boxing gloves out – 'blows away the cobwebs', he always said, often adding that it was 'important to keep the old ticker strong'. He brought his hands up in front of his face and his arm muscles bulged, his skin darkly tanned from the biceps down due to endless days tending the gardens at the Big House on the hill. Her father was the strongest man in the village, July thought with pride. With his shirt off like this, he looked like that Greek god in her encyclopedia, Zeus. The one with the lightning bolt raised above his head, who ate his wife because he was afraid their child would become stronger than him. This gruesome fact obsessed July and she frequently revisited the page to double-check it.

She couldn't imagine Daddy ever being afraid of her.

Her father shuffled his feet slightly. 'You want to land three to six punches at a time. Not just one or two. No more than seven, at a push . . .'

They all watched. Auntie Shell, Sylvie, July and Tim. What was Tim thinking? Probably what an impressive man her father was. Everyone thought so. That's why they called him Big Mick. But his large presence was about more than his physical size: everyone loved to talk to him and laughed at his jokes. A pillar of the community, they called him. July wondered if they realised, as she did, that this was only one side of him? That he was like one of the blood-red anemones she used to poke in the rock pools on the beach – morphing into two entirely different creatures, depending on their surroundings. Sylvie had laughed when July made the comparison – 'Only you could come up with something as dorky as that' – but July couldn't shift the idea from her head. When the anemones were submerged in water, their tentacles came out, wiggled around and grabbed on to your finger; but when they were exposed to the air, they hid away and looked like shiny little gobstoppers, clinging to the rock. When Daddy was outside their house and exposed to other people, he was the most charming man she had ever known and hid the parts of himself he didn't want to be seen; but when he was submerged in their home, his bad temper took hold. Did July have two sides to her, she wondered? She was tall like her father and they both loved white bread and watching *The Bill*. But were there bits of her mother in her, too? And if there were, how would she know how to spot them?

As her father grounded his feet, July closed her eyes and listened as he threw three punches. Smack, smack, smack. He paused, and she knew he'd be dancing on his toes. She heard his voice in her head: 'When you're not moving your hands, make sure you're moving your feet.' Then he grunted and there were another five punches in quick succession.

'See?' he asked.

July opened her eyes as he dropped his arms to his side.

'Three to six – it's enough to show your opponent who's boss, but you can get out of there before they come looking for revenge.'

'Bravo,' Tim said, clapping. 'You'll have to let me come and have a go some time.' He was being polite, July could tell. Tim didn't look like the kind of person who would be interested in boxing. But he liked her father, because he told him how to get the perfect lawn and what to spray on his roses to keep the aphids at bay. Tim turned to July. 'Happy birthday, Julie.' (He always got her name wrong.) 'Wait till you see what's under that.' He winked and pointed to the opposite side of the garden, where a green throw from the living room was covering a large object, leaning against the fence, next to Auntie Shell's cast iron bird bath.

'Don't you go anywhere,' her father said to Tim as he removed his gloves. 'Stick around for the big reveal.'

July stared at the throw as he walked over to it.

'A gift from your magnificent Gaga – sorry Tim, family joke, that's what we call her gran,' he said. (That wasn't strictly true – it was what *he* called her because he thought the name Yaya was 'insane'. When July was born her grandmother said she used to feel nauseous every time anyone called her Granny, so she'd chosen Yaya instead. 'But the woman has no Greek heritage to speak of,' Daddy would say. 'She should be sectioned.') He grabbed a corner of the throw and pulled it away.

Underneath was a shiny turquoise-framed bike.

'For me?' July ran forward and shrieked. 'Oh my God!'

'The Lord's name, July,' Auntie Shell warned from the patio.

'Sorry,' July muttered as she knelt and turned the pedals with her hand. She was still new to the whole church thing. Since Auntie Shell had convinced Daddy that he and the girls should come along with her to Sunday services, there were all sorts of new rules, including not using the Lord's name in vain, but Daddy still said 'Christ alive' and 'Jesus wept'. July couldn't work out if it was her father who was excluded from the rule, or Jesus.

There was a splash behind her. 'No way,' Sylvie said, emerging from the paddling pool. 'Shell, that's not fair.'

'It's *Mum* to you. How many times?'

'She probably can't even . . .'

But July was too in awe of her gift to pay much attention to her stepsister moaning to Auntie Shell. There was a huge pink bow tied around the handlebars, which was pretty enough to have been a wonderful present all on its own. Her own bike! She could go anywhere she wanted.

'. . . could share it,' Auntie Shell was saying. July was aware of their voices and the smell of Auntie Shell's cigarette smoke getting closer. 'What do you think? Sylv could show you how to ride it.'

'I know how to ride a bike.' July's voice came out even quieter than usual, and the others didn't hear her. 'I used to have one; I just got too big for it.'

'Freely you have received, now freely give,' her father said, and July turned to see him throwing his arms wide. He didn't notice Auntie Shell roll her eyes behind his back. 'Corinthians, that is.' This too was a new development in their lives since Church Sundays were imposed – he was forever pulling Bible quotes out of his back pocket and pinning them to whatever else he was saying.

Sylvie crouched beside July, putting her hand on the saddle. 'It's easy, really,' she said. 'It's all about balance.'

July grabbed hold of the handlebars.

'Play nice, girls,' her father said. 'I had a bike when I was their age. Didn't you, Tim? I used to go out with my mates every weekend. The adventures we had! Everyone had one.'

'Did Mum?' July couldn't help it – the words flew out of her mouth. What was wrong with her brain? It was like that lava lamp, with questions constantly bubbling to the top. But, unlike the strange moving shapes in the lamp, there was no stopping her questions – her brain had no off switch. *Stupid July. Stupid, stupid, stupid.* Everything had been going so well.

July looked at the bike, not daring to move.

But Tim was still there.

'Excellent question.' July could hear tightness in her father's voice. 'Do you know what, I have no idea.'

She moved her lips, but no words would come out. *I'm sorry, Daddy. I didn't mean to.*

Sylvie spoke instead. 'Don't be cross with July, Uncle Mick. She's probably asking because she's doing a project on her mum for school. She needs to find out about her.'

July turned to Sylvie, her eyes wide. What was she doing? Sylvie gave her a sly smile, pushed her out of the way and grabbed the handlebars.

'What a lovely idea,' her father said as July turned to face him – she knew she had to. His voice was bright, but his mouth was set in a grim line.

'I'd better be going,' Tim called over the fence. 'Dora won't walk herself. Lovely to see you all.'

'Good man. Let's grab a beer some time.' July's father didn't take his eyes off her as he spoke. When Tim had gone, he said, 'A project on your mother, is it?'

'It's not about her,' July stammered. 'Miss Glover said I should – but I – I don't want to write about Mum.'

As soon as the lie left her lips July felt a soft, cool hand slip into hers. She could see her mother standing next to her. 'Ask him about the car accident,' her mother whispered into her ear, although it wasn't her voice July heard – it was Miss Glover's. July shook her head in response. She couldn't ask that. He'd be too angry.

Her father stepped towards her as she knelt with her back to the bike, and she shivered as his body threw hers into shade.

'Time for cake.' His nostrils flared. 'Shall we?'

4

20 July 1995

'Wait a second.' Auntie Shell laughed as they stood around the two layers of chocolate sponge on the kitchen table. What was funny? Didn't she have that sicky feeling in her tummy like July? Didn't she realise something was about to go wrong? 'At least let me light the candles.'

'No need for that.' July's father picked up the knife from the table and stabbed it into the cake. 'I'm hungry, aren't you, Sylvie?'

Sylvie nodded.

'Candles drip wax all over the icing,' her father said. 'July? Close the doors.'

'Mick . . .' Auntie Shell looked at July, then back at him, smiling still.

'It's okay,' July said, tightening her grip on her mother's cool fingers. 'Daddy's right. I'm hungry too.' She shut the patio doors – or French windows, as Shell liked to call them – removing the layer of protection that her neighbours' listening ears offered. Whatever happened next would be contained within the four walls of the open-plan kitchen diner her father was so proud of. He handed Sylvie the first piece of cake, straight into her hands, then stuffed the second wedge into his own mouth.

'What are you two like? Animals, the pair of you!' Auntie Shell opened the crockery cupboard. 'Here, July, let's you and me have plates, like civilised people.' She cut two more slices and handed one to July on a chipped plate. July sat on the couch, and the large leather cushions became her mother's arms, embracing her as she sank into them. She forced herself to take a bite of the cake. Her mother's arms tightened around her waist, securing her on her lap.

'What's wrong with you?' her father asked. With every one of his words, the room temperature increased by a degree. *Hotter, hotter.* Any chance of breeze had gone when she closed the doors, and a spider of sweat crept down the back of July's neck, but she didn't dare move to brush it away. 'Why can't you be grateful?' *Hotter, hotter.*

She spoke through a mouthful of cake, staring at the plate. 'I am.'

'Girls, why don't we see if the lamp has warmed up yet?' Auntie Shell wasn't smiling or laughing now. July heard it in her voice. Out of the corner of her eye, July saw Sylvie move to the doorway.

'Stay where you are,' her father said. *Hotter, hotter.*

July still couldn't meet his eye. 'I'm sorry, Daddy. But Sylv got it wrong, honestly. I'm going to do it on Great-Grandpa Leonard. I told Miss Glover I wouldn't do my project on Mum. I explained—'

'What have I told you about discussing family business?' *Hotter, hotter.* 'I bet she loves sticking her pretty nose in. What does she say about us?'

Miss Glover's voice, from her mother's mouth, murmured again into her ear. 'Was there really a car accident?'

'Answer me, then. What does she say?' *Hotter, hotter.*

'Nothing.' July whispered the word. The sweat was trickling down her back now, getting blocked and absorbed by ripples in her school dress. The plate shook in her hand. 'I told her I couldn't do the project on Mum.' It was the truth, and it was the answer he would want her to give, wasn't it? So why did it make him so angry? That's what July asked herself later, as she rubbed the bruise on her face. That's what she thought about as Auntie Shell covered it with make-up the next morning before school. That's what she wondered as she sat behind her desk in their classroom, letting her hair hang in a side parting like Auntie Shell had shown her, so that nobody would know that she had been awful enough to deserve such a Lesson.

She didn't see her father lunge at her, but there would have been no getting away from him even if she had. His hand slammed against the side of her head as Auntie Shell shouted, 'Mick, don't!' The arm of the couch caught her as she toppled with the force of the blow, and her plate spun out of her hand, shattering as it collided with the floor. July made the mistake of looking around for her mother – but of course that meant that she disappeared. She was gone. Instead, July saw her stepsister by the doorway, staring at the ground and playing with the sleeve of her school dress.

Daddy didn't say anything else. Staying as still as possible, with her cheek pressed against the soothing cold leather of the chair, she braced herself for another slap as she watched Sylvie shift from foot to foot. He never hit her twice, not even when she had been really, really irritating, but there was a first time for everything.

'From now on, buy the cakes,' he said, jabbing a finger at Auntie Shell and wiping chocolate icing from his chin. 'Baking isn't your forte.'

July watched his back as he left the room, pushing past Sylvie. She listened to his feet on the stairs. Only when he arrived on the upstairs landing, did she sit up.

Another child might have fantasised about what it would feel like to shove him to the floor, or to pick up a plate and smack him across the head with it. But July never did, because she always knew she deserved the punishments he administered. Daddy only hit her to Teach Her a Lesson, that's what he always said. What could she possibly teach him, by hitting him back? He knew so much more than her, about everything.

Stupid, stupid July.

'You've really got to try and stop asking him questions.' Auntie Shell crouched next to her. 'Don't push his buttons.' Her tone was hard; the words felt more of a warning or a threat than benevolent advice. She held up a hand, as though she was considering stroking July's face, but then dropped it again. 'Sylv, get the peas.'

July remembered her stepmother's softness and smile as she had given her the lava lamp; she heard an echo of her shouting 'Mick, don't' a minute ago. She should have known better than to expect any protectiveness to continue. Auntie Shell's behaviour followed a pattern: she would spend a day or two being kind to July and then suddenly go cold for a while, before another brief thaw. It was like the bird bath in the back garden. On a cold winter's morning they would wake to find it had frozen over, then it would melt in the daytime sun before going solid again overnight.

She studied Auntie Shell's face, searching for traces of untruth. Why would she have lied about the way July's mother had died? It was so confusing.

Her stepsister wordlessly moved to the freezer, but July sniffed and shook her head when she pulled the peas out of the bottom drawer. She didn't like the numbness they left her with. 'I'll just go to my room.'

'You could do,' Auntie Shell said, her voice clipped. 'Or . . .' She looked out of the patio doors, towards the bike. 'Might be best to get out of his way for a little while.'

July stuck to the pavements. She was a little wobbly at first and had to put her feet down several times before she turned out of

Harmony Close, but she soon remembered what she was doing. It felt good to generate a breeze – the warm air blew through her hair and over her throbbing face.

She pedalled and pedalled, around trees planted into the pavement and past houses with the doors flung wide open. There was more life in the village than there had been an hour ago. On one driveway, children were running through a sprinkler set up on the paving stones; on another, two women in bikinis were sunbathing on beach towels laid out on the tarmac. She pulled over to let returning beach walkers and their panting dogs pass; she investigated cul-de-sacs she had never been to before; she noticed the houses with lush green lawns whose owners were obviously ignoring the hosepipe ban. She found herself on the other side of the village, cycling along streets she'd never visited before.

She nearly didn't see it.

ALMOND DRIVE.

She had been out for over an hour already when she spotted the sign as she passed the turning on the other side of the road. She braked, her neck jolting with the sudden movement.

Number 3 on her list of things she knew about Mum: They'd lived in a house on Almond Drive.

As soon as she stepped into Almond Drive, she felt strangely cold. Rubbing her arm to soften the goosebumps that had formed, July looked for something she would recognise, but there was nothing familiar.

What number had they lived at? Which one of these houses had she played in with her mother? In which one had Maggie Hooper rocked baby July to sleep in her arms?

It was then that she saw her. A woman emerged from a silver car parked a little way up the road. She had long red hair. No green skirt, but definitely the same red hair. July blinked. She looked alarmingly real. The woman opened the boot of the car, pulled out

38

a bag, and then got back into the driver's seat, before switching on the engine and driving down the road, away from July.

But why would her mother appear now, like this? July hadn't lied. She hadn't spoken to anyone since she left home. And this sighting was so unlike the usual ones she had. Her mother was never normally *doing* anything, let alone driving a car. Being here, so close to the home where they had lived together, made July desperate to see her mum again. Could she bring her back, in her car?

A lie was needed.

She leaned her bike against the front wall of the house next to her. Her hands had been gripping the textured handlebars so tight that her palms were covered with a pattern of tiny diamonds. She looked at the front door closest to her. All she had to do was knock and tell whoever answered that she was after her friend (Marianne? Joni? Emma?) and that she couldn't remember in which house she lived. Bingo. Lie complete. Mum would reappear.

But every time she tried to step on to the front path, her feet wouldn't move. She stared up at the house. It looked like it was about to fall down – it was sad and overgrown. Chipboard covered the downstairs windows. But what was garishly unusual about the place was its bright yellow window frames, visible around the ugly boards, and the matching door. The paint was peeling, but you could tell from that splash of colour that this house had once been full of joy. What had gone wrong, July wondered?

She took a couple of steps up the path. What if they guessed that she was lying? Or worse, what if they were extremely helpful and took her door-to-door asking everyone where Marianne or Joni or whoever lived? What if the person who answered the door was a child-murderer, and pulled her into the house? Nobody knew she was here.

She clenched her teeth and was about to take another step when she heard whistling. Turning to look where it was coming from, she saw a boy walking down the street towards her. July recognised him from school – it was Jacob Prince, from a couple of years below. She smiled – he was a much safer bet than the potential child-murderer.

She took up position on the pavement and was ready with her lie as he approached. But as she opened her mouth to speak, he lifted the box of Pop-Tarts in his hand to gesture towards the strange house with yellow window frames.

'You don't know him, do you?' he asked.

She shook her head.

'Right weirdo, he is. Scary. Nobody on the street likes him.'

She looked at the yellow door again. Thank God she hadn't knocked. (Was thanking Him allowed? Or did that also count as blasphemy? She would have to ask Shell.)

Jacob walked on.

'Hey,' she called after him. 'Wait.'

He turned.

'You've got pen on your face. Just there.' July tapped her own left cheek.

Jacob wiped his hand across the side of his face and examined his palm. 'Oh, right. Thanks.' He gave her a funny look before running off, the Pop-Tarts rattling in their box as he went, and pushing his way through the front door of a house further down Almond Drive.

She didn't care if he thought she was peculiar. She didn't care that he'd get home and look in a mirror only to find that his face was perfectly clean. All she cared about was that she could now see her mother's shape once more, on the opposite pavement. She was sitting on the low wall enclosing someone's front garden, watching July.

Without turning to look at her, July raised her hand at her side and gave a small wave. She had so many things she wanted to ask her. And, even though she knew no answer would come, she whispered, 'How come when I saw you earlier, when you were getting out of that car . . . how come I could stare straight at you and you didn't disappear?' If Sylvie had been with her, she'd have hissed the reply: *Because she's alive, dummy.*

She thought she saw her mother smile, before she slowly got up and walked away, in the direction of the main road. July knew it was pointless to try and watch her go, but she did so anyway – she'd been able to watch her get in and out of the car, hadn't she? But as she turned, her mother's form faded away into nothing.

She thought of Jacob Prince's Pop-Tarts, and her mouth began to water. What would Auntie Shell have kept for her tea? July pulled her bike away from the wall, swung it round and hopped back on. She took one last look at Almond Drive, then put her weight through her right pedal to move off.

As she cycled down the hill back into the centre of the village, she swerved to avoid a puddle of pink melted ice cream on the pavement, and something went wrong. The bike skidded, throwing her off and over the kerb so she ended up lying with her legs on the road. She screamed, clamped her eyes shut and saw her mother being hit by a car, bending double as her body bounced over the bonnet and off to one side. *She didn't die in a car accident,* Miss Glover had written. But it didn't make any sense, not when she had these memories. As quickly as the usual nightmarish vision came into her mind, it was gone again; her eyes were open and she was scrabbling back on to the pavement. Dumb bike. Dumb July for not concentrating. She sat next to the front wheel, thinking of her mother again, the ambulance crew working on her body to try and revive her. She vomited a little into her mouth, and tasted chocolate cake.

She dragged the bike home. *I'll never get back on this thing,* she thought to herself. *Too dangerous.* She threw it down with a clatter in the back garden after letting herself in through the side gate. Auntie Shell saw her through the patio door and glared at her.

'Dinner,' she said when July went inside, and handed her a cheese sandwich clingfilmed to a plate, with a pack of salt and vinegar crisps.

'Thanks.'

'Have it in there.' Auntie Shell tilted her head towards the living room. 'Sylvie's got something on the box.'

'Where's Dad?'

'Pub.' Without warning, Auntie Shell pulled July towards her in a tight embrace. Even if July wanted to hug her back, she couldn't because she was holding the plate and crisps, so it was awkward and uncomfortable – but then hugs with Auntie Shell always were. They happened so rarely that they always took July by surprise, and they were always unbearably intense, as if her stepmum was trying to squeeze the life out of her.

Auntie Shell stepped back, releasing her. Sure enough, as always after these moments, there were tears in her eyes.

These hugging incidents frightened July. They always made her think that one of them was about to die, and nobody had bothered to inform her. It was like an urgent farewell – as if they would never see each other again.

'Thanks for the sandwich,' July said, before making her escape into the living room to watch telly with Sylvie. She didn't ask Sylvie why she'd mentioned the project to her father, and she knew better than to expect an apology. The best thing to do was pretend it had never happened. They managed to sneak in an extra fifteen minutes of telly after the end of the film Sylv was watching before Auntie Shell popped her head around the door to tell them to get ready for bed.

'Oh, and July?' she said from the hall. 'Have you phoned your gran yet to say thank you for your bike?'

July called Yaya after doing her teeth, from the phone in her parents' bedroom. 'I love it,' she said, rubbing the sore patch on her thigh from her fall.

'You'll be able to cycle over to our house in the holidays,' Yaya said.

'Can't wait!' July said, though she could think of nothing worse than climbing back on to that death trap.

Her mother appeared by the window, watching her until she finished the call. Reluctantly, July mouthed, 'Night, Mum,' after replacing the handset, and made her way back downstairs to join Sylvie. They'd all been sleeping on the ground floor for the past two weeks, and it didn't look like it would be getting cool enough for them to move back upstairs any time soon. July missed having her own space, and Sylvie had made it very clear that she was not pleased with the situation either (an emergency addendum to the Stepsister Rules included an imaginary uncrossable line down the centre of the living room and a ban on July sleep-talking), but neither of them could face another restless night in their rooms. Their parents slept on a bed that pulled out from underneath the couch in the kitchen, which her father complained was doing his back in. None of them were getting much sleep.

Once she'd got changed, July was glad to finally lie down on her makeshift bed on the floor by the TV. It was too warm for her duvet, but she crept underneath it anyway – it felt like a hug. 'Happy birthday to you,' she sang, quietly, to herself, stretching her arms above her head and yawning. 'Happy birthday to you. Happy birthday, dear July, happy birthday to you.'

Sylvie threw a cushion at her. 'Shut up, would you? Your birthday's over.'

5

Darling girl,

Five things I want you to know about me

1. *I am dead. If you are reading this, and I am
    still alive, please stop. You're getting yourself
    into trouble. You've ignored my explicit
    instructions on the front of this bundle of
    letters – put them back where you found them.
    If I have passed away, read on. There are
    things I need you to know.*

2. *I am not sorry for what I did. Some people,
    I'm sure, would tell me I should feel remorse.
    They weren't there. Have the hundreds of
    church services I've attended been a waste?
    No, because:*

3. *God is on my side. I'd like to believe you will
    be too.*

4. *Regardless of whether you are, I neither want
    nor expect your forgiveness for what I am
    about to tell you.*

5.   *I killed someone.*

Give me time, I will explain.

All my love, always,
Mum x

6

21 July 1995

When Emma Glover had qualified as a primary school teacher, she wrote herself a list of rules. Which, nine years into the job, she regularly broke, mostly because she had failed to take into account the fact that she was human.

One of them was never to have favourite students. There had been a few over the years – brainy children, sweet children – but July Hooper was something else. Even before the head had sat Emma down to explain July's tragic family history, and the version of it that the girl knew, Emma had realised that she was a special one.

July Hooper had rescued countless bad teaching days and made them good again, with a simple question in class, a gesture towards a friend worthy of a stone in the kindness jar or a heartbreakingly innocent sentence in a piece of homework. But July Hooper also kept her awake at night, worrying.

Because Emma had seen a bruise, once. Then twice. Then three times.

'Protect your students' – that was another of Emma's rules, but when she had gone to the head, she had been told she couldn't go making accusations like this without evidence. Had the child complained to her? (No.) Had she actually seen either of the parents hurting her? (No.) Had she asked July how she came to be injured? (Yes. She'd said she had fallen at the playground, slipped in the bath, been fighting with Sylvie.) There you go then, the head had said, sitting back in her chair. All perfectly good explanations, she'd said. Children get bruises all the time, and some of them – July Hooper was obviously one – were more prone than others. Peaches, she'd said, in a way that told Emma this was the end of the matter. Emma had nodded. She couldn't deny that there was sense in what the woman was saying. Maybe she was being over-protective because she liked the girl so much?

Then, as Emma had stood to leave, muttering her thanks, the head had added, 'And Mr Hooper is so generous to the school, isn't he? We wouldn't have been able to resurface the playground if it wasn't for him.' And, as Emma walked out the door of the office, her boss had called after her. 'You're doing so well, Emma. You've settled here, haven't you?' Emma hadn't been able to answer, such was her shock at the thinly veiled threat.

It wasn't the first time Emma had been in trouble with the headteacher over July Hooper. When the woman had told her what July knew about her mother, she'd said it was for the best. They didn't want a young child to be unnecessarily traumatised, etcetera. As Emma listened to the justifications, she'd heard her late father's voice: 'The truth sets you free.' She had been raised to value honesty above almost anything else, which is how she found herself having a quiet word with July's stepmother one afternoon at pick-up time. Might July not be better off, knowing what really happened, she'd asked? She could handle it. She had a mature head on her shoulders, didn't she?

The stepmother had told the father.

The father had told the head.

Emma had received a written warning.

For the sake of her own young son and the roof over their heads she needed this job. Maybe it would have been different, if she hadn't been a widow or if her parents were still around.

But this is where she was; this was how it had to be. So she made an effort to stop worrying about the bruises in the middle of the night. The head was probably right, they were surely accidental. The parents seemed lovely, despite the dishonesty surrounding July's mother. And July Hooper wasn't the kind of child to lie to her teacher's face. But the more Emma made peace with ignoring the injuries, the more she felt compelled to help the girl in some other way. And that was how the idea for the project had been born.

It was too ambitious for year fives. She'd known that when she had set it. The head would have something to say about it, probably – maybe one of the parents would complain over the summer. But if it meant that July Hooper found out something about her mother, if she discovered one true thing, then it would be worth it.

Another of Emma's rules was just one word: 'Listen.'

Listen to other teachers, listen to your students. And she was listening the day after July Hooper's birthday, the final day of term, when the girl had come up to her at the start of their music lesson, recorder in hand, and whispered, 'Miss Glover, I have some questions about, you know . . .'

'About what?' she'd replied.

'Your note. I just wondered . . . The thing is, my dad . . . um . . .' July had lowered her voice even further, before attempting a couple more sentences. 'If she didn't . . . then how did she . . . Can you tell me any more?'

As Emma pulled out a pile of sheet music from the drawer in the music room, she had shaken her head. 'What note?' She handed the sheets to Darren Emerson and asked him to take one, then pass it on.

'Oh.' July had bitten her lip, then nodded. 'You don't want me to ask you. I get it. I'm sorry.'

'Wait,' Emma had called after the girl as she took her seat in the semicircle of chairs, but she hadn't turned back. Distracted by Neil Gibson attempting to play 'Hot Cross Buns' with his nose, Emma Glover had quickly forgotten all about July's mysterious questions. She had listened, but she hadn't really *heard*. She only remembered the conversation much later that summer, when she saw the news.

For now, after ordering Neil to wipe down his recorder, she led the class in an ear-splitting rendition of 'Scarborough Fair', not noticing that July, who usually threw herself into it, was biting the mouthpiece of her instrument rather than making any attempt to blow.

July chewed the plastic and stared at the sheet of music in front of her. The last day of term was usually so exciting. The year sixes would spend the day parading around, getting their shirts and dresses signed. July and Katie-Faye would finalise their summer holiday plans – when would they have sleepovers? What songs would they choreograph dance routines to? How many skits would they video with Katie-Faye's dad's camcorder? It was also traditional for each class teacher to bring in a cake to share.

But this year was different. The leavers had been banned from signing shirts after what happened to Laurence Bright last year; Katie-Faye was spending the summer at her grandparents' house in the Midlands, so there would be no sleepovers, no dance routines, no videos; and Miss Glover had brought in a fruitcake, of all things. Nobody liked fruitcake. And anyway, even if the day had been as thrilling as it usually was, July probably wouldn't have noticed, because she spent the whole of Friday thinking about Miss Glover's note, and about Almond Drive.

During 'Scarborough Fair', she replayed the whole experience of the previous evening several times. Instead of parsley, sage, rosemary and thyme she thought about: the vision of her mother, the strangeness of her being in a car, seeing Jacob and the long line of houses on either side of the road. As the class moved on to 'Frère Jacques' she decided that something wasn't quite right about it all. *Ding, dang, dong; ding, dang, dong.* But what?

That morning she hadn't planned to cycle to school – she hadn't been intending ever to ride that bike again – but Sylvie had commented at breakfast that she still didn't believe July could actually ride it and bet her twenty pence she couldn't get all the way to school without falling off. July had won the money, with Sylvie jogging all the way to the school gates alongside her. They'd even laughed together as they did it, at how silly Sylvie looked. And now July was glad she had her bike in the shed outside: as soon as Miss Glover announced the end of the last lesson, she was heading straight back to Almond Drive.

After music, as her classmates played hangman on the whiteboard back in their form room, made paper aeroplanes and watched *Beethoven* with the curtains drawn, July alternated between staring out of the window and at the clock, trying not to wipe the sweat off her face in case she dislodged the make-up covering her blooming bruise. When twenty past three came around, after a moment's hesitation as she considered asking Miss Glover about the note one final time, she ran out of the door, shouting at Sylvie as she went – a severe infraction of the Stepsister Rules – 'Tell your mum I'll be home by teatime!'

July rode along the length of Almond Drive, looking for the silver car, but it wasn't there, and neither was her mother. She leaned her bike against the wall of number 17 and made her way slowly past the odd-numbered houses, on the opposite side of the street to the one with the yellow door, which, she noticed this time, had a FOR SALE sign outside – who would want to buy a building in such a state of disrepair? She peered through the windows into front rooms with huge televisions, cats sitting on settees, heavenly shelves full of books. They were all so much bigger than their living room in Harmony Close. She and Sylvie would be able to sleep on the floor in one of these houses without rolling into each other all night long.

Pausing outside number 9, she looked up, taking in the whole building. It was enormous. In Harmony Close they had three bedrooms, but July's was really more of a cupboard. This house probably had at least four. And two bathrooms, July bet. It was a similar size to Katie-Faye's, where they had two bathrooms *and* a downstairs loo.

July crossed over to number 8, and as she passed from the sunny side of the street to the shade, a memory tiptoed into her mind. She was six, and she was crying because Sylvie had been teasing her, saying that she had the bigger room because she was the favourite. July had gone to her father and asked if it was true, and he'd told her to stop complaining. He had been out on the driveway, organising his gardening tools in the back of his van. 'You're lucky you don't have to share a room,' he'd hissed, spinning a reel of green twine around his fingers and looking over his shoulder to check no neighbours were within earshot. 'If we'd stayed at the house in Almond Drive there wouldn't have been enough space for you to have a bedroom to yourself. Why can't you ever show me some appreciation?' He'd thrown the twine at the back of her head as she'd walked into the house. 'Put it in the hall, would you?' he'd said, when she stooped to pick it up.

There wouldn't have been enough space for you to have a bedroom to yourself.

That was it. That was what had been bothering her all day. She had always imagined their old house to be tiny. A cottage or a bungalow.

She looked up at the building in front of her, its render

painted a fresh white, the wooden gables glossy black. Each house on the road was the same – all, without a doubt, much larger than their current home. Had she misunderstood Daddy? Slowly she moved on, past number 10, back towards her bike. Between numbers 10 and 12, she noticed something she hadn't seen when she was here the day before. A narrow alleyway. It was dark with overgrown weeds, but July glimpsed sunlight at the other end, and a sliver of another road, parallel to this one. She remembered cycling past it on the way here: Hollybush Avenue. Katie-Faye's road had an alley like this too. Hers had a gate in the middle to access a track running along the bottom of her garden. Maybe it was the same here? Perhaps the houses looked smaller from the back, and she could dismiss the niggling doubt in her mind about her father.

July swung her rucksack round to her side, pulled her perfume stick out of the front pocket and applied two streaks to her face, one on either cheekbone. The scent made her feel braver as she stepped into the alley, fighting her way past ivy and eye-gouging brambles reaching down from the trees above, and out-of-control spiky shrubs grabbing at her school dress. It was refreshingly cool in the shade of the trees branching overhead, but the relief from the heat was counteracted by the burn from the nettles nipping at the skin above her pop socks. This was a stupid idea. She sniffed, hard, but instead of her emboldening White Musk, she unintentionally welcomed an awful whiff of fox poo into her nostrils. She gagged. What was she doing? She should turn back.

But there, halfway along the alleyway on the right-hand side, was a gate. Through its black metal bars she could see a track, with the rear garden fences of Almond Drive on one side, and those of another road on the other. She gave it a shake, and it swung open.

As she carefully picked her way along the track, she craned

her neck to see over the fences. The gardens of Almond Drive were the same size as hers at home, but she had been right – the buildings were much larger, there was no getting round it. Still, she couldn't believe that her father would lie to her. She must have misheard him.

She carried on along the track, enjoying the chance to see into the lives of all these other families, with their neat vegetable gardens, gigantic nodding sunflowers and little ponds. Disloyally, she thought that some of them looked better than her father's garden at home.

The final house in the line of Almond Drive buildings was the one with yellow window frames. It had a matching drainpipe. She thought of Jacob's scathing comments again, about its inhabitant. As all the homes along here appeared to have, this one had a gate opening on to the track, but what set it apart was that, on the fence adjoining it, someone had used red paint to scrawl the word BASTARD.

This fence was slightly higher than the others, and unkempt bushes crowded over the top of it. If she was going to see what this man's garden was like, she would need stilts, or . . . She looked around. A few metres away there was a pile of old bricks and roof tiles. People at school sometimes called her a weirdo, she thought, as she dragged some bricks over to the fence to make a platform high enough for her to stand on. They never called her a bastard, but she suspected that might just be because it was a nasty word reserved for describing boys, wasn't it? They called her a square and a swot as well as a weirdo; it didn't mean that she was one. What would this man be like? She imagined him hunched, with a combover and thick glasses. Perhaps a brown cardigan. Maybe he snarled when he spoke, and had a stick that he waved at people he didn't like. She looked back up the track towards the gate she had come through, checking it was still open, then stepped on to the bricks.

As she did so, a loud shuddering sound came over the fence from the old man's garden. She peered over. Past a faded plastic children's climbing frame, the door to a shed next to the house was swinging open and – there he was. He wasn't what she had imagined, but Jacob was right: he did look scary. His clothes were tired – a faded blue T-shirt and grubby shorts – and his hair looked equally unkempt, a dark brown mess on his head and a thick, scraggly beard obscuring most of his face. It was hard to tell his age, but she was sure he must be older than her father by quite a long way – maybe about fifty-five? The only thing that seemed friendly about him was a pair of bright yellow flip-flops, but their brightness was counteracted by the toes in them, which she could see were filthy.

The most unnerving thing of all was the way he was muttering to himself as he searched around in his flower beds for something. She couldn't make out what he was saying, until he suddenly stopped still and growled, 'There you are, little guy.' Standing perfectly motionless, he began muttering again, but this time she could make out the words. 'Cruel to be kind,' he was saying. 'Cruel to be kind.' July squinted, shivering slightly at the sight of his strangeness. Who was he talking to?

She watched as the man lifted some sort of tool – a long wooden stick with a big rectangle of metal at the end, a bit like a hammer but larger and heavier-looking. He rested it against his shoulder for a moment, muttered something, and then with a grunt he lifted it above his head and drove it down towards the ground. There was a horrible noise – a kind of squeak, crunch and thud, all at once. She didn't know what he had done, but she had a feeling that it was very, very bad. Her face grew hot and she knew she should be running away, not staying to watch, but her feet wouldn't move.

He bent down. When he stood up again, he had something dangling from his hand. Deftly, he swung it behind him and threw it over the fence, straight towards July, who squealed and fell off her pile of bricks. Lots of things happened at once then: she looked at her feet and saw a dead and bloodied rat; she screamed again; the man shouted, 'What the hell?'; the man opened the gate.

'How did you get in here?' He was huge, towering above her as she lay on the dried mud of the track, which she dug her nails into. *He's going to kill me,* she thought. *And nobody knows where I am.*

'I said, how did you get in here?' He roared the words this time, and July whimpered.

'The gate was unlocked,' she managed to say, as she scrambled to her feet and backed away from him towards the alley. He was still holding that horrible tool, and his face looked like her father's did, right before his harshest Lessons.

When he replied, he didn't say what she was expecting him to. 'You?' he said, the rage in his expression mixing with confusion. He took a step towards her, getting terrifyingly close. She could see his eyes flashing with hatred behind his glasses, and a red, moon-shaped scar by his left eye, about the same size as one of his ragged eyebrows. He stared at her face for several seconds, before the confusion fled and the pure fury returned. 'Did he send you?' he snarled. 'Did he?' Some of his spittle landed on her face, but she was too afraid to wipe it away.

Had who sent her? She backed further away from him, shaking her head, feeling her heart pound in her chest. *I have to get out of here.*

His features shifted once more, though he kept staring at her. 'You can't be here,' he said, his eyes wide, his breathing becoming shallower. He no longer resembled her father. Strangely – very strangely – he looked at this moment much more like Auntie Shell when Daddy was about to smash a plate on the floor or push a chair over, in a Level Three argument. July had always

55

thought that expression was one of fear, but how could a grown man be afraid of a ten-year-old girl?

'Go. Get away from me. Out of my sight!' His eyes bulged as he yelled at her.

July didn't need telling twice, and finally her feet did as she wanted them to. She turned and ran as fast as she could for the alley.

'And close that gate behind you!'

7

23 July 1995

'God forgives us, so that means we have to forgive each other too.' July's father handed her the chocolate-covered bar of toffee he had just bought from the corner shop, and they carried on walking, side by side, up the street. 'Forgive, and you will be forgiven.'

July nodded, although she wasn't sure what God had ever forgiven her for. Would she know when He had?

'So how about it? Shall I forgive you? What's the word we say before we are forgiven?'

July had just taken a bite of her chocolate bar, and she chewed as hard as she could so that she could reply, but the toffee wasn't shifting. 'Um-hm,' she managed, stroking her fingers gently over the powdery make-up covering her now-yellowing bruise. 'Sorry, Daddy.'

'There's my girl.' Her father put an arm around her shoulder, and his hand dangled next to her face. His skin smelled of happiness: of the conditioner he rubbed into his boxing gloves when he was in a whistling mood. They took the path at the top of the hill through the dog-walking field. It was worth the pain of him hitting her, and the throb that had kept her awake the night of her birthday, for this touch of his arm across her back. She could barely breathe for the excitement of it, and grinned as she moved the sweet glue around her mouth with her tongue.

'You don't remember her,' he said. 'It's harder for me than it is for you. You understand, don't you.' He didn't inflect the final word; it wasn't a question.

They were on their way to the Sunday morning service at the village church, which perched next to the coast path, overlooking the bay. Sylvie and Auntie Shell had gone the normal way, along the main village road, but Daddy had wanted a 'special walk' with July. July had heard the vicar talk about the Calm before the Storm a few weeks ago in his sermon. But it seemed to her that the Calm always came after the Storm, not before it. These days after July 'lost her way' (as her father described it) were always the best ones – he was happy and fun, and bought her chocolate, and put his arm around her shoulder.

The pleasure of it almost made her forget about Almond Drive, but not quite. She had a lot of questions, some of which she had added to her Big List (Why had Gazza moved? Which house had Paul Nicholls lived in?) and others she kept in her head because she didn't have a list they fitted into. (Why had that horrible man recognised her?) But she knew it was pointless to try and find answers to them. She would probably never know anything more about Almond Drive, and right now, with Daddy's arm around her as they walked through the meadow down to the church, that was okay by her.

He stopped to look out to sea. 'Can't see the lighthouse. You?'

July lifted the peak of her baseball cap slightly, pressed her glasses up the bridge of her nose and scanned the horizon. 'Not today.' She crossed her fingers, hoping it was the right answer.

'Too hazy. The boys are out though, look.' He pointed towards the headland. Beyond the weathered stones of the church tower, two large grey naval ships were just visible on the glittering, still water, surrounded by dozens of little white triangles marking sailing boats out for the day.

'Wasn't Great-Grandpa Leonard in the navy?' She'd made a start on her project the evening before, but she only had a couple of lines about him so far.

Her father smiled, still looking out to sea. 'Sort of. Merchant Navy.'

'Oh.' She didn't know what that was, but instinct told her that asking him would make him cross. Should she tell him instead that the frigates and destroyers always reminded her of him: imposing, protective and strong? July could never predict whether her thoughts would please him. She mulled it over for slightly too long and the moment passed. Her father offered a solid nod towards the ships like the one he gave motorists when they pulled over to let him pass in his van, then set off down the hill towards the church.

Maybe the excitement of his touch got to her, maybe it was the sugar, or perhaps the already-hot sun on their heads. But when they made it to the bottom of the field and the rusted wrought iron gate which took them through into the graveyard, the horizon haze bled into July's brain too, and she felt light-headed. She clung to her father's arm as they descended the steep steps to the church, with ancient slanting headstones on either side of them as they went. July had never been in a grave-yard before – they had never walked to church this way since they'd started attending – and the crunch of her sandals on the gravel felt too loud. Disrespectful. There were bodies buried underneath them, and she had the horrible thought that they might be disturbed by her footsteps. The sound of children's laughter and gently breaking waves drifted up from the beach below – she was used to hearing this from the coast path, but here it was creepy and ghostlike, as if it was reaching them from another world. She gripped her father's arm tighter.

'Daddy,' she said, scanning the rows of grey slabs of stone, lined up like the chocolate bars on the shelf in the shop. He didn't hear her, so she repeated herself, more loudly. 'Daddy? Can I sit for a minute? I'm a bit dizzy.'

He looked down at her, and she saw a flicker of impatience cross his face, the dart of a grass snake's tongue. Already, the brief tide of calm was receding. The reversion to normal life always began like this, with her doing things to disappoint him. 'You can rest when we get inside.'

The congregation was gathering in the car park outside the church doors, and July knew it would be a while before her father had finished greeting everyone – she would easily make it into one of the pews in time. 'A minute? Please? You don't have to wait with me.' She let go of his arm.

'Make sure you're inside before the bells.' He cupped his hands over her shoulders and she tried not to shrink away as he squeezed. 'Promise me? Did you see how cross Mrs Peters was when that boy was late last week? I don't want to see her looking at you like that. Hoopers are never late.'

'I promise.'

She sat on a lichen-covered bench next to the steps, taking another bite of chocolate as she watched her father mingle – laughing and shaking hands with people he knew. She was always intrigued to see him with other grown-ups, moving smoothly and confidently through crowds like those naval ships through the swell. Trickles of conversation crawled back up the steps towards her: 'get you in to lay our new lawn' . . . 'you want to ask Shelley to put your bed linen in the freezer' . . . 'yes, I heard he was moving' . . . 'good riddance, I say.' The familiar feeling of pride steadied her spinning head; she loved to see him so confidently talking to people, and the way their faces shone with smiles as they listened to him.

Feeling a little better, she wandered along the grassy paths between the headstones. Some of them were toppling over, others were overgrown with weeds; some were tiny, neat rectangles about the size of one of her school exercise books, others were huge slabs of rock that were bigger than their fridge door. She stopped next to one which had a bunch of flowers in front of it, along with two mugs with DAD on them. There was a pile of papers covered with the scribbled drawings of a child younger than her and a small heart-shaped ornament with italicised writing on it: 'Dad. *When someone you love becomes a memory, that memory becomes a treasure.*' July pushed the final piece of her melted chocolate bar up out of the packet and into her mouth to help swallow the lump that had formed in her throat. She couldn't imagine life without her father.

There were many repeated names – Chenoweth, Blamey, Profit, Tregunna. She matched them all to the village families she knew as she watched a pair of cabbage white butterflies chase each other in circles towards the gorse that bordered the graveyard. How did they manage to sit on the shrub's needle-like foliage without tearing their wings? July knew if she was a butterfly she wouldn't achieve it – she was far too clumsy. And how did they know how to fly so gracefully, as soon as they came out of their chrysalides? Maggie Hooper had been graceful. (It was Number 14 on July's list – a pink scrap of fabric gifted by Grandpa Tony as they had watched Yaya dive into the public swimming pool one Saturday afternoon. 'Isn't your grandmother graceful?' he'd shouted over the echoing hubbub of other children's shrieks. 'Your mother had that way about her too.') But July was definitely not. How was she meant to know how to be, without her mother to teach her? She hadn't passed any Hoopers yet, she realised as she got to the end of another row. Where was her mother's grave? *She didn't die in a car accident.* Miss Glover's voice was so clear that she checked over her shoulder to make sure she wasn't actually there. If she could find the right headstone, maybe it would explain what had happened, once and for all? She picked up her pace and had walked along all of the rows marking the deaths from the last decade when she heard the bells signalling the start of the service, ringing out clear and bright, slicing through the stifling air.

She ran down the remaining steps, her sandals slapping on the ground, and into the church. It was immediately cooler inside, but July started to sweat more with the panic of being late. Even standing on her tiptoes, she couldn't see her father or Auntie Shell. They must have found a seat near the front. July took a couple of deep breaths, inhaling the reassuring scent of blown-out candles and dust, trying to think what she should do. She was far too embarrassed to walk down the aisle to find her family.

A whisper came from the pews to her left: 'Juju!'

Yaya was there, in the back row, with Grandpa Tony, beckoning her over. She saluted with wiggling fingers when July saw her, and July returned the greeting – it was their special signal, perfected with years of practice. 'Come and sit with us,' Yaya mouthed, shifting up to make a July-sized space between her and a stone pillar.

She squeezed in next to them, the wooden pew refreshingly cold against her back. Grandpa Tony reached over to pat her leg, passing her a stick of Juicy Fruit gum which she pocketed for later, and Yaya gave her a big wet kiss on her cheek. Luckily, the bruised half of her face was on the other side, hidden from view – she didn't want Yaya to know that she had messed up and needed a Lesson.

'How's the bike?' Yaya whispered.

July gave her a thumbs up, and for a brief (foolish) moment considered asking about Almond Drive or about her mother's car accident. She slipped her sandals off and chilled the soles of her heat-swollen feet on the stone floor. Sylvie always did this, but when July had tried it once, her father had pinched her leg so hard, tears had sprung to her eyes. As always, it was one rule for her stepsister and another for her.

The vicar got up at the front of the church, beginning his sermon. 'My memory is terrible, as many of you know,' he said, his voice booming. July could only just see his face above the heads of the rows of people in front of her. 'It's taken me several years to remember all of your names. It does have its benefits though – I can hide Easter eggs for my own hunt and I have no idea where I left them.'

Yaya tutted, but the rest of the congregation laughed.

'God knows how short our memories can be, so he . . .'

It was always around this point that July let her mind wander. She'd rather listen to Grandpa Tony talk about longshore drift and tides and coastal erosion any day – as a retired geography teacher he was always keen to brush off his repertoire for July, who loved to listen to him. He made it fun and interesting, and crucially, what he said made sense – unlike most of these Sunday sermons. The vicar was kind enough, but she could never understand half of what he said. Today, his opening words made her recall the words she had read outside, on the grave with the DAD mugs.

'Yaya?' July whispered as she leaned towards her, tapping her hand. Her grandmother smiled. 'Do you think . . .' She knew she shouldn't be doing this, she knew it would be upsetting for her grandmother. But sometimes the desire was too consuming to consider anyone else's feelings. 'Do you think Mum turned into a memory when she died?'

The smile dropped off her grandmother's face. She began to twist her wedding band around her finger. 'I . . . I'm trying to listen to the vicar,' she whispered back, her voice wobbling. July knew she didn't really care about offending the vicar – Yaya was not a believer. 'I only come for the hymns,' she always insisted. Her grandmother stared resolutely ahead of her for the next ten minutes, sniffing loudly and fidgeting with every piece of jewellery she was wearing, while the vicar explained that the Lord had left them the Bible to remember his words by. July should have known better than to ask Yaya about her mother. She would never hit her in response to a question, but she was as unlikely to answer as her father was. Instead of a slap, Yaya replied with tears, or wide eyes and a quivering lip that promised they would come if July asked any more.

July liked the idea of her mum having transformed upon her death, of her having become a memory. She imagined that memory like one of those cabbage whites she'd seen outside, fluttering around in her mind. But could Mum be both a memory and the angel she saw every day? This whole new religion thing was so confusing. She studied the magical stained-glass windows for the rest of the sermon (her favourite was one split into pink and yellow squares, like an enormous glowing Battenberg) and was only jolted out of her reverie when everyone around her stood up and chords rang out on the organ.

Grandpa Tony opened a hymn book and passed it to Yaya, who blinked and pulled a face (she refused to 'surrender' to glasses, though her eyesight was rapidly failing her, and relied on a magnifying glass to do her daily cryptic crossword). Tony pointed at the page with 'Be Thou My Vision' in bold type across the top. It was a new one to July, and she liked the stirring tune, but there were so many thys and thous and arts that she couldn't quite understand it. In the third verse Yaya hugged July to her side and pushed her lips up against her ear. July leaned into the soft familiarity of her grandmother's violet perfume.

'She didn't turn into a memory,' Yaya said carefully. 'But I do have lots of memories of her.'

July caught her breath, unable to continue her attempts to sing along with the rest of the congregation. She hugged her grandmother back in gratitude. She could hear Yaya battling through the emotions that usually prevented her from talking about July's mother.

'This was one of her favourite hymns when she was a little girl like you,' Yaya whispered, wiping away a single tear from her cheek. As she handed July this new fact, she fiddled with the red silk scarf she wore twisted around her cropped silver hair. She always did this on the few occasions she talked about her daughter, and she always wore the scarf in her hair. July always wanted to lift her hand to touch it too – what was it about that material that coaxed Maggie on to Yaya's lips? *Number 19*, July noted. *Mum's favourite hymn was 'Be Thou My Vision'.*

'She would get all tongue-tied and sing the wrong words, like you,' her grandmother said, wiping away more tears but smiling. Number 20! It was rare to get two new facts in such quick succession. 'You remind me so much of her,' Yaya added.

July pulled away and gaped at her. Nobody had ever said anything like that to her before. She was desperate to ask for more, but she hated to see her grandmother so sad as a result of her questions. And she had Grandpa's voice in her head too. 'We have to look after your Yaya,' he'd told her last year, after she'd become particularly upset when telling July about the July-bear nickname. 'Her weak heart won't take it.' July had been extra careful ever since.

Yaya held July's hand for the rest of the service, her many bulky rings digging into July's fingers in the way that she loved, and after it finished July stood by quietly as people in the pews in front of them turned to say things like 'Lovely to see you, Mrs Warren' and 'How are the cottages?' It was strange to hear people address her by this name, and it made July look at her grandmother through curious eyes, wondering what these other people made of the 'Mrs Warren' they knew. The name was too formal for all her exotic jewellery, her nose ring and her bare feet (she never wore shoes, not even in shops, not even to drive). She was only ever Yaya to July – nobody at home even referred to her as Kay, let alone Mrs Warren – and it felt perfect for her.

Mrs Warren must have been what she had been called at school before she retired last year, finally leaving her beloved maths department at the secondary school in town, which was when she'd stopped wearing shoes. When July visited her grandparents, she noticed that Tony, who had married her grandmother fifteen years earlier, called her 'Sir', and Yaya did the same for him. July had no idea why. So which was the real Yaya? The one she knew? Tony's 'Sir'? Mrs Warren in shoes at school, teaching quadratic equations? Or the barefoot Mrs Warren currently talking to the woman in a purple blouse about sightings of dolphins in the bay?

As much as she wanted to keep watching her grandmother and thinking about these things, July knew she had to find her father and apologise. She kissed Yaya goodbye and fought her way to the front rows of pews.

'I was in before the start, Daddy,' she said when she found him collecting up the blue hymn books. 'I sat at the back.' If he heard her, he didn't acknowledge it, instead placing a firm hand between her shoulder blades and shepherding her out of the church behind Sylvie and Auntie Shell. The doorway was an arch of blinding light against the darkness of the church, and stepping through it into the summer reminded July of something Katie-Faye had said once, about getting off an air-conditioned plane when she arrived for a holiday in Tenerife, and how the hot Spanish breeze had felt like a blast from a hairdryer.

Once outside the church, Daddy left the three of them so that he could chat to some other acquaintances. He knew so many people – she hadn't realised until they had started coming here. That first Sunday they had said things to him like 'Good to have you back, Mick' and 'At last, we've missed your baritone!' and slapped him on the back or hugged him.

The vicar was the last to step outside. He spoke to many of the congregation as they chatted, including Auntie Shell. After he asked how she was getting on, and something about the doctor's surgery where she worked as a receptionist (July tuned the details out, as anything to do with her parents' work tended to be tedious and not worth knowing), there was an awkward pause where the conversation ran out.

'Excuse me, Mr . . .' July paused. What was she supposed to call him? 'Vicar?'

'July Hooper.' He smiled. 'You know, you can call me Paul. Everyone else does. How may I be of assistance?' As he peered down at her, the sun shone through his prominent ears, making them glow red. *Green man go, red man no.* July chewed her lip. Was he someone she could trust not to fly off the handle at her? He had always seemed kind.

'Why is there no headstone for my mum?' July felt Auntie Shell bristle at her side and saw Sylvie snap her head round to watch her.

Confusion passed over the vicar's face, and he looked at Auntie Shell rather than July as he answered. 'For your mum?'

July got the impression he was about to say something else, but her stepmother cut him off: 'Because she was cremated, July. Not everybody has a grave. You know that.'

But July didn't know that. Why would she?

Auntie Shell grasped July's arm firmly. 'Now let's stop bothering the poor man and let him speak to someone else. Enjoy the rest of your weekend, Paul.' She pulled July away and Sylvie trotted after them. July thought she was in for an earbashing, but her stepmother said nothing more about it. Instead, she left the girls on the shady verge at the edge of the car park with strict instructions to sit down and not wander off, and went to speak to her friends.

'What if I don't want to sit here?' Sylvie moaned, stamping her foot as July sat down, flicking a cigarette butt off the grass and into the gorse. 'This dress is new,' she shouted after Shell.

'I'll get stains, and you'll be the one who complains about having to wash them out.'

'I think it's too dry to stain anything.' July patted the crispy tufts of grass.

'Are you sure?'

July wasn't. She had no idea why she'd said it, but right now she wanted some peace. 'Totally.' July's mother appeared at her side, lying on her back with her arms outstretched. July drew her feet out of her sandals and wriggled her toes closer to the hem of her mother's skirt.

Sylvie took her sunglasses off to investigate, and brushed her hand over a patch of grass before easing herself down on to it. July never had this problem, she didn't care about grass stains or mud splatters or creases or rips like Sylvie did. But then she really wasn't bothered about fashion like Sylvie was. Her stepsister had about twice as many clothes as her. Auntie Shell would probably buy July the same endless piles of skirts and vest tops and maybe even a denim jacket with a diamante heart on the back, like Sylvie's, if she wanted them. But she wasn't interested. July knew that all she would wear this summer was her rainbow tie-dye T-shirt, her denim dungaree shorts, her pink baseball cap and some sandals. She'd put them on this morning but been told to change into something 'less garish, please' by Auntie Shell, so opted for yellow shorts and a white top instead. Sylvie was in a new blue T-shirt dress with a pink star embroidered on to the centre of it, and wore a thin black choker to finish off the look. 'Really, Sylvie?' Auntie Shell had asked when she came downstairs that morning, pointing at her neck. 'For church?' But Daddy had stood up for her, which he never did for July. 'Let the girl alone, Shelley. She looks nice.'

And she did always look good, you had to give her that. 'I'm probably going to be a model or something, one day,' she'd say, as if she didn't really care for the idea but if she chose to do it then it would just happen with the click of her manicured fingers. Which, today happened to be her favourite shade – Midnight Blue. For some strange reason, despite the Stepsister Rules being very clear on who could use Sylvie's make-up, she had let July borrow the nail polish once, quite possibly because it gave her an opportunity to laugh at her lack of skill as an amateur beautician. 'Did you have your eyes closed?' she'd asked, which made July giggle, though she suspected it was intended to make her cross. Sylvie could be really mean, but she was funny too. When Yaya had seen the result, she'd commented that it looked like July had a strange disease, but July was pretty sure she meant it as a compliment, because she had said it with a smile on her face and gave her a kiss straight afterwards.

Once Sylvie had resigned herself to sitting on the grass, the two girls picked daisies. Sylvie fashioned hers into a chain long enough to encircle her head, lying over her fringe; July plucked petals and silently played He loves me, he loves me not. The girls at school often did this to determine whether the boy they had a crush on liked them back. July only ever wanted to know what her daisy surmised about her father's affections. Today the verdict was: he loved her. She clutched the bare yellow disc and its stalk in her hot palm and smiled, holding it out for her mother to see before scanning her eyes over the dwindling crowd to find her dad.

'I'm so hungry,' Sylvie said, 'I could eat that.' She pointed at a brown banana skin a couple of metres away from them on the verge. 'It's going to be ages till lunch. I don't see why they have to do this every week.' She waved a hand at the chattering adults.

July spotted her father as Sylvie spoke, in the middle of the group, as usual, holding court.

Then something else caught her eye, over by the church door. Auntie Shell was talking to the vicar, and it didn't look like a friendly conversation. They both appeared to be angry, and Auntie Shell was gesturing crossly in a way July never saw her do, even with her father. She strained her ears but couldn't hear what they were saying.

What could they possibly have to argue about?

8

23 July 1995

'I can do those too, if you want?' July pointed at the pile of plates and cutlery in Sylv's hands, as she arranged the glasses, salt and pepper on the table outside, freshly varnished by her father the previous weekend. Every small thing in the garden had to look perfect, he reasoned, in case anyone ever came round. Who would give a landscape gardener work if their own garden looked a mess?

Sylvie shrugged and handed the plates over. 'Whatever, Trevor.' She lay back on her towel on the lawn and reopened her magazine ('Down Boys!' were the words splashed across the cover. 'Gorgeous male models + cute dogs = amazing posters'. By the time Sylvie let her read it, all the posters would be torn out, but July couldn't complain – her stepsister always gave her the old ones she removed from her walls to make space.)

Their parents were upstairs changing out of their church clothes, and the girls had been left with their usual Sunday Lunch chores – laying the table, pouring the drinks. A chicken was in the oven – Daddy had insisted on a roast the last two weekends, despite the temperature. 'It's all right for you,' Auntie Shell had complained to July last Sunday as she pulled out a tray of golden potatoes and waved the steam away from her face. 'You're hot all the time anyway. This heatwave doesn't make any difference to you.' July, fanning her stepmother with an oven glove, had tried to explain that it was, in fact, worse for her. In the summer she was even more uncomfortable than everyone else because the heat merely added to her existing levels. 'I don't think anyone could possibly be any hotter than I am right now,' Auntie Shell had said. In an inexplicable turn of events, July's father had then laughed and said she had a high opinion of herself, and Shell had stormed out of the kitchen in tears. (Grown-ups, honestly.)

July laid the knives and forks out carefully, aligning them with the grain of the wood. 'What do you think your mum was talking to the vicar about, after church?'

'Probably what a horrible stepdaughter you are. I don't know why you're her favourite.'

'I am not.' July dropped a spoon. 'I'm not either of those things.'

'You are.' Sylvie inspected the polish on her nails. 'You know, it's disrespectful to talk about your mum in front of mine.'

'When did I talk about her?'

'Don't you remember? All that stuff about where she was buried.'

'But you talk about your dad all the time.'

'Not when Mick is around.' Sylvie huffed, stood up and pushed her way through a fringe curtain of long white cotton straps dangling from the washing line – the wraps July's father used to protect his hands under his boxing gloves. She resettled herself in the chair by the paddling pool, her feet dipping in and out of the water while she continued to admire topless men cuddling puppies.

Sylvie talked *about* her father, but never to him. There was one occasion when Auntie Shell had taken her to meet him for the first time since she was a baby, but it had gone so badly that neither of them had spoken about it since. Sylvie wet her bed every night for a month afterwards. ('If you tell anyone, I'll shave off your eyebrows in your sleep.') When Auntie Shell had married July's father, she had changed her surname to Hooper but decided that Sylvie should keep her real dad's name. July could never understand this. Why, in fact, had Sylvie even been given his name in the first place, if he had left so soon after she was born? 'Isn't it obvious?' Sylvie had said when July asked her. 'Sylvie Rose?' She said the two words as if they were a question and an answer at the same time, which gave July an instant headache like the ones she got when Yaya tried to explain a clue in her cryptic crossword. 'Sylvie. Rose,' her stepsister had repeated, slower this time. July shook her head, and Sylvie threw her whole body into a sigh. 'It's poetry, don't you think?' she'd said. This statement raised two issues for July: for one thing, she hadn't realised book-hating Sylvie knew what poetry was, and secondly, it still didn't explain anything. Sylvie had flung herself back on to her bed at the sight of July's baffled expression. 'Better than plain old Sylvie Hooper,' she'd explained to the ceiling. 'Do you know any film stars called Sylvie Hooper?'

July went into the kitchen to fill a jug with water. Was it really that disrespectful to talk about Mum in Auntie Shell's presence? Was there anybody who didn't have a problem with her bringing her mother up in conversation? She put the jug down and opened the fridge, sticking her head inside, then pulled her top up to expose her stomach and pushed that towards the bright white chilled interior too.

'Weirdo,' Sylvie called from the garden. 'I can see you.'

Ignoring her, July reached over to turn the tap on and resumed her position in front of the fridge. She had explained to Sylvie on countless occasions that if you cool your stomach, you bring down the temperature of your whole body. Yaya had told her. 'It's on account of all the blood vessels in that area,' she'd said.

As she let the tap run to get to the cold water, July heard Auntie Shell's voice, above her in their parents' bedroom. She was close to shouting. '. . . because I'm not her aunt!'

'Calm down,' Daddy said. 'It's only a name.'

'I know that. Fine. Forget it.'

'You were the one who brought it up. What do you want her to call you? Mum?'

July dropped her top back down, closed the fridge quietly and shut the tap off.

'You do, don't you?' her father said, not waiting for a response. 'You're not her mother, though, are you? Nothing like her.'

'Oh yes, how could I forget? Nobody is as good as *her*, are they?' Shell asked, her voice heavy with sarcasm. 'Maggie Hooper, that perfect saint of a woman? Flawless. Could never do wrong.'

'What's your point?'

'Forget it.'

'No, go on. What do you think you know about her? I want to hear this.'

So did July. Why was Shell being so mean about her mum?

Auntie Shell didn't reply.

'Spit it out.'

'July's asking questions, you know.' Whatever Shell said next, she spoke so softly that July couldn't make out the muffled words.

A moment of silence followed, then her father said, with a snarl in his voice, 'And what did you tell her?'

July held her breath. Was this about the conversation after church?

'You can't seriously be blaming me?' Auntie Shell snapped. 'You are, I can see it in your eyes.'

'I've told you before, you just have to shut these conversations down. What she doesn't know—'

'She's going to work it out, Mick! She's not stupid. Far from it.'

Auntie Shell really shouted this bit, and then the voices stopped, and there were footsteps on the stairs.

July quickly filled the jug and took it outside. She was pouring

74

water into the glasses when Auntie Shell came into the kitchen. July's hand shook as she poured, and water splashed on to the table.

Auntie Shell pulled the chicken out of the oven and July's father joined her in the kitchen. They didn't speak to each other. They were both very careless with the pots and pans, banging them around. July straightened the cutlery again, keeping an eye on them from the patio. Sunday lunch always used to be at midday, but since they'd started going to church, they'd been eating later and later. The smell of slowly crisping chicken skin floating around the house (or, today, into the garden) drove July and Sylvie half-mad with hunger. But after overhearing her parents' row, the rumbling in July's stomach had been replaced by knots. She wasn't hungry any more.

What did Auntie Shell think she was going to work out?

It was nearly two o'clock when Auntie Shell finally called out to them, 'Table, girls.'

Daddy brought the chicken out on a board and started carving, while a red-faced Auntie Shell set the veg and gravy boat in front of Sylvie. 'Thank you for laying the table, you two,' she said with a forced brightness.

The uncomfortable silence continued once they had all spooned carrots, broccoli and roast potatoes on to their plates, and July's father had given them all a few slices of meat. He had both the legs – nobody else ever dared to suggest that he might share one with the rest of them.

'This water's warm,' Shell said, taking a sip from her glass, then turning to July and making a face. This, from the woman who drank steaming mugs of tea when it was thirty-one degrees outside. 'It's not been sitting out here in the sun, has it?' She must have known it had as neither of the girls had been inside since their parents came downstairs.

75

July pushed her chair back. 'I'll get more.'

'Throw in some ice chips, as well,' her father said. 'Sylvie, you go and help her. And fetch the bread while you're at it.' He ate at least two slices with every meal. Usually July did too, but today she didn't have the appetite.

Inside, she tapped some ice cubes out of the mould in the freezer and wrapped them in a clean tea towel, as her father had taught her. She had asked him once why they couldn't simply put the cubes into the jug as they were, but he told her to stop being a smart arse. 'Who's had more life experience?' he'd shouted. 'I always know best – remember that.'

July held the bundle against the counter and bashed it with Auntie Shell's rolling pin, carefully aiming each blow.

'Let me help,' Sylvie said, covering July's right hand with her left one, over the rolling pin. 'We'll get it done quicker.'

Together, they smashed the rest of the ice into shards, giggling as they tried to coordinate their arm movements.

'What's so funny in there?' Daddy shouted. 'Get a move on.'

Sylvie took the white loaf outside, stuffing a slice into her mouth as she walked – typically, she got away without any hint of a reprimand for eating away from the table. While July refilled the jug at the sink and added the ice, she heard Auntie Shell saying, 'I've been having nightmares that the reservoirs will dry out. What would they do?'

July's father and Sylvie ignored her, so when July stepped back outside, she said, 'Did you know you can only survive for four days without water?'

Auntie Shell made a face at her as she sat down. 'I'm not sure we need to think about that.'

'It's true.' She'd read it in her encyclopedia. The water page was terrifying. 'WE ARE SURROUNDED BY WATER,' it yelled, then went on to outline disturbing facts such as: 'Seventy per cent of the earth's surface is covered by oceans and seas.'

There was also advice concerning thunderstorms, namely that you shouldn't go anywhere near the sea or a lake during one. Another reason not to trust the ocean.

'Where's the orange squash?' her father asked, mopping up some gravy with his bread. 'I told you to bring that out too.'

July looked at Sylv, who shrugged. She didn't remember him asking for it, but she got up without a word and fetched it from inside. When July set it down next to her father, he didn't add any to his water, and the bottle sat there, untouched, for the rest of the meal. She watched him in snatched glances over her plate. What didn't he want July to know? What exactly had he and Auntie Shell been arguing about? She thought about the pink, looping handwriting on the heart-shaped note, still stuck in her exercise book. How *had* her mother died?

Daddy and Sylvie continued to shovel food into their mouths, and July ate her potatoes, but Auntie Shell only picked at her dinner. 'School holidays at last,' she said, pushing a disc of carrot around her plate. 'Is there anything particular you two want to do? Within reason.'

'Within reason' was her catchphrase for this summer's break. Sylvie and July were being left home alone for the first time, and a very satisfying list of rules had been drawn up. July had approved – it was the closest she had ever felt to her stepmother, she'd decided, as she had copied it into her notebook. They were allowed to eat whatever they wanted for lunch, *within reason*. Nothing that required the kettle, oven or hob. They were to answer the phone and take messages. They were to stay together at all times, *within reason*, leave a note if they went out (the corner shop and friends' houses were approved locations) and lock the front door. They weren't to climb on furniture.

'When do we ever do that?' Sylvie had asked. 'We're not boys.' Auntie Shell had looked pointedly at July. 'I've seen your sister climbing up the outside of the bannisters, like a monkey.' Sylvie rolled her eyes and started to say something mean but Auntie Shell had cut her off. 'I also need you to promise to get along.' Finally, they were not to answer the door to strangers. 'Within reason?' Sylvie had asked, her mouth twitching with a smile. 'Don't joke,' Auntie Shell had spat at her, muttering something about Fred West.

July knew exactly what she would be doing this week. 'I've got two Judy Blume books from the—'

'Don't talk with your mouth full!' Auntie Shell shook her head. 'How many times?'

'Sorry,' July murmured, still with half a roast potato left to swallow.

Sylvie made a big show of opening her mouth wide, displaying that there was no food inside. July's father laughed. 'I have quite a bit of shopping to do,' she said, counting out the items on her fingers. 'Oyster Shell nail polish, some new earrings – maybe dangly ones, if you ever get round to deciding if I'm allowed.' She gave her mother a meaningful look, tipping her chair and balancing it on its back legs.

'Have you got anything in your piggy bank to pay for all of that? I'm not made of money.' Shell leaned over and pushed on Sylvie's thighs, bringing the chair crashing down.

July swallowed her last bit of potato. 'I'd like to get some incense.'

'That's a nice idea,' Auntie Shell said.

Sylvie mouthed across the table at July: 'Favourite.'

July's father wiped his chin with a piece of kitchen roll. 'Make sure there's none of that rubbish burning when I'm anywhere nearby,' he said. 'And open the windows. It's bad enough living with Fag Ash Lil, without you stinking the place out too.'

'I will, Daddy.' July smiled across the table, hoping for one in return, but it didn't materialise. Her father returned to devouring his chicken.

At the mention of Fag Ash Lil, Auntie Shell gave up on her lunch entirely, dropping her cutlery with a clang. 'So, shopping and reading. Anything else?'

'We've got our projects to do for Miss Glover,' Sylvie said.

'Oh yes.' Auntie Shell shifted in her chair and looked nervously between July and her father. 'But let's not discuss boring school matters over—'

'How's yours coming along, July?' Sylvie asked.

July tried to keep her voice steady. 'Good.'

'Who wants pudding?' Auntie Shell stood up, carrying her plate into the kitchen.

'Daddy?' July turned to her father, determined not to let Sylvie get her into trouble today. 'Was Great-Grandpa Leonard . . .'

His smile caught her off guard and she stumbled over her question.

'Was he cremated?' As soon as the words had left her mouth, July heard something clatter to the floor inside.

'Cremated?' Her father wiped a finger over the surface of his plate, scooping up the last of the gravy. It seemed to take forever. July hated these moments, when she was left wondering if she'd said the wrong thing again. 'No. He was killed at sea. The Krauts blew them up when they were delivering coal to Argentina. Why would he have been cremated?'

'Sylvie?' Auntie Shell called from the kitchen. 'You didn't open the peaches.'

'I told you, I can't use that can opener,' Sylvie shouted back. 'You need to get me a left-handed one.'

'I don't want peaches, anyway, if I'm honest,' July's father said over his shoulder to Auntie Shell. 'Get those chocolates out of the fridge, would you? The ones Mrs Porter gave me?' He was always getting treats and tips when he wrapped up the smaller jobs he did on days he wasn't up at the Big House. 'They love me,' he'd say when he brought home another bottle of wine or six-pack of beer. (*Anemone*, July would think to herself.)

'Poor old Leonard,' Daddy continued. 'Your gran will be so pleased to know that you're taking an interest in him. I'll tell her.'

For a moment July thought he was talking about Yaya, because she was the only grandmother she really knew. But no – of course he wouldn't refer to Yaya with that hint of fondness in his face and tone. He meant his own mother, July's Granny Orla. Still, it was unusual for her father to mention her, and July wasn't sure how to respond. His mother and Shell didn't get on, and neither of his parents had visited for several years. July could barely remember what they looked like. Sylv had told July once that Granny Orla 'didn't approve' of July's father remarrying, and they'd all fallen out over it. As far as July knew, Orla had only ever been kind to Sylvie, but Sylv, through loyalty to her mother, always referred to her as Granny 'Eurgh-la' and made a face as though she'd just smelled something awful whenever she was mentioned – as she was doing at this precise moment, in fact.

The fridge door slammed.

Auntie Shell reappeared with the box of chocolates and dropped them on to the table. 'Pudding,' she said, flapping her blue folding fan by her face. July watched, mesmerised, as its decorative pink cherry blossom fluttered rhythmically. 'Maybe July should call and tell her herself?' Shell added, her voice oddly light. It was a strange thing for her stepmother to say. She never willingly entered into a conversation about her mother-in-law, and if she did, it was only to say how much she disliked her. Behind the fan, Shell flashed a peculiar smile at July's father, her eyes bright with unmistakable provocation.

A cloud passed across July's father's face. 'July doesn't like talking on the phone, have you forgotten?' he asked, his own eyes responding with a message of their own – a challenge, July recognised, with panic rising in her chest.

Were they still cross with each other after the row upstairs?

She scrabbled to change the subject and avoid another argument. 'So . . . cremation,' she said. 'You didn't explain what it was.' She had looked it up when they'd got home earlier, but there was nothing in her encyclopedia. The only thing she could find about death was a small bit about Viking burials, which wasn't much use.

'I need a lie-down,' Auntie Shell said, squeezing July's shoulder firmly before stepping back into the house. July watched her go. It felt like she could do nothing right these days. Shell was clearly angry with her for asking about the cremation thing, that's why she'd grabbed her like that. Why was it such a problem? She was the one who had mentioned it in the first place. Did she think July was going to bring up her mother in front of Daddy again? She wasn't that thick. It would be at least another few days before she slipped up again; right now she was in that alert stage that accompanied the Calm, where she was extra careful.

'Some people are buried,' her father said. 'Others are cremated. It means they burn the body.'

'Yuk,' Sylvie said, popping a chocolate into her mouth. Why did *she* never get told off for talking with her mouth full? 'That's gross.'

July's father laughed. He always laughed at Sylvie. July wouldn't be surprised if he wished Sylvie was his daughter, instead of her. She took a cold, shiny truffle from the box and let it melt on her tongue as she thought about her mum's body being burned. She imagined it on top of a big bonfire like the one they had on the beach on Fireworks Night. The truffle suddenly tasted very bitter, and she winced as she swallowed.

'Come on then, girls,' July's father said, standing up. 'Help your old man clear away.'

As July picked up the serving dishes to bring through into the kitchen, she started humming. She kept the tune going as she returned outside to collect the glasses, and when she passed her father in the doorway, he ruffled her hair. She stood still, her scalp tingling with that rare sensation of a kind touch from him. Twice in one day! His arm around her shoulder, and now this. Her mouth filled with the memory of white chocolate mice and strawberry Millions.

'Don't stop singing,' he said as he disappeared back into the kitchen and ran hot water into the sink to wash up.

She started her tune again, and it was only then that she realised what it was – the hymn that Mum had liked, 'Be Thou My Vision'. That must be why her father had reacted as he did. Of course! Why had she wasted any time trying to imitate Sylvie? If she could be a little more like her mother, he would surely care for her more.

But how could she be anything like her, when she knew so little of her?

Once everything had been cleared away and washed up, July's father let her and Sylvie take a couple of chocolates each up to their bedrooms. July shut her bedroom door behind her, opened the curtains which Auntie Shell had made her close before church, then pulled out her List of Mum and notebook from her pants drawer, and her project notes from underneath her reading den cushion in the wardrobe. She sat cross-legged on the floor, surrounded by a sea of brown carpet speckled with Sylvie's nail polish stains (Sylv liked to paint her nails in here, so she wouldn't mark the new carpet in her own room). In front of July was the handout from Miss Glover, all about their summer project, and the notes she had started making about Great-Grandpa Leonard the day before.

After a few minutes of leafing through them, taking tiny bites of her chocolates to make them last, she opened her notebook and added Number 19, 'Be Thou My Vision', to the List of Mum, before climbing up on to her bed frame, carefully balancing on the slats in the absence of her mattress, and lifting the lower edge of one of the posters stuck to her wall – the one of a huge smiley face and the words 'Have a great day!' She reached up the back of it and unpicked a couple of strips of tape, pulling out the photo they secured in place, hidden from her parents. It was of her mother – the one Yaya had given her, and the only photo of her mother she had. Daddy said he didn't have any; there were none in the house. This single image held almost everything she knew about Maggie Hooper. In it she was sitting at a wooden table, behind a sewing machine (Number 9: she made all her own clothes), looking up at the camera and laughing. She wore a white blouse with black polka dots. On a shelf high above her head was a row of different coloured spools of threads and reels of ribbon. In her hands was a red sock, which she was darning. July's diligence in school sewing lessons was entirely due to this image. She was the only person in the class who cared about the difference between a running stitch and a backstitch, and her teacher said she had a talent for buttons. She had stolen a needle from the box at school to practise threading it, alone in her bedroom after lights out, whispering a small lie into the darkness to summon her mother to her side so she could watch her lick the end of the thread, press it between her teeth and push it through the eye.

July held the photo to her lips, before turning it over to examine the back. In an elegant, slanting script, her mother had written, 'Ten things worth loving'. Below that was a list – the one that had inspired her to start all of hers. 'My hair,' it read. 'My eyes. My generosity. My kindness. The birthmark on my right arm. My optimism. My sense of humour. My . . .' There were only seven points. Around the outside of it was a border, made of thin pink-striped paper, which had wrinkled a little where the glue had dampened it. She smoothed her fingers over the stripes, imagining her mother doing the same all those years ago when she pressed the paper down.

July stood up to look in the mirror on her chest of drawers. 'My hair,' she whispered, running her fingers through the tangled mess of her own. 'My eyes . . .' She resembled her mother a little, it was true. But that gap between her front teeth was not in her mother's perfect smile. She was nowhere near as beautiful as her. She wiped away a streak of sun cream next to her ear. How could she ever be like her mother? How could her father ever love her as much as he had loved Maggie Hooper? She felt like there was something missing in her, as if she had a hole in the middle of her tummy. Lifting her top a little, she tilted the mirror down to view her stomach. She couldn't see it, but she knew it was there. When she closed her eyes and breathed in and out, she could feel the air whistle through it, as it did through the gap in her front teeth when she parted her lips. She was incomplete; she was unworthy of his love. But holes could be fixed, couldn't they? Like the one in that sock, being darned by her mother's gentle fingers.

July hesitated, thinking of the way Daddy had smiled when she'd mentioned his grandfather this morning, and again at lunch. But then she felt that tingle on her scalp again, like a thousand tiny kisses. She quickly lifted a pen from the pot on top of her chest of drawers. Before she could change her mind, she crouched on the floor, picked up the page with a couple of lines about Leonard on it, crossed out his name from the title and replaced it with two words.

Maggie Hooper.

9

24 July 1995

The person Shelley Hooper was most angry with was herself. She was starting to think that this was true of most people. The very worst of Mick's fury, for instance, was directed inwards – she could see that much. He had never recovered from whatever really happened back in Almond Drive, and she knew he would never tell her what had gone on there.

Shelley was angry that she had let herself get into this situation, not once but two times. True, Sylvie's father had not been as physically aggressive as Mick, but his words had been bullets of brutality, and shots had been fired every minute of every day. For the second time in her life, Shelley knew she was bringing up her only daughter in a house where she wouldn't be safe, and now she had July to consider too.

When July was smaller, Shelley had told herself that Mick's take on discipline was just different to her approach. And July was his daughter, after all – not hers. She tried to talk to him about it, but when he made it clear that he wasn't interested in her advice, she tried to *show* him a better way, with how she parented Sylvie, hoping he might learn from her example. But as the years went on, and the incidents became more frequent, she couldn't stop herself from bringing it up with him, usually in the hours straight after he'd hit the girl. He was risking destroying his relationship with July, she told him. He was risking hurting her, badly. Was that what he really wanted? There were, incredibly, times when he did listen. He would crumple in her arms and tell her what his own father had been like – beating him, forcing him to eat food he hated, even making him sleep in the shed one night. There had been one or two times when he had cried, as he admitted that he knew no other way to be a father. She was so sure, as she held him in those moments, that he could change. That *she* could change him. But then, a few weeks later, it would all happen again. She had had to accept the truth: Mick Hooper was Mick Hooper. There would be no changing him.

Every night before she went to sleep, she prayed that someone would notice. She had started to do a deliberately cack-handed job of the make-up over July's bruises. Surely one of her teachers would see? Or the girl's grandmother? But months passed, and still nothing. She prayed that someone would send them help, even though she knew she risked punishment too, if the police or social services didn't believe that she had not been involved.

Shell prayed to her God because she still Believed, despite everything. But she had a back-up plan, in case God didn't come through. She had no idea if she could pull it off, but she had to try. She had to find a way to keep the two girls out of harm's way, out of Mick's way. Even if it killed her, she had to try.

She stared out of July's bedroom window over Harmony Close, the street still quiet as its residents slept. She had once believed this would be a happy place for her, fooled by the street name as much as she had been by Mick. In the dawn light she tried to think of the right words, resting her pen on a scrap of paper on her stepdaughter's windowsill. The note she was about to write, and the gift she had hidden in July's drawer, were steps towards convincing her that she was on her side. It was a tiny part of the plan, but a necessary one.

But how could she best explain this bundle of precious treasure? It held no value to most people, but to July, she knew, it would be the most special thing she'd ever held. How could she tell her stepdaughter why it had taken her so long to do this? How could she be as kind as she wished to be while also including enough of a threat so that July wouldn't put herself into more danger?

As she settled on the right words, picked up her pen and began to write, a floorboard creaked behind her. Shelley turned from the window and locked eyes with July.

What was she doing here, July wondered? Auntie Shell never came into her room, or so she had thought. July and Sylvie cleaned their own bedrooms (much to Sylvie's displeasure), and Auntie Shell would leave July's clean laundry on the floor outside her door instead of putting them away herself. What was she doing in here now? She glanced around the room, and noticed her pants drawer had been pulled open. *What's going on?*

Shell spoke first. 'I was . . .' She picked up a piece of paper from the windowsill and scrunched it into a ball. 'Close the door, would you?' she said quietly.

This couldn't be a good thing. Wishing she had forced herself to lie under her duvet in the living room for a bit longer, July stepped into her bedroom and shut the door as softly as she could.

'I'm not snooping, if that's what you think.' Auntie Shell was in her pyjamas and had no make-up on. July rarely saw her like this. She looked younger, but more tired. 'Aren't you going to ask me what I'm doing?'

July shook her head. 'I believe you.' She took a step towards her chest of drawers, feeling exposed with the top one open, but as she went to close it, she saw a pile of what appeared to be white cards, wedged in between her pants. They were near where she kept her List of Mum facts and notebook full of questions hidden. Had Auntie Shell found it?

Shell noticed her looking, and put her hand on the edge of the drawer. 'He's a complicated man, your father. Reminds me of a starling.'

'A starling.' July nodded, pretending to understand.

'From a distance, he looks black and brown, you see? Simple. But close up, you get to know him, and he's . . . he's . . .' Shell paused. 'Glossy.'

July took a step towards the closed door and pressed her back against the wood. When Auntie Shell didn't expand on her comparison, July felt obliged to say something. She cleared her throat. 'Glossy?'

'Yes. With shimmering greens and purples.'

'You mean . . . the colour of bruises?'

'Hm.' Auntie Shell put the pen and ball of paper down on the chest of drawers and pulled the cards out. Except, they weren't cards, they were photos. July could see that now. 'You should have these.'

Auntie Shell pressed the bundle to her chest before July could see the one on top. She looked hard at July.

'If you tell Mick I gave you them, there'll be no TV for a week.' She paused. 'Make that two weeks.'

July didn't like the sound of this deal. She hadn't asked for these photos, she hadn't asked for Auntie Shell to sneak into her bedroom – and now she was being threatened with sanctions? But she was intrigued. 'I won't,' she said, pulling at her lip.

Her stepmother held the bundle out towards her.

July glanced over her shoulder. Was that a noise downstairs? Was her father up? Was she going to get into trouble simply for touching these, whatever they showed?

'Take them, then,' Shell said, pushing the photos into July's hands. 'I've got to have a shower before work.'

July looked down. There were about twenty in the pile, held together with a thin, faded red rubber band. As she slid it off, it snapped in her fingers. Each image showed a woman she recognised as her mother, but she had never seen any of them before. The paper felt different to the photos they had these days – thicker, less shiny. Had her mother once touched these very pieces of paper? The thought made her skin go cold, despite the muggy warmth of her bedroom. She remembered her father, telling her that he had no pictures of her mother.

As July slowly shuffled through the photos, she saw pictures of her parents together, some smiling, some not. There were others of Maggie Hooper on her own – there was one of her in a garden with her head tied in a scarf, the same red scarf, July was sure, that Yaya wore every day. Another where she was sitting on an orange settee holding a bunch of daffodils, and a close-up of her, apparently asleep. She really was beautiful. July wanted to look at each one for a day, at least.

'Remember, not a word.' Auntie Shell moved past her, gently turning the door handle.

July grabbed her arm. She couldn't let this moment pass without trying to get more out of her. 'How did she die?' she asked, forcing herself to be brave.

Auntie Shell blinked, and her cheeks reddened a little. 'You know how. She was hit by a car.' She pulled the door open a little, taking a step out of the room.

'But what exactly happened? What killed her?'

Shell looked over her shoulder. She seemed nervous.

Then a new question occurred to July, one so obvious she wondered why she had never thought of it before. 'Who was driving the car? The one that hit her?'

'He wasn't anyone – it was nobody . . .' Shell broke off. When she spoke again, her voice had hardened. She sounded more sure of herself. 'It was just a kid, nineteen he was, speeding through the village. He wasn't from round here.' She shook her head. 'You're too young to be talking about any of this.'

July was sure she knew more, but could feel the distance opening up again between them; she needed more before Shell left, before things went back to normal. Reluctantly, she changed tack.

'What was she like?'

'I never met her, July. You know that.'

Did she know that? July couldn't remember ever having been told so before.

Auntie Shell crossed her arms over her chest. Without her make-up, it struck July how much she looked like her mother, but with straight blonde hair instead of her mother's auburn curls.

'What were her favourite flowers? Daffodils? What bedtime stories did she read me?'

'July . . .'

'Please. You must know something.'

Auntie Shell came back in and closed the door again, checking the landing before she did so. 'She wrote to you.'

'What?'

'Letters, notes. Something.'

'How do you know?'

'Keep your voice down,' Auntie Shell whispered. 'I heard your dad arguing with Yaya about it once. "All those bits of effing paper" he called them. Your grandmother was saying, "But they're July's!" They both thought the other had kept them, thought the other was lying.'

'And who had them?'

'Neither of them, as far as I could tell. They couldn't work out where they had ended up.'

July stared at the photos in her hands. The one she'd got to as she looked through them was of her mother alone, on a boat, coiling a rope over her arm. She was effortlessly stylish in a denim shirt and shorts, with her hair tied in a high side ponytail with a huge pink scrunchie – grinning with white film star teeth. *You wrote to me?*

'Look,' Auntie Shell said, keeping her voice low.

July held her breath – what else was she about to find out?

'If you go digging around, just make sure he doesn't find out, okay? Remember what happened when Katie-Faye's mum told him about that ridiculous séance?'

July nodded. It had been Katie-Faye's idea. 'Your mum will talk to us, I'm sure of it!' she'd said. July hadn't been convinced, but when the glass started to move under her hand she'd promptly vomited on the carpet in Katie-Faye's bedroom.

'That's how angry he would be, do you under—'

'I get it.' July's mind was flooded with memories of the second time a Lesson had taken place in the bathroom. Water up her nose, in her eyes, in her mouth. Coughing and spluttering. Her father's words: 'Do you have any idea how good my life was before I had you to deal with? Is this how you repay me for all my sacrifices? You do nothing but disappoint me.' She shook her head to get rid of them, and looked up at Shell. 'I'm not an idiot,' she said.

'I know. And you're a good kid. It's just . . .' Auntie Shell reached out and did something she never, ever did. She stroked July's face, the way she stroked Sylvie's. Her fingers smelled of lavender hand cream. July's body went rigid, and her muscles only relaxed when Auntie Shell pulled her fingers away and turned to leave.

'Thank you,' July said. She tried to say 'Mum' too, but the word got stuck between her tongue and her lips.

Once the door closed behind her stepmother, July clambered into her wardrobe and got comfy in her den, pushing her encyclopedia into the opposite corner next to her school shoes before examining each photograph in turn. She felt like she had a whole reel of ribbon in her hands, a precious and rare prize. The quality wasn't great in many of the images, but her mother definitely had the same small, pointed nose as July. She had the same freckles too, and July marvelled at one particular close-up which showed the Cassiopeia cluster next to her mother's left eye. July had never seen it before; she had only heard about it from Tony.

But more than her appearance, her mother had some of the expressions July recognised as her own. The way she raised one eyebrow slightly, and the curl of her lips when she smiled – the way the left side went higher than the right. July had seen these things in the few photos she had of herself too. There was one black-and-white picture of a girl, who July assumed must be her mother, grinning on a seesaw. A stern-looking woman stood behind her in a miniskirt and thick black eyeliner, a protective hand placed on her shoulder. Her face held some resemblance to Yaya's, but was that really her? In those clothes? With long hair, in pigtails, of all things? As she got to the bottom of the pile, July wondered why there were no photos of herself as a baby or small child with her mother. Where were the pictures of July on a seesaw, her Mum's hand on her shoulder, like Yaya's?

The final photo was of her parents, standing with their arms around each other's waists. Her mother was pregnant – this was the only photo of the three of them July had ever seen. She had a thick silver bangle on her wrist, which July immediately recognised as one that Yaya often wore. As she peered closer, July realised they were standing outside the front door of a house. The style of the porch and the small window to the left of the door were familiar – it was the same as the design of the houses in Almond Drive. This must be the house where they'd lived, with her. Between her parents' heads, she could just make out the number on the door: 4.

Which meant their house had been next door to the one where that crazy rat killer now lived.

IO

HMP Channings Wood
2 September 2001

Dear July,

I'm so glad you did decide to write. For six years
I've thought about you: what would our life have
been like, if I'd been less of a coward?

You say you're angry. Fair enough. I am too.
I hate myself for what I did to you, for what I put
you through. I could give you excuses, but you
don't deserve them. I messed up, didn't I? A little
girl should be able to count on her dad. I should
have kept you safe, not put you in harm's way.

What I keep thinking is, what if I'd faced up
to the truth? Who knows where we would be now?
You ever think about this kind of thing? The deci-
sions and mistakes we make, and where we end
up because of them? My cellmate used to call me
the Philosopher (now it's just Phil) because I don't
shut up about this kind of stuff. It's helped me, I
reckon, to work out where I've been going wrong

my whole life. I'm not the same person that jury found guilty.

Do you believe someone can change? No pressure, of course . . . but you could visit me, and see for yourself? It would be good to see you again. I miss you. I can imagine you rolling your eyes as you read that. I know you'll think that's impossible. But I mean it.

Anger is one thing, but please don't hate me. The rest of your letter makes me hopeful that you don't – am I imagining it? Thanks for telling me what you've been up to. It may be boring to you, but hearing about your world was the highlight of my week. Learning to play guitar, hey? Nice one. I used to play a bit, before my father told me he couldn't stand to hear any more Dylan songs being murdered and stopped me practising in the house. And those GCSE results! Well done. Better than anything I managed in my exams.

You say you have questions: go ahead. Just remember that my post will get read by prison staff. It's not private, not just between you and me, you know? So think carefully about what we want other people to know.

And July, I'm so sorry for everything. You didn't deserve any of this.

Love,
(I'm not sure I have the right
to call myself this, but here goes . . .)
Dad

Ps. Your sister wrote to me last summer and told me you two were getting on well now. I didn't hear from her again. Is she okay?

II

24 July 1995

July pretended to be disappointed when Sylvie told her she was going out with Helen that afternoon, and that July wasn't invited. (According to the Stepsister Rules, July could not spend time with anyone Queen Sylv was friends with or wanted to be friends with.) Auntie Shell had managed to borrow a bike from someone she worked with for Sylvie for the summer, to placate her after July's birthday gift was revealed.

'But your mum said we should stick together,' July said, watching her stepsister across the dining table and trying not to grin. She took a bite of one of the cheese sandwiches she had made for them both, shaped into hearts with a cookie cutter which had been a hand-me-down from Katie-Faye. (July always got first dibs on Katie-Faye's family's unwanted items. How did one family end up with not one, but two sets of novelty cookie cutters?)

No sandwich had ever tasted this exciting. Her chance to check out the house where she'd lived with her mother had come sooner than she'd expected. She had spent the morning in her den poring over the photos of her mother, looking for tiny details that might give her clues about her and writing notes under her project title. She tried her hair in some of her mother's different styles, attempted to recreate her facial expressions and lay on the floor imagining her father's reaction when he realised she *was* exactly like his darling Maggie, after all. She fantasised about day trips they might take together: the cinema again? A zoo? She pictured him laughing at her jokes and giving her a kiss as she left for school in the morning.

'Shelley says a lot of things.' Sylvie picked the slices of Edam out of her sandwich and licked the marge off the bread. Why did she have to eat so slowly?

July leaned her elbows on the table, put on her best forlorn look and gazed out of the patio doors into the sun-drenched garden. The outside world glowed even more brightly than usual today, full of promise. Something about the way the light seeped into the room triggered a memory: Mum, serving her a soft-boiled egg in a red cup. July had first remembered this on an equally sunny day a few years ago, recalling her own giggles at the silly name her mother had given the meal as she cracked her egg open with the back of a spoon. Number 10: Mum loved dip dip eggs.

July dragged herself back into the present. 'But I thought we could do each other's hair, and do makeovers and stuff.'

'Jeez. Stop being so pathetic, January Hooper.' Sylvie got up, opened one of the kitchen drawers and pulled out a plastic bag, shoving the remains of her sandwich inside. 'I'm not sticking around to listen to you whinge at me.'

'Wait, please. Don't go.' If Sylvie had listened carefully enough as she stomped out of the door, she would have heard the wobble of a laugh in July's voice.

The idea of being so close to the place where she had lived with her mother was intoxicating. Harmony Close was home, but her old house in Almond Drive was a slice of wonder, a deliciously tangible part of her past.

It felt different this time, as she cycled round the bend. She wasn't looking at two rows of anonymous homes, facing each other across blank tarmac under an equally featureless, bright blue sky. This was the road where she had lived, and now she knew exactly which house she'd been in.

Number 4. She'd barely noticed it when she was last here. She stood at the gate, trying to see past the windows' reflections into the front room. It wasn't familiar. How old had she been when they moved away? As hard as she ransacked her memories, the earliest one she could shake to the top of the pile was of her choking on a barley sugar and her father tipping her upside down to dislodge it, in the living room of their current home. She couldn't remember anything from this house. The front door looked the same as the one in the photo, which she pulled out of her pocket to compare as she stepped on to the front path. In the photo the door was painted black, but now it was a light blue, which made her hopeful. You had to be a nice person to paint your door a pretty colour like that, didn't you? The kind of person who would let a little girl in to see the house she grew up in?

July rang the bell and waited, breathing hard. She wouldn't run away.

But nobody came to the door. She rang again, and knocked in case the bell wasn't working. Still, no one.

Instead, an upstairs window at number 6 was flung open, and a white-haired woman poked her head out. 'They're not there, love,' she said.

'Oh. Do you know . . .' July trailed off. What exactly *did* she want to know?

'They left yesterday. You one of Olivia's friends, are you? I shouldn't really tell people they're away, I suppose.' The woman laughed. 'But you don't look like the burgling type.'

'When will they be back?'

'End of the summer, I'd say. He's Italian, see – still has family out there.'

July didn't see, but she nodded anyway.

'Sorry, love. You'll have to find someone else to play with today.' The woman began to pull her window closed.

'Wait,' July said. Maybe the woman could help her with her project in some way. It seemed unlikely, but she didn't have a long line of candidates wanting to tell her about her mother, so she was going to have to ask anyone she could. 'How long have you lived here?'

'Two years. Retired down here, didn't we, Bill?' A man grunted from inside. 'Nottingham, originally. Makes a nice change, you know?'

July smiled. She'd never been to Nottingham. She'd barely been anywhere else in the country at all. 'Thank you,' she said, a familiar surge of disappointment washing her back down the front path towards the gate, like a grain of dirt in the water tipped out of a mop bucket. Two years wasn't long enough. The woman wouldn't have known her mum. 'Bye.'

She took one last look into the front room. Maybe it didn't matter that they weren't here. What was she hoping for, anyway? They hadn't known her mum. They wouldn't be able to tell her anything that could help her be more like her. It was only a house. Wasn't it?

She wandered towards the alleyway entrance and discovered that the gate into the track along the back of the houses was still unlocked. She thought of the weird bearded man with the dead rat and paused with her hand on the bars of the gate, but then she remembered the feeling of her father's fingers ruffling her hair and pushed. She crept along the track until she was at the back of number 4. Straining to see over the fence, she looked up at the first-floor windows. Which room had her mum slept in? Which room had been July's? There were bright, striped curtains in one of the bedrooms, confirming her theory that they must be a nice family.

'You again.'

July jumped back from the fence. She hadn't heard the gate at number 2 open, but there he was – the rat killer, wearing a tattered wetsuit rolled down to his waist, with a stained yellow T-shirt covering his upper half, dark in patches at the shoulders where his wet hair had dripped on to it. When she looked up at his face, he was staring at her with that unsettling intensity again, like her skin was tissue paper which he could see straight through. She pulled her cap down to shield her face.

'How did you get in this time? Pick the lock?' He moved towards her, so that he was only a metre away: close enough for her to smell the dampness of his wetsuit, close enough for her to see some caked-on food near the hem of his T-shirt.

She shook her head, looking over her shoulder. 'I should . . . I should go.'

'You should. After you've told me how you got in.'

She couldn't meet his eye and fixed her gaze instead on his grimy bare feet. His big ugly toes were encrusted with red dust from the cracked mud in the alleyway 'I-I think the lock is broken,' she stammered.

He looked past her to the gate and swore under his breath. 'Perfect,' he said, and she felt his glare land on her for another long moment, before he turned and stepped towards a long blue and white surfboard which was leaning against a tree in the alleyway. He picked it up and carried it into his garden. 'I'll be in trouble,' he said, 'if you're found back here.' He threw the words at her, gruffly, over the fence. 'So, like I said the other day, you'd better go.' He reappeared at his gate, scowling at her.

July felt sick with fear in his presence, her stomach churning. But there was something about him, despite that. Something that made her want to talk to him.

'H-how come you've been surfing?' she asked, kicking at a stone on the path. 'No waves today.'

He laughed, a mean kind of laugh. 'I went for a paddle. Is that allowed?' July looked up at him for long enough to see him shake his head, but glanced away again when he tried to meet her eye. 'Why do I get the feeling you don't know who I am?' he asked.

The unexpected softness of the way he spoke caught her off guard. It was the first thing he'd said to her without sneering or shouting. She felt heat rise in her face. What did he mean? Who *was* he?

'Of course I do,' she said. Her mother stepped out of the shadows, giving July such a fright that she looked straight at her, catching a shimmer of green as she disappeared. Goosebumps crept down her body, from her neck to her ankles.

'Sure,' the man said, slamming his hand against his fence, making her jump again. 'Time's up, young lady. Go on, sling your hook.'

She felt suddenly angry. Why couldn't he just leave her alone? 'You don't have to talk to me,' she said, trying to sound more confident than she felt. 'I'm not here to see you.' She glanced back up at number 4. From this angle, standing closer to his house, she could see some of the ground floor through a gap in the fence: a large pair of patio doors revealing glimpses of the kitchen and a little window over the sink which was slightly ajar. 'My mum used to live there.'

When she turned, he'd gone. She looked round his gatepost to find him hunched over the board, which was lying on the ground, scraping at it with a bar of wax.

'Why did you ask me last week if someone had sent me? Who did you mean?'

He stopped what he was doing but didn't look at her. She took the opportunity to study the odd scar by his eye and wondered how he had got it. Maybe in a surfing accident? Or perhaps somebody had smashed a bottle in his face in a fight? 'Let's just say I know your father. I've seen you in the village with him. We . . .' He threw the wax to the ground with sudden, chilling ferocity. July stepped back. 'I'm not talking to you about this,' he said, spitting on the ground between them.

But July couldn't stop herself. *He knows Daddy.* 'Did you know my mum too?'

'You can't be here,' he hissed. 'Do you ever lis—'

He was interrupted by a woman calling to her children in one of the other gardens along the track. 'Snacks!' she cried brightly. The children laughed and shrieked back at her, 'Ice cream? Can we have ice cream, Mummy?' July imagined her mother doing the same when she was out playing, right here – in the garden a few metres away. She wouldn't have cared if it was ice cream or a plate of mushrooms – she would have given anything to be called inside by her mother.

The man sighed, rocking back on his heels, and the stare returned, attempting to pierce her skin. July looked away and backed out on to the track.

'Maggie Hooper.' The way he said her mother's name – unhurriedly, with a sigh – made her shudder. 'You could say I knew her, yes.'

July tried to ignore the way her skin was crawling. He might have information that could help her. 'And d-did you live here at the same time as us?'

'I did.'

July glanced at his face again, only to find that he was still watching her closely. *Run,* a voice in her head told her. *This is the kind of man you're supposed to run from.* But she was intrigued by him. He wasn't just looking at her eyes, she noticed now; she felt his scrutiny dart across her face, settling repeatedly on her mouth.

'She died,' July said, watching as he narrowed his eyes, staring intently at her lips as she parted them to speak.

He nodded. 'She did.'

She expected to see the mix of pity and awkwardness in his

eyes that she was used to seeing when she told people this. But his expression was entirely different to that of anyone she'd ever spoken to about it. Sad, yes. But not sorry for her. He looked . . . *disgusted*. That was the best way she could think to describe it when she thought about it later. His mouth turned down at the edges like he'd just bitten into something rotten.

Worried she was running out of time, July battled on. 'How exactly did she die? What do you remember about her? Did she like The Beatles? Did she . . .' July searched around her for inspiration. 'Did *she* surf?'

At that, he stood up and stepped towards her, ushering her away from his gate. 'I've got stuff to get on with.'

'Just tell me one thing.' July stood firm, clenching her fists. 'One thing about her.'

He laughed his strange, mean laugh again, and July forced herself not to allow tears to well in her eyes. How could he laugh at this request? She'd had people ignore her and refuse her, but never laugh. 'Only one thing about Maggie Hooper?' He shook his head. 'I have a shift in a few hours. I don't have time for this.'

'Nobody ever wants to talk about her.'

His lips stretched into a line and his eyes grew darker. 'That's not my problem.'

'Forget it.' She walked away from him, back towards the alley.

He called after her. 'Ask your bloody father, if you want to know what she was like.'

Ask Daddy? It wasn't this man's fault. He couldn't know what a ridiculous suggestion that was. But she couldn't help shouting back at him in frustration, 'It's not fair!'

As she slammed the alley gate behind her, she heard him yell, 'Life isn't fair, Jenny!'

Jenny?

The more time she spent with this creepy man, the more questions she had.

12

24 July 1995

Judy Blume had done her best to distract her for the rest of the afternoon, in the shade of the pear tree in the garden at Harmony Close. But July couldn't lose herself in the plight of Jill and poor, terrorised Blubber, not while the occupant of number 2 Almond Drive kept elbowing his way into her thoughts every three sentences. At one point she'd misread Jill's name as Jenny; later, she found herself reading the same page four times. And even the unnerving familiarity of the novel's class bullies, Wendy and Caroline, couldn't draw her in enough to make her forget that her project was sitting upstairs in her wardrobe, with only a few sentences written below the title. She was already three whole days into the school holidays – last summer she had finished all her homework within forty-eight hours of the final school bell. She hated seeking help with schoolwork, but she would have to overcome her aversion if the Maggie Hooper project was to progress beyond a title and a handful of photographs.

And so she found herself that evening lying as motionless as a shore crab buried in sand, hiding from its predator. Only she lay on her makeshift living room bed, not the bottom of a rock pool, and she was trying to trick her stepsister, not a hungry cormorant. She had spent more than three hours playing dead, waiting for the perfect moment to emerge and ask Sylvie for a favour. She tried to hypnotise herself with the blurry sight of the ceiling fan, attempting to guess how many thousands of times it spun each minute, grateful that the breeze it generated was just enough to necessitate covering her chilled legs with her treasured *Little Mermaid* duvet. Sylvie hated it, of course, and called her a baby for admitting to liking anything Disney-related, but July couldn't bring herself to take Shell's offer of getting something 'more grown-up'. July had no desire to paddle in the shallows, let alone live underwater, and yet she experienced a keener connection to the mermaid princess than the majority of her real-life acquaintances. After being played a hundred times after school, on rainy weekend mornings and sick days on the settee, sections of her video copy were now fuzzy, with lines of static across the screen. It wasn't only Ariel's red hair that made her feel familiar, or even that the girl didn't have a mother. It was the way in which nobody even mentioned her mum in the film that struck July's heart, and the way her father King Triton only told her off because he loved her so very much. She had tried to explain to Sylvie once, but her stepsister had entirely ignored her point, replying simply, 'Yeah, but who would want to stop being a mermaid? As if!'

Patting her hand on the floor to find her glasses, she slipped them on and looked across at Sylvie now, deep in sleep, strands of her fringe stuck with sweat to her forehead, and her pale arms and legs flung over either side of her mattress. July's own limbs were aching from the effort of not moving, but she didn't want to wake her stepsister up until it was *really* late, or cause all the sweet packets she had hidden under her pillow to rustle.

She held her watch up towards the window so she could see the hands illuminated by the faint glare of the street light shining through the gap in the curtains. 11.57 p.m. This would have to do – she couldn't wait any longer.

'Sylv?' she rolled over to the edge of her mattress and tapped her stepsister on the shoulder. 'Sylvie? Wake up.'

Sylvie groaned and batted her away with her hand. 'Sleeping. Leave me 'lone.' She rolled away from July and on to her stomach, burying her head in her pillow.

July slid her tub of Millions out from behind the cushion on the settee and shook it, so that all the tiny pink strawberry-flavoured balls rattled around inside. Sylvie didn't stir, so she unscrewed the lid, took out a few of the sweets and climbed on to Sylvie's mattress, pushing them against her stepsister's lips.

That did it. Sylvie sat bolt upright, spluttering and squinting. 'What you doing?'

July covered Sylvie's mouth with her hand. 'Shh. You'll wake them.' She gestured towards the kitchen. Her father's stuttering snore could be heard through the wall – even in sleep, his presence dominated the house.

'I was dreaming.'

'I've got everything. Chocolate, Flumps. These.' July held out the plastic tub.

Sylvie hesitated, but not for long. 'Okay, weirdo.'

'I've been saving them under my bed for a special occasion.'

Sylvie snatched the Millions out of July's hands and dug out a handful. 'Was this what you were shoving between my lips? Gross. God, you're such a freak.' She stuffed them into her mouth and smiled.

July opened the Flumps and took one out, squashing the marshmallow softness between her fingers. But now that she had instigated their midnight feast, the thought of actually eating any of the sweets made her throat constrict. What if Sylvie refused? What if she told July's dad what she was doing?

She squeezed the Flump hard between her thumb and forefinger. 'I wanted to ask you to do something.'

'I can eat sweets in the day too, you know.' Sylvie whispered the words as she chewed. 'You didn't have to wake me up to bribe me.'

'I didn't want to risk them hearing us.'

Sylvie's eyes narrowed and she scooped out another handful of sweets.

'I was thinking, I could do your project for you. And your maths homework. And clean your bedroom for four weeks.'

Sylvie screwed up her nose and shrugged.

'Six weeks,' July offered.

'What do you want?'

'It's easy. Ask your mum something for me.' July had squashed her marshmallow so hard that its intertwined strands had separated. She dropped it on to the carpet and wiped her sticky hand on her mattress. 'You can ask her anything and get away with it.'

'What exactly?' Sylvie snatched the Flumps, lifting the bag up to her nose to inhale. Her bare leg emerged from underneath her duvet, exposing a penny-sized birthmark on her calf shaped like a heart. July liked to think of it as her stepsister's benevolence trying to show itself – her body's way of saying, 'I'm all right, really.' As she tried to form the words of her question with her dry tongue, she focused on the heart's imperfect edges. Sylvie was a good person, deep down. She'd want to help.

'Ask her what she knows about my mum. Especially what she knows about the accident,' July said, glancing at Sylvie's face just in time to catch the end of an eye roll. She dropped her head and refocused on the heart, willing Sylvie's kindness into existence. 'She'll tell you,' July whispered. 'You know she will.'

'I don't know.'

'Please.' July fished another two bags of Flumps out from under her pillow and threw them on to Sylvie's bed.

'I'm not talking to Shell about it, okay? She gets really funny when I bring your mum up. But—'

July snapped her head up. *But what?* Sylvie looked like she was thinking hard. She rubbed at her forehead.

'What if I knew something that I could tell you? Like, now.'

July enclosed her thumbs into her fists and squeezed. 'Go on.'

'It'll change everything. Are you sure you want to know?'

'You *do* know something,' July said. 'That stuff you were saying on my birthday—'

'If I tell you, I want more than you doing my stupid project and all that.'

'Like what?'

Sylvie held July's gaze for a moment, the two grey pebbles of her eyes glinting in the peach glow from the streetlight. 'You'd need to move out.'

July sat back, the unkind edge of the settee base needling her spine, and laughed. But Sylvie didn't. 'You can't be serious.'

'This –' Sylvie waved her hands around in circles '– isn't working. You don't want to be here. It's so obvious that you hate my mum.'

When would Sylvie break into a grin? July studied her closely, looking for signs that she was about to bend double with repressed giggles and take the mickey out of July for being so gullible. 'Where do you want me to go?' July asked, her voice low and her words careful. 'This is my home.'

'Go live with your mum.'

July screwed her eyes shut. Had she fallen asleep by mistake while she was waiting for her opportunity to wake Sylvie up for the midnight feast? Was this a dream? July knew Sylvie didn't like her, but she'd never expected her to pull a stunt like this. Demanding she move out? The problem, July had heard Auntie Shell telling Sylvie's grandma on the phone once, was that Sylvie had never been keen on younger children. She wasn't the kind of girl to coo over babies; she didn't make friends at the park with anyone smaller than her. That summer when July and her father moved in with Shell and Sylvie, before they'd bought the Harmony Close house, July had been three years old. Sylvie was a much older and wiser four years old. There was a mere ten months between them, but 'Sylvie always was that bit more mature, you know?' said Auntie Shell on the phone. July had thought Sylvie was her new best friend. 'Look at my kitten stickers, Sylvie! Do you prefer my hair in a plait or a pony, Sylvie? Do you want to dance with me, Sylvie?' Pre-school Sylvie's answer was always 'No.' Nothing much had changed since then. But did she really hate her this much?

Sylvie moved towards July and knelt on her mattress, placing a hand on each of her shoulders. 'Do you promise that if I find a way for you to live with your mum, you'll do it?' Sugary whispered breath hit July's face, its unsettling sweetness contradicting the sour edge of Sylvie's demand. 'You've got to promise before I tell you.'

'You're making no sense.'

'Promise!'

'To do what?' July hissed. 'Go and live with my dead mother?'

'You've got to swear.'

'You're mental.' July shook her head, but Sylvie was still holding on to her and staring at her with an intensity she'd never seen before in her stepsister. 'Okay, I promise. I will . . . move out.' It didn't seem to matter, promising to fulfil an impossible demand. Maybe Sylvie hadn't properly woken up yet. Or she was actually insane.

Sylvie let go of July's shoulders and held out her little finger. 'Pinky.'

Now it was July's turn to roll her eyes. 'This had better be good.' She linked her own little finger around her stepsister's to confirm their deal, muttering 'Pinky promise,' then Sylvie pulled away and lay back on her own bed, exhaling.

July waited, tucking her feet under her duvet, making Ariel's green fishtail flip up. She wanted to hide behind a cushion until Sylvie finished what she was going to say – like she did during the scary bits in the film, such as when King Triton went to smash up his daughter's collection of human trinkets pilfered from shipwrecks. She could never watch that part.

Eventually, Sylvie spoke. 'Don't scream or anything, okay?'

July pulled at her lip.

'Your mum's not dead.'

'My . . . What did you say?'

July pinched her leg. She must be having a crazy dream. But when she pinched, nothing changed. She was still there, in their darkened living room, listening to her bonkers stepsister.

'It was a couple of weeks ago,' Sylvie whispered, leaning close to July. 'I wanted to call Helen, but when I picked up the phone downstairs, *he* was already on the line, on the bedroom phone. I hadn't realised and—'

'My dad?'

'Yes. With your Granny Orla.' Sylvie put her fingers into her mouth and pretended to vomit. 'I listened for a bit, but they weren't talking about anything interesting, so I was about to hang up.'

'But you didn't.'

'No, because suddenly your Gran says, "So how's Maggie?"'

'What?' July grabbed a handful of her duvet.

'Yep. Then your dad goes, "Good, as far as I know." Something like that.'

'What did he say *exactly*?'

'Stop interrupting,' Sylvie hissed. 'I'm trying to remember.'

'Sorry.'

'Orla says, "Tell her I still wear that dress she made me." And your dad goes, "I don't really see her that often, Mum. We've talked about this."'

'I don't believe you.' July swallowed. Her head was swimming. 'You're making this up.'

Sylvie reached for her hand and squeezed it before continuing.

'Then she says, "You shouldn't have given up on her, Michael. Maybe you could still make it work." '

'Why are you doing this?'

'I think I might have gasped then, because he goes, "What was that?" So I put the phone down.'

July reached over for the tub of Millions, dipped her hand in and shovelled some into her mouth. She needed the sugar to help her process what she had heard. She chewed and swallowed, before whispering into the dark, 'You probably misheard him. He was talking about someone else.'

'I didn't, and he wasn't. You need to find her.'

'If it's true, why hasn't she been to see me? It's been years.'

'And Mick still meets her. Can you believe it? Do you think my mum knows?'

'He still . . . what?'

'Weren't you listening? He said, "I don't really see her that often." '

July suddenly remembered Miss Glover's handwriting. *She didn't die in a car accident.* 'The note . . .' she said. Was this what her teacher had wanted her to find out? Was Sylvie actually telling the truth?

'The note,' Sylvie repeated.

'The one from Miss Glover, remember? It said that Mum didn't die in a car accident. She must know that Mum's alive. I have to try and speak to her again. How am I going to find her?'

Sylvie picked at a fingernail. 'I don't think that's a good idea.'

'Why not? She *knows* something, Sylv! And she wants me to know it too. Maybe she has Mum's address, or—'

'It was me. I wrote it.'

'But . . .' July stared at her stepsister. 'But the paper. The handwriting.' She shook her head. It must have been from Miss Glover.

'It was easy to nick one of those stupid little hearts. And her writing isn't exactly difficult to copy. I slipped it into your book first thing that morning, the day you found it.'

July pressed her fingers into her eye sockets. 'Why didn't you just tell me?'

'I knew you wouldn't believe me. I was right, wasn't I?' Sylvie moved on to her toenails, flicking the end of each one. 'But you trust her. And anyway, even if you had believed me, you'd have gone straight to him and dropped me in it. Imagine how furious he would be if he knew I'd been eavesdropping.'

'So why tell me now?'

'Because you've got to find her, July. You've done nothing about it, and it's been what? Five days? It's been excruciating, the waiting. Watching you do *nothing.*'

'And this bothers you because you want me to find my mum, who I've believed was dead for the last eight years, or because you want me out of here?'

'Can't it be both?'

July still didn't know whether to believe her. In her mind she raced through possibilities, reasons why Sylvie would make this up. 'You just want to get me into trouble. You love it when my dad's angry with me.'

'I do not.' Sylvie spoke through a mouthful of Flumps. July could see them, bright pink and white, like big, soft lies filling her stepsister's mouth. 'Seriously, I have better things to do than make up stories about your mum.'

'But she died in a car crash on my second birthday. I remember it.'

'Maybe the car crash happened, but she didn't die. I don't know. But I know what I heard. She's definitely alive.' Sylvie paused. 'I thought you'd be pleased.'

'I would be, if it was true.'

'It is. Listen, why don't you do that thing Miss Glover was

going on about? Go to the library in town and look in old news-papers. See if there's an article about the crash.'

'I suppose.' Where was Mum now, and why hadn't she come back?

'You know the date. It won't be hard to find – if it happened.'

'Can you get your mum to take us into town?'

'She's working every day this week.'

'Saturday, then.'

'Okay.' Sylvie yawned. 'You're all right, aren't you?'

July nodded into the darkness. 'Yeah, I . . .'

'It's good news, right? She's out there, somewhere.'

Sylvie rolled over and July was left alone again, with a pecu-liar, light feeling in her chest, staring at the spinning ceiling fan. It felt like it was pulling her mind with it, in dizzying circles. What if Sylvie was telling the truth? Where was her mother now? Was she also lying awake somewhere, watching a ceiling fan? July took off her glasses and laid them carefully on the floor.

Had her mother left them, or had they left her? And why?

She was certain she wouldn't sleep the rest of that night, but as the sun started to paint the dawn sky pink, she did drift off. She dreamed of a quilt embellished with an intricate pattern of stitches, each one a lie, with one of them unpicked, the ripped thread begging to be tugged free, to pull the rest of the stitches loose too. She dreamed of moving in with her mother. Of hold-ing her hand, of finally finding answers to her Big List of Questions, of sharing a can of Diet Coke and laughing together when the bubbles went up their noses. And of learning how to be the perfect daughter that her father wanted her to be.

13

HMP Channings Wood
4 October 2001

Dear July,

My daughter, going to the theatre! There was none
of that in my school days. Sounds like a fun trip.
I don't know any Shakespeare plays; I'll try to
find that one in the prison library. You made my
mouth water with the description of your interval
feast. What flavours did you have? Let me live a
little through you – we get nothing recognisable as
ice cream on our dinner trays.

Now . . . on to your questions. When I think
back, yes – I reckon your mum knew. As for why
she didn't tell me, I have no idea. I suppose she
thought she was doing the right thing.

And no, YOU ARE NOT A BAD PERSON.
It breaks my heart to see you write that. You did
nothing wrong.

Love,
Dad

14

25 July 1995

The beach was busy as Kay looked out of her bedroom window, even though it was barely half past nine. Families had set up camp for the day with windbreaks, towels, folding chairs and picnic blankets. It was too painful to watch. She had moved to the old coastguard cottages overlooking the small, sheltered beach in the winter, not realising the torment that peak season would cause her. 'That used to be us,' she murmured to herself, feeling a fresh wave of sobs coming.

This was interrupted by the sight of July, freewheeling down the hill. Kay ducked beneath the windowsill and crawled across the floor, making sure she was out of sight. Had Tony locked the door when he had left? Would July come in and find her?

Yes, she'd given July the bike, but Kay hadn't expected her granddaughter to use it to visit unannounced.

Oh July, Kay thought. *Any day but today.*

Every Tuesday Tony went out for the morning 'to run errands'. Silently, they had fallen into this routine, this parting of ways which allowed Kay time to shuffle around the house, letting the tears flow, so that she could just about hold it together for the rest of the week.

She simply couldn't let July see her like this.

Kay listened as July knocked on the back door. She imagined her, wrinkling her nose at the damp smell that lingered on the path along the rear of the houses, as she always did. 'They never see the sun,' Kay whispered in explanation, as she curled her body up into a ball at the foot of her bed. She knew what July would do next, as she waited for one of them to answer – she would inspect her grandmother's line of beachcombed limpets on the windowsill and stack them into towers.

Her granddaughter knocked again.

'Yaya?' she called. Then, to Kay's shock, she shouted, a little more loudly, 'Mum?'

It was too much for Kay to bear. She only had these few hours each week, only this short time to mourn the loss of her best friend. People rolled their eyes when she said her daughter was 'her person' – the one human being who understood her, more than any other. She's your child, not your friend, they told her. They were jealous, she knew; she pitied them. But that past smugness was no use to her now, as she spent these short hours wrapping herself in her guilt and grief. With July here, she felt an extra layer of shame, pulled tightly around her shoulders. She saw the girl so rarely, what with Mick's warnings and threats not to come to their house, and all the obstacles he put in the way of July visiting them at the cottage. This kind of visit was so uncommon, she should be welcoming her in, and yet she couldn't force herself up. What did that say about her?

She didn't deserve to be a grandmother. Hadn't deserved to be a mum, either.

Everywhere around her, she saw mothers and fathers who were doing a far superior job to her. It shamed her to admit that even Mick bloody Hooper seemed to be a better parent than she had been. For everything awful that had gone on between her daughter and that man, and despite the way he had treated Kay herself, she had to concede that he was a decent dad. She didn't see much of him with July, but when she did he was always loving, always protective. Everything to his child that she had not been to hers.

Outside the back door, July considered turning around and going home. She could shut herself in her bedroom for the rest of the morning, while Sylvie and Helen crimped each other's hair on the settee and watched daytime television with the curtains closed. That's how she had left them half an hour ago. They never paid her any attention when they were together – they hadn't noticed the front door close when she left, and they wouldn't hear it when she arrived home. She could try ringing Granny Orla again to ask about her mother – she'd called this morning but there had been no answer – or she could bide her time; wait until the weekend and consult the newspapers at the library.

Impossible! That was four whole days away. Ninety-six hours. Five thousand, seven hundred and sixty minutes of waiting, stuck in the Wilderness of Not Knowing, bordered on one side by the world she'd known before the midnight feast and on the other by a new, sparkling realm where her mother still danced and laughed.

July kicked at the letters lying next to the basket. Where *was* Yaya? It was the first time she had ventured further than the village boundary on her bike, and her bravery had been for nothing.

Feeling guilty for her strop, she picked up the post to make a neat pile of it again. At the bottom, beneath a couple of boring white envelopes, was a holiday brochure with a note stuck to it. 'Enjoy!' someone had written in cramped handwriting. 'No rush to give it back.' The front cover featured a photo July knew to be of Venice – Yaya (who had been twice) had described it to her enough times. Seductively dazzling turquoise water littered with gondolas cut through old, intricate buildings. July didn't trust it. How could people live like that? Surrounded by water? In bold white letters across the top of the cover were the words 'Discover Italy'.

July wondered again where her mother was. Maybe she'd been travelling the world? Perhaps she could take July with her on the next leg of her journey. They would travel light, like Yaya was so proud to do, only taking one small rucksack. She scuffed her feet back along the path to the road, where she had left her bike. They would steer clear of Venice. They certainly would not travel by boat. But perhaps they could go to Italy. Maybe she was *in* Italy right now?

Italy.

July chewed at her thumbnail.

A path appeared in the haze of her mind, winding its way out of the Wilderness towards that magical land where Maggie Hooper wasn't an angel who visited July when she lied, but a flesh and blood human being she could look at, touch and talk to.

Jumping back on her bike, July pedalled as fast as her legs would let her – all the way to Almond Drive.

She slipped round the back of the houses. The man from number 2 hadn't fixed the alleyway gate yet; it was secured with a rope tied with several half hitches, but they were easy for her to undo. Once she was through she tried the gate at the bottom of number 4's garden but it was locked, so she dragged some grubby bricks to make a step. She looked over. *Yes.* The little kitchen window was still open. Was she really going to do this?

Climbing over the fence was easier than she thought it would be. She dusted herself off, ran up the garden path and – again, with surprising ease, perhaps she was born for a life of crime – slid her hand through the ajar window, lifted the latch and swung it open fully, before squeezing in, head first, and falling on to the draining board next to the sink.

Standing in the kitchen of the house where she'd spent her earliest years, her heart beat as fast as the wings of a hovering kestrel, and she cast her eyes around with the hunting-sharp focus of one too. But instead of voles, mice and shrews, she looked for one thing only: Maggie Hooper, Maggie Hooper, Maggie Hooper. Her mum had stood here, on this very spot, and cradled baby July in her arms as she cried. At a dining table like that one over there, July had sat in a highchair and her mother had spoon-fed her mashed banana. July had learned to crawl on this floor as her mother clapped and cheered her on. But the place didn't feel like home to July. She couldn't remember it. She was most unnerved by the smell: the strong floral scent of an alien perfume, which hung in the stuffy, warm air of the closed-up house. They hadn't left their curtains and blinds closed against the heat, like Auntie Shell would. July pulled at her lip. She had hoped to feel more of a connection to the place.

What was she hoping to find? Now that she was here, the escape route from her confusion was fading – had it simply been a cruel mirage? July tried to rebuild it, piecing together the thoughts that had brought her here. She had seen her mother here, the first time she had found herself on Almond Drive. What if it wasn't simply one of her usual apparitions? What if it really had been her? July thought of what the neighbour had said yesterday, leaning out of her window. 'I shouldn't really tell people they're away . . . He's Italian, see – still has family out there.' Standing outside Yaya's cottage, July had felt certain that the Italian was her mother's new husband and that Maggie Hooper had never left this house. Seeing the holiday brochure, she had convinced herself that her mother was on holiday in Italy, which accounted for why July hadn't seen her since that first day, when she'd spotted her getting into the silver car. But now that she was here, she felt less sure.

The kestrel of July's heart swooped, dropping after the disappointment of a failed kill, but she forced herself to continue looking for evidence of her mother's presence. A sewing machine? Cans of Diet Coke? Handmade clothes? Photos?

On the mantelpiece was a framed black-and-white family portrait, in which they were all grinning – the parents appeared to be enjoying their children's company, which was an unimaginable concept for July. Was that her mum in the photo? She squinted. No. Maybe it wasn't the family that lived here? Could it be their cousins, or friends?

She turned her attention to the pinboard on the wall in the kitchen, sliding her fingers over business cards, receipts and leaflets, until they stopped at a small scrap of paper with a handwritten phone number on it. She read the number once, then again, and a third time. That was her phone number. Hers, her father's, Auntie Shell's and Sylvie's. What was that doing here?

Before she could think any more about it, something brushed against her leg and she jumped backwards, knocking her elbow against a solid object. There was a loud crash, and she turned to see what she'd hit. A large green glass vase lay in pieces on the floor. A fluffy white cat skittered underneath the dining table.

July crouched and started picking up the shards of glass. What should she do? She could tell the vase was expensive, even in its broken form. Dread trickled into her limbs, like it did when she was near water or when her father flexed his fingers before a Lesson. She shouldn't have come here. She searched the cupboard beneath the sink and pulled out a dustpan and brush, as the cat emerged from under the table and curled around her legs again, mewing. She kicked at him gently, but he wouldn't leave her alone. 'Go away,' July hissed, as she attempted to sweep up the glass, and he rubbed against her shins, purring.

And then, turning in a flash, he scampered away for the second time since her arrival. This time, though, he hadn't been spooked by a falling vase.

This time it was the turn of a key in the back door which had frightened him.

15

25 July 1995

Before the door opened, she flung herself under the dining table. A tablecloth hung low over the edge – she hoped it would conceal her from whoever was coming in. As she crouched, peering under the edge of the plastic-coated material, she saw a pair of men's feet walk in – large and ugly. She squeezed the handle of the dustpan as she recognised the yellow flip-flops. The man from next door.

Please don't find me.

She pressed her cheek against the wooden frame of the table. It felt cool against her panicked skin – she was sweating profusely, and now she could feel it dripping down her back. What excuse could she give for being there?

The man said nothing. He slid his flip-flops off and stepped slowly, deliberately across the black-and-white checked lino, stopping right next to the table. The cat poked its head under the tablecloth, rubbing up against her again, appraising her with unfriendly eyes. She tried to shoo him away with the brush, scowling at him. But then he started mewing.

'Mitten?' the man said. His voice was groggy, and he coughed to clear his throat. 'What's up, buddy?'

I'm going to prison. Daddy's going to kill me.

The edge of the tablecloth lifted, and a man's eyes met hers, but it was not the person she was expecting. This man was clean-shaven and looked much younger than the rat killer from next door. But when she studied his swollen, worn-out eyes, she realised it was him. The glasses were the same. The eye colour was the same. The hair on his head, though shorter, was the same shade of dark brown. In her confusion, she couldn't bring herself to speak.

'I should have known,' he said, dropping the cloth and laughing. 'Planning to stay under there all day?'

'Of course not.' What was she going to do? She was in so much trouble. And in a house with this weird man. Beard or no beard, he made her feel uneasy.

'I'll go then, shall I?' he asked. 'Leave you to . . . what were you doing?'

She looked at the dustpan and brush in her hands. 'If you must know,' she said, trying to sound annoyed rather than scared, 'I'm cleaning.' Her mother joined her under the table, her hand on July's back. *How can you be here?*

'Really.'

She imagined his eyes watching the table, staring through it, at her. She shuddered. 'It's my holiday job,' she said, flattening her forehead against the table frame as her mother stroked her hair. *But you're alive. You're not an angel.*

'Bit young to be working, aren't you?'

'I'm twenty.'

'Twenty? So you should know what breaking and entering is, then?'

Her mother kissed her shoulder. *How are you here?* July turned sharply to face her, sitting up straight and banging her head on the underside of the table. She tasted blood in her mouth and dabbed at her tongue with her finger, staring at the empty space in front of her.

'You all right?'

Why didn't he sound angry? He seemed more amused than

anything else, and it was unnerving her. She remembered his horrible laugh yesterday – his sense of humour creeped her out. She crawled awkwardly out of her hiding place, wiping the blood from her finger on to her leg. 'If you're thinking,' she lisped, sucking her sore tongue, 'of calling the police, I wouldn't. It would be embarrassing for you.'

He laughed again. 'Not much chance of that.'

What did that mean? She hated the way he talked in these riddles. He treated everything she said as a joke to which only he knew the punchline. She glared at him, taking in his new look. He still looked dishevelled, even without the beard. His hair was sticking up in all directions, and she could see the label poking out from his T-shirt at his side. *What a state*, she thought. July's father wouldn't be seen dead looking as sloppy as this. But without that mess of hair hiding his face, he did look like a different man, she had to admit. He looked . . . normal. She wouldn't avoid him if she passed him in the street, but she would have done if he'd still had the beard.

'It wasn't you who untied the rope on the gate then?' he asked, raising an eyebrow.

'Of course not. I have keys. For the front door.' Her mother returned, her bare feet wiggling as they stuck out from underneath the table. July forced herself to look away.

'Sure you do.'

She bit at her thumbnail. 'Why would you tie a gate up with rope, anyway? Wouldn't a burglar just undo the knots?'

'It's not burglars I'm worried about.'

'Then who?'

He bent to pick the cat up and stroked his head. 'I just want to make it more difficult for—' He stopped. 'I didn't have time yesterday to fix the lock before my shift. All I had was some rope.' He gave her one of his funny looks again, staring hard at her face.

'Your T-shirt is inside out,' she said, to interrupt his gaze, pointing at the label.

'Is it?' He held the cat out at arm's length and peered down at his own stomach. 'Hm. Well, you did wake me up.'

'But it's . . .' she checked the clock on the wall. 'Ten fifteen!' ('Lie-ins are for deadbeats,' her father always said if they slept past eight o'clock.)

'I was at work until seven this morning.' He yawned.

July didn't know what to say to that and poked the glass around in her dustpan with the tip of the brush. What job did he do, working overnight? The only people she knew who worked nights were doctors. And policemen. She felt her cheeks flush. *I'm going to prison.* 'I'd better be getting on with my cleaning,' she said, the pan shaking in her hand.

'Of course. I'm sorry, I forgot. Carry on, don't mind me.' He laughed again. 'Cleaning,' he said, shaking his head. He lowered the cat to the floor.

'What are *you* doing here?' she asked, putting the dustpan on the table, picking up a tea towel from beside the sink and using it to rub at non-existent stains on the kitchen surfaces. 'How come you have a key?'

'This lock hasn't been changed in years. I heard something.' He looked around and spotted the smashed vase on the floor, behind the table. 'Ah.'

'It was an accident.'

'Tell that to the judge.'

She clutched the towel in her fist. 'You said you wouldn't call the police.' Her voice came out too squeaky. 'Please. My dad will kill me.'

The man's face darkened, and all trace of the earlier laughter disappeared. 'I'm not calling anyone,' he said softly. 'Don't worry. Leave the vase. They'll think Mitten did it.'

She watched as he picked up the dustpan, emptied its

contents back on to the floor next to the rest of the broken remains. He handed the pan and brush back to July, and she stowed them under the sink.

'Listen, I know why you're here.' He rubbed his eyes with the heel of his hand. 'I know you're not cleaning—'

'I am. I—'

'But you can trust me. I'm not going to drop you in it. If I told them you'd been here, I'd have to admit I was too, wouldn't I?' He paused, tilting his head to the side. 'Want to know a secret?'

Auntie Shell's voice came into her head. *Never trust a grown-up who wants you to keep a secret.* She shook her head.

This made him smile again. 'No? First child in history to turn down a perfectly good secret. Have it your way, then.'

Now she wished she had said yes. What would he have told her? But then she thought again about Auntie Shell's words of warning. She knew nothing about him, other than where he lived. Sweat pricked at her back again. She was alone in a house with a stranger. Nobody else knew she was here. He could murder her, right here, and nobody would know. If he was a policeman, he would know how to hide a body.

'I've got to go.' She moved towards the door.

'In a minute,' he said, standing in her way. The smile left his eyes. 'You're here because of your mum, I take it?'

He knew something. July was conscious of how loud her breathing sounded in the silent room. What should she do? She glanced at the door handle, then back at him. 'She lives here, doesn't she?'

'If you're who I think you are – July, is it?'

She nodded.

'Then yes. Your mum lived here once, a long time ago.'

'No. Not *lived*. I mean, she lives here now. Don't lie to me. I know she does. I saw her last Thursday, when I first came back here. She was getting into a car.' She clenched and unclenched her hands, and wiped her sweaty palms against her shorts.

'You can't have seen her.'

'Long red hair, getting into a silver car. It was her, I know it was.'

'Silver car . . .' He rubbed at his temples. 'You mean the woman who lives at number 16. She has hair a bit like your mum's.'

'N-no. It was her. She's alive, isn't she?'

He leaned against the back door. 'No.'

'You can't know that for sure.'

'I do. It wasn't her that you saw. It couldn't have been.' He looked sad now but was still staring at her.

She didn't believe him. 'Did you see them burn her body?'

'Burn?'

'Cremate her.'

'Is that what they've told you? I . . .' He shook his head and muttered to himself, 'Why would he do that?'

'She wasn't cremated?'

'No. She's buried, at the church. She loved that graveyard. Lots of people do. Best cemetery in the country, I reckon, with those views.'

July's heart leaped. Number 21: Mum loved the graveyard. But then it hit her, what he was saying. Her face grew hot. 'But my stepsister, she heard . . .' She trailed off. What *had* Sylvie heard, exactly? Could she have got it wrong? Perhaps July's father had been talking about somebody else?

'I'm sorry.'

'Who are you? How do you know this? Are you a policeman?'

He laughed. 'Policeman? No. I work in a care home, night shifts.' He looked out of the window. She got the feeling that he didn't want to meet her eye. 'You know who I am. I live next door to this house you just broke into. I think I'm the one who should be asking questions here, not you.'

She ignored him, blinking hard to counter the threat of tears. 'How do you *know* she's there?' She spoke quietly. 'In the ground?'

He smiled sadly, turning back to her. 'You are certainly your mother's daughter. She always questioned everything, drove people mad.'

Number 22. July felt a fresh rush of joy as she tucked away the information, but then it backed away, like seawater retreating from the shore to form the next wave. She had another fact, but she didn't have her mum. She would never see her again.

'I don't know for sure, you're right,' he said. 'I can't be absolutely certain that she is in that grave.'

Another wave, hope foaming on its lip, broke against her heart. 'She could still be alive?'

'No. I'm sorry, I didn't mean that. I was being literal. Look . . .' He sighed, knocking the knuckles of one hand against the palm of the other. He looked like he was deciding whether to tell her something. 'I don't know for certain that she is in the ground, but I know for sure that she is dead, because I saw her die.'

16

25 July 1995

'You saw her being hit by the car?' July asked. Could she trust him?

He shook his head. 'What car?'

'The car that hit her. On my second birthday.'

He fixed his eyes on her face; her whole body went rigid under his scrutiny.

'That's what you think happened?' he asked. 'A car crash?'

'Yes.'

He sank into a bright red velvet armchair in the corner of the kitchen, leaned his head back and looked at the ceiling, drumming his fingers on his thighs. July wanted to shake him. Why did he keep stopping like this?

'I was there. I remember it,' she said, hoping to spur him into conversation again. There was something hanging between them in the muggy heat of this kitchen, she could feel it – the tension that accompanied new information about her mum. What did he know?

'I'm not sure what it is that you remember,' he said. 'But she didn't die in a car accident. I don't know why they've told you that.' As he spoke, he grimaced as if he was in pain, rubbing the smooth skin on his jaw. He was still examining the ceiling, reclined in the chair. 'She died of natural causes. She got ill, suddenly.'

Now it was July's turn to pause, to leave him waiting for a response. In a daze, she picked up an apple from the bowl on the dining table. It was lighter than any piece of fruit she'd held before. Lifting it up to her nose, she sniffed, but it had no aroma. She turned it in her hand, taking in its unusual shine, and tapped it with her nails. Fake. She tossed it back into the bowl to join what she now realised were plastic pears and oranges. Fake, false, pretend – she mouthed the words in disgust. There were lies everywhere in this world. She should have known this wasn't her mother's house any more, she thought bitterly. She may have known very little about her, but she was sure she wouldn't ever display fake fruit.

She skimmed her finger around the rim of the bowl. 'Was this after the crash, then? She didn't die, but got ill later?'

'No . . . I—'

'Why should I believe you?' The words shot out like bullets. He sat up and looked at her.

'You don't have to. But it's the truth. There was no car crash. Not that I remember. She was here.'

She slid her hand into her pocket and stroked her Diet Coke slammer. All she had of her mother was an object the woman had never even touched and a handful of blurry photos her father would beat her for looking at. Now this man was telling her that her memories were false too? 'What was wrong with her?'

'Something happened that – well . . .'

'Was it cancer?' There was a girl at school whose mum had cancer in her lungs and died. July had tried to feel sorry for her, but she couldn't. She'd had her mum for a whole nine years before it happened.

'No. It . . . it was bad luck.'

She wanted to ask how someone died of bad luck but didn't want to sound stupid, so instead she asked, 'And you were there?'

'You mustn't tell anybody that I told you this, okay? Do I have your word?'

She ran her tongue against the gap between her front teeth, back and forth.

'Do I?'

'Yes. I promise.'

He stood and moved to the large window overlooking the garden, touching a hand to the frame. When he spoke again, the words emerged slowly, as though each was a fragment of sea glass he'd searched through hundreds of pebbles to find. 'I heard her.' (The first piece, bright green, rectangular.) 'From my house.' (Another, darker in colour, polished into a circle.) 'She was in pain.' (Jagged, ugly and brown.)

'What was she saying?' She threw the pieces of glass back at him. *These aren't enough.*

'What do you mean?'

'You said you heard her.'

'She . . . she wasn't saying anything.' He leaned his forehead against the window. 'She was . . . Christ. I don't know if I should be telling you this.'

'Please. I want to know what happened.'

Without turning to look at her, he nodded slowly. 'She was . . . er . . . she was shouting. For help. I let myself in. Your parents gave me a spare key for when they went away and stuff like that, you know.' He held up the key he'd used to open the back door a matter of minutes ago.

'And was I here too?'

He snapped his head round and she saw that his face was flushed. He looked straight past her, as though she wasn't there. 'Yes. You were . . . really small. You didn't know . . .'

July waited, but he didn't finish his sentence. 'What didn't I know?'

'You had no idea what was happening.'

July imagined herself as the chubby toddler she'd seen once in a photo, the only picture she'd seen from her childhood years. In it, her face was screwed up as she bit into a large wedge of lemon. July winced at the imagined sourness. She was only two, Daddy had said. He had discovered the photo tucked inside the Bible on their shelves. Two: the age she'd thought she was when her mother had died in the car accident. But it wasn't a car accident; she had been unwell. *Bad luck*. Had she been scared by her mother's screams? Did she realise that something was wrong? Where had Daddy been?

'Then what happened?' she asked.

'Look, I told you,' he said, his words no longer meticulously sought-out sea glass but sharp kicks of shingle. 'She died. That's it.' He used the hem of his T-shirt to wipe the greasy mark of his forehead from the window, rubbing at it so hard she thought he might crack the pane. Then he thrust his feet back into his flip-flops and opened the back door. It banged against the wall.

'In this house?' July looked around her. Where had it happened? In this kitchen? Her eyes fell on the red and white cabinets, like something out of an American diner in the telly shows she and Sylvie watched. Bright blood red. Was there a lot of blood when you died of bad luck?

'I've said too much already. You really should ask your family about this.' He tapped the door. 'Come on. Be as quiet as you can.'

'But they won't talk about it,' July whispered, taking one last look around the room. On the wall there were two painted plates, with tiny baby feet imprinted on each one. Where were these family treasures in Harmony Close? They had no photos on the walls, no baby feet on plates, not even a creepy box of milk teeth like Katie-Faye's mother had on a shelf in their living room. It was as if she and Sylvie hadn't existed until their two families had merged.

'I won't tell anyone you were here, if you don't tell anyone what I told you.' *Never trust a grown-up who wants you to keep a secret.*

'I won't.' She walked past him as he held the door open. The searing heat hit her like a slap as she stepped outside, the sun cruelly cheerful. She tugged at her cap to shield herself from its glare: she was being forced the wrong way out of her Wilderness, back into her old life, with no mum. It was not a day for sunshine. She ran down the garden path, unable to avoid the spitefully sweet smell of simmering roses. They were taunting her too. *Your mother planted us. We knew her better than you do. Look at us. Look!* She kept her eyes trained on the paving slabs. It wasn't a day for roses either.

She threw herself against the fence at the bottom of the garden, grateful for its indifferent beigeness stretching like a frown in front of her, soothed by its discreetly rotten scent.

'The gate's open,' the man from number 2 hissed after her as he locked the door.

July nodded, pushing her way through. She was so confused. She was pleased to have more information, but she had no more understanding of her mum's death. *Bad luck.* July had never heard of someone dying from bad luck before. Cancer, yes. Car accidents, yes. Heart attacks, yes. But then, what did she know?

And why had her father let her spend so long believing that her mother had died in a car crash? 'Why would he lie to me?' she muttered to herself as she kicked at the weeds on the path. It was a foreign sensation, questioning her father: one that made her feel untethered, like a dinghy cast off from its mooring without a sail. But as soon as the words left her mouth, she realised her error. Her father wouldn't lie to her – no way. She must have misunderstood him.

The man locked the gate behind them as she made her way back towards the alley.

'I'm sorry I can't tell you more,' he said, keeping his voice low. 'It's not my place.'

'Not your problem.'

'Good luck. But don't let me find you here again. Your mother doesn't live here any more. You believe me, don't you? That much I can tell you.'

July looked up at the house. 'I guess.'

'Take care.'

She paused by the alley gate, playing with the length of rope she had untied to open it. 'What's your name?' she asked.

He squinted at her. 'Why?'

'Just . . . because. I don't know your name.'

'Rob. My name's Rob Salter.'

'Thanks, Mr Salter.'

He laughed softly.

'Why do you always do that?'

'What?'

'Laugh at me?'

'You're a funny kid.'

'I'm not.'

He held his hands up. 'Okay, okay. You're not funny.' But he laughed again. Then his face dropped, and he was serious once more. 'I'm not joking around now, though. I never want—' He stopped abruptly, wincing as though he'd stood on something sharp. 'I never want to see you back on Almond Drive again, understand? You're going to get at least one of us into big trouble.'

'It won't matter though, will it? You're moving.'

'You saw the sign.'

'Couldn't exactly miss it.'

'That won't be happening for a few months. Let's not give my neighbours something else to hate me for. Even as a leaving gift.'

She lifted a hand to wave goodbye and shut the alley gate behind her. He was still standing on the track as she did so, watching her.

July meandered home, words spinning in her head with each downward stroke of her feet on the pedals. *Rob – Salter – Rob – Salter – Rob – Salter.* She knew that name. Where had she heard it before?

17
26 July 1995

There were those who said one shouldn't interfere, especially not if one was a man of God. But Paul didn't tend to
listen to those types of people. In his experience, they were pre-
cisely the ones who *did* interfere, and he had no time for
hypocrites. As Jesus said, first, take the log out of your own eye,
etcetera.

And, besides, he couldn't stand by and watch as this little girl
was strung along like this. She deserved to know the truth, even
though he knew it would upset her. It had been bothering him
since Sunday. But how was he going to help her? How could he
get to her without arousing the suspicion of her parents?

As it happened, God delivered her to him. He was good like
that.

Paul was weeding the oldest section of the graveyard when he
heard the girls coming. The weeds looked lovely – a mixture of
golden dandelions and shocking-pink herb-Robert – and it was
a shame to uproot them. But he was procrastinating heavily,
avoiding the weekly chore of labouring over his sermon, which
everyone seemed to suppose was his favourite part of the job (it
wasn't – his favourite part of the job had been eight years ago
when his teenage daughter and her friend had spiked the com-
munion wine with Drambuie. It had all been downhill since
then.)

He heard the other one first – Sylvie, was it? The two girls were relatively new to his flock, and he didn't know them very well. He hadn't known July Hooper's mother, either – he'd only moved here in the late 80s – but of course, he had heard the rumours about what she had done. And he'd heard about the events of '85. Lorraine, the churchwarden, had reliably informed him that a number of his congregation had been involved. Many of them were the type who would be so bold as to suggest one oughtn't interfere in another's business.

Sylvie's voice carried through the still air as the pair of sisters cycled up the lane. 'He definitely likes me?' she yelled.

Still gripping a handful of flowers, Paul hid behind a large lichen-covered stone cross and watched the girls approach.

'Why else would he want to see you?' July Hooper replied.

Paul wiped the back of his hand across his brow, his mind racing to formulate a plan. He'd need to slip back into the church, but yes – he knew what he would do. There was a red leather bound book on the shelf in the office which would do the trick quite nicely.

And if that didn't work? He would try something else. He wondered how much the girl knew and how much he should help her find out.

Today would be a start, he thought, as the giggles grew closer.

'Are you sure this is the way?' Sylvie asked. 'Are we getting married?'

July had told her that she'd bumped into Sylvie's crush, Nick Hanson, the day before, and he'd asked her to bring Sylvie to meet him at a surprise location. (July's mother had sat in the corner of the living room, listening to their conversation, curling a strand of her hair around her finger.)

July raced ahead of her stepsister, singing the wedding march into the trees lining the road. When she arrived at the church gates, she parked her bike. 'Nick wanted you to meet him by one of these graves,' she shouted over her shoulder to Sylvie, who was still puffing her way up the lane – the bike Shell had borrowed for her was old and unloved, and stuck in a high gear.

As Sylvie reached her, she eyed July suspiciously, but she leaned her bike against the church wall and followed her up the bank into the graveyard. 'Are you serious?' she asked, panting. 'Here?'

'Definitely.' July started searching. *Maggie Hooper. Maggie Hooper.* Or perhaps she'd be under 'Margaret'?

'What name are we looking for then?'

'It's a surprise.'

'Tell me, September.'

'No.'

'Tell me.'

'No!' July found a row of 1980s deaths. ANITA SUMMERS. CORA GREENE. DANIEL WARD.

'Tell me tell me tell me.'

July paused and closed her eyes, starting to regret bringing Sylvie along. But she needed her there; she needed her to see why July would not be moving out. She lifted her wrist to her nose for a hit of White Musk, to give her courage. 'I think it might be Margaret.'

'Margaret who?'

'Hooper.'

'Hooper . . .'

'Yes.'

'Wait.' Sylvie grabbed July's arm and stopped her as she neared the end of another row of graves. 'Margaret as in Maggie? Maggie Hooper? She isn't here. She can't be. I heard your dad, remember? Talking about her. In the present tense.'

July shook her arm loose and walked away, continuing her search. HANNS LEEDS. JOYCE HOWARD.

'Why would Nick want to meet me next to a non-existent grave?'

'Help me look, would you?'

'He's not coming, is he?'

July was reading the epitaph on the headstone of a beloved wife and mother called Rosemary Simpson when she felt pain between her shoulder blades. A hard shove sent her flying forward on to the path.

'What are you playing at?' Sylvie shouted. 'I knew Nick wouldn't have talked to you. I didn't believe it for a minute.'

July stood, brushing gravel off her dungarees, picking pieces of dusty grit off her tongue. She spat a few remaining bits on to the ground, wiping her mouth.

'I'm going home. Never do this to me again.' Sylvie stomped down the hill. 'In fact, don't even speak to me for the rest of the holidays.'

'Just help me find her, will you? Don't you want to see it?'

Sylvie stopped next to a line of older graves, surrounded by daisies and buttercups. 'How do you know she's dead?' she asked, turning slowly. 'Who have you been speaking to?'

'You take those ones, over there.' July pointed to a group of stones on the opposite side of the steps.

'You went somewhere yesterday morning, didn't you? I knew I'd heard the door go.'

'Can you be quiet? I need to concentrate.' July worked her way steadily along another row. These were 90s deaths now, and still no sign of her mother.

'You sound like Shelley.' Sylvie snorted, but did as she was asked and started to make her way along the graves she had been assigned. '*Be quiet, Sylvie, I can't hear myself think. Does my head in.*'

'Hm.'

'I absolutely do not want to be anything like her when I grow up. In my house I won't make anyone take their shoes off to sit on the settee. My kids will be allowed to eat chocolate spread straight from the jar, and . . .' She crouched to read the words on one of the headstones. 'Look, a baby. She died before her first birthday, it says here.'

'Why would you not want to be like your mum?' July couldn't understand. She had no desire to be a clone of Auntie Shell either, but she'd love to be exactly like her own mother. She had styled her hair this morning like her mother's in the boat photo – a high side ponytail with the biggest scrunchie she could find among the mess of her bedroom. 'Who will you take after, then? Your dad?'

'Myself, dummy. I'll be me.' Sylvie spread her arms wide, making a proclamation to the entire churchyard.

'But surely you'll be a bit like one—'

July was interrupted by someone shouting, 'Hello, girls!' Paul the vicar was standing by their bikes at the bottom of the steps, wearing his dog collar with a short-sleeved shirt and knee-length black shorts. July couldn't help but gawk, her jaw hanging slightly open – she had never seen him without his flouncy white robe on, and had assumed he always wore it, maybe even to bed. He looked almost normal. 'Would you young ladies be kind enough to give me a hand in here?'

Could they tell him they were busy? She glanced at Sylvie, who pulled a face. But July wasn't convinced she could say no to a vicar – not even one wearing shorts. 'Okay.'

They followed him into the church. The divine cold of the building's interior soothed her impatience at having her task interrupted. They'd had the dogged sun in their faces on the ride over, and on their backs as they peered at the headstones. July had never been inside without dozens of other people, and the silence and stillness stunned her. It was the quietest place she had ever been.

'If you'd make a few tidy piles of those leaflets over there, I'd be eternally grateful,' Paul said, pointing at a table covered in scattered pieces of folded green paper. Before July and Sylvie could respond, he clapped his hands once and said, 'Excellent. One less job for me!' He paused, and his smile slipped into a straight line. 'I . . . You know, girls, if there was ever anything bothering you, or that upset you, you are welcome to talk with me.'

July didn't know what to say to that. She nodded but knew she would never take him up on his offer.

'Or your teacher!' Paul clapped again. He looked relieved, as if he had just stumbled across the answer to a question that had been bothering him for days. 'Yes, your teacher is always a good option. Very trustworthy, teachers are. Very helpful. I'd best be letting you get on. Thank you, young ladies!'

With that, he strode off towards the other end of the church and disappeared through a door beneath the red and blue bell ropes.

Queen Sylvie rolled her eyes at July. 'What was that about?'

'No idea.'

Sylvie sank into a pew. 'First you drag me here under false pretences, then you get me lumbered with a church errand, and now the creepy vicar is trying to be our new best friend. Remind me never to listen to you ever again.'

'He's not creepy.'

'No, you're right. Everything he just said was totally normal.'

July collected up the leaflets, which detailed the different services on offer in August, as well as events coming up in the community hall, and arranged them into batches of twenty.

'Look, there's a flamenco dance class on the sixteenth,' she announced to Sylv. 'It's only two quid!'

'Like Mick will let you go to that,' her stepsister replied, raising an eyebrow.

July stuck her tongue out and picked up a few of the leaflets. She spread them into a fan shape, lifting them above her head, then raised her chin and rotated her wrist like the flamenco dancers on the video Katie-Faye had brought back from her holiday in the Canary Islands. Sylvie sniggered as she pulled a series of dramatic poses: both her arms in the air as her feet stamped across the stone floor.

'Why would he ask us to do this, anyway?' July whispered, returning to the table, slightly breathless. 'It's not exactly a difficult job.'

As she gathered the last of the leaflets, she uncovered a large book which lay open underneath them. Pushing the leaflets to one side, she took in the list scrawled across its pages. Each line had the name of one man and one woman, and one date. As she looked even closer, at the top of the open page she saw her father's name. Michael Hooper. 'Look, here's my—'

But she stopped herself.

'What?' Sylvie asked.

'It must be the weddings they've had in the church . . .'

'And?'

'My dad's here, but the name next to his is Peggy Elliott. This can't be right.'

'Do you know her?'

'February 1983,' July read. 'Do you think he left it open on purpose?' she whispered, as Sylvie came to look over her shoulder.

'Maybe.' Sylvie ran her finger along the line next to July's father's name. 'You know what, I saw a Peggy out there somewhere.'

'What do you mean, out there?'

'A grave, dummy.'

'You sure?'

'I remember thinking I liked the name. It's kind of normal

but glamorous at the same time, don't you thin— Where are you going?'

July ran from the church, Sylvie following close behind, and up the bank to the graves her stepsister had been checking.

'Do you think he married someone else then? What about your mum?'

'I don't know.' July's mind raced. Could he have married this woman, then her mother afterwards? Or was he never married to her mum?

'Your mum isn't dead then? I was right?'

'No . . . she's definitely . . . she is dead.'

'So what was your dad on about?' Sylvie sighed with a big heave of her shoulders. 'I really thought . . .' She trailed off, sticking her bottom lip out.

July stopped, her chest heaving – partly from the exertion of charging up the bank, but more because of the beast of her rage, which threatened to take a swipe at her stepsister. She glowered at Sylvie, who was still walking along the row, and bit her lip hard. Why was Sylvie disappointed? It was July who had lost her mother – not once, but twice.

But she couldn't keep quiet for long. 'You really thought what?' she snapped, storming after her. 'That I'd move out? That you'd finally get my bedroom?'

'Bedroom?' Sylvie asked airily, barely paying attention to July as she searched for the headstone.

'You've always wanted it, haven't you? So that you can have that walk-in wardrobe you harp on about.' July clenched her fists. Everything that had been building inside her since their midnight feast was churning up, fighting to be released. How could her stepsister have asked her to leave?

'Here it is.' Sylvie stopped in front of a headstone. 'Peggy Elliott.'

July read the name – plain white letters cut into glossy black stone – but she was too cross to concentrate on it. 'Or is it that you were pleased because I'd be joining your sad little club?'

'What are you on about?' Sylvie frowned.

'I've seen you. At school. Talking to Hannah and Lois. Your little gang of girls whose parents didn't love them enough to stick around.'

Sylvie stared at her.

It felt good to shout at someone, so July kept going despite the glint of tears in her stepsister's eyes. 'You're jealous, is that it? Because my mum didn't leave me, like your dad did. She died. She didn't give up on me.'

'Are you out of your mind?' Sylvie asked, her voice rising. 'There's no club. I don't want your stupid bedroom. I thought you'd be able to escape, that's all.'

'From what?'

'July. He *hits* you.' Sylvie all but screamed the words at her.

July crossed her arms and looked out at the bay. A couple of kayakers were out, fishing rods trailing lines behind them as their orange hulls sliced through the blue; the flat water sparkled as though millions of tiny diamonds were floating on its surface. The serenity of the view jarred against her galloping heart and roaring mind, but she couldn't look away. 'Not often,' she said, following the kayaks as they glided towards the estuary. 'And I deserve it. He's trying to Teach Me—'

'Forget it. Have it your way. Stay, let him beat you up. See if I care.'

July turned to see Sylvie throw her hands in the air. *Drama queen.*

'Anyway,' Sylvie said, her voice levelling out. 'How do you know she didn't leave you?'

'She died.'

'People kill themselves, you know.'

'Not my mum. She died of natural causes.' July hoped she sounded more sure than she felt.

'How do you even know this? Seriously, who have you been talking to?'

'Someone who *knows* stuff about her, all right? She was ill. It was bad luck. I was there when she died. I was like, two, or something. And she really, really loved me.'

Sylvie turned to look at the headstone.

July grabbed her shoulder, but Sylvie shook her off. 'She did not kill herself,' July said, trying to get in front of her, into her eyeline. 'You can't say things like that.'

Sylvie pushed her away and squatted down. July looked back out towards the sea, but her kayakers had disappeared. *Do not cry. Do not cry.* There was no way her mother would have taken her own life.

'July.' The startling softness in the way Sylvie spoke made July spin round. 'Your birthday!'

'What about it?'

Sylvie was still crouching next to the headstone. July's head swam as she read the carved words again. PEGGY ELLIOTT. Who was this woman? Where was her mother's grave? Had Mr Salter lied to her?

'Twentieth of July, 1985, right?'

'Sylv, it was only a week ago, how could you not remember the date?'

Sylvie stood, facing her. 'Would you give me a break? I'm trying to help.' Her grey eyes were dark – she looked even angrier than when she'd realised Nick Hanson wasn't coming. 'I was just checking—'

'What's this got to do with anything?' She wasn't having this. Why should Sylvie be the one to be cross? After everything she'd said? 'What are you on about?'

'Why are you being such a cow?' Sylvie left July standing by Peggy Elliott's grave, her feet crunching back down the gravel path. 'Take a look at the date, would you?'

'What date?' July muttered to herself, bending down, sweaty hands gripping above her knees, reading the words underneath Peggy's name. ALWAYS LOVING, NEVER LOVED ENOUGH.

As she listened to Sylvie climbing on to her bike and pedalling off along the lane, July scanned the next few lines on the headstone. When she got to the final one, the world around her stilled, except for the sound of her pulse in her ears. Reaching out to trace the engraved letters, she snatched her fingers away when the dark stone bit at them with its absorbed heat. 20 JULY 1985.

Peggy Elliott had died the day July was born.

18

Darling girl,

Five things I've been thinking about death

1. *I might never meet you. I have the most awful apprehension that my life will end as yours begins, and I'll never get to count your tiny army of eyelashes or know the hook of your fingers around mine.*

2. *A punch in the windpipe, that's what I get when I envisage a blank page in history instead of an account of our first meeting. I gasp at the notion that I won't cradle you in my arms. Please, please – let me hold you.*

3. *And yet, I'm at my most vital as I crouch here, in the jaws of lurking oblivion. Each day is a gift I unwrap, second by second. I marvel at everything nobody notices any more: a dull sky, footprint patterns in the mushed mud, the sand clinging to limbs of torn seaweed on the beach. Perhaps it isn't morbidity that inspires me to gaze in awe at my world, but*

your presence inside me, lending me your child's wonder eyes? Either way, your father barks at me to snap out of it, to stop dwelling on my mortality. I appreciate him for this more than I can tell you. In time, you may tumble into love. I hope that person is forthright with you, as he is with me. Loving someone who speaks frankly is a sharp walk on the coast path in a February easterly. It burns your eyes and skin and throat, but you return home, to yourself, invigorated.

4. *I once believed in Heaven, but now I can't be sure. If I die before I get the chance to hold you, what good will Heaven be to me, anyway? All I want is to be with you. And besides, I have to ask myself, am I welcome there? I trust God is on my side, but if he isn't, then I'll spend my eternity elsewhere. Wherever I end up, I want you to know I am not afraid of the dying, as such. No. My mouth only goes dry when I contemplate never touching my lips to the sinless soles of your feet, never tracing the whorls of your ears with my little finger.*

5. *It is not extraordinary. When I was a girl, I assumed death was magical, spiritual and mysterious. But when I saw it flooding the body lying next to me, it was none of those things. It was quiet; it was simple. It was necessary.*

All my love, always,
Mum x

19
26 July 1995

With her teeth gritted and her feet pedalling furiously, July went straight to Yaya's. This time she was there. July didn't even have to knock on the door, as she could see her grandmother lying outside the front of her cottage, roasting herself – doing her crossword to the soundtrack of dozens of small children squealing on the beach as they alternately built and flattened sandcastles. Their mothers' voices also swooped up the rocks, reflected off the bright corrugated steel of the cottages' roofs and dripped down the white render in a melted mess of laughter and reprimands. So, when July called 'Hello?' her grandmother didn't notice initially – it was just another voice in the throng. July climbed the steps to the garden and called out again, and when Yaya looked up, July lifted her hand in their special salute.

'What a lovely surprise.' Yaya pushed herself up on to her elbows, wiggling her fingers by her forehead in response, and pulled her bikini straps up over her golden shoulders. Looking at her own creamy, freckled complexion, even paler than usual with smears of factor thirty, July sometimes wondered how they could be related. It was the first time July had seen her since Shell had given her the photographs; the first time she had seen her mother's red scarf on Yaya's head and the silver bangle on her wrist and known their significance. Why couldn't she have something like that – a piece of her mother to hold close? She wished she could tell Yaya about the pictures. 'I know why you wear those,' she could say if they lived in a different version of this world, one where she didn't have to constantly deny her mother's existence.

'Come on your bike, did you?'

'Yes. I need—'

'Sir!' Yaya called into the house, leaning over the back of her lounger to ring a little bell which hung from a potted olive tree. 'July's here. Can you bring the Rich Teas out?'

July sat cross-legged on the dry grass in the shade of Grandpa Tony's frayed sun umbrella and took a deep breath. 'Yaya, who was Peggy Elliott?'

Her grandmother pushed her sunglasses up on to her forehead and swung her legs round so she was sitting on the edge of her chair. She studied July, her green eyes dark, shining with sudden sadness. July hadn't meant to make her upset. What had she said?

Yaya sighed. 'Get a move on with those Rich Teas,' she called without looking away from her granddaughter. 'I may need another Baileys too. On the rocks.'

Yaya picked at the corner of the sun-bleached cushion on her lounger, and a thread came loose. 'I'm sure I've told you before.' Her voice was so quiet, July had to lean forward to hear her.

July shook her head. 'Never.'

'I . . . your . . .' Yaya pinched the bridge of her nose. 'I'm sorry, my darling. I find this so hard.' She exhaled slowly. 'Hasn't your father . . . ?' Yaya tilted her chin up to the sky and blinked a few times, wiping at the corners of her eyes with the heel of her hand. 'He hasn't told you?'

'I know she was married to him.'

Yaya twisted the silver bangle around her wrist. July's arms ached with the effort of not reaching out to touch it. She wanted to run her fingers over the ridges decorating it, like the ribs of a scallop shell. 'What's brought this on?' her grandmother asked, sighing deeply again.

'I went looking for Mum's grave, but then I saw this book in the church and I saw who Daddy married and then I found Peggy Elliott.' The words came out in a rush.

Yaya slipped her sunglasses back on, and July noticed that her hands were shaking.

'Don't you . . . don't you know what my name was when I was married to your grandfather? Not lovely Tony in there –' she nodded towards the cottage '– but your mother's father?'

'Kay?'

'Yes, Kay.' Yaya laughed sadly, pulling at another thread on the edge of the cushion. 'But what was my surname?'

July had never really thought about it. Yaya was just Yaya. Her surname now was Warren. July had no idea what it had been before she married Tony.

'Elliott. I was Kay Elliott. Your Grandpa Joe, God rest his soul, was Joseph Elliott. He died when your mother was a little older than you are now.'

Number 23! July smiled to herself. 'But who was Peggy? And what does it mean when it says, "Always loving, never loved enough"?'

Yaya lay back in her chair, adjusting her red scarf and turning away from July. 'I don't know . . . I don't know if I can do this. Tony?' she called into the house, her voice tight with panic. 'Are you coming?'

July patted her hand on the lawn, scared to look at her grandmother, as Tony shouted from the kitchen that he was nearly done. Who was Peggy? Why was Yaya acting like this?

Her grandmother murmured something, and July looked up, waiting for a moment for her to repeat herself. 'Yaya? Did you say something?'

Yaya turned to face her. 'I said, *we* all called her Peggy.'

'Who? Who did you . . .' July stopped, realising who Yaya was talking about. 'Mum? But her name was—'

'Her name,' Yaya interjected, her voice suddenly clear and strong, 'was Margaret. Peggy is short for Margaret.'

'It is?' July picked a few blades of yellowed grass and squashed them between her fingertips. *Number 24*, she thought, letting the miserable grass drop to the ground. How could she have lived for ten whole years and not known this? 'But—'

'Enough now.' A rogue wave crashed on the beach below them, underlining Yaya's demand with the gentle snarl of pebbles dragged against each other. 'Sorry, darling, I didn't mean to snap . . . It's just . . .' Yaya sobbed, and July looked up horrified to see that her grandmother had tears streaming down her face. 'She was everything to me. We were always so . . . so close, you know that. She was my best friend. I lost my best friend.'

July hadn't meant to bring up her mother. She'd thought she was asking about Peggy Elliott. How was she supposed to know that the two were the same person? *Always loving, never loved enough.* What did that mean? Who hadn't loved her mother enough? She thought about her mother's headstone as Tony came outside in a pair of swimming trunks and his favourite orange utility shirt, its four pockets stuffed with Juicy Fruit and sunglasses, pens and scraps of folded paper – it was comforting among all this bewildering new information to see him unchanged. He was carrying a plate of Rich Teas in one hand and a drink in the other. As he handed Yaya the glass, ice clinked and made July's mouth water. 'Oh,' he said when he saw his wife's face. 'Oh dear.'

Yaya took a sip of her drink. 'I'm okay,' she said after she had swallowed. 'We were talking about . . . July's mum.' She struggled to say the final two words.

'I see,' Tony said. 'Canapé?' he asked, offering July the plate.

She took a biscuit, smiling up at him. Something about his kind face – the reassuring uniformity of his teeth, his pearly white beard or the twinkling of his eyes – coaxed words on to her tongue.

'But Yaya,' she said quietly, 'she died the same day I was born.'

She'd always believed that she'd had a couple of years with her mum before she had died. What did this mean? That there had been no mashed banana fed to her on a spoon in her high chair, no clapping when she crawled? No cuddles, no singing her to sleep? July wrapped her arms around herself. Had her mother even held her, before she died?

Yaya nodded.

'But I always thought she'd died in a car accident. On my second birthday.'

'Is that what he told you?' Yaya shook her head. 'I'm sorry, July, I thought . . .' She struggled to find the next words. 'I never thought to ask you what you knew. If I'd realised he'd lied to you like that . . .'

Tony leaned over to squeeze Yaya's hand.

After a couple of deep breaths, her grandmother spoke again. 'She died . . . she died the day you were born, yes.'

July remembered the dream she'd had a couple of nights ago, of the embroidered deceptions coming loose. Her mother may not have turned out to be alive, but there were other lies lurking. A secret name and a devastatingly different date of death. Why had everyone let her believe that she'd spent the first couple of years of her life with her mother?

July got up, mumbled, 'Toilet,' and ran inside.

In the bathroom she ran the tap and held her mouth underneath it to get a drink. Once she'd dried her face, she tiptoed into her grandparents' bedroom, looking at them through the window. They were sitting in silence, sunglasses on, holding hands. Then Yaya stood, and walked inside.

July rushed from the bedroom as her grandmother called up to her. 'July?'

'Coming,' July replied, running down the stairs. Yaya was waiting for her at the bottom, and put an arm around her, squeezing tight. She planted a kiss on top of her head. 'How about two more questions. I'll give you two, okay? Ask me anything you want about her. But after that, I really do need a rest.'

'Are you feeling well enough? We don't have to.' July remembered Tony's warning to her: 'Her weak heart won't take it.'

'You know I can't normally . . . I . . . It's so hard, darling, you understand, don't you?'

July nodded.

'But this is important. I can . . . I will try to . . .' Yaya paused. 'I'll do my best.'

Two questions! July nearly tripped on the doorstep with the excitement of it. They were barely out of the door when she blurted out, 'Why isn't her real name on her gravestone?'

Yaya sat down and patted the sun lounger, making a space for July to join her. The cushion was crispy in the heat, and burned into the backs of July's bare legs, but she didn't care.

'It *is* her real name.' Yaya picked up her drink and a Rich Tea, dipping the biscuit carefully into the Baileys before sucking it. Her hands were still shaking, July noticed.

Tony leaned forward. 'Your grandmother chose the name they used because she paid for the headstone,' he said, glancing at Yaya, who nodded for him to continue. 'And her funeral, for that matter.'

'Everything,' Yaya added. 'I paid for everything.'

'But she was called Maggie Hooper when she died.' July

looked through the picket fence into next door's garden, at the tired upturned dinghy they'd had on their lawn for as long as she could remember. She felt a new sympathy for that poor boat – she knew what it was to be upside down and abandoned. Nothing made sense right now.

'Only your father . . .' Yaya took a large gulp of her drink. 'Only your father called her Maggie, short for Margaret. And she wouldn't have wanted his surname on her headstone.'

'But I've got his surname.'

Yaya sighed. 'It's getting harder to protect you from this, now that you're older.' After a moment's pause, she added, 'I know you love him. I know he is good to you. But they weren't happy, your mum and dad.'

The draw of the decrepit boat was getting stronger. Could July crawl underneath it and have a lie-down? 'No.' She shook her head and couldn't stop once she had started. 'No. I don't believe you.' Shake, shake, shake. 'No.'

Yaya slid along the lounger, closer to July, so that their knees were almost touching. 'I'm sorry, my darling. Your mother and I, we used to . . . we used to tell each other everything. She told me things weren't good between them.'

A drop of water splashed on to July's thigh. She looked up to find Yaya was crying once more, tears leaking down her cheeks under her sunglasses.

'Why do you think . . . why do you suppose he hasn't told you that your mum died on the day you were born?'

'I don't know.'

'He should have told you. He's ashamed.'

'Of what? I don't believe you. They loved each other.' July thought of the photo of the pair of them, smiling outside the house in Almond Drive.

'It wasn't her time to die. He could have prevented it.' Yaya's words were beginning to slur.

Grandpa Tony leaned forward in his chair once more, handing Yaya a tissue. 'Kay, I think that's—'

'She might . . .' Yaya's voice wobbled more. 'She might have still been here.'

July tried to follow what her grandmother was saying. Grownups were infuriating. *It wasn't her time to die. She might have still been here.*

Yaya downed the dregs of her drink and pressed her sunglasses firmly against her face, wiping her face with the tissue.

July sensed that her time might be almost up. *Next question, next question.* Her last one. Something Auntie Shell had said surfaced in her mind. 'Where are the notes my mum wrote me?'

'Notes?' Yaya looked at Grandpa Tony, who shook his head. 'She didn't leave you any notes, Juju. Not that I know of.'

'Oh. But—'

'I think . . . I think I have to stop there, for today,' Yaya said, biting her lip.

'But—'

'I was going to say the same,' Tony said. 'We don't want to put you under too much strain.'

Yaya burst into tears again. 'God, I miss her. Tony, I miss her so much.'

July looked longingly at the dark underbelly of the upturned boat.

July stayed with her grandparents for another half-hour, but Yaya barely spoke. The only thing she did other than eat biscuits, each dipped in her topped-up Baileys, was hold July close to her in another embrace and whisper into her hair, 'I love you, darling girl.' July pulled away from her grandmother's sticky bare skin as soon as she could, wondering why she was being nice to her. Kindness always unnerved her.

Grandpa Tony joined her in the lane when she was getting ready to leave. 'You must be upset,' he said.

'I don't know.' (She was.)

'It must be a shock. To find out she died when you were . . . so small.'

She shrugged. (It was.)

'You can always talk to us about it, you know. If it bothers you.' He pulled a stick of Juicy Fruit out of his top left pocket and handed it to her.

She took the gum, unwrapped it and folded it into her mouth, before hopping on to her bike.

'Don't you have a helmet?' he asked.

'No,' she replied in between chews. 'It's finc, though.'

'Your mother never wore one, either. Used to drive your father mad.'

July closed her eyes as her thumb found the lever on her bell, flicking it a couple of times. She saw her mother on a bike, helmet-free, hair and skirt flowing out behind her, coasting down a hill. Number 25.

'Well, go safe. And it's probably best if . . .' He mimicked a zip closing his lips. 'Don't mention our conversation back there to your old man.'

'I won't,' July said. She laughed inwardly at the absurd thought of telling her father, then pushed herself off and cycled away up the hill. 'Bye, Grandpa,' she called over her shoulder, catching a final glimpse of him waving, framed on either side by tall clumps of gently swaying pampas grass. It whispered to her, *Don't tell.*

When she got home, she went straight up to her bedroom to change out of her T-shirt. The lanes were thick with dust, and her skin was covered in a fine red film of it where the tiny particles had clung to her sun cream. ('Skin cancer is no joke, girls,'

Auntie Shell told them regularly.) She'd have a bath later, to wash the dust, and the day, off. Scrub away the dirt, the secrets, the sweat and the unknown; be free of them for a few short minutes, before they started to form new layers and smother her again. For now, though, a change of clothes would have to do.

But when she stepped into her dark bedroom, she immediately knew that someone had been in there. Her top drawer was open. *Sylvie*. Without stopping to switch on a light or open her curtains, July frantically pulled out most of her pants, throwing them on to the floor. But her fears were confirmed: her photos were gone. She should have realised her stepsister was angry enough to want to take revenge.

As she wondered how she would retrieve them, a deep voice behind her asked, 'Missing something?'

20

26 July 1995

July could just make out her father, lurking in the shadows of the corner of her bedroom, shoulder against the wardrobe. She blinked a few times as her eyes adjusted to the low light. He was wrapping his right hand with one of the long cotton straps he wore underneath his boxing gloves for bouts with his pear tree punchbag; the strap glowed white in the darkness. Loop on to the thumb; around his wrist three times; spread fingers; around the knuckles three times. She had watched him do this on hundreds of occasions.

'You're back early.' His van hadn't been in the driveway, and she hadn't been expecting him home. She forced a smile to her lips, but he wasn't looking at her to see it. He was standing right next to her reading den, and she longed to push past him and climb inside, closing the door behind her. She felt comforted by her mother whenever she sat in there, because of Number 11 on the List of Mum. One of the rare, perfectly shiny buttons of memory Yaya had slipped her had been a description of July's mother, aged eight, getting caught in the middle of the night reading by torchlight in the wardrobe of her childhood bedroom – all the clothes tossed on to the floor and replaced by cushions and blankets.

July scratched a clean white line through the dirt on her arm and asked, 'Have you been at the Big House today?'

'Aren't you happy to see me?'

'Of course.'

'Left my van at the garage and walked home, didn't I? Thought I'd surprise you girls, take you for a walk to get an ice cream. Imagine *my* surprise when you weren't here.'

She'd missed out on an ice cream? July's heart sank. She'd messed up.

'What have you lost?' He looked towards her drawer, binding his thumb and then passing the strap through each of his fingers. Was he the one who had taken her photos?

'I thought maybe Sylv had borrowed some of my clothes,' she said. Immediately, her mother appeared by her chest of drawers, another shadow in the gloom. It felt good to have her there, next to her. *What happened to you, Mum? Why weren't you happy with Daddy?* She heard Yaya's words, from earlier: 'He could have prevented it.'

July had a million questions for each of them. She followed the movement of her father's hands as he switched to wrapping his left wrist, afraid to continue to watch his face in case she wasn't able to stop herself asking. *Why didn't you tell me that Mum died the day I was born? What happened?*

'Hm,' her father said, apparently satisfied by her excuse. As he threaded the strap between each finger of his left hand, he paused. She felt his eyes on her. 'Where've you been, without your sister?'

'For a bike ride. I thought it—'

'Shelley won't be happy.'

'Please. Don't tell her. I won't go on my own again.'

'And what have you done with your hair? It doesn't suit you. Take it out.'

July glanced towards her mother's feet, her skin startlingly white – perfect and pure – next to July's grubby dust-caked toes. *I only did it to become more like her. So that you would like me more.*

'Did you not hear me, July? I won't ask again.'

She pulled out her scrunchie, balling it up in her sweaty palm at her side, and her hair fell heavily over her shoulder.

'Sit down.'

July perched on the edge of her bed frame, and he took a few steps forward into the room as he finished wrapping his fingers. He held both hands out in front of him, examining his work. July allowed herself a peek at his face and saw something she had not expected – a strange, small smile. It made her want to cry.

'I've been waiting for you to come and ask me about Great-Grandpa,' he said when he finally dropped his hands to his sides.

July played with her hairband, twisting it and pulling at the elastic. 'I'm not meant . . .'

'Speak up.'

July cleared her throat. When she spoke her voice was louder, but shaking. 'I'm not meant to get help from an adult.' Her mum drifted across the room to sit on the floor at July's feet.

'How are you supposed to find it all out then?' her father asked.

July swallowed. How to answer? She knew he was trying to catch her out. There was a Lesson coming. 'I—'

'Is he buried in the graveyard down the road?'

'I don't know,' July said, stroking the soft fabric of the scrunchie between her thumb and forefinger. What would today's Lesson comprise? Was he just going to hit her? Or would he drag her to the bathroom, to hold her head under the shower? She interpreted his silence as dissatisfaction with her answer, and tried something else. 'I . . . I don't think so?'

'No. He's not.' He spoke slowly. 'Look at me. Stop fiddling with that thing.'

She lifted her chin, and with a huge effort raised her eyes. His nostrils were flaring, the strange smile still on his lips.

'What were you doing there this morning?' he asked.

How did he know? July didn't know what to say. She'd run out of lies.

He looked away, moving to the window, where he yanked open the curtains. She winced at the sudden brightness. As he smiled and waved to someone out in the street, he said, 'You need to stop asking questions about your mum. Ask and it will not be given to you. Seek and ye shall not find.'

'Did Sylvie tell you?' July asked, rubbing her eyes. She knew the answer.

He slammed his hand down on her windowsill. July flinched. 'At least *she* is a good girl.'

In that moment July experienced a new sensation: a mirroring of emotion she had never been seduced by before. For the first time in her life she met his anger with her own. Her chin floated higher, and her breathing slowed. She had to bite her lip to stop herself shouting, *I did this for you!*

'I'm protecting you,' he said in response to her unspoken words, stepping towards the chair next to her chest of drawers. He leaned down and picked up a small pile of papers from the seat. 'You won't like what you find out. Believe me.'

Yaya's voice reverberated in her head. *He's ashamed. He could have prevented it. She might have still been here.* She hadn't allowed herself to believe her grandmother when she'd said those things, but now, with him standing here in front of her, she knew they must be true.

I already know, July wanted to shout, tilting her head back in defiance. *I know when she died. I know you did something.* She couldn't resist any longer, and looked directly towards where her mother was sitting. *Mummy . . .* She squeezed her eyes shut as her mother disappeared, imagining her wrapping her arms around her, holding her tight.

A soft thud forced her back into the room. Her father had

dropped the pile of papers on to the bed frame by her side. July lifted them off the slats and flicked through the top few sheets. There were some typed pages, some handwritten notes, some photos. All about her great-grandfather.

'Those should help,' her father said as he walked out of her bedroom, tugging at his hand wraps, adjusting them by millimetres.

July listened as he descended the stairs, then pushed her door closed and went through her drawer again. Whoever had taken her photographs had left her lists at least. July pulled out her notebook and turned to her Big List of Questions.

'What really happened to . . .' she wrote, looking around her bedroom as she searched for a celebrity name to use. She settled on a Nirvana poster stuck to her wall, given to her by Katie Faye's brother when he got given two of the same for his fifteenth birthday. She met the lead singer's eyes, before bringing her pen back to the page to write, 'Kurt Cobain?'

July knew who would have the answers. If Yaya refused to explain, there was only one other person she could ask. But she couldn't go today. She wouldn't be able to go anywhere now that her father was home.

She put her glasses in her pocket and pulled her T-shirt up over her head, taking a new one from the clean pile on her floor, taking a moment to inhale its promising freshness before heading into the bathroom with her toilet bag. Her father said he hated their 'millions' of shampoos, conditioners, soaps and creams lying around in 'his' bathroom, so she, Sylvie and Shell each kept their toiletries in their bedrooms. Sylvie always moaned about it to July, but July defended her father. 'He just wants to make the house nice and tidy for everyone,' she'd say, or, 'This way, you don't have to worry about me stealing any of your body wash.'

As she squeezed some facewash into her hands and reluctantly splashed her face with water, she listened to her father in the garden, through the open bathroom window: the sharp in and out of his breathing as he shadow-boxed with an imaginary opponent. In her head she also heard his vicious tirades, which haunted her whenever she washed. *You're a disgrace. Do you have any idea how good my life was before I had you?* She felt his rough hand on the back of her neck, as he ran the gushing hot water over her face, and she gasped for breath. The memory of those moments stopped her from showering more than once a week or going anywhere near the sea, even for a paddle. *You're a disgrace. You do nothing but disappoint me.* Water everywhere hissed those words to her, telling her it wasn't finished with her yet; it threatened her and warned her of more to come.

She pressed a towel to her skin as, outside, her father moved over to the bag. Thump, thump, thump. Two quick exhales. Thump, thump, thump. Pulling her face away, she put her glasses back on and stared at her pink towel's honeycomb pattern, like pieces of a puzzle slotting into place. Thump, thump, thump. She knew where she had heard the name Rob Salter before.

Sometimes, when her father was training like this in the garden, he muttered that name. Saying things like 'Fuck you, fucking Rob Salter. Fuck you.'

21

HMP Channings Wood
10 November 2001

Dear July,

That sounds like a bad week, I'm sorry. I hope
things are better by the time you read this.

Thank you so much for your letter. Your question made me smile for an entire day as I
considered how to answer it. Yes, your mum talked
about you, and to you, when she was pregnant.
She wondered what you might be when you grew
up – a politician? A musician? An astronaut?
She was always singing; she said it calmed you.
You're going to ask me what songs, aren't you? I
don't know exact names, but they sounded like
hymns to me. And I remember one afternoon in
the garden, I heard her describing the birds she
could see to you. She turned to me and said, 'She
likes the goldfinches best; her little feet flutter when
I mention them.'

But I have sad memories of her while she was pregnant too. She nursed a constant worry that she might never meet you; it was hard to convince her otherwise. I've often wondered, since, if she sensed what was to come.

So . . . on to Shelley. No, I don't think it would bother your mother that you are calling her Mum now. She'd understand. It's good, as you say, that you have been able to forgive her. From what I know, she never wished to hide the truth from you.

As for forgiving me? I'm no expert. I'd never properly forgiven anyone before prison. You could try something we do here, in a class I've been taking.

1. *Sit opposite an empty chair.*

2. *Imagine I'm in that chair.*

3. *Pretend that you want to forgive me.*

4. *Say out loud that you forgive me.*

5. *Imagine my reaction – it would be positive, I can tell you that much. Sit with it for a while. Does it make you feel good, does it reduce any of your pain?*

Love,
Dad

22

27 July 1995

Wendy was waiting for her horoscope to appear as the Teletext pages scrolled past with an agonising lack of urgency when a movement on the street outside prised her attention away from the TV screen. She saw a girl in dungaree shorts and a pink baseball cap emerge from the alleyway over the road and march her skinny white legs straight up to That-Rob-Salter's house. Wendy put the remote down and used two fingers to expertly separate two slats of her blind in order to get a better look.

The girl hammered on the door. 'I know you're there,' she yelled.

Thank goodness Wendy had the windows open wide! This could be interesting. Was that his daughter? She was about the right age. She looked back at the TV just in time to catch Gemini and the words 'amorous intentions' on the screen before Leo and Virgo took its place. Damnit. She would have to wait for the five other pages in the cycle to go past again. Amorous intentions? Did she have any of those left, she wondered? 'Must do,' she muttered to herself. 'If anyone would know, it's the stars.'

Over the road, That-Rob-Salter opened his obnoxious canary-yellow front door. She remembered the exact week they'd painted it, back in '83, because it was a few days after Shergar was kidnapped. Wendy, a keen horsewoman herself, had felt the lurid shade was a little disrespectful in the circumstances. There was a time and a place for those things, wasn't there? She should have known then that something wasn't right about her neighbour. Oh, and he looked shifty this morning, didn't he just? Nothing new there. He scanned up and down the road, checking to see if anyone was watching, no doubt. Well, they damn well are, Wendy thought to herself. They damn well are.

The girl said something Wendy couldn't quite catch, and That-Rob-Salter shook his head. (Wendy widened her peep hole, the blind slats bending obligingly – they knew the drill.)

'But I need to talk to you,' the girl repeated, loud enough for Wendy to hear this time. About what? Was that scoundrel not giving them enough money to put food on the table? She wouldn't put it past him.

'I'm busy,' he said. Up to no good, more like. The sooner he moved out, the better.

The girl took a few steps backwards, and Wendy thought she was about to give up and leave. (Too easily, Wendy thought, a little disappointed.) But then she started singing at the top of her voice.

'I know a song that'll get on your nerves, get on your nerves . . .'

She had a sweet voice, Wendy'd give her that, but she also knew from hearing this tune of torture warbled by her grandchildren that there wasn't an adult alive who, faced with a child preparing to sing the same lines ad infinitum, wouldn't immediately capitulate and give said child whatever they damn well wanted.

Sure enough, That-Rob-Salter lunged forward, grabbed the girl by the shoulder and pushed her into the house, checking the road again as he did so, and shut the door quickly behind them.

Wendy waited. What should she do? No point telling the police, they would never hear a bad word about Saint Robert

Salter. Oh no! Model citizen, he was, in their eyes. It was her duty, as a Founding Member of the Neighbourhood Watch, to place his house under surveillance and make sure the girl got out safely. And then Wendy would pop round to Jeremy-Next-Door and tell him everything she'd seen.

As Wendy pulled up a stool and settled in for her stakeout, July was steered behind the closed door of number 2 into Mr Salter's living room. 'Keep quiet until I come and get you,' he hissed. 'I've got a visitor.' He slammed the door to the hall, and she was left alone in one of the most extraordinary spaces she had ever set foot in.

She had arrived blazing with White Musk warpaint smeared across her face. She'd shaken the gate in the alleyway when she found it secured with a bike lock, and roared through its bars in frustration. She'd pushed past Mr Salter when he let her into the house, determined to extract answers. But now, here, in this peculiar room, her limbs softened; the roar slunk away and hid in her throat; her breathing slowed.

As she strained her ears to listen to what was being said upstairs – she could hear the voice of a posh man, a low drone of undecipherable words – she looked around. The only furniture was an armchair repaired with miserable patches of duct tape, a long coffee table with grimy bowls stacked on one end and small squares of colourful paper the size of CD cases on the other, and a tiny television on the floor in the middle of the room. This much, she realised as she looked at it all, didn't surprise her about Mr Salter. Nor was the dinginess unexpected – despite the light being on and no shade present to diffuse the bulb's bare glare, the boarded-up windows made it feel like the middle of the night. What she had not been ready for, and couldn't have imagined even if you'd given her one million pounds and a hundred and forty-six years to think about it, was the rainbow flocks of tiny paper birds hanging from the ceiling.

There must have been hundreds of them.

Dozens of lengths of string, more than two metres long, were stapled in concentric circles around the light fixture and hung all the way down to the floor. Each one was threaded through about twenty of the folded birds – greens, pinks, blues, purples, every colour July could think of. They all had elongated necks like the tar-black cormorants she liked to watch ducking under the water in the bay and long pointy tails like stingrays. July had never seen anything like it – she had never seen paper used in this way to make even one of this kind of bird, let alone a room full of them. Gently, in their beaks, they took the fire in her heart and the knots in her stomach, and returned them as something new. Wonder, calm and hope, a small smile plucking at her lips.

She touched one, its wings thick with dust and secrets. Why had Mr Salter, who her father swore about when he was sparring with invisible opponents, made all these delicate creatures?

Floorboards creaked above her head, and the movement made the threads of folded birds sway like the branches of a weeping willow tickled by a breeze. She heard Mr Salter's voice, and another man's but not the low droning tones she'd first heard. Did he have more than one person with him? *Hurry up,* she thought, checking her watch. She had told herself she would be no more than an hour; she didn't want Sylvie getting home from Helen's house before her and asking questions, and she certainly couldn't risk her father getting back early from work again and noticing she'd been out on her own.

She drew her palms together behind her back into the prayer position as she waited. It was one of a sequence of stretches Tony had taught her – the very same ones he said he had shown her mother years earlier. (Number 15: her mother always had stiff shoulders from the hours she spent hunched over her sewing machine.) She pressed her hands together, opening her chest and easing the ache brought on by her sudden conversion to cycling, and listened. Mr Salter and the new man were now loudly discussing the size of the rooms. She could still hear the first man, talking in the background.

The new one said, 'Do all of the windows still open, behind these . . . uh . . . these—'

'Yes. Fully functioning.' Mr Salter sounded annoyed.

More footsteps, more birds swaying, and the sound of a door closing upstairs. *Hurry up.* The voices continued but July couldn't make out what they were saying. She opened the door to the hall as noiselessly as she could, and tiptoed past two surfboards propped against the wall and through into the kitchen. There were no birds hanging in the hall, but a quickly stolen glance up the staircase revealed hundreds more dangling from the walls at the top, dropping down to the skirting boards. *Why so many?*

The house had exactly the same layout as the one she had grown up in, but in reverse, giving the place the unnerving feeling of a dream: the blend of the familiar with the foreign. In this kitchen the shiny floor of number 4 was replaced with bare floorboards, grey and splintering. The sleek red and white cabinets were gone, and in their place were wooden cupboards, painted green. They were bleached pale, though what light had done that she didn't know – this boarded-up room was as dark as the other had been, with, again, only a bare bulb to illuminate it. It was as hot and airless in here as it had been next door, but instead of the floral perfume there was the lingering stench of burned onions. Where number 4's dining table had been, for July to hide beneath, were endless stacks of local newspapers. The *Morning News* as well as the *Herald*, the paper yellowed, crackling under her fingertips. How long had Mr Salter's home been like this, she wondered? Had her mother once stood in this kitchen and felt its heavy heart too?

July rescued some unopened envelopes from the chaos of the

counter – the surfaces were a mess of paperwork, dirty plates and cutlery, empty 7up bottles and microwave chip boxes. Her father would have had a fit if he'd seen the place. And to think he reprimanded her for leaving her plate by the side of the sink for five minutes! As she picked her way through the post, the man upstairs asked, 'And is that an original fireplace?'

She didn't hear Mr Salter's answer because at that moment, under the last envelope in the pile, she spotted a notebook. She began to flick through. Page after page was covered with stuck-in photos and neatly handwritten notes. The pictures showed smashed panes of glass in windows with yellow frames, scratches along the side of a dark blue van, graffiti on what she recognised to be Mr Salter's back fence and front wall. Among the graffiti were: LIAR (in red), THIEF (in blue) and KILLER (blue again). July felt heat rise in her face. Why would someone do this to him? Had he done all these things – lied, stolen . . . killed? She remembered the rat, and a shudder threatened to surge through her, but it was stopped in its tracks by the comfortingly systematic notes. They listed dates and times, and the meticulous columns went on for dozens of pages. Some of the earliest incidents were back in 1985. She savoured the enchanting order of it, the preciseness of the tidy lines of numbers.

There were footsteps on the stairs, and the voices became louder and clearer. July quickly backed her body into a space among the stacked newspapers and crouched, like a hermit crab retreating into its shell, sliding one copy of the *Herald* from the top of its pile to cover her head.

'I know what you'll have seen in the news about me,' Mr Salter was saying, as he descended the stairs. July ran her fingernail across the rippled edges of the papers by her nose. Was that why he had so many? Was he famous? Maybe she should have told Sylvie about him – she might have known who he was, if he was an actor or something.

The other man said something July couldn't make out, and then Mr Salter said, 'When my neighbour died.' Was he talking about her mum? She peered round the corner of the paper stack but couldn't see the staircase. Where was the third man – the first one she had heard talking? As she watched through the doorway, she noticed for the first time the fridge to the right of it. It was covered in faded children's drawings – felt-tip flowers and trees alongside indecipherable shapes and scrawls, with vast scribbled backdrops of blue-crayon sky. Her bewilderment (who had drawn them?) competed with longing (her father's fridge was too perfectly clean to ever have accommodated hers and Sylvie's artistic efforts), but both were quickly superseded by curiosity, as Mr Salter's companion spoke again.

'It's not that,' he said. 'You could think about tidying the place up a bit. People like to see what it could—'

'They're getting a bargain as it is,' Mr Salter snapped. 'I'm not making it any easier for them.'

They fell silent, and she heard the front door open.

'Be in touch,' the other man said.

If Mr Salter responded, she didn't hear him. All she could make out was the slam of the door again and the slide of bolts being drawn across it. She realised she could still hear the low murmur of the first man drawling on upstairs.

'Where are you, then?' Mr Salter called out. 'I can see you're not where I told you to wait.'

Was he talking to her? Or the man upstairs?

'July? I know you're here somewhere.' His voice got louder as he walked into the kitchen.

She stood up and stepped out of her hiding place, the *Herald* slipping from her head to the floor with a smack. 'Sorry,' she mouthed. 'I thought you were talking to him.' She pointed upstairs.

'What?' Mr Salter looked shattered. His face was yellowish, his hair wasn't brushed.

'Isn't one of your friends still here?' July whispered, pointing upstairs again.

He turned to look where she was indicating, then laughed. 'That's the radio.' He ran the tap and washed his hands. 'When you get your own place, remember that trick. Always keep a radio on. Puts intruders off.' He laughed again. 'Nice to see that it worked. On you, at least.'

'Oh.' Now that he'd explained, it was obvious that it was a radio. She blushed.

'I thought I told you not to come back here again? At the risk of sounding like a broken record.'

He opened the back door and the room suddenly came to life. It was still filthy and strewn with rubbish, but the detritus had colour to it instead of consisting of brownish greys and blacks. It was still dusty, but with the influx of hot air racing in to find new spaces to scorch, this dust swirled up in busy motes, seeking sunlight. The drawings on the fridge fluttered; the newspaper towers stood proud, casting straight shadows instead of lurking in them.

'Who was that man?' July asked, running the toe of her sandal along the dark seam between two of the floorboards, wondering what lay beneath.

'You said you had something you needed to talk to me about?'

'Who was he?'

Mr Salter sighed. 'The estate agent.'

'Oh.'

He turned his back to her and ran the tap again. 'Thirsty?'

'I shouldn't . . .' She checked her watch as he got a couple of glasses out of the cupboard. Still twenty-five minutes before she'd promised herself she'd be home. 'Do you have lemon barley?'

He froze with two tumblers in mid-air, then soundlessly placed them on the counter. 'I don't have any kids' drinks here. It's water or milk. Tea, if you want.'

'Water, please. Did I say something wrong?'

'No.' He filled her a glass and handed it to her. 'Just reminded me of something.'

'Sorry.'

He smiled. 'You apologise for that, but not for snooping around my house?'

Later, she would wonder why she did it. Later that day, later that year, in ten years' time. Twenty. In that moment, though, what she did next seemed unimportant, an impulsive act.

She stepped forward and embraced him – briefly, awkwardly. Her cheek brushed the soft red marl of his T-shirt; she smelled the same neoprene scent she recognised from the surfer kids in her class after weekends spent in their wetsuits; one hand, holding her glass, pressed into his back, and the other hung inertly at her side; the metal buttons on her dungarees clinked against the buckle of his belt. 'It's a sad house,' she whispered, her words skating over his frozen rigid body (he made no attempt to return the hug). Then she released him, shuffled backwards and took a gulp of water.

He coughed. 'You didn't like my cranes? They're not so sad, are they?'

July looked at him. His cheeks had coloured; she'd embarrassed him with what she'd done. *Stupid July.* 'Cranes?' she asked. What was he on about? She would have noticed a crane outside the front of the house.

'The origami.'

Origami? There was still no answer in his eyes, so she looked for one in her water.

'Please tell me you know what origami is. Please. You have to. He should have . . .'

July swallowed and shook her head, still staring into her glass. Why was he so shocked that she didn't know this strange word? There would be thousands of words she wouldn't know the meaning of, if he asked her. *Origami*. Should she know it? Had she seen it in her encyclopedia?

'She –' He swore, but instead of finishing his sentence he suddenly leaned over the counter. With the removal of his disappointed gaze, she felt able to lift her own from her glass. He was studying something, and she stepped forward to see what it was. An ant, making its way towards the sink. She closed her eyes, waiting for the slam of his hand as he squashed it, as she knew her father would do. But when the slam didn't come, she opened them again and saw him tenderly coaxing it on to his palm, before taking it to the back door and releasing it on to a shrub outside. She blinked. Was this the same man she had seen beat a rat to death a few days earlier?

'The birds in the living room,' he said, interrupting her thoughts. 'Cranes. Made out of folded paper. Origami.'

'Oh, those!' July smiled, relieved to understand what he was talking about, finally. 'Yes, I saw them. They're amazing. Why did you make so many? Is it difficult?'

He gave her one of his under-the-skin looks, and she sought out the reassurance of the slammer in her pocket, looking down to obscure her face from his view, behind the peak of her cap. *What*, she wanted to ask? *Why do you look at me like that?*

He put his glass on the side, opened a cupboard and pulled out a few squares of paper like the ones in the living room. He handed them to her, keeping one for himself. July put her drink down too, pushing an empty ham packet out of the way to make room on the counter, and turned the paper over in her hands. It was thin, almost like tissue paper but shinier, and opaque. Each sheet was golden yellow.

Clearing more space on the counter, he laid his piece in front of him and started folding, his fingers moving quickly and expertly, like Sylvie braiding her hair. He pressed each fold, running his finger along each crease. The deftness of his movements was mesmerising. Within a couple of minutes it had taken shape, and he pinched the little creature's beak as a blackbird broke into song outside. She automatically checked to see where the noise had come from, but instead of the singing blackbird, her stare was met by the shabby climbing frame in the garden. As Mr Salter put the finishing touches to his handiwork, lifting it up to the light, July took in the bars of the frame's steps and the fraying green rope of its swing. *Where are your children?*

'Here,' he said, as if he had heard her question, making her jump. She stepped back, tripping over a bowl, and a few cat biscuits spilled out of it on to the grey floorboards. She recognised them as the same brand Katie-Faye's family fed their adored tabby, Skimbleshanks. So, Mr Salter *didn't* live here alone. She was thinking how glad she was that he had company to sit with in that dreary living room of his when he repeated himself. 'Here. Finished,' he said, handing her the golden crane. Putting the rest of the pieces of paper down and forgetting his pet, she turned the bird over, looking at it from every angle, trying to decipher the magic of it. Its head was held high – a graceful and courageous being, holding the secrets of its creation within itself, among its many folds. The beauty of its wings, lifted slightly, ready to aid its escape from the captivity of her hands, made her wish for a pair of her own. If only freedom really was as simple as a few folds.

'There's an ancient Japanese legend,' Mr Salter said as July continued to examine her bird. 'Anyone who folds a thousand of these little guys can make a wish.'

'Why a thousand?'

'The crane is said to live for a thousand years. It's a myth, of course. But . . .'

'How many have you made?'

He exhaled. 'Oh . . . At least that many.'

'And did your wish come true?'

He didn't reply. July looked up, and handed the crane back to him.

'Did it?' she repeated.

Slowly he pushed her hand away. 'Keep it.'

She lifted her crane in front of her face, holding it as delicately as she would a real bird. Once, she'd found a stunned goldfinch lying on the patio at home, a greasy feathered outline on the glass of Auntie Shell's French windows explaining how it had injured itself. She'd noticed it because its friend (or mate; she liked to think they were in love) had been hopping frantically on the edge of the lawn, chirruping shrilly, bobbing its little red lipstick face. When, with Auntie Shell's encouragement, she had picked up the tiny, dazed creature, she had been able to feel its heart beating through its soft feathers. She had been about to panic that she was going to crush it when it lifted its beak and broke out of her trembling grip, bouncing once against her father's lawn before taking flight into the pear tree with its relieved paramour.

'Why are you here, July?' Mr Salter leaned against the counter and took a sip from his glass. 'I don't have any more to tell you.'

She blew softly on to her bird and its wings quivered. 'What really happened to her?'

'I told you.'

'You didn't say she had died on the day I was born.' She carefully pressed the crane flat and slipped it into her pocket, then looked up at him.

He shook his head.

'Why doesn't my dad like you?'

A shadow passed across his face, and he looked like he might say something, but then he simply shook his head again.

'You're as bad as the rest of them.'

'It's not my place.'

'What would it matter to you? You're moving.'

He removed his glasses and pressed his thumb and forefinger into his eyelids.

July wanted to grab his hands and pull them down from his coward's eyes; she wanted to force him to look at her. 'I thought you were . . .'

What? What had she thought he was? Her friend? Because he hadn't turned her into the police? Because he'd made her a bird out of paper? *Stupid, stupid July. A disgrace.*

She ran from the kitchen, down the hall, and through a blur of tears she unbolted the front door.

'July, wait,' he called after her.

She turned. Had he changed his mind? He knew something. He had to. She lifted her glasses a little and wiped her lashes with her thumb. 'What?'

'I . . .' He scratched at the wax on one of his surfboards, avoiding her eye. 'I'd rather you left through the back door.'

It was her turn to laugh. 'I don't care what your neighbours think. Fuck you!' She'd never sworn before in her life. The words were popping candy on her tongue.

She swung the door open and stormed out on to the front path. As she strode away, she thought perhaps he would call her back again, but he didn't. Instead, she heard the slam of the door behind her.

As she retrieved her bike from the alley, her mind was a rush of anger and questions. He'd said more to that estate agent than he had to her. Why had he been in the news? What did it have to do with her mum? And then it struck her. Why hadn't she thought of the newspapers since Sylvie had mentioned them? There must have been something written about her mother's death, and now she knew exactly when it had happened, she could look it up.

In a couple of days it would be the weekend, and she could go into town with Auntie Shell and visit the library. The excitement soared in her chest once more, sending its tingling feelers out to her fingers and toes. She had a new plan, and she was sure this one would get her somewhere.

If she hadn't been blinkered, first by rage and then by hope, she might have noticed the eyes watching her as she cycled back along Almond Drive and towards home.

Two pairs of eyes.

23

29 July 1995

On the bus into town, July pulled the crane out of her pocket. How hard could it be to make? She turned it over in her hands as she listened to Sylvie and Auntie Shell chat in the seats in front of her. Or rather, she listened to Auntie Shell talking to Sylvie, who answered in monosyllables, if at all, while applying a million layers of strawberry-flavoured lip balm, which was stinking out the whole bus. 'And have you seen my fan?' Auntie Shell was asking as she searched through her handbag. 'I had it with me yesterday, at work . . .' She dropped her house keys in the gangway, and July watched over the wings of her crane as Shell apologised to the woman in the seat opposite her while leaning down to retrieve them, even though the other passenger had not been inconvenienced in the slightest. 'Sorry, so sorry. There we go, got them.'

July winced at the memory of her own fawning apologies in Mr Salter's kitchen and, replaying his words – 'It's not my place' – she wrenched the bird apart, not caring if she ripped it. She smoothed the square of yellow paper on her lap, pulling her irritation taut. What gave him the right to withhold information about her mother? With furious, sharp movements, she copied the first steps she had seen Mr Salter's fingers undertake – folding it in half on the diagonal and then in half again to make a small triangle. Now what? She studied the crease marks on the

181

paper, hoping to find the solution in them. But none of her attempts worked. She pulled it apart again and flattened the square up against the warm, fingerprint-smeared glass of the bus window. *Stupid July.* Stupid scrap of paper. It was as useless to her now as the limited facts she knew about her mother. Maggie Hooper, or Peggy Elliott, had been that crane – striking, admired, elegant. And to July nothing short of mythical. But July's list of twenty-five things was just a piece of crumpled paper in comparison – with no folds to give it form. It would float away pathetically, without a fight, on even a whisper of breeze.

Auntie Shell turned in her seat, gaping in dismay at July's hand on the window. 'Oh, July, really? Think about all the hands that have touched that.' She dropped her voice. 'Think of what else they've been touching. Other people don't *wash*.'

'But I'm not touching the window. I'm touching the paper.'

'Less of that tone, young lady.'

July pulled the paper away from the glass and stuffed it back into her pocket, then dabbed her hand with the lemony wipe Auntie Shell passed her through the gap in the seats.

Shell sighed, taking the used wet wipe and dropping it into a plastic sandwich bag she kept in her handbag for such occasions (usually involving July). 'More books today, is it? You definitely need more? Have you read all the others in that pile in your bedroom yet?'

July had told her that morning that she needed to go to the big library, and had asked if she could accompany her stepmother and -sister on their Saturday shopping trip. She usually got her books from the truck that visited the village every couple of weeks, and preferred to spend her Saturdays at home with her father, in case he wanted to take her for an ice cream, or watch football on the telly together, or take her with him to finish a job. If she waited long enough, one day it might happen. Parents liked their children more as they got older, she'd once heard Katie-Faye's mum say as she'd clutched her daughter to her bosom. Katie-Faye's mother knew everything, so July was confident it was only a matter of time.

'They have a better selection,' July said, running a fingernail across the fuzzy fabric of her seat and flicking at the vinyl piping along its front edge, wondering how it was all sewn together and making a mental note to add to her Big List: 'Did Mariah Carey ever do any upholstery?'

'I haven't got time to come to the library with you, you'll need to go on your own.'

'I'll be fine.'

'*Thank you.* I'll be fine, *thank you.*'

It was July's turn to sigh. She shifted her feet, feeling the soles of her sandals slowly peel off something unpleasantly sticky on the bus floor. It was obviously one of those days with Auntie Shell. She'd been so nice recently; July should have known another freeze was coming. Take the books, for example. Only yesterday Shell had been saying how wonderful it was that July enjoyed reading so much. 'Of course, they're not *my* cup of tea,' she'd said, 'but it's the passion that counts.' But today she was all, 'Why have you got so many books?' Katie-Faye had confidently diagnosed schizophrenia. (Katie-Faye's father was a psychiatrist. She was always diagnosing people: their teachers, friends, friend's parents. When Miss Glover was off work with her broken leg, Katie-Faye said, 'It's probably psychosomatic,' as if July would know what that meant.) July tried to find out more about schizophrenia – or, more specifically, how she could engineer more of the thaw days than the frozen ones – but the condition wasn't mentioned in her encyclopedia. Mistakenly believing that the word began 's-k-i', she had been frustrated to find that the index skipped straight from 'skipping ropes' to 'skuas'.

*

'If there's an even number of steps, I'll go in,' July muttered under her breath as she stood, looking up at the sliding doors of the library entrance.

After she had waved goodbye to Sylvie and Auntie Shell, her mouth had immediately gone dry as though she had eaten a spoonful of Yaya's rhubarb compote the day she'd forgotten to add sugar. Now her legs were shaking, but she climbed and counted. At twelve, she reached the doors. She glanced behind her, checking she hadn't missed one, and then entered the building, her fingers crackling against the origami paper. How was she going to do this? She didn't know where they stored their old newspapers. Miss Glover had said they kept copies for years and years, but she hadn't said how to go about finding them. And even if she did manage to locate them, what would they say? What had happened to her mum? Did she really want to know? She heard her father's voice: 'You won't like what you find out. Believe me.'

She took a couple of deep breaths of the stuffy library air, calming herself with the friendly smell of books, and approached the ladies sitting behind the reception desk.

'If there's an even number of black tiles before the desk, I'll ask,' she whispered to her knees. She avoided the brown and white tiles in her chosen row and counted.

But before she reached the final few – she'd counted to thirty-one – one of the receptionists asked, 'How can we help?' She had kind eyes and short, spiky black hair, the sort of style her father would have made rude remarks about but July thought looked fun. The long, soft curls of the woman sitting next to her were getting blown all over the place by the small fan whirring away on their shared desk, but July's lady's hair was gelled in place and unaffected by the breeze. It gave July something to focus on.

'Where are your old newspapers?' July's voice was tiny. She pressed her toes against her sandals.

'Do you have an appointment?'

'No.' She stared at the hair spikes and tried to count them all. *One, two, three, four, five . . .*

'Well.' The woman tilted her head to one side. 'You're supposed to make appointments for the microfilm reader.'

'The what?' July abandoned her examination of the woman's gelled hair.

'The newspapers are all kept on microfilm.' July must have still looked confused because the lady went on, 'They're like photos of the pages in the paper. You view them on a special machine.'

'Oh.'

'So, would you like to make an appointment to come and look at them one day? It might be a good idea to bring your mum or dad with you?' The woman looked over July's shoulder, confirming that she'd come alone.

'I can't bring my mum.' There were times, very occasionally, when July let herself cry in public. There were times when, as a child without a mother, it felt okay to exploit that fact to get something you wouldn't otherwise get. July felt the tears start to roll down her cheeks and she didn't try and stop them. 'She's in Heaven.'

'Oh dear. Hold on, don't cry, you poor thing. Do you need a tissue?'

'I'm okay.' July wiped her face with her hand and sniffed.

'I tell you what . . .' The woman checked a sheet of paper on her desk, running her finger down a list. 'Why did you say you wanted to see the papers?'

'For a school project. I've got to look at the news from a week in 1985.' July's cheeks grew hot.

'And how old are you?'

'Ten.'

'Well. I—'

'Go on, Gloria,' the other woman behind the desk said, gently nudging her colleague with her elbow. 'I can manage here. There's a machine free until twelve.'

'I suppose I could . . . Come on then, missy. What's your name?'

'July. Thank you,' she said. 'Thanks so much.'

'An unusual name!'

'Yes.' She didn't feel in the mood to tell the story behind it today.

'Come on then.' Gloria came out from behind the desk and led July through the peaceful library to a large set of filing cabinets. 'Which newspaper did you want?' she whispered. 'The *Herald*?'

Once they had found the films with the 1985 newspapers, and Gloria had threaded the right one on to the spools to view it on the machine, they sat in front of its big screen and Gloria pressed some buttons. 'So, we're looking for the twentieth of July to start with?'

'Yes, please.' Images of newspaper pages scrolled past. There were lots of words and the occasional photo of people wearing funny old-fashioned clothes. July squeezed her fists around her thumbs, watching for a picture of her mother, and leaned closer to look over Gloria's shoulder. She smelled of mint humbugs.

'Here it is. A Saturday.'

Above a photo of football fans in England shirts, the front-page headline shouted, GET OUT!

'Is there anything particular you want to see?' Gloria asked, keeping her voice low. 'This looks like an article about hooligans being sent home from somewhere or other . . .'

'Can I go through the pages? You don't need to stay with me. I'll be really careful.' July pointed at the buttons Gloria had been pressing. 'I'm meant to write a report about the kind of things that happened during that week. Everyone has a different week

186

to research.' As she bent down to take her notepad out of her rucksack, July spotted a flash of her mother's red hair – she was standing next to the filing cabinet.

'I'm not sure that's . . .' Gloria tapped on the table. 'But you look like the sensible type. Don't press the red buttons, all right? They'll scratch the film. Or this handle here. If you use this one and this one –' she pointed to two black buttons with arrows on them '– you'll be able to flick through.'

'I'll be careful, I promise.'

Gloria stood up. 'You can always come and get me if you have trouble.'

She watched as July had a go with the buttons, and then, satisfied that she wasn't going to break anything, returned to the reception desk. July's mum came to sit on the chair next to her, keeping her company.

Each time she pushed on the right-hand arrow it made a little clicking sound, which in the library's silence felt embarrassingly loud. July was relieved whenever somebody coughed or spoke in hushed tones to a member of staff – it made her feel less conspicuous. Pressing the buttons as quietly as she could, she scrolled through. There was nothing on 20 July, but as she continued to the Monday edition, she was met with her mother's black and white face smiling out at her from the front page.

It was the photo on the boat that Auntie Shell had given her. She abruptly pulled her hands back from the machine, feeling a shock like the sharp pain of a pin prick, which she had experienced many times in school sewing lessons. Gingerly, she moved her hands forward again, reaching up to touch the screen, but thought Gloria might not like that, so hovered her fingers by the headline instead. MURDER PROBE AFTER NEW MUM'S TRAGIC DEATH, it said.

July picked at a scab on her elbow and read the headline again. This couldn't be right.

It was bad luck.

She read on. The article said that her mother, who they called Maggie Hooper, had died at home shortly after July was born. 'A man has been arrested on suspicion of murdering the 31-year-old,' the report went on to say. 'Her body was found at her home in Almond Drive on 20 July. An ambulance crew and police attended the scene, but she was pronounced dead.' July's mother's cool hand found hers. 'As of Sunday evening,' the report continued, 'the suspect remains in police custody while enquiries continue.'

Who was the man they'd arrested? The article didn't say. July read it all twice, but his name wasn't there. Who was it? She was suddenly very aware of the sound of her own breath.

'Daddy?' she whispered. *He's ashamed. He could have prevented it.*

July scrolled past more news, TV listings and the sports pages, through to the next day.

On page 3 the same photo of her mother was printed, under the headline, MAGGIE HOOPER: MURDER SUSPECT RELEASED ON BAIL. She knew what that meant from the hours she had spent watching *The Bill* with her father.

On the Wednesday the front page carried a new photograph of her mother, this time the one of her pregnant, standing on the doorstep of the house in Almond Drive with July's father. July read the headline several times. MAGGIE HOOPER 'WASN'T MURDERED', it said. July turned to her mother, desperate for someone to explain everything she had read. But instead of her beautiful smiling face, July saw Gloria waving from the reception desk, then giving her a questioning 'thumbs up' signal. July waved back before returning to the screen.

She read the black print under the headline. 'A man arrested on suspicion of murder following the death of new mum Maggie Hooper has now been "completely eliminated" from police enquiries,' it said. 'It is confirmed that the 26-year-old had no involvement whatsoever in the tragic death of Mrs Hooper. The police say that they no longer believe there were any suspicious circumstances surrounding her death.' July did some sums in her head. Her father had turned forty-one earlier this year, so he would have been several years older than twenty-six when she was born. Her shoulders relaxed. But she still couldn't understand everything that had happened. Why had the police initially thought someone had killed her mother? And what had made them change their minds?

'Following the results of a post-mortem,' the article continued, 'police have concluded that Mrs Hooper died after suffering a massive haemorrhage following the birth of her daughter. A police spokesman said, "We believe that Mrs Hooper lost her balance and fell down the stairs after experiencing a post-partum haemorrhage."'

July wrote the word 'haemorrhage' in her notebook to check in her encyclopedia later. She didn't understand – what had killed her mother? She read the article a second time. Whether she had been murdered or not, it all felt desperately sad. And why had Yaya said all those things about her father? How could he have prevented what happened?

Rubbing her eyes, which were starting to feel tired from focusing on the bright screen, July kept scrolling through the newspapers. On the front of the Saturday edition, a week after her mother's death, was another face she recognised.

Mr Salter.

He was younger and thinner, but it was unmistakably him. In the picture next to him was a woman she didn't know and a small girl, younger than July. This headline read, 'I DID NOTH-ING WRONG': MAN QUESTIONED OVER MAGGIE HOOPER DEATH SPEAKS OUT.

You.

Suddenly, his strange behaviour started to make a bit more sense. What was it he had said, one of those first times they'd spoken? 'Why do I get the feeling you don't know who I am?' She shivered, then began to make copious notes from this article, as it continued on to page 3. 'I did what anyone would have done,' she wrote, copying Mr Salter's quotes down. 'I helped a woman in need, I helped to deliver her baby girl.' And: 'Now my neighbours won't talk to me, and people spit at my wife in the street. The police have ruined my life. I did nothing wrong, but everyone thinks I am guilty.' July also wrote down two new names: Janine and Jenny. Mr Salter's wife and three-year-old daughter. She remembered the day he'd called her by that name. *Jenny*. Then she wrote, 'Did he do it?'

Next to the main article was a small box with a shorter piece of text in it. 'SHE WAS A WONDERFUL NEIGHBOUR', the title read. In it, Mr Salter's wife talked about July's mother. July bit the knuckles of her left hand to stop herself squealing with excitement as she copied out every single shining, priceless word.

On the way home later that day, Sylvie prattled on excitedly, loud enough for the whole bus to hear, about a pair of yin yang pendants she had bought, one of which she planned to give to Helen, the ingredients she had picked to bake a lemon drizzle cake (Sylvie was actually quite good at cooking, which was a constant surprise to July) and the nail polish she had chosen.

July nodded, half-listening, as she reread her notes, which she had clutched to her chest as she ran from the library twenty minutes earlier, already late for her arranged meeting with Auntie Shell under the clock in the square. She had spent nearly two hours, long after she had to give up the microfilm reader, going over the things Mr Salter's wife had said. In that small box of text was more about her mother than anyone had ever told her in one go in her ten years – she was now up to Number 34 on the List of Mum. Maggie Hooper had been the perfect neighbour, Mrs Salter told the reporter. She was always the first to take freshly baked oat and raisin cookies round to new residents of Almond Drive; her door was always open when you needed a cup of tea or a shoulder to cry on – she cared; she was great with the local kids and frequently made clothes for the children of a couple of families on the street, free of charge. But she was also a strong woman, she said, who stood up for people who couldn't do so for themselves. 'She was brave. She was fearless,' July had copied into her notebook. Part of her wanted to tell Sylvie everything she had found out, but officially they were still cross with each other after their row in the churchyard.

As they walked from the village bus stop back to Harmony Close, July lagged behind her stepmother and -sister, fanning herself with the notebook, wondering where Mr Salter's wife and daughter were now and repeating in her head the words she'd read. 'She was so looking forward to becoming a mother,' Mrs Salter had said. Her mother had made piles of baby clothes and quilts for her. She would often talk, apparently, about how becoming a mother was a 'dream come true' and how she couldn't wait to meet her daughter.

I was a dream come true.

July whispered the words over and over as Auntie Shell turned her key in the door, laughing at something Sylvie had said. 'Where on earth do you get these jokes from?' She kissed Sylvie's forehead, then pushed the door open.

Usually that kind of thing left July with a jealous pang, a sense of loss and longing. That kind of kiss on the forehead usually made her own tingle, thinking of the ones she'd never had from her father. But not today.

Dream come true. Dream come true. Dream come true.

Auntie Shell stopped abruptly as soon as she got into the

house and July crashed into her back. 'What . . . ?' She peered around her stepmother.

Sitting at the bottom of the stairs was her father, his forehead shiny with sweat, tapping his nails against the side of a can of Boddingtons. His boxing gloves were hanging over the bottom of the bannister. He glared at Shell, then July, his face hard and unreadable.

'How much of my money have you spent, then?'

24

29 July 1995

Tim was reading the Saturday papers in his armchair, with Dora sitting at his feet, panting in the afternoon heat, when he heard them start. Mick and Shelley next door, shouting. Again.

Mick asking to see receipts. Shelley shrieking something unintelligible. Mick demanding to know who she'd been meeting. Shelley retaliating with 'Nobody!' and Mick not waiting for her to finish the word before he yelled 'Liar!' (among other things).

Libby came through from the kitchen with a paintbrush in her hand, whispering, 'Don't they realise we can hear? Should we say something, do you think? We should say something. Or not?'

Tim set the papers down. Dora rolled on to her back, and he bent low to scratch her pink tummy. 'Good girl,' he said. 'Good dog.'

'Leave her alone!' Shelley's voice rang through the walls, and Dora's ears flicked up.

Libby pointed at the Hoopers' house with her brush. 'Timmy, you should go round there. I really think you should.'

He scratched Dora's nose and forehead.

Mick's deeper voice again, now: 'What are these?'

Tim picked up his newspaper. 'Don't let them upset you, Lib. Not when you're in the middle of your watercolours. Put the radio on, would you? It's none of our business; let's give them some privacy.'

Libby looked worriedly at the wall, back at Tim, then switched Radio Four on before returning to her half-completed beach scene at the kitchen table.

With the radio on, they didn't hear Mick shout, 'You bitch. You betrayed me.'

They didn't hear July shushing Sylvie as they huddled together on the settee in the living room.

In the comfort of their own home in Harmony Close, they didn't see Mick pin his wife's face to the kitchen counter.

They didn't see July covering her stepsister's ears to save her from having to hear the blows.

They didn't see the blood dripping from Shelley's nose.

They didn't hear Sylvie's sobs.

Instead, Tim and Libby heard Alun Lewis reporting on Huntington's chorea and brain grafts. 'Isn't science incredible?' Tim called through into the kitchen as, next door, Shelley started to mop her own blood off the floor, Mick went upstairs for a shower, and Sylvie fell asleep in July's arms.

The girls didn't leave the living room other than to go to the loo – and when they did, they went together, Sylvie squeezing the bones of her hand so tight July worried they might fuse together as they tiptoed through the house. Auntie Shell made them some ham and marge sandwiches at seven o'clock, opening the door just enough to slide a plate in.

'Mummy?' Sylvie had called out weakly.

'I'm not feeling well, all right?' Shell answered softly through the closed door. 'I'm off for a lie-down. You girls be good, watch some telly, then get yourselves to bed.'

Sylvie was too frightened to get her pyjamas and didn't want July to leave her on her own, so when they did eventually turn in for the night they were wearing the same T-shirts and pants they'd worn into town, a trip which now felt like it had been days ago. Long after Sylvie had drifted off, July lay awake, silently folding and unfolding the square of origami paper on her pillow. She had never known her father to hit someone else before. When it happened to her, it felt different to how it had sounded with Auntie Shell. When he taught July a Lesson, it sometimes felt unfair, and it often hurt, but she always knew, deep down, that she deserved it. Auntie Shell hadn't deserved it. She hadn't hidden any receipts, as he'd suggested. July's rucksack was not new, contrary to his accusation – Katie-Faye had given it to her at the end of term because she had been given two the same by separate aunties. (When her father finally seemed to accept this, he'd changed tack with his wrath. 'You think she's your friend, do you, this Kate girl? She feels sorry for you. She gives you her unwanted crap. That makes you think you're friends, does it?') Auntie Shell had not bought an expensive new dress and hidden it at a friend's house on the way home. ('Think you can fool me?' he'd snarled when Shell had cried, 'What friend? Tell me, Mick, what friends do I have?') Sylvie was the only one who had bought anything, and even then she'd only spent £9.50. (Her father had added it up, before throwing his calculator at July's ear and sending her running from the kitchen.) And, anyway, it was Sylvie's own money – a pretty twenty-pound note, slipped into a card sent by her grandmother the week before.

July had thought that he only hit her. The revelation that this was not true made her think about her mother. *Did he ever do this to you?* Something still didn't add up, even after reading all those news articles. *What really happened?* In the dusky light forcing its way through the thin curtains, July cast her eye along the rows of novels on Auntie Shell's bookcase. Her stepmother only read fiction written before 1900, she was always keen to point out. The shelves were full of Austen, Brontë and Dickens.

Shell said she had been disappointed once too often by modern books. 'Dickens never lets you down,' she'd say, pulling a couple of her favourites from the bookcase and pressing each of them to her lips. 'And what he writes is still relevant to this day. Take *Barnaby Rudge*,' she'd say, as if that would explain everything. Sitting in the half-light, propped up against the settee, July wondered if any of her stepmother's beloved novels were relevant to this. Were any of them about a man who hit his wife and child?

After another hour the house was dark and silent. July put her shorts back on and carefully opened the living room door, holding her sandals against her chest. From the hall, she could hear her father's heavy breathing in the kitchen and the occasional snore. Very slowly, she lifted her key off its hook at the bottom of the stairs and opened the front door. It clicked as it shut, and she froze, waiting for a sound from inside, but none came. Still clutching her sandals in her hand, she crept through the side gate and retrieved her bike from the back garden, wheeling it out on to the drive.

The air was wonderfully cool against the bare skin of her arms and legs, and smelled more strongly of the sea than it did in daylight. Before she climbed on to her bike, she slipped on her sandals and looked up. The sky was the colour of the ink they used in their fountain pens at school, and thick with stars. She looked north, above the tiled rooftops of the houses on the other side of the close, to find Cassiopeia. *Dream come true.*

It was strange being out when it was so quiet. She didn't see a single person on her road or the next one. A couple of men were walking back from the pub when she turned on to the main road through the village, but they didn't notice her. Auntie Shell was paranoid about July or Sylvie being out after dark on their own, but she didn't feel scared. All the lights had halos around them, which she knew was on account of her poor eyesight, and she had to squint to see clearly, but she didn't care.

The night was magical, she decided. A bat darted low in front of her face and she thought, *You've got the right idea.* Could a human be nocturnal too, she wondered?

In the alley at Almond Drive, she looked up at the spikes on the gate, glinting in the moonlight. She remembered Mrs Salter's words in the paper. *She was brave. She was fearless.*

Placing one foot on the handle of the gate, she managed to grab hold of the corner of the flat roof of the garage on one side of it and haul herself up and over.

Now that she was here, she wasn't sure why she had come; she only knew that the siren song of Almond Drive had called her, and that she couldn't stay away from this street, from this house.

She climbed over the fence into number 4's garden. The window was closed this time, and the blinds had been pulled down. She couldn't remember Mr Salter doing that before they left on Tuesday. Had someone else been here? She stood by the back door, pressing her face against the glass. She heard Shell's voice in her head and laughed to herself. 'Think about all the hands that have touched that. Other people don't wash.' She cupped the sides of her eyes with her hands to help her see better. Her life had begun here, as her mother's ended. What was the first thing July had seen? What was the last thing her mother had touched?

As she scanned the darkness of the room, something on the kitchen counter, just inside the door, caught the moonlight. She knew the shape – it was a fan like Auntie Shell's, folded closed. She hadn't noticed it the other day; she was sure that it hadn't been there. It was difficult to tell in this light, but it even looked the same colour as hers, a dark blue plastic handle, with a pale trim around the top edge of the material. Hadn't Shell said, earlier today, on the bus, that she'd misplaced hers? But this couldn't be it. Auntie Shell couldn't have been in this house.

Then July noticed something else strange. She squinted to make sure that she wasn't imagining it, but no – the shattered remains of the glass vase she had smashed were definitely gone from the floor. Someone had been here. Was the family back from holiday?

She wandered back through the garden. Would she ever know the truth? She kicked through a pile of rubbish next to the shed – empty compost bags, old plastic nursery pots and broken bits of terracotta tiles. She winced as she stubbed her toe against something hard, and bent down to see what it was. A long metal bar with a curved end was at the bottom of the pile. Her father had one of these in his van. A crowbar, wasn't it? She lifted it up and was surprised by its weight in her hands. She turned and looked at the back of number 4, then across to Mr Salter's house.

He would be out at work, she thought, as she ran her hand along the cold smoothness of the bar.

Why would the police arrest you if you'd done nothing wrong?

Why won't you answer my questions?

What have you got to hide?

As she thought these things, she climbed on to the water butt and dropped the bar on to the track before jumping down herself. After taking a deep breath, she pushed at the gate to Mr Salter's back garden. It wouldn't budge, so she climbed over the fence, dragging the crowbar with her.

At best, he'd lied to her. He knew so much more than he had told her. At worst, he'd been the one who had taken her mother away from her. Creeping through his garden, her fingers tight around the bar, July wondered whether she had been wrong all this time. She had always assumed that the problems of her world lay with her, that she wasn't good enough, that she had the hole in her tummy which needed fixing. What if the problem was with everyone else? With the likes of her father, and Mr Salter.

But as she reached the house, a light came on upstairs – she could see its glow around the edges of the chipboard. She stopped, trying not to breathe. Under no circumstances did she want to be caught by a potential murderer in his garden after dark. She quickly laid the crowbar in a flower bed by the back door and ran through the garden, clambered over the fence and sprinted along the track, wishing she'd worn trainers.

On her way back over the gate into the alleyway, she scraped her thigh on one of the spikes. She winced with the pain, but jumped down, retrieved her bike and set off for home.

25

Darling girl,

When I started writing these letters, I was address-ing myself more than you, making sense of everything as well as wanting you to understand the truth, something I have never told anyone else in my life. Not even your dad.

But with every passing day, you grow in my belly and in my mind. You are a proper person: you can breathe already; your eyes can focus. This sharpens my awareness of other things I must impart, in case we never meet. My past is insig-nificant compared to everything I need to tell you.

Six things I want you to know about life

1. *I love your father so much. Hold out for a pas-sion like that; refuse to settle for less.*

2. *Take leaps of faith. You've got fierce little dragon wings hiding under those shoulder blades of yours. Jump, and you might find you can fly.*

3. *Stand up for yourself and for others. For starters, bullies will poke fun at you because you have a month for a name. Ignore them. They have no idea why it is important to our family.*

4. *Stop saying sorry all the time.*

5. *Travel. Or don't. Have kids. Or don't. Read the classics. Or don't. There's no single correct way to live, but there's definitely a wrong way: measuring yourself against the standards of anyone else.*

6. *Be yourself. Promise me you won't change for anyone. ANYONE.*

All my love, always,
Mum x

26

30 July 1995

The pancakes woke her. The smell seeping under the living room door: batter dropping into the pan. The sounds: the whisk against the sides of the bowl, the sizzling butter, her father whistling 'Dock of the Bay'.

July smiled, stretching her arms above her head, then rolled over on her mattress, patting her hand on the carpet to find her glasses. The Calm had returned.

Sylvie was already up and dressed in yesterday's clothes, hugging her knees to her chest on the settee. 'I'm not going in there without you,' she said when July sat up.

'He'll be fine this morning.' July yawned. 'Can't you hear him?'

Sylvie glanced in the direction of the kitchen, listening to July's father whistling.

When she spoke, her voice was tiny, like a small child's. 'What about my mum?'

July looked away. She found her shorts underneath her duvet and pulled them back on, flinching a little as the material caught the scratch on her thigh. She remembered a series of images from the night before – the spike on the gate, the crowbar, the fan on the counter at number 4 – then stood up. 'Come on. He makes good pancakes.'

*

'Here they are,' her father said, throwing his arms wide as July and Sylvie stepped into the kitchen. The room was bright and hopeful, the patio doors flung open to let a change of air into the house. 'Sit down, sit down.'

Sylvie did as he asked, but July couldn't help herself – the promise of pancakes and her whistling father made her spin around between the table and the couch, slide from side to side on the smooth kitchen floor, click her fingers and wiggle her hips. She imagined her mother jiving on the table beside her. Number 13: her mother loved to dance on her kitchen table, with the radio turned up loud, according to Grandpa Tony. She never *saw* her mother when she imagined her doing this, not in the same way she saw her after a lie, but she felt borrowed energy in her feet and hands, in the movements she made with her body.

'Table, July,' her father ordered, and she collapsed into a chair, smiling.

He poured them both glasses of orange juice and handed them each a plate stacked with small, fat pancakes. 'Syrup's on the table. I made them just the way you like them, little Four Eyes.'

July grinned at his use of her special nickname, as he resumed his whistling.

'Can I have some caramel sauce, Daddy?' she asked, a little out of breath. 'There's some in the cupboard.'

Without turning, he replied, 'No, you prefer maple syrup.'

Sylvie picked up her first pancake and nibbled at it, eyeing his back cautiously as he poured more batter into the pan. She didn't say a word throughout breakfast, and shrank away from July's father every time he passed within half a metre of her. July drizzled her stack with syrup and tucked in, also watching her father as he moved round the room. What she wanted, more than anything, was to run over and wrap her arms around him; for him to bend down and kiss her forehead. Looking at him now, as she demolished her second pancake, it seemed silly to think that she had ever been cross with him for lying to her (there must be a perfectly good explanation) and ridiculous to think that she had thought him capable of hurting her mother – he loved her too much, didn't he? When she was on her third pancake, he turned the hob off and set down another plate of fresh ones on the table, before sinking on to the couch to rub conditioning cream into his boxing gloves. She watched the methodical, gentle motion of his hands, the care he was taking over the task, and questioned what she had heard the previous afternoon. Maybe he hadn't hit Auntie Shell?

She loved him on the chocolate days, the pancake days, the whistling and humming days: she loved him more than anyone in the world.

She had eaten too fast, or too much. Either way, a crippling stomach ache crept up on her all morning and now, at 10.30, she was sitting halfway up the stairs, leaning against the spindles as she half-heartedly attempted to apply sun cream to her arms.

When her father came down, still whistling, dressed in his shirt and church trousers, she croaked, 'Can I stay home today, Daddy? I don't feel so good.'

'Not you as well?' he asked. There was the smallest hint of impatience in his voice.

As well as who, July wondered?

'You do look pale,' he said, and she glanced up at him. He never said things like that. He smiled, and she let her lips mirror his. Today's Calm had been particularly good so far. She replayed the morning's events. Perhaps she had done something to remind him of Mum? Maybe she had also sat like this, on the stairs, when she felt poorly? Unable to go up, unable to go down; stuck in the peculiar wasteland between feeling well and being properly ill.

She tucked some hair behind her ear, and his expression changed, the smile very slowly collapsing into itself. His eyes followed her hand as she dropped it back to her lap. What had she done wrong? She looked down. Across her wrist was a bruise in the clear greyish-blue shape of three fingers. It hadn't registered with her until now. When had that happened? He must have grabbed her yesterday afternoon, during the receipts row.

He reached a hand towards her and, instinctively, she flinched away, but he didn't seem to notice. He laid his palm across her forehead.

'A little hot. Best stay at home, then,' he said, walking away.

July watched him as he doubled back at the bottom of the stairs and made his way to the kitchen without looking at her. *Stupid July.* Why hadn't she noticed the bruise before and put a cardigan on? He hated to be reminded of what he had done.

With a great effort, she heaved herself up and descended the last few stairs. In the living room she found her Discman under a pile of clothes, lay on her mattress and pressed her headphones over her ears, focusing on the pale blue walls. Auntie Shell said the shade was called forget-me-not, and July couldn't help but think of it as a message from her mother whenever she was in the room. But today she also hoped the tranquil shade would soothe her. She mouthed the words to every track on the album she was listening to, trying to distract herself, but the pain steadily worsened. She turned her attention to the photograph of Burgh Island above the telly, trying to divert her mind with attempts to remember the tiny details of a rare family trip there. They'd eaten vanilla ice cream with raspberry sauce in cones as the warm wind whipped their hair. A seagull had stolen a man's sandwich on the beach. (July's father had laughed, so July had too.) They'd crossed the sandy passageway over to the island for a long, hot hike up to the stony remains of a chapel at the very top. (Sylvie got blisters.) Her father had carried her on his shoulders across the water back to the main beach as the tide rushed in. She'd got sand in the back of his van, and he'd shouted at her for making a—

July heard the front door slam and sat up: she was alone. Maybe she'd feel better if she moved around? She liked having the house to herself. It felt like a happier place without the rest of its inhabitants, as though it breathed a sigh of relief whenever they left. As she wandered aimlessly into the kitchen, humming along to her CD, she remembered something from Mrs Salter's piece in the paper, about how July's mother's kitchen was always warm and welcoming. July looked around their own. It was spotlessly clean, as it always was after her father had cooked. It smelled nice, still – of the pancakes and her father's coffee. And it was certainly warm, in this weather. But welcoming? No. She didn't think any of them would describe it that way. It did its job, but there was nothing that made you want to hang around in it. The wicker in the chairs scratched at your legs if you sat for too long. The tiles on the walls were brown and orange, and she reluctantly tasted orange Club bars every time she looked at them. Everyone knew you were either Team Mint or Team Orange, and she and Sylvie were firmly on the former. The pine cabinets regarded you blankly, and if you stood in front of them for long enough, they whispered in their master's voice, *Go and do something useful. Stop moping around.*

Whose kitchen had Mrs Salter been welcomed into after July's mother had died? There was no sign of her or her daughter at Mr Salter's house – only the climbing frame in the garden and the drawings on the fridge. July couldn't imagine him as a father. What had happened? Where was Mrs Salter now? She wished she could speak to her and find out more about her mother. She seemed to have known her so much better than Mr Salter had.

But what if she *could*? July pressed Pause and pulled off her headphones.

On top of the small desk next to the kitchen couch, she found the phone book and turned to the 'S's.

'Sackville . . . Saint . . .' she whispered, running her finger down the list. 'Salter!' But there was no Rob or Robert Salter. There were other Salters listed in the area, but there was no Janine either.

July slumped on to the couch. This was one part of the room she did like – its black leather upholstery was shiny, with a tinge of brown, like the mermaid's purses that washed up on the shore and nestled among the seaweed and driftwood on the tideline. Sometimes, when she sensed a Lesson coming – not imminent, but steadily approaching – she liked to curl up on it and pretend that she was a baby dogfish, cocooned inside its egg sac, protected from predators. She kicked at her father's boxing bag, lying at the foot of the couch alongside two pillows and a folded blanket – her father put the bed away each morning and fastidiously tidied his and Shell's bedding. One of his white hand wraps fell out of the bag, unravelling as it bounced on to the floor. She picked it up and tried to wrap her own hand, as she had seen him do so many times, looping it on to her thumb to begin. It was like the long strips of fabric they had used to learn basic weaving techniques at school, way back in year one. Maybe she could keep it, she wondered, as she wound it round and round her hand. He had so many, he wouldn't notice if one went missing. She finished off by sticking the Velcro patch across her wrist and held it up to admire her work. He'd be proud of her, she was sure. She would borrow it just for a while, she decided. To perfect her technique and then show him. It also crossed her mind that she could try and weave it somehow, weave *him* somehow, into her collection of scraps of her mother. How did he fit in? What had they been like together?

She was about to get up when she noticed a small blue envelope inside her father's bag. Holding her breath, she pulled it out. Could this be one of the notes from her mother? Could he have been keeping them here, all this time? But when she turned it over, disappointment pushed her hopeful, leaping heart back into its place. The handwriting listing her father's name and address was shaky. The postmark over the stamp told her it had been sent from Cumbria. It was from her grandparents, her father's parents. She pulled a leaflet out of the envelope – 'What is dementia?' – stapled to a scrap of lined paper.

'Son,' the note said in blue biro. 'Thank you for the other day, for going along with what your mother was saying about your Maggie. She won't stop talking about her, convinced she is still alive. She's getting worse. Thinks I'm her brother sometimes. The simplest thing is to let her believe she's right – she's much less agitated when she isn't challenged on these things she gets confused about. Regards, Father.'

July returned the note and leaflet to their envelope, and shoved it back in her father's bag. She knew about this illness – it was the one that twisted up grandparents' brains, made them forget things and people. Ben White, in her class, had brought it up one day, and Miss Glover had discussed it with them all. Ben's grandpa couldn't remember his own name any more. July felt sad for her grandmother, suddenly remembering the way she had let July play with the pearls around her neck, and wondered if she still knew she had a granddaughter.

The simplest thing is to let her believe she's right. So that was why Sylvie had heard what she had. July's father probably *had* said everything she reported, but it wasn't because Maggie Hooper was alive. Even though July already knew for sure her mother was not coming back, she still felt the blow of this realisation.

Her mind wandered again, via her mother's memory, to number 4 Almond Drive. She stood and returned to her stepmother's desk, remembering the fan. It definitely hadn't been there when she broke in – she was sure she would have noticed. She ran her fingers along the handle of the desk drawer as she sat down in the hard plastic chair. This was Auntie Shell's domain. She and Sylvie knew they were not meant to go snooping through her belongings – she'd made that perfectly clear – but maybe there was a perfectly sensible explanation for the fan? Or perhaps she would find it in the drawer? It would be better to eliminate one question from her ever-lengthening list, wouldn't it?

Slowly, holding her breath, July pulled the handle. A few centimetres at first – but all she could see were a couple of biros and a pink highlighter. She pulled it out further. There was a small pile of papers – typed letters. Some bills, which she flicked past without removing them. There was nothing that linked her stepmother to Almond Drive. It was all pretty boring. But then, near the bottom of the pile, she saw a piece of paper with her name on it. She lifted the documents on top of it so she could see better. It was a letter to Auntie Shell referring to her 'application to adopt July Hooper'. It talked about assessments and meetings, and said, 'we will, of course, want to discuss it with July herself'. July shoved the papers back into the drawer and slammed it shut. Auntie Shell wanted to *adopt* her?

July's stomach suddenly cramped again and she ran upstairs to the bathroom, two steps at a time. She crouched by the toilet bowl, waiting to be sick, grimacing at the stench of stale urine, and remembered something Katie-Faye had said about her mum spreading sheets of toilet roll on the seat if they were forced to visit a public loo – which, apparently, they avoided. Had July's mother done the same? Shell didn't, but she did spray her perfume around liberally, insisting that the alcohol in it killed any lingering bugs. Sylvie and July would stand, squashed into the cubicle with her, choking on vaporised vanilla. Did she want to be adopted by Shell? What would that mean? And why would Auntie Shell want a daughter like July when she already had Sylvie?

After a couple of minutes, when July still hadn't vomited, she got up, unwound the hand wrap from her wrist and sat for a wee instead. She stared at her pants in horror as they stretched between her knees. There was a dark brown stain in them. Was that . . .? No, it couldn't be – she'd know, wouldn't she, if she'd done that? Then what was it? Blood? She gripped the edge of the sink, smelling her father's shaving foam, trying to allow its limey familiarity to comfort her. Nobody had ever said getting your period looked like *that*.

'No . . .' she groaned. 'I want my mum.' She never usually said it out loud, but nobody was in the house to hear her. 'Mummy!' she shouted. What was she going to do? She tried to remember anything useful from the page on reproduction in her encyclopedia but all she could recall was four little drawings of an egg – which was bright blue in the illustration – travelling from the ovary to the uterus. No information on how to get your underwear clean or where to find your stepmother's sanitary towels and tampons.

Then there was a knock on the bathroom door, and a woman's voice said, 'July?'

July looked up at the door handle as it twisted slightly. 'Mum?' she whispered.

27

30 July 1995

'July, are you all right in there?'

It wasn't her mother, of course it wasn't. The sound of Auntie Shell's voice had never been so disappointing – like when July plunged her hand into a fresh box of Frosties only to find Sylvie had got there first and claimed the free toy. That feeling times a million. July silently knocked the side of her forehead against the sink. One, two, three. *Stupid, stupid, stupid.* When would she learn? It would never be her mother. This wasn't a Disney film. No magical sea witch was about to appear and offer to grant her a wish. Instead, she was stuck with Auntie Shell, perhaps forever. *Application to adopt July Hooper.* Why hadn't either of them told her about their plan to erase her real mother for good?

'July?' The handle twisted again. Thank God she'd automatically locked herself in, rather than leaving the door wide open under the misapprehension that she was alone in the house. She watched the handle rattle uncannily, like something out of a ghost story. Nothing good ever came of opening the door in those tales – the girl trapped in the bathroom would be searching for somewhere to hide or for a window to climb out of. *I don't know if I can trust you.*

She stuffed her father's hand wrap into her pocket and flicked her thumb against the elastic of her pants, looking up at the reassuringly neat lines of the door panels and then back down at the mess her body had made. The handle shook again, and July knew she had to say something. 'Aren't you supposed to be at church?'

'Oh, goodness, July. You gave me a real fright.' Auntie Shell sighed heavily, and her shadow shifted in the centimetre strip of light creeping in under the door. 'What are you doing in there?'

'I didn't know you were here.' July spoke quietly, staring at the redundant keyhole beneath the sliding bolt, and had a vision of her stepmother on the other side, wafting her misplaced blue fan in one hand and dangling the adoption letter from the other like a set of jailer's keys. July blinked to see the white-going-cream emptiness of the door again.

'I didn't catch that?' Auntie Shell waited a moment for July to repeat herself. 'You've not been sick, have you?'

July really didn't want to have to talk to her stepmother about this, especially right now. But who else could she turn to? Sylvie would know what to do but she wasn't here, and anyway she hadn't got hers yet – nobody in their year at school had. She could ask Yaya, but what would she do in the meantime? 'I think I've got my period,' she said, burying her head in her hands. 'Or I'm dying. One of the two.'

'Let's hope it's the first one, hey?' Auntie Shell laughed. 'Can you let me in? It'll be okay, don't worry, sweetheart.'

Sweetheart? She had never, ever, in the seven years since Daddy had introduced her to July, called her that. 'Give me a minute.' July folded a wad of toilet paper, put it into her pants and pulled them up, before flushing the loo and washing her hands. She looked at her pale face in the mirror, pulling at the flesh of her cheeks. It most definitely was not the face of a woman – there must be some mistake. 'It's like a caterpillar, turning into a butterfly,' Sylvie had told her once. Sylvie knew all about periods and boobs and pubic hair from Helen Knight, who had two older sisters. Surely Sylvie would have been a better candidate for this to happen to first? 'One day you're a girl,' she'd said, chewing on the section of hair she carefully styled to hang down the side of her face each day. 'Then the next you're a woman. Personally, I can't wait to be on the rag. What? Don't make faces at me, July. Nobody calls it the p word, any more. That's just for mums.'

As soon as July opened the door, Auntie Shell bent down to put her mug of tea on the floor and pulled her in for a tight hug. There was no hint of her usual perfumed scent – only cigarettes and the sleep-smell of her dressing gown. 'You know, when I got mine, my parents all but threw me a party,' she said as she pulled away and retrieved some sanitary towels from the top cupboard in the bathroom.

'A party?' The thought horrified July. Was Auntie Shell going to do that for her? Was she going to tell her father? She'd die of embarrassment.

'We all went to the chemist to get some of these –' she placed the purple packets of pads in July's hands '– and then we went home for pizza.'

'That's weird.'

'It was, a bit. But also nice.' Shell retrieved her mug of tea and took a sip. 'It's a big day for you.'

'I guess.' She still didn't want a party, though. Or pizza, even. She wanted to pretend it hadn't happened – there was enough going on without this. 'How long can I leave these in?' she asked without looking at Auntie Shell's face. She couldn't stand the humiliation and fought a sudden urge to wrap herself in the plastic shower curtain.

'What do you mean?'

July backed away from her stepmother on to the bath mat, which was unnervingly damp. Her father insisted that it was hung to dry after use and was quick to punish July if she forgot, but she was sure he was the only person to have showered in here today. She wiggled her toes against the wet cotton and stared at the packets in her hands.

'July, what do you mean?' Shell repeated. 'You can ask me anything, no matter how stupid you think the question is.'

Stupid, stupid July. 'Sylv said . . . she said you could get some kind of illness. If you left them in too long.' July flicked at the little white tab on the top packet. 'Said it can kill you.'

'That's tampons,' Auntie Shell said, sounding like she wanted to laugh. July was grateful that she didn't. 'You change these whenever you need to.'

'I thought I was too young.'

'My sister got hers at your age. A bit younger, actually.'

'But I don't want it yet.'

'Nobody ever does, sweetheart.'

That word again! What was going on? She looked up at Auntie Shell's face for the first time since she'd let her in, hoping to see something there that might account for all the strange things that were going on with her. But there were no explanations etched across her cheekbones, down the bridge of her nose or across her forehead. All July saw were bruises. A split lip. Dark brown patches of skin under her eyes. July's mouth formed into a silent 'Oh.'

Auntie Shell turned away, straightening the towels on the rail above the radiator. Dark green for Daddy, pale pink for Sylvie, cream for Shell. July's was a darker pink version of Sylvie's – they'd come as a set (Sylvie had got to choose which ones she wanted first). 'Don't worry about me,' Shell said. 'How's your wrist?'

'Fine. You . . .' July wanted to say something, to help. 'He—'

'You know none of it is your fault, don't you?'

July dug her nails through the plastic wrappers into the sponginess of the pads contained within them.

'Do you think your friends' dads hit them?' Auntie Shell asked, spinning round. 'Katie-Faye? Caroline?'

'If they've been naughty. If they need to be Taught a Lesson.'

'No, July.' Auntie Shell grabbed her shoulders and brought her face down to July's level. Up close, July could make out constellations of blue and green stars in the darkness of the bruise on Auntie Shell's jaw. Not Cassiopeia, but perhaps Leo if she squinted a bit. 'That's not how it is. Other families are different.'

July wasn't sure she understood what Auntie Shell was saying. She'd never spoken to Katie-Faye about it, but had always assumed that her father must hit her too. How else could he make her into a better person, like July's father said he was trying to do?

Was Shell suggesting there was another reason for her father's behaviour?

'Then maybe he's really sad?' July offered. As soon as she said it, she realised it must be true. 'Did you know Granny Orla is ill? He must be upset about it.'

'I didn't know he'd told you,' Shell said, releasing July and stepping away. 'That's good. I've been on at him for ages to say something. I told him you deserved—'

'What happened yesterday? Did you ask him a question about my mum too?' July interrupted her stepmother, unable to take her eyes off the bruise on her jaw. 'Is that why he . . .?'

Auntie Shell smiled, but it wasn't one of her usual ones, framed by frosted pink lips stretched wide. Her mouth twitched at the corners and her chin crinkled. She pinched July's cheek. 'Kind of,' she said, turning to leave. 'Now, why I don't I let you—'

'I know what happened to her.'

Auntie Shell stopped, her fingers on the door frame.

'She didn't die in a car crash,' July said.

A moment passed. Then: 'No.'

'Why did you both tell me she had?'

'We . . . we didn't.'

'You did! You—'

'Your dad told you she'd gone to Heaven when you were old enough to start asking. That was all he said.' Shell paused. 'Then, one day, when you were about five, you started telling people she had died in a car accident. We just . . . we never corrected you.'

The simplest thing is to let her believe she is right.

'We meant well,' Shell said. 'It seemed the kindest thing to do. Why upset you even more?'

'So why do I remember it? If there was no accident, what do I see whenever I close my eyes?'

Shell leaned her forehead against the door. 'That must have been me. I was hit by a car when you and Sylvie were little.'

July screwed her eyes shut, trying to summon the images she had believed for so long. Could it be true? Could it be Shell, not her mother?

A woman's body, bouncing over the bonnet and off to one side.

The crunch of metal.

The ambulance crew trying revive her.

She wanted to think about it more, to understand the shifts this new information caused in her mind, to interrogate other memories she had always relied upon being true, but instead she forced her brain to change gear. She had other questions to ask while Auntie Shell was in an answering mood. Some big, some important, and some . . . some that would seem less pressing to most people. But to July all her questions were equally weighted. Each answer gave her part of her mother. 'And why – what – how come I remember her liking boiled eggs? She called them dip dip eggs. I remember sitting at the table with her on a sunny morning, with white toast soldiers and . . .' The image was so vivid, so real, she could almost reach out and touch the egg cup on the table in front of her; she could feel the warm sun on her face. 'That, and the car crash. Those are the only two things I remember about her. The only memories of my own.'

Auntie Shell rolled her forehead from side to side against the painted wood of the door, still not turning to look at July. 'I'm sorry, sweetheart. That was me too. With the eggs.'

You? How could July have mistaken Shell for her mother? She felt like she'd let her down, terribly.

But there wasn't time to dwell on that now. She eyed her step-mother's hand, still on the door frame. It was poised, ready to move to the handle in a flash, and then she'd be gone. The answers would leave the room with her.

'That man next door,' July said, blinking hard to gather her thoughts. 'Mr Salter. He killed her. They said he didn't, but he did.'

Auntie Shell's hand dropped, but she didn't turn back to look at July. 'July . . .' She was about to cut her off, tell her to drop it, stop asking questions. July knew the exasperated tone. But then she said, 'This conversation didn't happen. What I am about to tell you, you didn't hear it from me.'

July waited, holding her breath.

'Okay?'

'What?'

'The things I'm about to say to you, I never said. Okay?'

'Right.'

Auntie Shell sighed, still facing away from July. 'That's what your dad thinks, yes. That Rob Salter killed her.'

July's stomach churned. She'd spent so much time talking to that man. She'd started to like him. And all along, he was the person responsible for her losing her mother. She dropped the pads on to the closed toilet lid and thrust her hand into her pocket, pulling her Diet Coke slammer free of its crumpled yellow companion. The paper crackled against her fingers like an electric shock, and she snatched her hand and the slammer away, out of her pocket. *I betrayed you. I'm sorry.*

'He thinks that man was harassing your mum, and when she turned him down, he got angry.' Auntie Shell turned and tightened her dressing gown around her waist, but awkwardly, with one hand; the other still held her mug of tea. 'He thinks that when she . . . He thinks Rob Salter killed her and made it look like she died . . . naturally.'

'She died because of Mr Salter.'

'Maybe. Look, July,' Auntie Shell tugged at the hairs of her eyebrows. 'Nobody really knows what went on. Your dad has his theory. Your gran thought . . .' She trailed off. 'She thought something different happened. But the police . . . How do you know all of this, anyway? Has Yaya been talking to you about it?'

'I read it, in the newspapers. At the library.'

Auntie Shell drained her mug. She didn't seem cross, July thought with relief.

'What exactly does Yaya think happened?'

'She doesn't like your father much,' Auntie Shell said, 'but that doesn't mean . . .' She shook her head. 'He couldn't have had anything to do with it. He wasn't there.'

Yaya's cryptic comments began to make a little more sense, but Auntie Shell was right. He wasn't there. How could he have been to blame?

'But that's important to remember when you consider what your dad thinks happened too,' Shell went on. 'It's important to remember he wasn't there. He is absolutely convinced that Rob hurt your mum, but that doesn't mean it did happen like that. You see the difference, don't you? It's like, you know that time when he yelled at you because he thought you'd left your wellies in the porch?'

'But it wasn't me.'

'Exactly. It was my fault – you left them outside like he wanted but I'd brought them in and then forgotten them.'

'But he wouldn't believe me.'

'No. Once your father gets an idea in his head, it gets wedged in there, doesn't it?' She looked July straight in the eye. 'Rob Salter didn't kill your mum. The police thought he had, but they changed their minds. You've got to trust that – they know what they're doing. The evidence showed he didn't do it.'

'But how *did* she die, then?'

'Sometimes people just do. Women, having babies.' Shell's voice grew quiet. 'Sometimes things go wrong.'

July hadn't considered this option before. 'I killed her?' The slammer grew suddenly hot in her hand. Accusatory. She loosened her grip.

'Lots of women die in childbirth.' Auntie Shell ran a finger along the edge of the sink, avoiding looking at July. 'It's one of the most dangerous things you'll ever do as a woman. But it's not the baby's fault.'

'So if she hadn't had me, she'd still be alive?'

'It wasn't your fault.'

The room started to spin. July grabbed at the shower curtain to support her, before sitting on the edge of the bath. 'I killed her.' It made sense. Mr Salter didn't seem like a murderer. 'I killed my own mother.' She slid down into the still-damp bath, hugging her knees to her chest. She didn't care that her shorts were getting wet. She didn't deserve any comfort in life. She didn't deserve anything good. She dug her nails into her leg until she wanted to cry out from the pain, and held them there. 'She must have hated me in those final moments, knowing she was dying and I'd killed her.'

'It isn't like that,' Shell was saying, but it sounded like she was a thousand miles away. 'I shouldn't have told you. This kind of thing hap—'

'Stop it!' July screamed. 'I'm a murderer. Stop trying to make me feel better!'

She was vaguely aware that Shell had started to cry, and touched a hand to her own face. It was wet, but she couldn't tell if it was because of tears or because her fingers were wet from the puddle in the bath. *You don't deserve to cry.*

'She must have hated me!' July yelled, smacking the edge of the bath. '*He* must hate me.' It was all starting to fall into place. Of course her father didn't love her. How could he, after what she had done?

'Oh, July. No. He doesn't hate you.' Shell tried to put a hand on July's head, but she pushed her away. 'He hates Rob Salter, not you. That's why you moved away from that house.'

July caught her breath and steadied her voice. She'd been right. 'I knew it. It's so much bigger than this one. Daddy said—'

A strange look passed over Auntie Shell's face. 'You've been there?' she asked.

July nodded, wiping her eyes. 'Just to look.'

'Promise me you won't do that again?' Shell's tone had changed. The softness had gone, replaced by a tightness. A nervousness.

July bit her lip. Should she tell Shell she'd seen her fan on the counter? Impossible. Shell would be furious that July had been climbing fences and snooping around. Instead, she said, 'Shell? Why didn't Daddy tell me any of this? About what happened?'

'He doesn't like to talk about it.' Auntie Shell leaned over the bath and pulled July towards her for another hug, but her voice was still strained. 'Promise me you won't tell him I said anything?'

July tried to shake her head, but Auntie Shell was holding her too tight, July's face squashed against the soft fluffy cotton of her dressing gown. Did her mother wear dressing gowns like this? With small pink flowers? Would she have made her own?

'Don't go back to Almond Drive. Promise me? It's not safe for you to hang around there.'

28

31 July 1995

J uly had spent several hours lying awake overnight, watching the lime-green minutes tick by on the digital display of the video player underneath the TV, toilet paper stuffed into her pants alongside the pad, terrified of falling asleep in case she woke up to find blood on her bed. Could it soak through her mattress on to the living room floor?

And she couldn't stop thinking about her mother. Her *victim*. She had got her period one day, many years ago (what had Yaya said to her about it, July wondered?), which had meant she'd been able to have a baby. That baby had killed her. Her own daughter had killed her. At 1 a.m. July had buried her face into her pillow and screamed until her throat was raw.

She had found herself, surprisingly, missing Sylvie, who was staying the night at Helen's. July wanted to tell her stepsister everything that had happened while she was at church – about the note in Mick's bag, her period and, worst of all, about how her mum had died.

When she got up in the morning, her first morning as a woman, she had climbed the stairs to her bedroom and lain down on the floor, shuffling her body back so that her head was underneath the slats of her bed frame, like a car mechanic investigating the undercarriage of a car, surrounded by her diminishing stash of sweets. This was where she kept her secret display: limpet shells that had been tossed by the sea until they had lost their apexes, worn down into rings and abandoned on the beach in their millions. She had dozens of them, each the colour of vanilla ice cream, stuck with Blu-tack to the underside of the frame, where she knew nobody would look. Her collection had begun the same day Grandpa Tony gave her Number 12: her mother adored these 'sea hoops', as she'd called them. Now, lying with her neck itching against the scratchy brown carpet of her bedroom floor, she traced the circles of her dozens of shells with her little finger. She could barely see them in the darkness of her room with the curtains drawn, but she felt the ridges of each hoop, thinking about the much larger, much less tangible circle of life. Thinking about the overlap of her first breaths with her mother's last. How many gulps of air had they shared? Ten? Twenty?

Tears rolled down July's face, pooling in her ears before overflowing on to the carpet. Had they shared enough breaths for her mother to have had the time to hold her? How was it fair that July had lived, but her mother had died? Yesterday she had thought about her father, and immediately understood why he detested her. Now she considered Yaya too. July had killed her only daughter. Was that why she couldn't stand to talk about it with her? When she looked at July, was she filled with loathing?

July knew that she had to go back to the scene of her crime, back to Almond Drive. Her stepmother had told her not to but hadn't given any good reason. July could still feel the pull of the place, calling her there, to where her mother's heart had beaten its last, and July's had fluttered for the first time outside the protection of the womb. To where the last person to see her mother alive was to be found. She had to speak to him again. Had her mother even seen her, she needed to ask? Had she realised that she had been right in predicting that she would have a daughter? Had she spoken her name?

Eventually, hearing Sylvie arrive back as Helen's mother dropped her off, July had pushed herself out from under the bed and found the paracetamol Auntie Shell had given her for the cramps. She swallowed a couple of tablets with warm water from the plastic bottle on her windowsill, then slowly made her way down the stairs to the kitchen, where the rest of them were having breakfast.

'Toast?' Auntie Shell asked without a smile. Her bruises were covered in thick make-up, her hair loose around her face, ready for her shift at the GP surgery. She pushed a plate across the table with a slice of barely browned bread on it.

'I'm not hungry.'

'Suit yourself.' Shell snatched the plate back with a huff. The softness of yesterday – the 'sweethearts' and the hugs – had gone. She had frozen over again. Then, with a lowered voice, she asked coolly, 'How are you feeling today?'

July felt her cheeks redden, and she picked nervously at the scabbed-over scratch on her thigh.

Don't ask me that, she wanted to say. She had made Shell promise not to say anything to her father about her period. *He'll know something is going on.* He didn't notice, though. He was eating his toast, slathered thickly with strawberry jam on both the top and bottom, studying the tough-skinned pears ripening on the tree. She watched his eyes flitting from fruit to fruit. Taking stock, predicting which might prove the most useful, which might let him down by dropping silently to the grass and allowing itself to be carried off by a rat in the night. He looked at the three of them like that sometimes too – her, Shell and Sylvie – assessing what was his.

'Can I go out?' July asked. 'Just for a little bit, on my bike. I'll be careful.'

'Fresh air might help, I suppose,' Auntie Shell said, seeming relieved. July often got the feeling that she was glad not to have her around when she was in this kind of mood. 'But not without your sister, obviously. Do you want to go, Sylv?'

Sylvie scowled over her cornflakes, shaking her head. '*Big Breakfast*'s on.'

'Be nice out there though, before it gets too hot?' July was surprised to hear her try to persuade Sylvie on her account – was today a freeze or a thaw? She didn't understand this woman at all.

'It'll be nice here too.'

'But—'

July's father slammed his hand on the table, giving Sylvie such a fright, she dropped her spoon on the floor, causing milk to splash July's leg. When July looked up at her, her own mouth dry with the dread that escorted an imminent Lesson, she saw tears pooling above her stepsister's lower eyelashes. 'For Christ's sake, woman,' her father said through a mouthful of food, spitting crumbs, 'let the girl stay at home.' He turned to July, pointing at her with his half-eaten toast, jam dripping off the bottom in huge globs on to the tablecloth. 'Don't be too long. Don't leave the village.'

July jumped up, forgetting for a moment that she had asked to go in the first place, just desperate to obey his commands promptly. As she walked out of the patio doors to get her bike, she felt his eyes on her back (would she be a useful pear or a rotten one?) and was grateful that he hadn't asked where she planned to go. She hadn't lied since Auntie Shell had told her she'd killed her mother. She couldn't bring herself to see her.

Mr Salter was outside when she arrived in Almond Drive, squashing a bag of rubbish into his bin. He saw her, shook his head and looked away.

'Why didn't you tell me?' July gripped her handlebars to stop her hands trembling.

'I got back from work half an hour ago. I'm dog tired.' He lifted a second black bag into the bin and pressed it down. 'It's not a good time.' The stench of hot waste wafted over to her, but she refused to turn away.

'I know what happened.' She squeezed her handlebars tighter. 'Why didn't you just tell me the truth?'

Mr Salter walked to his front door, but she couldn't let him go. 'Where are Janine and Jenny?'

That did it. He stopped with his hand on the door handle.

'Why have I never seen them here?'

Without turning, he spoke, just loud enough for her to hear. 'Cycle round to Hollybush Avenue. Come through the alley. I'll open the gate.' He slammed the door shut behind him.

Hollybush Avenue was the road parallel to Almond Drive. She got back on her bike and did as he said, parking her bike as she watched him walk down the track to open the gate. He put a finger to his lips as he unlocked it, and ushered her through, leaving it unlocked.

Only when they got into his house did he speak, over the quiet voices on the radio upstairs. (A woman today, with a foreign accent, talking to a whinging man.) 'Why are you here?'

'She died giving birth to me,' July said. 'You were with her.'

He nodded, slightly. 'I delivered you.'

'But you're not a doctor. Why didn't you take her to hospital?'

'You were too impatient to wait for hospital. Too impatient even to make it to the bathroom floor. I delivered you in the middle of the landing.' He smiled. 'You'd decided you were coming out, and there was nothing we could do to stop you.'

'Did she hold me? Was there time?'

He leaned against the door frame, his features dark against the bright backdrop of the garden drenched in morning sun. 'You had a few minutes together; she kissed you, stroked your face. But then . . .' He paused, took a deep breath. 'There was a lot of blood, suddenly. She panicked, I think. She handed you to me, and before I could stop her, she stood up. That was when it happened.'

'She fell.'

'They think she must have passed out. She'd lost so much blood.'

July swallowed, reaching out a hand to touch the nearest stack of newspapers. She remembered the police quote in the news article, the notes she had made and read hundreds of times since. *We believe that Mrs Hooper lost her balance and fell down the stairs after experiencing a post-partum haemorrhage.*

She wanted to ask more: *Did she hate me? Did she know she was dying?* But the words lodged in her throat against the roughness caused by her screams in the night. Instead, she said, 'I guess I know now why you don't like the police.'

Taking a piece of origami paper from a pile on the counter, he started to fold. 'They took a very simple situation and turned it into a massive, complicated mess. Like these birds, you see? You take a piece of paper: it's simple, a square; not many people would be interested in that. But fold it in all these different ways . . .' He kept folding, pressing shapes open and closed with his fingertips. He held up another perfectly formed crane. 'It turns into this complex, fancy shape. Much more interesting for everyone. So, it must be true.'

'My dad thinks you hurt her.'

Mr Salter stroked the wings of the crane in his hand. 'And you believe him?'

'Why did he never get the key back off you, for the back door? If he thought that?' It was one of the things that had been bothering her – Mr Salter dangling that key and smiling at her in the kitchen of number 4.

He looked up at her. 'He didn't know I had it.'

'You said my parents had given it to you?'

'Your mum.'

He set the crane down on the counter, in a stream of sunlight seeping in around the edge of the board on the window. July waited for him to elaborate, but he didn't; instead, he washed his hands in the sink, carefully rolling a bar of cracked white soap in his hands. She stared at his fingers. Had they been the last thing to touch her mother before she died? Had she been afraid?

'But the police knew you had the key? The day Mum died? They would have told Daddy, and he would have got it back.'

As she said the words, she felt stupid. What did this matter? This wasn't what she wanted to ask him. *Did she know I had killed her? Did she say my name?*

He kept rubbing his hands together in the running water. 'I told them, and I guess your dad told them, that the door had been open when I got there. That your mum had it open. It was a hot day.'

'But it wasn't open.'

'No.'

'Okay.' But it wasn't quite okay.

There was a squeaking sound, and July looked down to see next door's fluffy white cat skipping in, heading straight for the bowl of cat food.

'Morning, buddy,' Mr Salter said, turning the tap off and wiping his hands across the front of his shorts.

'Why did you lie to them?' July asked as Mr Salter crouched down to scratch the cat's head. 'The police? Why would you lie?'

'They don't look after you, do they? Poor old Mitten.' The cat mewed, looking up at Mr Salter. 'Going away on holiday and leaving you all alone.'

'Won't your cat mind, her eating all the food?'

'Him. And I don't have a cat.'

July looked from the bowl to the cat flap in the back door and back again. Mr Salter must have read her thoughts. 'They don't deserve him,' he said defensively. 'They don't look after him. He prefers being here.'

July shrugged. She hadn't come here to talk about a cat.

'I don't know anyone called Jenny Salter,' she said.

He took a spoon out of a drawer next to the sink. 'No, I wouldn't imagine you do.'

'She must be about thirteen now,' July said, watching him open the fridge door. As he took a saucepan out, she saw that there was very little else inside – a half-empty bottle of milk, some cheese, a box of tomatoes, some brown bread. 'It said in the newspaper she was three. Three plus ten is thirteen.'

'Aha.' Mr Salter elbowed the fridge shut and dug his spoon into the pan, lifting out a lump of pasta in a white sauce. It looked like macaroni cheese. 'The newspaper,' he added. 'That's how she knows all of this, Mitten.' He put the spoonful of food into his mouth.

July looked over her shoulder at the cat, and back to Mr Salter. 'Why don't they live here any more?'

'Jenny Davey. That's her name. Not Jenny Salter.' He poked his spoon back into the pan.

July wished she hadn't skipped breakfast. She loved leftover pasta, and could taste each mouthful as he devoured it – the rubberiness of the macaroni, the cold saltiness of the cheese sauce. Her mouth filled with saliva.

'Janine didn't believe me. Didn't believe the police would make a mistake.' He leaned against the countertop, facing her once more.

'So she left?'

He spooned more pasta through his lips and pointed at a cupboard in the corner of the kitchen. A calendar was stuck to it. She'd seen it when she was here last time. How was this an answer? But as she looked more closely, she saw that it was from

228

1986 and open at February. 'That was the last time I read my daughter a bedtime story,' he said. '*Each Peach Pear Plum.*'

July's stomach flipped. She hated hearing about families that had split up. Why did they do that? Why would you not want to all be together? She'd give anything to be together with *both* her parents. 'But Davey isn't your name,' she said, also thinking that there was no Jenny Davey at her school. She didn't know her.

He picked something out of his mouth and flicked it into the sink. 'No. Janine changed their name back to hers.'

'Do they still live around here?'

'Yes.'

Ask him, July thought. *Ask him now. Did my mum realise she'd had a—*

'How did you get that bruise on your wrist?' He pointed at it with his spoon, his voice suddenly steady and serious.

'I . . .' July looked down to the floor, where Mitten had started rubbing his soft coat against her bare calves, looking at her with big green eyes. *Think quickly*, he urged her. She heard the pips of the news bulletin on the radio upstairs. 'It was . . .'

Mr Salter put the saucepan down and stepped towards her to take a closer look, pushing his glasses up his nose and reaching his hand out but stopping short of touching her. 'Are those finger marks?'

Mitten mewed.

'Did *he* do this to you?'

The lie wouldn't come. She couldn't bear to see her mother.

'He did, didn't he?'

'Did he ever hurt my mum?' July closed her eyes. She wasn't sure she wanted to know the answer, but it had been on her mind ever since Saturday night as she'd listened to Auntie Shell whimper in the kitchen.

'May I?' Mr Salter pointed at her arm, and July held it out towards him. Very gently, he took hold of her wrist, turning it over to see the extent of the bruise. 'What am I going to do?' he muttered. 'I'll fucking k—'

'Don't do anything. Please. He'll get so angry.' She yanked her arm out of his grip. 'Please, you have to promise me. It was my fault, I upset him. He thought I'd spent too much money in—'

She was interrupted by shouts coming from the road at the front of the house. 'July? July!'

She turned to Mr Salter. Her legs felt suddenly weak, and she clutched at the kitchen counter. 'That's him.'

July stared into the hall, imagining her father bursting through the front door. She could already feel his fists on her face, his palms pushing her to the floor and his kicks to her back. She hunched her shoulders, instinctively covering her head with her arms. He was coming for her.

29

31 July 1995

Vanessa was bundling her kids into the car when she saw Mick Hooper banging on the door of number 2.

'Mum?' Jacob asked from the back seat. 'What's going on?'

'Don't stare, it's rude,' Vanessa said as she watched the commotion through the windscreen. 'Help your sister, would you? Strap her in.' She wound down her window.

'I know you're in there,' Mick was shouting.

'Isn't that Mr Hooper?' Jacob asked.

Everyone knew Mick Hooper, mainly because of what had happened shortly after Vanessa had moved to Almond Drive. She'd known Maggie too, of course – the wife. They hadn't been friends as such, but Maggie had brought flowers over a few days after Vanessa and Ben had moved in. 'If you need anything, you know where I am,' she'd said, smiling. 'You'll love it here, such a friendly street.' A few weeks later, she was dead.

It wasn't the first time Vanessa had seen Mick back here, though normally when she spotted him it was in the middle of the night, when she pulled at the edge of her curtains to check the road after hearing a strange noise. She'd seen him painting words on Salter's wall, leaving things on his doorstep, dousing the front lawn with weedkiller. She was sure many of her neighbours had seen him too (she'd noticed other curtains twitching), but, like her, they'd all gone back to bed and slept soundly.

Because Salter – well, he was a nasty piece of work, wasn't he? They all knew it. They all remembered what he had done. But, as she'd whispered to her sister one night a few years ago, after getting smashed on a couple of very drinkable bottles of Sauv Blanc, she also remembered other things. Stuff that occasionally, if she wasn't careful, had made her question Mick's version of events.

It wasn't anything serious enough to tell the police, though, you know? Because they'd just think she was a gossip, and anyway she didn't talk to the police. That was how her father had raised her, she thought proudly. That was how she was raising her two kids.

She held the car keys in her lap, making no attempt to put them in the ignition. 'We'll be late for swimming at this rate.'

'But what's he doing?' Jacob asked again.

Inside number 2 Mr Salter was asking the same question. Also high on his list of hissed queries for July was: 'How does he know you're here?' He looked past her, towards the hall and front door.

'He doesn't.' July's toes curled in her sandals. With a great effort, she straightened up and stared at Jenny's childish drawings on the fridge. The faded lines took on new forms: a monster, a murderous man, a cowering girl. Her father was going to kill her if he found her. Why was he here? Shouldn't he be up at the Big House today?

'Have you told anyone else that you come here?'

'No! Nobody.' It wasn't a lie. Auntie Shell knew that she'd been to Almond Drive, but not to this particular house.

More shouts came from outside. 'July Hooper! I know you're here somewhere.'

Mitten dashed out of the back as the front door rattled with her father's blows, but July stayed, the soles of her sandals

fusing with the grey floorboards. She looked at the newspapers –
somehow, she didn't think her hiding place among them would
be enough to fool her father. Where else could she go? She
glanced into the hall, up the staircase strung with multicoloured
cranes. Was there a cupboard up there she could slip into? Or
should she face her father now? She could open the door, let
him take her away. Surrender to the Lesson. She winced at the
thought of it.

'Okay, okay.' Mr Salter paced the kitchen floor. 'So, he doesn't
know for sure that you've spoken to me?'

'Yes. I mean, no.'

Mr Salter looked at her wrist again. 'Your dad would hate it if
he knew you'd been talking to me. He can't ever know about
this.'

July pointed towards the front door. 'I think he knows already.'

'No. He *thinks* you're here. We have to make him believe that
he's wrong.'

July tried to think of words to explain to Mr Salter that nobody
ever told her father that he was wrong.

'I'm going to distract him, then you go out the back gate, take
your bike out to Hollybush Avenue and get home.'

'What will you say?'

'I'll think of something.'

She stepped reluctantly towards the back door, nervous to
leave the safety of the dark kitchen. She gripped the edge of the
counter with both hands, as if holding on to a cliff edge to stop
herself from falling to the rocks below, or worse, into the sea.

'Look at you; you're terrified of him.' He shook his head, then
touched her shoulder. 'I'm going to help. He can't do that to
you.' He nodded towards her wrist. 'I'll . . . I'll work something
out.'

She tried to say 'okay' but her mouth was too dry. She let go
of the counter and took another step towards the door.

'Go on.'

July ran as quickly and as quietly as she could down through the garden and out along the track. Just as she reached the main alley gate, she heard Mr Salter open his door and shout, 'This has to stop!'

'Where is she?' Her father's voice was louder. July tripped when she heard it, and she steadied herself against the fence. Sweat beaded on her forehead as she stood in the sun.

'I know it's all you,' Mr Salter said, his voice carrying clearly through the still morning air. 'And now this? Showing up here, shouting, disturbing the whole road.'

'I don't know what you're talking about.' She could hear the sneer in her father's voice as she slipped out of the gate into the refreshing shade of the alleyway.

'Sure. It's somebody else throwing bricks through the windows. Covering my walls with graffiti.'

July thought about the notebook she had found, listing dates and incidents. All those nasty things in such beautifully ordered lists. They were down to her father?

'Too much of a coward to admit it?' July had never heard anyone dare to speak to her father like this.

'Where is she?'

'It fits. All bullies are cowards.'

'Where is she?' her father repeated.

'Who?'

July knew she should be getting home, but she wanted to hear what else they said. She crept up the alleyway towards Almond Drive, staying out of sight. As she peered around the corner, she saw her father on the path to Mr Salter's front door, his face red with rage. She remembered him shadow-boxing in their back garden at home. *Fuck you, fucking Rob Salter. Fuck you.*

'My daughter, you bastard. Where's my daughter?'

'Not here,' Mr Salter said. 'Why would she be? Now get off my property before I call the police.'

'How many police officers have you got in your pocket, hey?' her father asked.

Mr Salter stepped into July's view, and her father backed away from him out on to the pavement.

'Or maybe you've got a girlfriend on the force? Or you've got some dirt on someone? Which is it?'

Mr Salter shook his head as he walked further away from his front door. He yanked at the post attached to his wall, pulling down the FOR SALE sign.

'What are you doing?' July's father asked.

'You'd like this, wouldn't you? You'd like me to leave?'

'Nobody wants you here.' Her father turned towards the alley, and July ducked back quickly. She shouldn't be here.

'I've changed my mind,' she heard Mr Salter say as she grabbed her bike. 'I'm staying. I'm not done here.'

She pedalled along Hollybush Avenue as quickly as she could, her thighs burning. But when she pulled on to the main road through the village she slowed slightly, trying to catch her breath, replaying something her father had said to Mr Salter.

Where's my daughter?

It wasn't the words that had stuck in her mind, but the way he had said them. There was a ribbon in them, she was sure of it, hidden in her father's intonation. *Where's my daughter?* A ribbon of her mother scratching at the hard confines of those three words, a truth fighting to escape. She repeated them over and over, all the way home, hoping to wear the words' exoskeletons thin, desperate for one of them to crack open.

30

HMP Channings Wood
14 December 2001

Dear July,

I did care. It is possible to love two people simultaneously. Life and love are wild and complicated beasts. I'm not saying I didn't make mistakes – I caused hurt. Undeserved suffering. But I cared for her.

Love,
Dad

31

31 July 1995

With a shaking hand July sat on the floor in her bedroom, making notes about her great-grandfather from the pile of papers her father had given her. When she'd returned home, she was surprised to find Auntie Shell still there. She and Sylvie appeared in the hall as July climbed the stairs – Sylvie's face puffy and tear-stained, Auntie Shell's pale. 'Where have you been?' her stepmother had asked. 'Did you see your dad?' July hadn't known what to say. What had happened since she'd left? Why wasn't Auntie Shell at work? Her stepmother continued: 'He knows you've been going to Almond Drive. I told you to be careful. I told you not to go back there. Didn't I tell you not to go back there?' Her voice became increasingly shrill with each reprimand.

July had picked at a flake of white paint on the bannister. 'Can I go to my room, please?' she asked, turning to walk up the rest of the stairs.

'Tell him you're sorry,' Auntie Shell had called after her. 'I'll try and talk to him, but . . .' July knew the end of the sentence without having to hear it . . . *he won't listen.* 'Just tell him you're sorry,' Shell repeated as July closed her bedroom door.

The first thing she had done was apply some White Musk across her cheeks and on her wrists, inhaling deeply. She then dragged her curtains apart and opened her windows to alleviate the stuffiness. Finally she took her Diet Coke slammer and the square of crumpled paper out of her pocket and laid them on the floor next to her, pulled her project notes out of her wardrobe and got to work on a blank page. She could barely concentrate; the words blurred on the paper in front of her. She still hadn't eaten and her stomach snarled.

And then the front door slammed.

'*My Great-Grandpa Leonard was one of six children,*' she wrote, the black biro letters jumping on and off the line.

'July?' her father shouted up the stairs.

'*His father died in a mining accident when he was nine years old.*'

Auntie Shell's voice pleaded, 'Mick, wait a minute.'

'Not now, Shelley.' Footsteps creaked and thudded on the stairs. 'July? Where are you?'

'In here,' she croaked, gripping her pen between her fingers. '*Leonard was in the Merchant Navy and killed at sea.*'

She felt a rush of air as he pushed her bedroom door open and squeezed her eyes shut.

'Look at me when I'm talking to you.'

She turned round, but she couldn't force her eyes to focus on anything higher than his chin. She could see the dark pores and hair follicles; he'd shaved that morning and there was a small cut on his jaw.

'What were you doing in Almond Drive?'

'I'm sorry . . . I . . .'

'Answer me.' He was rubbing his hands together hard, as though he was trying to scrub something off them.

'I'm really sorry.' July's mind was split like the yin yang necklace Sylvie had bought in town. The white teardrop: she knew she deserved this. *Stupid, stupid July.* Of course he was angry; she would be too, in his position. The black teardrop: but she also wanted to shout at him, *All I wanted was to know what my mum was like. You don't tell me anything.*

'How many times have you been? Sylvie says she saw you there last Thursday.'

Sylv. Had she followed her? July couldn't believe her stepsister would betray her like this. She knew she didn't like her much, but this? She must have known how angry it would make him.

'You will answer me!' he bellowed. She flinched; it was only a matter of time. He was building up to a Lesson. She heard Mr Salter's words: 'He can't do that to you.'

'A few – a – not many times, Daddy, I promise. I'm sorry. I went to see our old house.' She hunched her shoulders, waiting, still gripping her pen in her hand.

'I thought I had made it clear that you shouldn't be digging up the past?' His voice was quieter now but no less terrifying.

'I want to understand why you loved her so much.'

She stared at the dry patches of skin on his knees, ingrained with dirt, and waited for his response, but it didn't come. Instead, he kicked his foot out, sending the slammer skittering across the carpet, and bent down to pick up the yellow piece of paper. July's hand shot out after the slammer, but she didn't dare move to retrieve it from under her bed.

'What's this?' He pushed the paper in front of her face, only centimetres away from her nose. She blinked as she took in the pattern of creases on it. *He can't do that to you.*

'Origami paper.' Why would he be angry about this? Had he been inside Mr Salter's house? Would he know about all the cranes, would he know that Mr Salter had given it to her?

'How long have you been doing this?'

'I can't do it. I was trying to—'

'Do you do these things deliberately? Did Gaga put you up to it?'

July tried to follow what he was saying. Why was he so cross?

'Have you got more?' He swept his hand across the top of her chest of drawers, sending her mirror flying towards her bed frame and her pot of pens rolling to a stop by her stack of library books. 'Have you?'

'No. Only that piece. I'm sorry.' When he didn't reply, she went on: 'I didn't mean to make you cross. I wasn't asking *you* questions, I thought it would be okay. I—'

It happened quickly. He spun round and she brought her arms up to protect her head, but the Lesson never came. The door shut with a bang, and she heard his footsteps move into the bedroom he shared with Auntie Shell. What would he do next? He never left her like this, without finishing things off.

As she waited, she looked up at the stars on her ceiling. She remembered her father lugging a step ladder into her bedroom and spending a whole glorious hour helping her stick them up there. He hadn't done Cassiopeia; she had piled boxes on to her chest of drawers a day later, so that she could reach and do it herself. She smiled at the memory of his (as yet unfulfilled) promise to take her camping under the real stars. As long as they had moments like those, there was hope, wasn't there? Hope that she could be the daughter he wanted her to be.

She heard his footsteps coming back and his laboured breathing. Then a key turning in the lock of her door.

'Daddy?' she whispered.

'I wish you hadn't made me do this,' he said from the landing. 'I love you. You know that, don't you? I'm doing this for your own good.'

July got up and went to the door, stroking the painted white wood panels.

As she listened to him descend the staircase, she pressed her cheek against the wood. She tasted white chocolate mice and strawberry Millions on her tongue.

I love you.

It was the first time he'd ever told her that.

32

1 August 1995

July was allowed out of her bedroom to go to the toilet, but that was it. She had looked around her bedroom on that first day for ways to keep the boredom and, by lunchtime, the jagged hunger, at bay. She'd hauled her fluorescent pink inflatable armchair out of the wardrobe and blown it up the best she could (it was a hand-me-down from Katie-Faye, and one arm had a puncture), but when she collapsed into it, practising binding her fingers with her father's boxing hand wrap, a glue of sweat stuck her hot skin to the pink plastic within minutes. She lay on the floor with her ear against the carpet, trying in vain to hear snippets of conversation from downstairs – she had seen Auntie Shell leave for work early in the afternoon (how would she explain her tardiness to Dr Mushtaq?), but her father and Sylvie stayed home the rest of the day. Using Sylvie's nail polish stains as position markers, she made up new dance routines, despite not having her Discman, which was in the living room. The radio stood in for her CDs, but it wasn't the same – she needed to be able to play a song on repeat to really perfect her moves. She tried reading her encyclopedia in her wardrobe den, but it was too hot in there, even with the door open. For a good hour or so, she watched her neighbours' children across the road – Lynsey and Nick Tingle in their swimmers, having a water pistol battle on the lawn outside the front of their house. July waved, and they waved back, asking her if she wanted to come down and join them. She said she was busy and reluctantly left the window, dropping down to the floor below it to listen to their games instead. Once, she'd watched as Mr Tingle, their father, plaited Lynsey's hair for her in her bedroom. It was one of the most extraordinary things she had ever seen (her *father* doing her *hair*) and ever since she had she always made sure to say an extra bright 'Hello' or 'Good morning' or 'Have a fabulous day, Mr Tingle' whenever she saw him.

July's father had unlocked her door briefly to bring her some dinner – her first meal of the day: ham omelette and baked beans, which she'd seen off in less than ninety seconds. He'd also dragged her mattress and duvet back up to her bedroom. She was glad of Ariel's company. King Triton had probably locked her in her underwater bedroom a few times, she reasoned.

She'd slept surprisingly well, despite the upstairs heat, tangled up with the mermaid's tail. In the morning, when she was playing pogs on the floor of her bedroom, Auntie Shell brought her some cornflakes, though her father had been the one to unlock the door – he clearly didn't trust anyone else with the key. When Auntie Shell asked if July was okay and reached to stroke her cheek (a thaw!) Daddy had said, 'This is supposed to be a punishment, Shelley.' Auntie Shell had blown her a subtle kiss as the door had closed, and then July was alone again. After her cornflakes, she'd stood in front of her mirror, using her fingers to trace over her face gently, then wrapping her arms around her body in a hug. *I love you.* She couldn't believe he'd actually said it.

As soon as Auntie Shell and her father left for work that morning, nearly twenty-four hours after she'd been locked up, Sylvie sprinted up the stairs and tapped on July's door. 'I would have come sooner but he said not to,' she said.

July turned her back to the door, knelt on the carpet and

returned to her pogs, stacking them high. She clenched her teeth together until they ached.

'I get it. You're mad at me.'

July fired her Diet Coke slammer at the tower of pogs, and they scattered across the floor. What made Sylvie think she'd want to talk to her? It was her fault she was in here.

'I made you this.'

July turned to see a chocolate cookie sliding through the gap under the door, alongside some of the missing photos of her mother. She grabbed the pictures and held them to her chest. 'I'm sorry, Mum,' she whispered, before flicking through. There was the black-and-white one of her mother as a child on a see-saw, the one of her gardening with her head tied in a scarf, the one of her parents outside the house in Almond Drive, her mother pregnant. It was so difficult to understand – how could a baby kill such a vibrant woman? Someone so full of life? 'Where are the rest?' she asked.

'I gave them to Mick,' Sylvie said. 'I was really cross with you. And I . . . I wanted to show him that I was on his side. I wanted him to like me. But this was days ago, before . . .'

July sighed. She knew that feeling all too well. She leaned against the door, knowing that Sylvie was on the other side, doing the same. 'He does like you,' she said, picking up the cookie. 'Sometimes I think he'd rather you were his real daughter, not me.'

'It didn't work,' Sylvie said. 'He hit Shell when he found out about them.'

'When?'

'Saturday, when we got back from town. That's why they were really rowing – it was nothing to do with the shopping. I'd left a few of them with a note for him, told him where I found them.' She paused. 'I'm sorry. I wanted to get you into trouble after the graveyard thing.'

'I do a good enough job of that myself.' It all added up now. His rage on Saturday afternoon had seemed unusually irrational – there had to be more to it than a few quid spent in town. July took a bite of the cookie, chewing slowly, savouring the sweetness.

'I didn't know she was the one who gave them to you. How was I supposed to?' Sylvie sniffed. 'I thought you'd found them somewhere in the house.'

'This is good,' July said, crumbs of chocolate falling from her mouth to the floor. 'The cookie,' she added, remembering that Sylvie couldn't see her.

'You think?'

July rescued a chocolate chip from the carpet and let it melt on her tongue. 'Why did you follow me to Almond Drive? To get me into more trouble?'

Sylvie gasped. 'What was that?' she whispered, sounding afraid. 'I've got to go. He can't find me here.'

July hadn't heard anything – no voice, no footsteps, no van door slamming. As Sylvie ran down the stairs, she went to her bedroom window to see if her father had indeed returned. But there was no sign of his van on the drive. She would have heard if he'd pulled up – she'd tell Sylvie, if she came back. One of the perks of having a bedroom facing the road was being able to hear who came and went very clearly. She also heard conversations: like the day before, when Shell had gone out to her father's van to suggest they took July some lunch, and he'd said, 'She isn't hungry.'

After a few minutes, Sylvie returned. 'Sorry,' she said.

'Why did you follow me to Almond Drive?' July repeated, keen to pick up where they'd left off. She didn't require an apology from Sylvie for being afraid of her father, but the same could not be said for other things Sylvie had done.

'I was just . . . bored. I saw you heading off and I thought I might as well see what you were up to.'

'And why did you tell him?'

'I didn't know this would happen,' Sylvie said. 'I was trying to . . .'

July waited, but Sylvie didn't finish her sentence. 'Trying to what?'

'It was yesterday morning. They were arguing again after you left on your bike.' July remembered the way her father had snapped at Shell, the jam dripping from his toast on to the table. 'They were yelling at each other about whether we should be allowed out on our own.'

'Doesn't explain why you'd tell him,' July said. 'And anyway, how did you know that's where I'd be?'

'I didn't. I – I wanted to stop them shouting. I wanted to distract him so he wouldn't hit her again, so I thought I'd tell him that you were up to something. I didn't know that road was where you used to live. Honest. I didn't know he'd react like that.'

'Thanks a bunch.'

'I'm sorry, okay? I didn't know this would happen.'

'What did you say, exactly?' July ran a finger along the thin scab on her thigh, resisting the urge to pick at it.

'I asked if they knew who lived in Almond Drive. That got their attention. He got really mad after that, like, really quickly. Asked where you were. I said I didn't know, but I'd seen you there, and—'

'He came to find me.'

'I guess.' Sylvie sniffed again. Surely she wasn't crying? 'I really am sorry,' she said. 'It's not *you* we need to get out of this house; it's him. I hate him. I really, really hate him.'

July's father's voice filled her head. *I love you. You know that, don't you?* 'But he's my dad.'

'Why are you *still* defending him?' July heard a soft thud as if Sylvie had slapped her hand against the carpeted floor of the landing. 'He's locked you in your bedroom for a whole day. So far. God knows how long he's planning to keep you in there.'

'He'll calm down. I'll stop asking questions.' It was true. July had decided, that moment when he'd told her he loved her, that she was done. 'What does it matter anyway? My mum's dead. Because of me. None of this will bring her back.'

'What do you mean, because of you?'

July sighed. 'I killed her.'

'Don't be ridiculous.'

'She died giving birth to me. It's the same thing.' July dug her nails into her leg, biting her lip to stop herself making a sound as the pain hit.

'Oh my God.' Sylvie paused. 'When did you find this out? Why didn't you tell me?'

'Saturday, at the library.' She released her leg and traced a finger across the pattern of red half-moon indentations on her skin. 'Then your mum explained a few things. I killed her, Sylv, I killed my own mum.'

'You did not.' Sylvie sounded cross. 'Women die having babies. It happens all the time. Helen's mum is a midwife. She told us.'

'But—'

'Stop it. Right now. I mean it. You didn't kill her. It wasn't your fault.'

July didn't want to hear it. 'Anyway,' she said, 'she's dead. What's the point in finding out more about her?'

'You don't mean that.'

'I'm serious. I don't care any more.' The Lessons were one thing, but she couldn't have him hurting Auntie Shell because of all this too. She might freeze over a little too often for July's liking, but she was all right underneath.

'But you do. And I don't think this will blow over. He's pretty mad this time, June.'

July smiled at the name.

'He was ranting yesterday afternoon, something about a piece of paper? A Japanese thing?'

'Origami,' July said quietly.

'That was it! He was stomping about in the kitchen, ripping this little piece of yellow paper up, saying that your mum used to do it, and that you're tormenting him, deliberately trying—'

'He said my mum used to do origami?' A rare breeze made her curtains billow. July closed her eyes momentarily, enjoying the brief refreshment, then looked out of the window. Was there a storm coming? There were no black clouds that she could see.

'Yes. She loved it, apparently.'

Number 35: her mother did origami. But why hadn't Mr Salter told her that? She would never know now as there was no way she could go back there. She wished she'd taken greater care of the crane he'd made her.

'And he's been making phone calls.'

'Who to?'

'I don't know. He asks the people on the other end of the line things like have they seen you in Almond Drive? And if you've been seen anywhere near "that bastard's" house. Who's he talking about?'

'The man who used to live next door to us. The last person to see my mum alive.'

'You've found stuff out, haven't you? More than what her favourite colour was.'

Could she trust Sylvie? She wanted to.

'I wanted to give you something else. To say sorry.' Sylvie's fingers appeared under the door, and when they pulled away again, in their place was a small white teardrop attached to a black leather cord – one of the yin yang pendants she'd bought at the weekend.

'You know you're speaking to July, right? July Hooper? The

stepsister you hate? The one you told to move out?' She lifted it in her palm. It smelled of sandalwood incense, as everything did in the little shop Sylvie had bought it from.

Sylvie laughed. 'I know you can't see me but I thought you'd be able to recognise my voice by now.'

July smiled, putting the pendant around her neck and closing the clasp. 'I thought it was for Helen.'

'I'd rather you had it.' Sylvie tapped gently on the door, three times. 'I still hate you, obviously.'

July laughed and tapped back.

'Shell says you got your period.'

'I thought that word was just for mums.'

'Do you believe everything I say?'

July lay on the floor and stretched out. 'It's rubbish. I don't want it.'

'But it means you're going to get boobs before, like, everyone else.'

July put her hands to her chest. 'I don't want them. You have them.'

'I don't think that's how it works.'

They sat together in silence for a couple of minutes. July knew Sylvie would want to know more, but she wasn't about to volunteer information about what was going on in her pants.

Sylvie was the first to speak. 'Can I ask you something?'

July groaned, rolling on to her stomach. 'It's really not that interesting. And it's pretty gross, to be—'

'What? No. Not about that.' Sylvie paused. 'What do you think your mum would want you to do right now? Do you think she would want you to give up on her?'

July said nothing, but she thought about it, her cheek pressed against the rough carpet. And what occurred to her was that her mother wouldn't want Mr Salter to be so sad. She thought of his ex-wife's words in the newspaper: 'Her door was always open

248

when you needed a cup of tea or a shoulder to cry on. She cared.'
Her mother wouldn't have wanted him to have got into trouble
when he hadn't done anything wrong, and to still be suffering
for it. If she tried to fix things for him, that wouldn't count as
asking questions about her mother, would it? 'Sylv,' she said,
tapping on the door again.

'What?'

'Can you help me with something?'

'He keeps the key around his neck, and he's taken it to work.
There's no way—'

'Not that. Something else.'

33

1 August 1995

Five minutes later Sylvie was back outside July's door, sliding another chocolate cookie underneath. The freshly baked smell was impossible to resist, and July immediately took a large bite. Its crisp base was a little salty, and she craved a glass of ice-cold milk to wash it down.

'I've got it,' Sylvie said, sitting down on the landing with a creak.

July picked up her biro and scribbled a few lines on the pad of paper next to her. 'Go to Davey – D, A, V, E, Y.' She crossed her fingers.

'What if she doesn't still live round here?'

'She does.' July took another bite of the cookie and jotted a question down with a big star next to it.

'Are you writing something?' Sylvie asked.

'You'll see in a minute.'

'What if she's ex-directly?'

July smiled. 'It's ex-directory, Sylv.'

'Okay . . . D . . . So she and her daughter moved out?'

July heard her sister flicking through the pages of the phone book. 'Yes.'

'Even though he'd done nothing wrong?'

'Have you got it yet?'

'Okay . . .' Sylvie flicked through another couple of pages. 'That's awful for him. And his daughter. What a cow.'

July winced. Sylvie was right – it was awful – but this woman had said such nice things about her mother. July didn't think of her as being a cow. 'Can you see the name Janine Davey?'

'Here she is.'

'Really?' July put her pen down, her heart pounding.

'Janine Davey. It's got an address and a number.'

July stood up and started pacing by the door. 'Right, now you need to call her.'

'Why me?' Sylvie whined.

'How are you planning to get the phone under the door?'

'Can't I hold it up and you speak through?'

'The cord won't stretch that far.'

Sylvie huffed. 'Fine.'

July listened as Sylvie scrabbled to her feet. 'Hang on a sec.' July picked up her pen again and started writing, leaning her pad of paper against the door.

'What am I meant to say to her?'

'Give me a minute,' July said, biting the pen top between her teeth. 'I'm just finishing. I'll pass it under the door.'

'Finishing what?'

'Your script.'

'It's ringing!' Sylvie shouted from their parents' bedroom. 'I feel like DC Carver!'

July shook her head and smiled. Sylvie had a bit of a crush on *The Bill*'s DC Carver. If July ever got the chance to go to Sun Hill, she'd rather hang out with June Ackland. She reminded her of Miss Glover – they had the same flicky blonde hair, the same kindness.

'She's not pick—' Sylvie called, stopping abruptly. 'Yes, hello there.' She had put on her grown-up voice: slightly breathy and much posher than anyone they knew. 'I'm calling from the police, about the case of Maggie Hooper's death. We owe you and your husband an apology.'

July dropped her head into her hands. Couldn't Sylvie put some more feeling into it? Make it a bit more natural? It was obvious she was reading from a piece of paper. *I thought you wanted to be an actress.*

'Sorry. Former husband,' Sylvie said. 'We have been reviewing old cases and we realised we made a mistake with our investigation. She died of natural causes, and your – I mean, Mr Salter – should never have been brought in for questioning. We wanted to let you know, in case you wished to move home. He misses—'

Sylvie stopped. July wished she could hear what Janine was saying.

'Yes but—'

July pressed her ear against the door.

'But he didn't kill her. So, if you wanted to, you could move—'

This wasn't going well.

'Your daughter probably really misses her dad.' Sylvie's voice faltered, and she lost her silly accent for a few words.

'Sylv!' July hissed through the door. This was not on the script.

'Having a stepdad is *not* the same.'

'Sylv, stop it; she's going to put the phone down on you,' July whispered, but Sylvie couldn't have heard her, because she carried on.

'But he didn't do it,' Sylvie said, then let out a frustrated sigh.

'Hang up!' July shouted this time, desperate not to waste her chance with Mr Salter's ex-wife. 'DC Carver, you're needed in interview room ten!'

July heard the rough sound of a door sweeping across carpet

and then the click of it shutting – Sylvie had closed their parents'
bedroom door. July leaned her head back against her own door,
straining to hear what Sylvie said as she continued.

'Okay . . . moving on, Ms Davey . . . some questions about . . .'

What was Sylvie playing at? July let her back slide down the
door until she was sitting on the floor again.

'. . . you were friends with her?'

This was definitely not what July had asked her to say. She
picked up her biro and started doodling around the edge of the
scratch on her thigh, pressing the pen gently into her pale skin
as she joined the freckles together with straight black lines.

Sylvie barely gave Janine a chance to respond before she continued, although July couldn't make out the first bit she said,
and suspected Sylvie had dropped her voice on purpose so she
couldn't hear. '. . . tributes to give to her daughter, seeing as it is
the ten-year anniversary . . . never knew her . . .'

July abandoned her stars and wrote a big 'NO' instead, across
the top of her knee. Surely Sylvie knew the police would never
do something like this? Mr Salter's ex-wife would definitely
know. Hadn't Sylvie been paying attention to DC Carver?

'No, I am.' Sylvie's voice rose. 'I'm an actual detective. It really
won't take long, Ms—' She went quiet.

July waited a moment, then hissed, 'What's going on?'

The door to their parents' bedroom opened. 'She hung up,'
Sylvie called out. 'Shall I ring again?'

'No.' July threw her pen at the wall, where it bounced off Kurt
Cobain's nose. Sylvie had really blown it. 'What were you doing?
Why didn't you stick to the script?'

'I just went with it.' Sylvie's voice got closer again, until she
was right outside July's door. 'It's an acting thing, it's called
improvising.'

July could imagine Sylvie saying that with a toss of her blonde
ponytail.

'And anyway,' she went on. 'I thought you'd be grateful to know some more things about your mum.'

July bit her lip. It was great that Sylvie was being nice to her for a change, but she'd ruined the chance to fix Mr Salter's marriage. 'What did she say before she hung up?'

'Oh, something . . . I can't really remember.'

July recognised that voice. It was the one Sylvie employed when she was trying to hide something from her mother. 'Try.'

'I've got to go.'

July banged on the door. 'Where?'

But Sylvie was already running down the stairs.

'Sylvie!' July shouted. 'What did she say?'

34

1 August 1995

Oliver gave his two whippets a quick rub down with the towel he kept in the car, the wet sand falling to the tarmac, and looked towards the horizon as they hopped up into the boot. The rumbling thunder was drawing closer, and the sky was as inky dark as Monty's soft coat. The sea was a shade he'd never seen it before, a deep, dull green. When he'd arrived a couple of hours ago, it had been flat as a pancake, but now it was churning up in the gusty breeze – a bay full of chop. Monty and Luna were cowering in the boot, eyes wide, and Oliver patted each of them. 'Nothing to worry about,' he said. 'Only some clouds. Let's get you two home.' If he hadn't had them with him, he'd have stayed to watch the storm crack across the bay, relieved that the tyrannical heat of the last couple of weeks was finally being overthrown, and he loved to see lightning grab at the ocean. Reluctantly, he put his key in the ignition and looked over his shoulder to reverse out of the parking space.

Everyone else was doing the same. The car park was teeming with dog walkers and young families packing up and abandoning the beach before the rain hit, and there was a queue to get out of the car park.

The only people going against the tide were a large, tanned man and a red-haired girl jogging alongside him, trying to keep up as he strode from their car down towards the beach. 'Where are those two off to?' Oliver asked Monty and Luna. The dogs whimpered in response. 'They've not even got coats on.' The purposeful way the man walked, without talking or looking at the girl, and the way she kept her head bowed as she trotted along, one hand deep in her pocket, fiddling nervously with something, made Oliver's toes curl as if he'd heard nails scrape across a blackboard. He hadn't thought of his father for a while, but seeing these two made him feel eight years old again, in shorts and long socks which kept slouching to his ankles, running to keep pace with his old man. He'd always known he would be barked at, or worse, if he didn't keep up. The memory caused a ripple of shivers to course across his skin, forcing him to turn away. 'There, there,' he said, as much to himself as to his thunder-shy companions.

Instead of watching the curious pair pick their way across the beach to the bottom of the cliff path on the other side, Oliver joined the queue out of the car park and drove slowly up the road through the village, going the opposite direction to July and her father, who had driven down the same road a few minutes earlier, on their way from Harmony Close.

July's father had arrived home from work shortly after midday. Sylvie had only provided lunch a few minutes before, passing July a piece of 'illegal bread – he said not to feed you', and July had to run a finger along the rough, unpainted underside of the door to clean off the margarine and strawberry jam that had caught on the wood as it was delivered. Hearing the slide and slam of her father's van door, she wolfed down the second half.

Outside, the summer brightness was disappearing behind black clouds. The air was thickening. July couldn't help but feel excited – she loved a good thunderstorm, when watched from the safety of her bedroom. She had pulled her encyclopedia out of her den and turned it to the right page. 'A common weather system,' she read. 'Thunderstorms are usually violent and short-lived.' She was leaning out of her window, sniffing the promise in the air, when the lock on her door clicked, and her father staggered in, his physical presence stalked closely by the stench of alcohol.

'Come on, kiddo,' he said with a slight slur, disappearing out of her bedroom as suddenly as he had arrived. 'We're going on a mission.'

She didn't need him to ask her twice. A mission with her father! *Kiddo!* He must have forgiven her. She hopped around her room as she pulled her trainers on (a mission might require trainers, mightn't it, and sandals weren't adventure-ready enough) and ran downstairs. Sylvie was curled up on the settee in the living room, reading the latest edition of *Smash Hits*, whose pages were flickering in a breeze generated by the ceiling fan. It was the one with Ant and Dec on the cover. Dec was licking Ant's face, and the words 'I love you!' were scrawled across the image in red text. *I love you,* July grinned. *Kiddo, I love you.*

'Are you coming?' July asked her stepsister.

'Don't think I'm invited,' Sylvie said. 'He's in the van.' She lowered her magazine. 'You sure you want to go with him?' she whispered. 'Is everything okay?'

'Of course I do!' July laughed. 'It's fine. I told you it would blow over.'

'He smells a bit . . . you know.'

'He probably had a beer with lunch.' July didn't believe the words as she said them. 'Or two.'

Sylvie raised an eyebrow. 'I'm calling Shell as soon as you go.'

'Honestly, Sylv, it's fine. See you later.' She skipped from the darkened room – the curtains were drawn as usual. 'Have you seen, there's a storm coming?' she called back as she ran out of the front door. 'Don't miss it.'

She climbed up into the passenger seat of her father's van

and couldn't help but grin again. 'Where are we going?' she asked.

'Video City.' He started the engine and reversed out of the driveway before she had a chance to do her seat belt. 'Let's get something to watch tonight, hey?'

'Seriously?' she asked. 'Yes!' She let the final 's' drag out and clapped her hands.

Through the insect-splattered windscreen, July could see Sylvie standing in the window, poking her head between the curtains, watching them go. July lifted a hand to wave goodbye, mouthing, 'We're getting a video! VI-DE-O!' and pretended to crank an old-fashioned film camera as if she had a movie title clue in a game of charades, but Sylvie didn't wave back. *Suit yourself*, July thought, and turned to look out of her window at the ever-darkening sky.

They turned left out of Harmony Close, when July had been expecting them to turn right – the way you'd go to leave the village.

'I thought we were going to Video City.' She tried to keep her voice light. In the last thirty seconds she had already set her heart on microwave popcorn, a bag of marshmallows and that film Katie-Faye had seen the other week. 'Daddy?'

'Scenic route.' He laughed as he turned on to the beach road and headed down the hill, before reaching into the storage compartment in his door, pulling out a grimy cloth he used to wipe away windscreen condensation and throwing it into her lap. 'Get that muck off your leg. You told me you thought tattoos were chavvy; don't go getting any stupid ideas now.'

July spat on the cloth and rubbed at the biro on her thigh. She couldn't remember ever having a conversation with her father about tattoos, she thought as they turned towards the bay. It was the first time she had seen the sea since yesterday morning. She didn't like the look of it – storms may have excited her, but the sea under those furious clouds was a different matter entirely. She recalled the water page in her encyclopedia, and the little box about thunderstorms: *Stay away from open water.* She liked the look of her father even less. They weren't going to Video City, were they? Things hadn't blown over after all.

'Is this part of the mission?' she asked, her voice little more than a squeak.

'Could say that,' he said as he pulled into a parking space overlooking the agitated waves.

She got out straight away, knowing that any dithering would only make him more cross. Was this all still about her going to Almond Drive? Or had she done something else wrong? Had he found out about them phoning Janine earlier?

He locked the car and paced down the hill towards the beach. What were they doing here? People were getting into their cars, not getting out of them. Everyone was heading home. It was obvious that rain was coming – when you lived by the sea you learned to smell it in the air and spy its diagonal smudge on the horizon. July hadn't brought her coat, but then neither had her father, she noticed, as he marched away from her to the coastal path on the other side of the beach, towards the horse paddocks.

Where are we going, she wanted to ask, but his tightly balled fists told her not to. Keeping an eye on the sea to her left, unable to trust it, she remembered another sentence from her encyclopedia: 'We are surrounded by water.' She shuddered. *You're a disgrace. You do nothing but disappoint me.*

He turned back to her. 'Keep up, would you?'

The air grew heavier as they walked. They didn't pass a single soul on the usually busy path. Eventually they got to one of the narrow tracks that cut down from the coast path on to the quieter sections of beach below. Without uttering a word, her father turned along it, easily striding down the bed of the dried-out stream that ran through the middle of the track in the winter. July found it more difficult to descend, keeping one foot either side of the stream bed and straddling it awkwardly all the way down to the beach, her legs repeatedly getting stung by nettles.

He didn't stop at the bottom but carried on to where the waves were sucking and frothing at the pebbles. July hung back, the gusts of warm wind whipping her hair against her face.

'Think you're so clever, don't you?' he shouted back over his shoulder.

She wasn't sure what to say to that. He always wanted her to get good marks in her tests and school projects. Was the right answer 'Yes' or 'No'?

'Don't you?' he repeated.

She gambled. 'No, Daddy.'

'Don't you have any friends your own age?'

She kicked at a piece of tyre rubber nestled among the pebbles at her feet. 'Yes.' Again she was unsure whether this was the correct answer.

'That Kate girl?' he asked. 'I've told you before, she's not a friend. You need to get your eyes checked.' He glared at her. 'In fact, give me your glasses – I'll clean them for you.'

Her hand trembling, she took them off. He stepped forward to snatch them from her. Without making any effort to wipe them, he slipped them into his shirt pocket. Was he not going to give them back?

'Any other friends?' he asked.

'Yes.' She watched, her world now badly blurred, as he picked up a large rock from the shallow water and launched it in a great arc out into the bay. 'Why've you been hanging around with him, then?'

He knew she'd been with Mr Salter. She'd hoped he only knew she had visited the road. How had he found out?

'I'm sorry, Daddy,' she said, taking a step back, glancing over her shoulder, hoping someone else might clamber down the track behind her. She knew how this went, now. She knew that there was only one thing she could do: grovel and hope it worked. 'I'm sorry. I was stupid. I love you.'

'Do you?' he sneered at her. 'Come and stand with me, if you love me so much.'

She hesitated.

'As I thought.'

She edged closer, blinking as she tried to see the ground clearly. He was standing in the water, even though he was wearing trainers. She stopped a couple of feet away from him, but he grabbed her arm and dragged her so that she was in the water too. She yelped and looked back over her shoulder. She couldn't make out any shapes of other people on the path above them. *Help*.

'I still have friends on Almond Drive, you know. Thought you could fool me, did you?'

'No, Daddy.' She pressed the back of her hand into her eyes to stop the tears.

'Been laughing at me, have you?'

'No, Daddy.'

'You have. Laughing at me. You . . .' It was only then that she looked up, squinted and realised he was crying too. Big, fat tears were streaming down his face. 'No respect. After everything I've done.'

'I'm sorry, Daddy.' The cold waves licked her calves.

'Stop it!' He kicked at the water, splashing her face. She blinked but didn't turn away. 'Daddy this, Daddy that. I'm sick of it.' He leaned forward so that their faces were close and jabbed a finger at her. 'You're nothing like your mother.' He spoke quietly, but she felt spittle land on her skin and smelled the sweetness of whisky on his breath.

Later, she didn't know quite what had come over her. But

something happened in that moment. *You're nothing like your mother.* She thought of the photo of her mother on the boat coiling a rope over her arm; she heard Mr Salter say 'He can't do that to you'; she saw Janine's words in the newspaper – 'She was brave. She was fearless.' She remembered Auntie Shell telling her that other children's fathers didn't beat them, heard the thud of her father's fists against her stepmother's face, and started to list all the lies he'd told her about her mum.

You're nothing like your mother. His words were the lightning forks in the storm that had been brewing all her life. She paused as the sound waves caught up, then delivered her thunderclap.

'I am.' She didn't say it quietly. She said it loud, because she meant it, and she wanted to be sure he heard.

She turned her cheek, ready for the Lesson, but it didn't come. It was as if he hadn't heard her or wasn't listening. 'She was an incredible woman. Incredible.' He stumbled over the word, twice.

'Is that why you don't like me? Because I'm like her?'

And again he didn't hit her. This made her braver and more afraid in equal measures. What else could she say to him? But also why wasn't he hitting her? Did he have something else planned?

He staggered slightly. 'You can never go back there.'

A roll of real thunder rumbled in the distance. *Stay away from open water.*

'Give me your word.'

July shook her head slightly. Everything happened very quickly after that.

She felt pressure on the back of her neck, and then water on her face and up her nose, saltiness in her mouth and a sting in her eyes. She couldn't breathe and swung her arms around madly, trying to grab hold of something. *You're a disgrace. You do nothing but disappoint me.*

Her father pulled her head back up out of the water. July

spluttered as she tried to get some air; she was on her knees and her whole body was soaked. 'Give me your word,' he said again, before slamming her face back into the shallow water.

This time the pebbles and sand clashed against her teeth. She shook her head, but it made him grip harder.

'I promise,' she gasped when he finally brought her back up, blinking furiously to get rid of the saltwater sting on the insides of her eyelids. The sky flashed white with lightning, and a few seconds later more thunder rumbled overhead. She braced herself to be plunged back into the water, but he held her there, his fingers snarling in her hair and his nails biting at her skin.

'Tell me what you know,' he said from behind her.

She stared out towards the sea. She couldn't focus on the headland, but she could make out the dark shadow of rain growing closer. *I know thirty-five things*, she thought. 'About what?'

'Don't mess around, July,' he said. 'I'm not in the mood.'

'I know she died the day I was born,' she said. 'I know the police thought Mr Salter killed her.'

'Mr Salter, is it?' He spat into the shallows at her side and clutched her neck tighter. She winced.

'I wanted to know more about her,' July said. 'I never wanted to make you angry.'

'What did your Mr Salter tell you then?' He said the name in a nasty, sing-song way. 'What did he tell you about your darling mother?'

'He . . . he . . .' Even if July had wanted to tell her father what Mr Salter had said, her mind suddenly went blank.

'Well how about *I* tell you something, hm?' He thrust her face towards the water again, but this time he held her above its surface. The tip of her nose dipped into its coolness, but the rest of her face hovered. She threw her hands out in front of her, pushing back against him, but he held firm. 'It's me or her, July. Do you hear me? It's time to choose.'

'I don't understand.' She dug her fingers into the shingle.

'I won't have you living in my house, making a fool of me. If you want to carry on with this crusade of yours, you can go and live with your old bitch of a grandmother and I will *never*'– he pushed her face down slightly, so that her forehead was in the water too – 'have anything to do with you, ever again. Do you hear me?'

'Yes.'

'What's it to be then?' He let go of her neck with one final shove, and she fell forward into the water, landing awkwardly on her side. 'Me or her?'

It's time to choose.

She hesitated for a moment too long.

At the very moment she said 'You' he swung his foot back. She scrabbled to get away from him, but he stopped its low arc just before it reached her, covering her in more water, not connecting with the ribs that she had fully expected him to crack. He laughed and spat in the water again.

'Too bloody right, it's me,' he said. 'I'm going to have a quiet word with your Mr Salter. Filling your head with bullshit.' He turned and tramped up the beach back towards the path as the first spots of rain started to fall.

July lay back in the water, her chest heaving with laboured breaths, her ears ringing with the punches that never came, her mouth full of sand, and her heart split in half: two valves of a mussel shell ripped apart to expose the vulnerable, soft body inside.

It's me or her.

35

Darling girl,

We don't have long to go now, only a matter of weeks. You weigh as much as a honeydew melon, but you aren't smooth and round like one – you're all elbows and knees, little nudging hands and stamping feet trying to get comfortable as I search for slices of sleep.

Those hours lying in bed, too hot and too awake, give my mind acres of space to wander. It ambles off in many directions, but there's a favourite path it likes to tread. Edging closer to becoming a mother has made me think more and more about my own mum, God rest her soul.

I wish she was here now, to hold my hand, to touch my belly when it twitches with your hiccups. I wish she could have met you.

All my love, always,
Mum x

36

1 August 1995

I t was a long walk back from the beach.

A few cars drove past her, but nobody stopped to help – she was soaked to the skin but that wasn't odd, given the torrential showers coming through every few minutes. July trudged up the hill, feet squelching in her shoes, T-shirt sticking to her skin. She kept slipping on the wet road.

It's me or her.

Her limbs ached, and she felt like she was dragging a ton of bricks. She couldn't see clearly – everything was a blur of shapes without her glasses – and she couldn't think clearly about anything either, because all she could hear in her head was her father's voice, on repeat.

It's me or her. It's me or her.

She had told him that she chose him, so why hadn't her mother appeared when she said it? Had July simply not noticed her? She didn't realise her words had been a lie until she got back to the house, kicked her sodden trainers off, and climbed the stairs to her bedroom, her feet leaving wet footprints on the carpet. She didn't realise who she had really chosen until she pulled her school rucksack out of her wardrobe and started packing some clothes, books and the photos of her mother, squinting in an effort to see what she was picking up. Something had changed in the last hour, since he had forced her head into the water. *She had changed.*

She was vaguely aware of Auntie Shell calling up to her from the kitchen. 'July? Is that you?'

But she ignored her stepmother, her mouth set in a straight line, and kept packing. Could she really do this?

'Oh my God,' Auntie Shell said when she appeared at July's bedroom door. July could smell cigarettes – Shell always smoked when she was anxious. 'Sylvie, get a towel, quick. I can't believe he left you out in this rain.'

July zipped up her rucksack, dragged her swim bag out from under her bed and started stuffing that too. Pants, socks, pyjamas. Notebooks, a hairbrush, her pogs. She found her old glasses in a drawer. One arm was broken, and they were held together with garden twine, but they were better than the blurry mess she saw without them.

'What happened?' Auntie Shell asked as she wrapped July in her pink towel. 'Come on, why don't you get out of these wet things?'

But July shook her head and shrugged the towel off so that it fell to the floor at her feet. She didn't care about her wet clothes; she didn't have time to worry about them. She would be getting much wetter in a minute, when she left this house, for good. There wasn't much time, she knew. Her father may have gone to see Mr Salter, but he would be home soon, and she didn't intend to be here when he got back.

'Where did he take you?' Shell asked. 'What are you doing with these bags?'

So many questions.

Then it was Sylvie's turn. 'You can't go.' Her voice was much quieter than her mother's.

'I'm moving to Yaya's.'

'No, you're not. No.' Auntie Shell grabbed her shoulders now and spun her round, but July refused to look at her face. 'You're staying here. What did he do to you? Are you hurt? Stay here, with us. I can look after you, I promise. I'm going to get us all out of here. You can come with me and Sylvie.' She wiped some sand from July's cheek. 'I just need a few more days to get things sorted.'

'What you mean, Mum?' Sylvie asked. 'Where are we going?'

Auntie Shell turned back to Sylvie, and July finished packing her second bag, wedging her pencil case in before she did up the zip.

'We can't stay here, darling,' Auntie Shell was saying.

Sylvie was crying now. 'But . . .'

'Isn't that what you want, July?' Auntie Shell asked. 'We can be a family. You, me, Sylv. You can still see your grandmother.'

July paused for a moment, for a couple of breaths. But no, she didn't buy it. 'You'll never leave him.' For a terrible, short moment, she also felt as though she was saying it to herself, but she shook her head to banish the idea.

'I will. We . . .' But Auntie Shell trailed off. She knew it, and July knew it.

'We're stuck here with him,' Sylvie said in her small voice. 'Aren't we?'

'You want to leave, I believe you,' July said to her stepmother as she took the photo of her mum from behind her smiley face poster. 'But he won't let you. And I can't stay here with him any more.'

'You can't go. There's something I need to tell you.' Shell pulled Sylvie in from the landing and shut the bedroom door.

'I know,' July said.

'No, you don't. I've been trying to adopt you. I—'

'Shell, I know.' July paused, swinging her bags on to her shoulder. 'Thank you for trying.'

268

'Oh.' Shell's mouth hung open. She put a hand to her chest, plucking at the material of her blouse, and to July's horror she saw tears in her stepmother's eyes. 'I see.'

July swallowed, wishing she hadn't admitted to knowing anything about what Shell was planning. She hadn't meant to upset her. She was about to reach out to hug her stepmother when Shell pushed her shoulders back a little and blinked a few times, seeming determined not to show her distress.

'What happened out there?' she asked after clearing her throat. She sat on the bed frame and July thought of all the sea hoops underneath it. There wasn't time to pull them all off – she would have to start a new collection at Yaya's. 'He came home, so angry.'

'He went out in the van,' Sylvie said, wiping her tears away. 'He said, "I'm going to kill him. I'm going to fucking kill that man."'

'Sylvie!' Shell said. 'Please don't . . . please don't swear like that.'

'Seriously, Mum? That's what you've got a problem with right now?'

'Mr Salter,' July whispered. Her father had said he was going to have a word, not hurt him. Why did she believe that? How stupid could she be?

'Sylv told me, you've been talking to him,' Auntie Shell said, picking at her cuticles. 'Is that true? Is that why you've been going to Almond Drive?'

What was she going to do? She couldn't let her father hurt Mr Salter.

'What did he tell you?' Shell asked. 'The thing is . . .'

July fiddled with the zip on her bag. She couldn't listen to her stepmother as she spoke, let alone answer her – not with her head full of images of her father with his fists clenched and fire in his eyes . . .

'. . . whole road is like a millstone round your father's neck,' Auntie Shell was saying, quietly. 'He can't let it go.'

'He never sold your old house, did you know that?' Sylvie asked. She had climbed on top of July's chest of drawers and was playing with a hairband.

'Sylvie!' Auntie Shell scolded.

'What? You didn't say I couldn't tell anyone.'

'Yes, but . . .' Auntie Shell sighed, shifting her weight on the edge of the bed.

'What's she talking about?' July asked, moving the bags to her other shoulder.

'He didn't sell the house after you moved out. We kept it on as the landlords. We rent it out.'

The fan on the counter. So Auntie Shell *had* been there.

'Your father is obsessed with the place, and with that man.'

July fought the nausea rolling in her stomach. 'What are we going to do?'

Auntie Shell stood up and brought her hands together in a single clap. 'You get changed. I'm going to make some toast and hot chocolate, warm you up. You're not going to your grand-mother's until you've had something to eat.'

'But what about Dad? And Mr Salter? Shouldn't we call the—'

'We shouldn't get involved, that's what we shouldn't do. He's not going to . . . People say things all the time, when they're in the heat of the moment. He's not going to hurt him.' Auntie Shell's voice was firm. 'Now, go on. Get out of your wet things.' She left the girls together in July's bedroom.

'I've got to help Mr Salter, Sylv.' July grabbed her stepsister's arm when she heard Auntie Shell reach the bottom of the stairs. 'This is all my fault.'

'But it's dangerous. *He's* dangerous. You don't go looking for him, not when he's like this.' Sylvie bit her lip. 'Can't we ask my mum?'

270

'You heard her. She said she didn't want to get involved.'

'Your gran? We could call her?'

'It would take too long for her to get here. I need to go now.'

'What about you moving out?'

July let the bags slip to the floor. 'I can make it back for these afterwards,' she said, unconvincingly. 'There'll be time.'

'But what will you do?' Sylvie whispered. 'How will you stop him?'

'I'll think of something.' She picked up her baseball cap from the windowsill and put it on over her wet hair.

Sylvie swung her legs over the side of the chest of drawers. 'Your dad locked our bikes in the shed before he left,' she said softly. 'But I have the spare.' She pressed a key into July's hand.

July hugged her. 'Where did you get this?'

'Shell's bunch in her handbag. I took them earlier. Figured you'd want your bike.' She took the rest of the keys out of her pocket. 'I don't know what half of them are for.'

'How am I going to get out of here without your mum seeing?'

'Leave that to me,' Sylvie said, hopping to the floor. 'Are you ready to go?'

July gripped the key tightly.

'There was one more thing I needed to say,' Sylvie said, biting her lip again. 'I never told you what Janine said on the phone. I wasn't sure if I should, but . . .'

'Go on.'

'She said, "That bitch got what she deserved." ' Sylvie looked at the floor. 'I'm really sorry. I don't know why she—'

'It's not your fault,' July said. Why would Janine say such a thing? Her mind raced as she tried to figure it out. 'I've got to go. What's the plan?'

Sylvie grinned, then shouted, 'Yes, okay!'

July looked at her, confused, picking up her sandals.

'I'll run you a shower,' she yelled. 'You get out of those clothes!' Then Sylvie mouthed at her: 'Go.'

As July tiptoed down the stairs, she heard Sylvie turn the water on, and as she let herself out of the front door, Sylvie noisily pulled the shower curtain across and shouted, 'Stay in there as long as you want, warm yourself up. That's okay isn't it, Mummy?'

'Of course, darling,' Auntie Shell replied from the kitchen as July softly closed the door.

37

1 August 1995

The shed padlock took so much rattling to open that July was sure Shell would hear her and come outside, but they were in the midst of another downpour, so the noise of the rain bouncing off the patio covered for her.

Eventually she got the door open and rolled her bike out. She didn't stop to lock the shed back up or close the side gate. She pedalled quicker than she ever had before, sometimes barely able to see through the rain lashing at her face and covering her glasses with water, which she repeatedly and fruitlessly tried to wipe away with her finger. On the tarmac beneath her a small river ran towards a huge lake which had formed around the drain by the corner shop, and she swerved to avoid it.

That bitch got what she deserved. What did Janine mean by that? Nobody had ever said anything horrible about July's mother, ever, and it hadn't occurred to her that anyone could have possibly not liked her. But all this did was make July love and miss her more. With every day that had passed since her birthday, with every piece of information she had prised loose, her mother was becoming a real person, not just a spectre who appeared when July summoned her with a lie. Real people weren't liked by everyone, July realised as she cycled, her teeth crunching on a few lingering grains of sand in her mouth.

The rain stopped as she turned the corner into Almond Drive. It was unnervingly quiet. She could see that Mr Salter's house was intact – its window boards hadn't been splintered by her father's gardening tools, as she'd thought they might have been – and there was no shouting to be heard. Maybe Daddy wasn't here? Then she spotted his van parked at a funny angle with the driver's door hanging open.

But where were they? When she'd left them arguing the day before, they'd been shouting on Mr Salter's doorstep, and she'd assumed they would be outside in the front garden again, yelling at each other, maybe with some neighbours standing around watching. She'd imagined she would run up the front path and get between them; tell her father that it wasn't Mr Salter's fault, that he had told her she needed to leave him alone, but she had kept asking questions. She was pretty sure that her father would hit her then, but he had to understand, didn't he? He had to understand that it wasn't Mr Salter's fault.

She didn't run up the front path to fling herself between them, because they weren't there. Instead, she stood by the front wall, staring at the house and listening as she wiped her glasses with her T-shirt. Nothing. No shouting. No glass smashing. What was going on? Slowly she made her way to the front door and knocked. She waited, then tried again, but Mr Salter didn't answer.

Backing out of the front garden, looking at the upstairs windows as she went – could they be up there? – she suddenly heard something from inside. A thump, like a door slamming maybe? She ran round to the alleyway, but the gate still had Mr Salter's bike lock securing it. As she looked at the spikes on top of the gate, she lifted her sodden shorts a little to rub at the graze on her cold thigh. She didn't want to climb it again, but she didn't feel she had a choice.

She managed to get over, but was extra-careful this time.

Next, she climbed Mr Salter's garden fence as quietly as she could and crept up towards his back door, which was slightly ajar. That was when she heard them. Whether or not they had been shouting earlier, they definitely were now. She stayed close to the fence bordering number 4's garden, trying to stay out of view.

'You killed her,' her father was shouting. 'You murdered her!' He was crazed, wilder than she had ever heard him. Whipped up like the waves in a winter storm, building and building in strength until they crashed themselves down on the rocks.

'You of all people know that isn't true.' Mr Salter's voice was quieter – he sounded more weary than angry. 'But if you want to bring that up, I've got a question for *you*: did she really die because of some complication having July –'

'Don't say her name.'

'– or because you'd hit her?'

'I never laid a finger on my wife.'

July moved closer to the door, her back flat against the wall of the house. If she leaned forward a tiny bit, she could see them, standing in the kitchen. One of Mr Salter's surfboards lay on the floor, propping the door open.

'But you did, didn't you, Mick?' Mr Salter said. 'Before that. And you're clearly abusive towards your own child. I mean, what kind of a man—'

Her father laughed. 'If you thought that, why didn't you come and rescue her? What kind of a man knows that a child is in danger and does nothing about it?'

'So she is in danger? You're admitting that?'

'I'm admitting nothing.'

'I *saw* Maggie. I saw the bruises down her arm and her bust lip.'

July pressed her hands against the damp render of the wall and shivered in her wet clothes.

It was her father who spoke next, so softly she almost couldn't hear. 'That was an accident.'

'And the day she died, was that an accident too? I saw the cut on her cheek.'

'I didn't do anything.'

'You expect me to believe that?'

'Believe what you want.'

'You know she was leaving you? That day? She was packing a bag.'

Her father started shouting again. 'She was going to her mother's for a couple of days. Not leaving me. You know nothing.'

'That's what she told you, was it? And you believed her? But even that, even your pregnant wife going away for a break, that was enough to piss you off so much you hit her? What would you have done to her if you'd known the truth, that she was leaving you? She was moving to her mother's house permanently. You drove her away.'

'You don't know what you're talking about,' her father yelled. 'And all of this is irrelevant. She died because of you. She died having that baby, and that's tantamount to you killing her.'

'You've got to be kidding.'

'She's your bastard child.'

July didn't think she had heard right. Who had said that? It had sounded like her father. She held her breath.

'Come off it.' Mr Salter paused. 'You're . . . you're joking, right? This is your twisted idea of a joke.'

'Do I look like I'm laughing?'

There was silence for a moment, and then Mr Salter spoke quietly. 'No.' July could hear the irregular rhythm of his ragged breaths. 'No,' he repeated. 'I . . . What? I can't . . .'

'You must have known.'

'I . . . N-no,' Mr Salter stammered. 'Maggie, she said . . . She told me that—'

'It's pretty fucking obvious,' her father said. 'The girl looks exactly like you.'

'Shut up, would you? Give me a . . . Just give me a minute. I need a minute.' All the anger had seeped from Mr Salter's voice, just as the blood had drained from July's face.

But still her father taunted him. 'Surely you guessed?'

'I wondered . . . but only, only recently.' Mr Salter sounded confused, his voice light. 'Only when she turned up here.' He muttered something July couldn't hear. 'I'd not – I'd not seen her up close before that. She looks a lot like my daughter – their faces, the gap in her teeth . . . But I thought I was imagining it. Seeing Jenny . . . going mad . . .'

July let herself breathe out and ran her tongue against her front teeth, feeling the space between them. Mr Salter was her father? Her mind raced. Was Daddy joking? Was this all an awful hoax?

'Maggie didn't tell you?' her father asked, laughing. 'Can't have cared about you that much then, can she?'

'Why . . . why did you take her?' July couldn't see Mr Salter's face but she could imagine it clearly, screwed up in bewilderment. She knew exactly what it would look like because her own face was doing the same thing. 'Why have you kept her away from me all this time, if you knew?'

Yes, Daddy. Why? Why have you done this? July pushed her thumbs into her fists and squeezed her eyes shut to stop the garden spinning. How could this be true?

'So that you couldn't have her,' her father said, his voice chillingly steady. He sounded about as mean as she'd ever heard him. *Daddy.* She wanted him to say he was lying, but she felt the truth of it in her heart. What did this make him? If he wasn't her father, who was he? She mouthed a single word in the silence. *Mick?*

'Was it really?' Mr Salter said, anger returning to his words once more. 'Not because you didn't want to have to admit that Maggie never loved you?'

July stepped away from the wall, into the doorway.

38

1 August 1995

'How long have you been listening?' Mr Salter asked, turning to look at her. He was still Mr Salter. She couldn't quite think of him as her father. She stepped past the surfboard, looking from one of them to the other, waiting to be told it was all a misunderstanding. The smell of the room was a disconcerting mixture of both men – her father's sopping clothes combined with Mr Salter's wetsuits and burned onions. Upstairs, she could hear the radio on loud, as usual – the calm, steady voice emanating from its speaker at odds with the taut hostility in the kitchen.

'What the hell are you doing back here?' Mick said. 'And what have I told you about eaves—'

'Is it true?' she asked, every muscle in her body tensed, ready.

Outside, there was a rumble of thunder: quieter, further away. The storm was retreating.

'Go home,' Mick said. The slur had disappeared from his words. His clothes, like hers, were clinging to his skin. His red forehead shone in the light from the bare bulb hanging from the ceiling above him. Surrounded by the darkness of the rest of the room, he looked almost like he was in a spotlight, and she couldn't take her eyes from him. She wondered what he made of the boards across the windows and imagined the kind of comments he would have made on another day, in another time, if

they'd passed a house like this. 'Crackpot.' 'Fruitcake.' 'Nutjob.'
But Mr Salter wasn't any of those things.

'Go on. Home,' Mick spat.

Mr Salter stepped towards her. 'July, I . . .'

She glanced his way but couldn't deal with him yet. She
needed to speak to Mick first.

'Is it true that you hurt Mum?' The fear of Lessons, the fear
that she had felt all of her life, had dissipated as she stepped
through the door on to the grey floorboards of Mr Salter's kitchen. She looked directly at Mick for the first time in months.
She wasn't shaking.

'Go home,' he repeated.

'Tell me.' She said it calmly but firmly, clenching her fists at
her side.

Mick looked at her, surprised, before his mouth turned into a
horrible sneer. 'I'm not answerable to a nine-year-old.'

'Ten.'

Mick snorted.

'Is that why she died? Because you hurt her?'

'Don't be ridiculous.' He turned to stare out of the window.
'She was unlucky, they said.'

It was bad luck. July shot a look at Mr Salter.

'Could have happened to anyone,' Mick added.

'A slap round the ear didn't exactly help her though, did it?'
Mr Salter said. 'Who knows what impact the stress—'

'And is it true?' July faced Mr Salter properly for the first time
since walking in. 'Are you my dad?'

'Don't pretend you didn't know,' Mick muttered, flicking one
of Jenny's drawings as if it was a piece of rubbish he wanted to
get out of his way.

Mr Salter ran his hand over the stubble on his chin, meeting
July's eye. 'It would appear so.'

That bitch got what she deserved. Janine must have known. July had never found something out about her mother that she didn't like, until now. Number 36 – she had been unfaithful. This was a piece of black, coarse thread made up of strands of shame and disgrace, and July didn't want to touch it. She didn't want anything to do with it.

'She did a bad thing. You did a bad thing.' She didn't understand what they would have done, not completely, but she'd watched enough television dramas to know that her mother and Mr Salter must have had an affair, and that affairs hurt people.

'Exactly,' Mick said. 'Thou shalt not commit adultery.'

Mr Salter laughed bitterly. 'Thou shalt not bear false witness against thy neighbour.'

'Thou shalt not covet thy neighbour's—'

'Stop!' July slapped her hand against one of the stacks of newspapers, and it toppled over, newsprint pages spreading across the floor next to the surfboard. She considered apologising but thought better of it. At least it had the effect of making both men shut up for a moment. She kicked at the nearest newspaper. She hated this room, she suddenly decided. She hated the mess of it, the disorder and dustiness, the awful smell, the dirty plates and cutlery strewn across the counter. This realisation confused her. She preferred her father's spotless work surfaces, the gleaming stainless steel of his polished hob. *Not my father's*, she corrected herself. *Mick's*. Could this house have been her home? Could this grubby chaos have been her life?

'Why did you keep me?' she asked Mick, twisting her cap round backwards so she could see him better, so she could closely watch his reaction. She needed to know what was behind the decision that had given her one house, one father, and not the other. 'It wasn't because you loved me.'

'I did, but then . . .' Mick trailed off. 'I thought you'd remind me of her. But all I saw was him. Every single time I looked at you.'

Mr Salter saved July from having to respond. 'You kept her because you couldn't stand Maggie to have anything that she wanted,' he said. 'Not friends of her own, not a job that you hadn't approved—'

'Every time I saw those ugly glasses of yours,' Mick continued, ignoring Mr Salter and pointing at July. 'Hereditary, they said it was. The astigmatism. Except I don't need glasses, and neither did Maggie. Strong eyes we had. Healthy.'

'So you hit me? And Auntie Shell?' July moved towards him, further into the gloom of the kitchen. 'Like you hit her?'

'Someone needs to keep you on the straight and narrow. You'll thank me one day.'

Mr Salter laughed again. 'You're a bully, Mick. A weak, inadequate bully – always were.'

July looked at Mick. His feet were beginning to shuffle from side to side on the floorboards, like they did when he stood in front of his punchbag. *When you're not moving your hands, make sure you're moving your feet.* His eyes were darkening – steady and focused like a bird of prey the moment before a kill – and his nostrils flared slightly. 'Mr Salter,' she tried to whisper, to warn him, but the words were too afraid to leave her mouth. She recognised the look on Mick's face – she knew a Lesson was coming, though not for her, not this time.

She tried again. 'Mr Salter.'

But, even though the words were brave enough to emerge on their second attempt, they still went unheard, because Mr Salter spoke over her. Slowly looking Mick up and down, he said, 'That's why she never loved you.'

In one swift movement, Mick swooped. He shot out his arm and grabbed the bread knife that was lying on the counter, before turning to face Mr Salter, pointing it at his heart. July couldn't breathe as she watched them, their eyes locked across the small distance separating them, Mick's feet still restless and dancing, Mr Salter's rooted to the spot. Upstairs, classical music began to play on the radio, and for a moment the house was silent but for a progression of light, elegant piano chords and the soft whine of Mick's rubber-soled boots against the floor.

Mr Salter raised his hands in front of his chest, palms facing each other. 'Steady, Mick,' he said. 'Don't be . . . Don't do something you'll regret. Steady.'

Mick didn't respond. Upstairs, strings joined the piano, and the melody soared.

'Put the knife down.' Mr Salter pushed one hand behind his back, shooing July towards the door. She couldn't move. 'Mick, put it down. There's a child in here. Someone's going to—'

July screamed as Mick launched himself at Mr Salter. 'Don't you fucking tell me what to do!' he shouted as the two men fell to the floor at her feet.

'Stop it. Get off him!' July didn't know she could shout so loud, but it made no difference – Mick showed no sign of letting up. She stepped back towards the open door, watching the grunting, writhing horror in front of her, accompanied by the most beautiful piece of music she had ever heard spilling down the stairs from Mr Salter's radio.

As it crescendoed, Mick and Mr Salter rolled towards the kitchen cabinets, leaving a smear of blood on the floor behind them. Whose was it? She couldn't see the knife and couldn't see a wound on either of them. 'Daddy, stop!' she screamed.

It was the last time she would ever call Mick that.

She caught glimpses of the silver blade as the two men grappled with each other, but she still couldn't tell who was holding it until Mick reared up, the knife quite clearly in his hand, and plunged it down into Mr Salter's side as he lay beneath him.

39

1 August 1995

'You're going to kill him!' July threw herself at Mick's back, pummelling it with her fists.

She tried to pull him away, but he pushed her to one side and lifted the knife again. With it raised by his side, and Mr Salter pinned under his knees, Mick paused to wipe his hand across his face, and then, in perfect time with the music, he sank the knife twice more into Mr Salter's body, below his ribs.

'Fucking . . . bastard . . .' Mick muttered as Mr Salter roared in pain, drowning out the rise and fall of the final bars of piano, the music slowing as if taking its final breaths.

As voices on the radio began to discuss the life of the composer whose masterpiece they had just played, July looked around the room for something she could use to distract or stop Mick.

Then she remembered.

She ran out into the garden. Where had she dropped it? She scanned the flower beds as Mr Salter screamed again in the kitchen. *There.*

July picked up the crowbar and ran back into the house.

'Get off him!' she shouted, trying one last time to get through to Mick. 'You're going to kill him.' But he ignored her.

She raised the bar at her side as she stood over the two men on the floor, tasting sand in her mouth.

One last time, she thought. *I need you one last time.*

'I never loved you,' she said loudly and deliberately.

Her mother immediately appeared by her side and grasped July's hand holding the crowbar. 'Never,' her mother said as she helped July bring the bar down, her strength combining with her daughter's to deliver a single blow to the back of Mick's head.

'You wouldn't let me,' July whispered as she waited for the tears that would never come and watched the man she'd spent her life believing was her father slump to one side, then roll on to the floor.

July looked away from him and turned to her mother. But she wasn't there. In her place stood Sylvie, soaked to the skin, her left hand still covering July's right one on the crowbar.

40

HMP Channings Wood
15 January 2002

Dear July,

To answer your questions, I need to explain the situation your mum and I found ourselves in. It's time I told you what happened.

Janine and I sometimes socialised with Maggie and Mick. We had barbecues, shared fireworks in the back garden, walked to the beach together for the New Year's Day swim. Your mum was kind, fun and clever. And she was stunning; I mean, she was the most intoxicating woman I'd ever seen. She had this way about her – a constant smile that made you feel at ease, forced your shoulders to drop; eyes bright with joy and wit; wild hair which danced with the sea breeze. I wondered what might have been, if I'd met her before Janine, and before she'd met Mick. Like I told you in my last letter, I loved her. Even before we spent any time alone.

Janine and I were trying to salvage our relationship, but we argued non-stop. I missed having a laugh with her; I missed the easier times, when we could decide between chicken curry and fish pie for dinner without a shouting match. Loneliness followed me around like a hungry dog. I was aware of trouble between Mick and Maggie too, so neither of our marriages was thriving. That's not an excuse, none of this letter is; I'm simply telling you how it was.

Then one day I was putting the rubbish out and I saw your mum arrive back home. She was crying as she dragged herself out of her car, and it would have been impossible for me to ignore her. I asked what was wrong, and she looked at me with such sadness smeared across her face – I'll never forget it. 'Mick,' she said. 'I'm never good enough.' I slammed down the lid of my bin so hard that the plastic split. I told her she shouldn't put up with it and she replied, 'Neither should you.' Our eyes met over the bloody bins – the setting hardly lent itself to romance. (Ever since, I've not been able to smell rotting fruit without thinking of her. She'd find that hilarious.) Then she said, 'Do you have any Earl Grey? We're all out and I'm gasping for a cuppa.' She liked hers black. Did you know that? Black, no sugar. I remember little things from that day, things that I hold close. For example, she asked me how I got the moon scar by my eye, and I told her how my father kicked me with an ice skate, by mistake, when I was four. We laughed because I had the moon, and she had the stars – you know, the freckles on her face? The ones that looked like a constellation? After the tea . . . You're sixteen, so I'm guessing you know by now how babies are made. It only happened a few times. We both knew it was a mistake.* We both wanted our marriages to survive, or at least I thought we did.

We ended things and kept our distance from each other, only spending time together when Janine or Mick were there too. But it was around then that I started noticing things, and so did Janine. Loud arguments and noises coming from next door, and your mum sometimes trying to hide a bruise or a cut on her face. When Janine told me Maggie was pregnant, I followed her to the beach one day so I could talk to her alone. I asked if the baby was mine; she said the dates didn't work. I've given days of thought to how our lives could have been different if I had questioned that and I'm sorry I didn't. And I'm sorry I didn't help her escape from that house, from Mick. I should have called the police, spoken to her, done something. I worried Janine might guess the reason for my concern, and it made me a coward.

I was there when you arrived, as you know. I delivered you. Janine was at work, Jenny was at nursery, and I was just getting up after a night shift when I heard your mum calling for help. When I got there, there was a lot going on. She was clearly in labour. I asked where Mick was, and she said he had stormed off after they'd had a row. She thought the labour might have been brought on by their argument, and she was worried the stress of it had upset you or harmed you in some way. She told me she had called an ambulance and they were on their way. 'If anything happens to this baby,' she said, 'he'll have her blood on his hands.' He did have blood on his hands in the end, didn't he? But not yours. She had a cut on her face. I assume he had hit her, but I didn't get a chance to ask, everything happened so fast. I told the police all this, but they were never interested; they thought I was trying to get myself out of trouble.

We were trying to get her to the bathroom when you were born, so we were at the top of the stairs. After I cut the cord, she had a little cuddle with you, leaning against the wall, lying on the floor. She kissed you and said, 'Hello, July-bear.' Did I tell you that? Then suddenly she handed you to me – she seemed really panicky, it came out of nowhere – and tried to stand up. But she'd lost a lot of blood. It seemed a lot, but I didn't realise how bad it was until later. I was more focused on making sure you got out okay. When she tried to stand up, she just collapsed and then fell down the stairs. There was no time for me to do anything, it all happened so fast. I promise you, if I could have done something to prevent it, I would have done.

I remember running down the stairs, holding you tight against my chest as you cried, wrapping you in a coat and laying you on the floor next to her. Then I tried to revive her. July, I did my best,

I promise you. I did everything I could think of, I even tried pressing your little face against hers. I thought I saw her lips move when I did that. But then there was nothing. She was gone.

Lots of people arrived in quick succession afterwards. First the ambulance. Then your grandmother, Maggie's mum – she was coming to collect her, she said, once I had calmed her down enough that she could speak. They had planned to go back to her house, because Maggie was leaving Mick. She had come so close to getting away from him. The police arrived next and started asking questions, followed by Mick himself, who began accusing me of all sorts. When they told him that your mum had fallen down the stairs, he accused me of pushing her, said I was harassing her and he didn't trust me. The police arrested and questioned me on suspicion of murder. They released me when the post-mortem found that the haemorrhage killed her, but the damage was already done in the village. The police no longer thought I'd played a part in her death, but nobody else believed that. We should have left then – maybe Janine would have stayed with me if we had – but I was stubborn. I didn't want them to force me out of my own home.

It was hard enough for me, but Janine found it impossible. We grew further and further apart. One day someone accosted her in the shop and asked if it was true that your mum and I had been having an affair, and she came home and confronted me. I couldn't deny it. I assumed she would leave immediately, but she stayed for a few more months. It was Mick who tipped her over the edge.

He had taken you to live with his parents for most of your first year, but then he returned to Almond Drive. He'd shout at me as I got into my car or walked to the shop, ask me how I slept at night, call me a disgrace. Our bin would be emptied over our doorstep at two in the morning, urine sprayed over the front garden, 'murderer' written on pieces of paper I found glued across my car windscreen. The police did nothing. I told them it was their fault for arresting me with no evidence, but they washed their hands of me. Then, one day, he spat at Janine in the street and called her an accessory to murder as she walked Jenny back from nursery. They moved out the next day. Since then she has only allowed me to see Jenny a handful of times.

Does that answer all your questions?

Love,
Dad

PS.
*When I say our affair was a mistake, I don't mean that you were one too. You're anything but. Just because our marriages were failing, we shouldn't have cheated. But if we hadn't done it, you wouldn't exist. I'm so glad that you do and that you found me, and I know Maggie was so happy to be your mum too.

41

1 August 1995

Mr Salter rolled over, groaning. He saw Mick lying on the floor next to him, unmoving, and looked up at Sylvie and July.

'What . . . what did you do?' he asked, grimacing in pain. 'What the hell have you done?' His eyes dropped to the crowbar in their hands. 'Which of you—'

'Both of us,' Sylvie said. Her face was as pale as July felt hers to be.

Mr Salter looked at them for a moment before pulling himself up to sitting. 'Fuck,' he muttered. 'Why would you . . .' He winced as he clutched at a bloody patch on his T-shirt, then turned to Sylvie. 'You her sister?'

July felt Sylvie's fingers tighten over her own. She searched herself for any feelings of fear, remorse or guilt but couldn't find any. All she felt was peace, the still clarity of looking into a rock pool on a sunny day. Did that make her a bad person? She pulled the bar away from her stepsister and let it drop to the floor with a clang.

'I'll say I did it,' July said to Sylvie. 'Nobody has to know you were here.' She looked back at Mick, lying face down on the floor. At the blood trickling from the wound on his head.

'Like hell you will,' said Sylvie as Mr Salter stretched a couple of fingers towards Mick's neck, feeling for a pulse.

He grunted as he rolled Mick on to his side. 'Come on, man, come on.' He slapped Mick's cheeks. 'Mick? Can you hear me?'

July stared at Mick's face. His eyes were closed; he could have been sleeping. Would he wake up? She shuddered as she realised that she didn't want him to.

'Okay . . . okay,' Mr Salter said to himself, taking some deep breaths. 'It's going . . . be okay.' But he didn't sound like he believed it. He sounded like he was freaking out. As he spoke, July felt the grubby walls of the room close in around her. 'I don't think . . . I don't think I can manage CPR.' He tried to kneel up, then collapsed back down on to the floor. 'We should . . . we should call an ambulance. Christ, I think he's dead.'

'How do you know?' Sylvie asked. She sounded unshaken, hardened and pragmatic. Somewhere between five and ten years older than she'd been an hour ago. 'How can you be sure?'

'I've seen a lot of dead people at work,' Mr Salter said, lowering his body to put his cheek next to Mick's open mouth. 'Nothing. He's gone. Jesus . . .' He sat back against the kitchen cabinets, clasping his hands at his side. 'Think,' he whispered to himself. 'Think!' His face was getting greyer by the second. 'You need to go,' he said, closing his eyes. 'Don't tell any—' He screwed up his face in pain. '. . . anyone you were here. Don't let anyone . . . see you leave.'

'Okay,' Sylvie replied for them both and headed for the door. But July hesitated. Could they really do that? She thought of the police detectives on *The Bill*. They'd figure it out, wouldn't they?

Mr Salter pointed up at the far corner of the kitchen counter. 'Pass me that tea towel.'

Sylvie did as he asked. He grabbed the crowbar, dragging it across the floor and wiping it down before holding it in his hands across his lap.

'What are you doing?' July asked, although she knew the answer.

He pressed the towel to the wound on the side of his abdomen, blood soaking through it in an instant. 'You could end up in . . . prison for this. Your mum wouldn't want that. I'll tell them . . .' He shifted his weight, inhaling sharply and grabbing at his side. '. . . I did it. Self-defence.' He arched his back in pain. 'It'll be all right. I'll only get a few years, if that.'

'But if we tell them the truth, they'll see – they might not – maybe we're not old enough—'

'Can't take that risk,' he said. 'You saved my life. He would have . . . would have killed me. Let me do this for you.' He closed his eyes again. 'Get me the phone.'

As July reached for it, above his head, plugged in next to the kettle, he suddenly shouted, 'Wait – no. Don't touch it.' With an enormous effort, he leaned to one side, reached up and grabbed the phone himself, bringing it crashing to the floor.

As he dialled, then asked for an ambulance, July kneeled.

She kissed Mick on the forehead – that kiss she had always wanted from him – and began to sing softly, 'Be thou my vision, O Lord of my heart . . .'

Mr Salter tapped her on the shoulder, and she looked up to see him holding a finger to his mouth. He pointed at the phone.

'They'll hear,' Sylvie mouthed.

July looked back down at Mick and slid her glasses out of his shirt pocket.

'Number 2, Almond Drive . . .' Mr Salter was saying. 'There's been a fight. A man is dead. I've tried, but he's . . . I think he's gone. I'm injured and . . .' He winced again, muttering some more swear words under his breath. As he spoke, he pointed emphatically towards the kitchen unit next to the fridge. July got up and went over to it, and he pointed at the top drawer, nodding for her to open it.

'Come as quickly as you can,' he said into the phone, and, 'Yes, I've got a towel, I'm keeping it . . . under pressure . . .'

Inside the drawer was a bundle of folded pieces of paper, tied together with a length of green string.

'For you,' Mr Salter mouthed.

July shrugged, trying to show him that she didn't understand, but she untied the string and looked through them. There were birds, fish and flowers; all different colours, all perfectly crafted. There was an elephant made of pink striped paper – the same pattern that was on the back of the photo she had of her mother. She pointed at Mr Salter. *You made these?*

He shook his head, trying to smile. She remembered what Sylvie had said she'd overheard Mick saying to Auntie Shell. *My mum did origami.*

Sylvie grabbed July's arm, trying to pull her out of the door. 'We don't have much time,' she muttered in her ear.

Mr Salter held out a hand, indicating that they should wait. 'I've got to hang up,' he said into the phone. 'It's hurting too much . . . I . . . How long will you be?' He nodded, holding up four fingers to the girls. Four minutes. 'No, I can't . . . I'm sorry, I need both hands to hold the towel . . . Just tell them . . . get here as soon as they can.' He put the phone down and looked up at July.

'What are they?' she asked.

'The day you were born . . .' He grimaced, shifting his weight on the floor. He was getting weaker. 'After Maggie had died, after the ambulance came . . . before the police, before Mick . . . I went to get extra blankets for you . . . and found those . . . next to her suitcase. I took them, to remember her.' He paused to take a few breaths. 'Later . . . I . . . I realised that maybe she had made them for you. Your name is on one of them . . . the bear.'

July-bear. 'But why did you keep them?' July asked. Ten years had passed.

'I couldn't return them . . . Mick would have . . .' He winced. 'And they were all I . . . had left of her. After she died I learned

295

how . . .' Mr Salter croaked, lying down on the floor, pointing out of the kitchen towards the staircase, towards his hundreds of birds. '. . . like she was still here . . . teaching me.' He shook his head. 'I'm sorry.'

July clutched the bundle of folded shapes to her chest as he pointed at the back door.

'Go,' he whispered.

'But . . .' She stared at him. There was so much she wanted to say.

Just because she had stopped Mick didn't mean she forgave Mr Salter.

You don't know, she thought. *You don't know what I like in an omelette. What my favourite film is. That when I was seven, I broke my arm in two places.*

Those are the things she would have said to him, and more, if the ambulance hadn't been a matter of minutes away, and if Sylvie hadn't dragged her out of the house. What she wouldn't have said was that all those things were also true of Mick. He had known nothing about her either.

She turned and ran.

42

1 August 1995

Nikki was doing deliveries when she drove past the two girls on bikes and the woman on the pavement shouting for them to stop.

She had been doing this job for long enough to recognise the women who got sent the kind of flowers she had in the back of her van and those who didn't – and the one on the pavement was in the second category. There was something in the way people held themselves: the angle of the chin, the curl of the shoulders. Women who received bouquets from Flowers by Frankie had an air about them, a sure knowledge that they were loved enough to be the lucky recipient of a Peach Perfection or a Floral Fantasy.

But a woman's category could change, Nikki reminded herself as she looked back at the trio in her wing mirror. Hers had, hadn't it? From being the black sheep of the family and the superfluous twin of her adored sister, to the head of her own small clan with a husband so lovely she had to make up negative anecdotes about him to stop her friends cursing her good fortune. She checked her mirror again. Judging by the way the two young girls had thrown their arms around the woman's neck and waist, Nikki would be on her doorstep in years to come with a Mamma Mia or a Make her Day.

The next day she would see the news and realise how close

she had been to the road where the man had been killed, and around the same time it had happened too. It made her shiver. It was all over the TV news and on the front page of the papers. DECADE-LONG FEUD REIGNITED, that kind of thing. Ironic, wasn't it? How she had spent that very moment thinking about love and about the visibly strong bond between those two girls and their mother, while a few streets away there had existed hatred so strong that it had led to murder.

But for now she was oblivious to the death that was to shake the village. She had no idea that she would be on this woman's doorstep sooner than she thought, within the next few days in fact, delivering two bouquets: a Thinking of You and a With Sympathy.

A woman's category could change, sometimes overnight.

On the pavement July and Sylvie clung to Auntie Shell, and she held them close. July never wanted to let go. 'Tell me you didn't go looking for him,' Shell said, panting slightly. She must have run all the way there.

'I'm sorry, Mum.' Sylvie was the first to pull away.

'What were you thinking?' Shell shot a cold look at July, who registered it but did not realise that it would be the last one. That, now Mick was dead, Shell would no longer feel compelled to keep her stepdaughter at arm's length whenever she could muster the strength, just in case her plan failed, and they were separated.

'July wanted to talk to him, and I thought I could help.' Sylvie shrugged. 'Sometimes he listens to me.' July couldn't believe how calm her stepsister was. July thought she was a good liar, but Sylvie's skills were on another level. The words slipped off her tongue like cubes of ice without even a flicker of deceit crossing her face.

After the sisters had left Mr Salter's house, their hearts

galloping in their chests, Sylvie had helped July climb over the fence into the back garden of number 4. 'I've got the house key,' she'd said breathlessly, pulling it out of her pocket. 'It was one of the others on the bunch I nicked from my mum.' It had a tag attached, which read '4AD'. 'I was coming to give it to you. I thought it could help,' she'd explained as they crept through the house. When they were sure the coast was clear, they had left through the front door. They found their bikes in silence and pedalled away from Almond Drive. Just before they spotted Auntie Shell, Sylvie had slowed, so that she was level with July. 'Mick would never have stopped,' she said. 'You know that, don't you? He would have killed Mr Salter. He would probably have killed you too, one day. Or my mum. We had to do it.' July had nodded as a florist's van drove past them.

July relaxed her grip on her stepmother and took a step back. Auntie Shell's face was red and shiny, but soft – she wasn't too angry with them. For a fleeting moment July considered telling her what had happened.

'And? Did you find him?'

July looked at Sylvie and they locked eyes. 'No,' they said together. Sylvie spoke firmly, but the same syllable from July's mouth was a feeble croak. She didn't look for her mother to appear this time. Maggie Hooper hadn't been in Mr Salter's house; she had sent Sylvie in her place. July couldn't say how she knew, but she did, that her mother wouldn't be appearing to her again. Heaven had called her home. And, while July would give anything to have her back alive, she knew she was going to be okay without her visiting angel. She rubbed at the slammer in her pocket, her thumb dragging across the damp metal.

'You're both so pale,' Auntie Shell said, squeezing their cheeks in turn. 'It's these wet clothes. Let's get you home.'

'We heard him though,' Sylvie said a little too loudly.

July shook her head behind Auntie Shell's back. What was Sylvie doing? They'd agreed not to say anything, even to her mum. Something flickered across Sylvie's face – a look of, 'I know what I'm doing'. July turned away from her to watch the steam rising from the wet tarmac in the baking sun, which had reappeared as they had crept out of the front door of number 4 Almond Drive, as if shining a searchlight on them. *It knows*, July had thought, covering her face as she ran to retrieve her bike. *It knows what I've done.*

'We heard his voice inside the house,' Sylvie said. 'They were shouting, him and the other man.'

'Shouting.'

'Yes.'

'We should . . . What if he . . .' Auntie Shell dropped her head into her hands.

July shot another look at her stepsister, shaking her head again, but Sylvie wouldn't meet her eye.

'We called for him to come out, but he didn't hear us,' Sylvie said. 'We should leave them to it. He'll be home soon.'

'I really would like to get you two back,' Auntie Shell said reluctantly, looking in the direction of Almond Drive as if seeking Mick's approval. 'Get you changed . . .'

'I'm pretty cold.' Sylvie rubbed at her bare arms and pulled the damp cotton of her vest top away from her stomach. July knew she was lying – a few minutes in the scorching sun had already dried most of her clothes, and her skin felt like it was burning.

'Come on then,' Auntie Shell said, turning her back on Almond Drive. 'Do you want to ride your bikes, and I'll catch you up?'

'It's okay, we can walk with you.'

Auntie Shell's eyes widened in surprise at her daughter wanting to be anywhere near her, but she didn't say anything.

As July wheeled her bike along the pavement behind Sylvie and Auntie Shell, she heard the distant sound of sirens. Steadily, they got louder, as her heart thudded more rapidly. *They know. They're coming to arrest us.* 'Sylvie?' she said.

Her stepsister turned and gave a slight nod, hanging back to walk alongside July as the noise crescendoed. Auntie Shell stopped, looking up the main village road as a police car and ambulance pulled on to it, lights flashing, sirens wailing.

'Oh God, Mick,' she whispered, the colour draining from her face. 'What's he gone and done?' When the ambulance turned into Almond Drive, she started running.

July looked at Sylvie.

'We didn't go inside,' her stepsister said softly, reaching a finger out to scratch a smudge of dried blood from July's arm, then grabbing her stepsister's hand in hers.

'We didn't go inside,' July repeated, and they walked side-by-side back towards Almond Drive, watching as their mother ran around the corner and disappeared from view.

43

Darling April,

You're here! And you are astonishing. As I write this, you are napping in the sling on my chest. Your pink marshmallow cheek presses up against my skin; your mouth is open, revealing your toothless gums; your little fingers are grasping the silver chain around my neck, squashing the small 'J' hanging from it into your fist. As my pen moves across the paper I sway, as I did for all those months that I carried you even closer than this, rocking you in my belly. Hello, April. I'm so glad we both made it here. I used to think I was immune to worrying but that all changed with you. As soon as I fell pregnant, all I could think about was what happened to your Auntie July's mother. And then I started seeing news stories everywhere about women dying in childbirth. I couldn't bring myself to name you out loud or on paper until you were born – it felt like inviting bad luck into my home, into my womb. But now I sing it to you every day. Prince, Simon and Garfunkel, Ella Fitzgerald – they all knew how beautiful your name was. April Shelley Carver, we first met you on 2 April 2019.

I didn't have time before you arrived (three weeks early!) to write the most important letter of all, the one containing The Truth. It's not just my truth – it is as much your Auntie July's as it is mine. (It was July's idea for me to write to you, by the way. I told her I feared dying without meeting you. She said, write her letters or lists – five things you want to tell your daughter about yourself, that kind of thing. She has always loved lists.)

Ten things I've never told anyone else

1. I saved someone's life once. His name was Rob Salter, and he was your Auntie July's father.

2. But to do that I killed another man, called Mick Hooper. He was my stepfather.

3. I helped July hit Mick over the head as he attacked Rob. One of them was going to die that day, with or without us. I think that is worth remembering.

4. Rob took the blame – he wanted to protect July. He told the jury that he was defending himself, but they didn't buy it. We talked about it once, he and I, much later, only a few years ago. He told me that the jury suspected he wasn't telling the truth – which of course he wasn't, because in reality he hadn't done anything other than let the man into his house. The prosecution convinced them that Rob

had made the first move, threatening Mick with a crowbar because he'd had enough of being harassed. The barrister did a good job of persuading them that if Rob had really been scared for his life, he would have run out of his open back door rather than attack Mick. They found him guilty of murder, and the judge sentenced him to twenty years in prison. He was out on parole after ten.

5. Mick used to beat July and my mother. They didn't deserve it, though they both thought they did. He was that kind of person, you know? He somehow made them love him and hate themselves, forcing them to live in a negative image of their world where everything was reversed. If they'd seen the picture the right way round, they would have saved their hatred for him, and sent their love inwards. They would never have blamed themselves, or thought they were stupid or ugly, or counted themselves lucky that he ever spoke to them. Actually, what am I saying? I hope you know nothing of this type of man. I hope you never meet a Mick Hooper.

6. Love (for my mother, my sister) made me brave. When we brought that crowbar down on the back of his head, I wasn't thinking of how much I hated him; I was thinking of how much I loved them.

7. I nearly went to the police many times, especially in the first year. But how could I? If I

had handed myself in, I would have impli-
cated July too. What would the ramifications
have been? I had no way of knowing. I
couldn't ask anyone, and I was terrified. July
and I never spoke of it, and we still don't. I
realise now that they could have charged us —
we were old enough. Rob reckons we had a
strong defence, but he maintains that he
couldn't have risked it.

8. *I think July felt the same guilt in those early*
   years. We often laugh about being able to read
   each other's minds, but we never speak about
   the pinpoint in time when this psychic ability
   began. In that moment, with the crowbar
   lifted, we became proper sisters. As close as
   twins.

9. *These days I am not sorry for what I did, but*
   I do pity Mick and the way he lived his life
   before he died. A trauma or a cruel figure in
   his past must have turned him into the mon-
   ster I knew. That said, his actions as an adult
   were his own. He could have chosen differ-
   ently. July isn't sorry either. Sometimes she
   grabs my hand in hers and squeezes, and I
   know that is what she is telling me.

10. *I do feel sorry for what happened to Rob*
    though. Handing ourselves in now wouldn't
    give him back the time he spent in prison, so I
    do what I can to repay my debt to him in
    other ways. When he was released, July and I
    found him a flat and decorated it. She used to

make him dinner a couple of times a week when she was home from university in the holidays. During her term time, I taught him to cook, going over to his flat after I finished work. I was with him (he cooked his first perfect omelette that evening) when I got the call to tell me that my mum had been taken into hospital after her stroke. He waited while I sat at her bedside until dawn; he called July for me; he stood at my side in my mother's last moments because July couldn't get there in time. It was Rob who encouraged me to use my inheritance to open the café. I gave him a job in the kitchen. Sometimes customers would glimpse him back there, recognise him and say nasty things, but he never reacted. How did he stay so calm? These days he doesn't work for me any more, but we do family Sunday lunches – him, me, July, your dad, your Uncle Marcus, your cousin Pegs. July and I tracked down Rob's other daughter, Jenny, and persuaded her to write to him in prison and see him when he came out. She has always found it harder to have him back in her life, I think because she doesn't know the truth about Mick's death. Rob wouldn't tell her, and made us promise not to either. But sometimes she comes for lunch on Sundays too. I suppose I've treated him like my own father. You will call him Grandpa. They say you can't choose your family, but I have chosen him to be part of mine.

So, there it is. I hope you have done as I requested with these letters, and have not opened them until both July and I are gone. This information is now yours, to tell anyone you wish.

All my love, always,
Mum x

44

2 August 1995

There was a soft knock on July's bedroom door before it opened a crack. She curled into a ball on the floor and shut her eyes tight.

'Can I come in?' The voice was not one she was expecting.

She opened her eyes to find Yaya's bare, tanned feet in the doorway, her toenails painted turquoise. She looked up to see her grandmother wiggling her fingers by her forehead in their special signal, above a sad smile.

'How come you've been allowed into the house?' July asked, pulling herself up as Yaya sat down on the floor next to her. It was strange to see her there – like June Ackland showing up in Ramsay Street.

'Because he isn't here any more,' Yaya said quietly, pushing a strand of hair from July's face and tucking it behind her ear.

He isn't here any more. The peace that had enveloped July the previous day still hadn't left her. It was strange to think that the Lessons were over; strange to think that she had no idea when someone would next hit her. In the past she had always known that a blow of some kind would come within the next couple of weeks. Three, at most. She knew she should be feeling guilty, but no matter how hard she tried, she couldn't. The older she grew, past this day, into her teenage years and beyond, the more she thought about what had gone on between her and Mick

Hooper, the less sense it made. She had loved him so much. Surely she should have, at the very least, felt some kind of confused *mix* of feelings? Or even a sea of relief, with just a small oil slick of remorse floating on its surface? But no – she felt only lightness, the sense of possibility, of a life wrenched open like a fissure in the rocks Tony told her about – where the pressure had built and built until it had broken apart.

July waited for Yaya to ask if she was okay. That's all Auntie Shell had been saying since they'd watched the police storm into Mr Salter's house the previous afternoon. *Are you okay are you okay are you okay?* July wasn't okay, but not for the reason Auntie Shell thought. She'd barely been able to say a word, too afraid she would blurt out the truth.

'I know he and I didn't always see eye to eye,' Yaya said, smoothing the thin material of her trousers over her knees. 'But I'm sorry about your father.'

'Shell didn't tell you?'

'Tell me what?' Yaya asked. 'She said there was something you'd want to talk to me about but I assumed—'

July took a deep breath as her grandmother spoke and then cut her off. 'Mick wasn't my father.'

Yaya frowned. 'He – what?' She scratched at her cheek, still staring at July.

Her reaction was different to Shell's. When she'd told her stepmother last night, she had nodded and said, 'I always wondered.' She'd heard about the affair a few years ago, Shell explained through her tears.

But from Yaya's bewildered expression, July could see that this was all news to her. She gave her grandmother a moment to consider what she had said, then continued. 'Mr Salter is my father. Not Mick.'

As Yaya pressed at her eyes with her fingertips, whispering, 'What . . .?' and 'Surely . . .?' and 'How . . .?' July looked out of the window. What would be happening to Mr Salter now, she wondered? What had he told the police? And what was she supposed to feel about him? Should she have felt love for him as soon as she found out the truth? Because she hadn't.

Yaya eventually managed to drag a sentence together. 'How do you know this?'

July turned back to face her and prepared the story she had fed her stepmother and the police the day before. 'Mr Salter told me a few days ago,' she lied, fighting the ingrained habit of looking for her mother as she did so. *It's okay. I don't need you by my side.* 'And Da— Mick confirmed it was true. Before he died. Before he went round there.'

'Hang on, let me get this right.' Yaya's eyes were wide, searching around the room frantically as if July's curtains or wardrobe would explain what was going on. 'You've been spending time with him? With Rob Salter?'

Carefully, July continued with her script. 'I went round a few times. He told me things about Mum.' She picked up her hairbrush from the floor and started tugging the knotted hair out of it.

'And you're sure? He's sure that he—'

'Yes.' She rolled the gathered strands of hair into a ball the size of a large pebble and threw it into her bin. Her grandmother's shock was starting to irritate her. 'I thought you were best friends,' July said. 'You said she told you everything. But not this?'

'Oh, Peggy.' Yaya leaned back against the bed frame and fanned her face with her hands, wafting her violet perfume towards July. The previous day's thunderstorms had done little to dissipate the lingering heat in the house. 'We *were* best friends. We were. But this . . . no. I had no idea.'

'None at all?'

'No. I promise.' Yaya turned to face July. 'I would have told you.'

'Would you?' July snapped. She couldn't help herself.

'Of course.' Yaya's brow furrowed. 'Juju, you're very upset right –'

'But you know lots of other things that you haven't told me.' July stood up and moved to the window, where her mother's origami shapes were stacked on the sill. She started laying them out, one by one, in a long line. Outside, she could hear birdsong. A robin or a blackbird. She didn't remember hearing any during her confinement in her bedroom. Or over the last couple of weeks, in fact. Had the previous day's storm caused them to start singing again? Or had the birds too been afraid of Mick Hooper?

Yaya's burgundy Ford Sierra was on the driveway where Mick used to park his van. The police had taken the van, and July wondered if she would ever have to see it again.

After a minute or so had passed, Yaya asked quietly, 'What do you want to know?'

'Was my mum really leaving Mick? The day she died?'

'Yes.' Yaya sniffed.

July laid a blue crane between the pink striped elephant and an orange bear decorated with the letters of her name in gold pen. Her mother had touched these the day she died. Running her own fingers over them was the closest she had ever felt to talking to her.

She turned to look at her grandmother, who – as July had expected – was crying. Behind her, on the bedroom wall which Mick had painted pink, although she'd asked for yellow, tiny rainbows danced as sunlight refracted through Yaya's dangling glass earrings. July couldn't stop looking at them. How could beauty like that co-exist alongside Yaya's pain?

She crouched next to her grandmother, and Yaya took her hand, squeezing it tight.

'She was coming to stay with me,' Yaya said through her tears, mascara smudged under her eyes.

July nodded.

'There's something . . . something I need to explain to you,' Yaya said. 'I know I told you we were best friends, and it's true, we were, but we . . . we weren't actually that close in the last year or so. Did . . . did you know that?' Yaya squeezed July's hand more firmly. 'Did you know we hadn't been talking? I don't know what Mick's told you, what Rob's told you.'

July shook her head, trying to remap the stories she'd heard, the limited comments her grandmother had made over the weeks, months and years. Trying to piece together a different world where her mother was not on speaking terms with Yaya.

Her grandmother continued, 'We didn't get back in touch until a few weeks before you were born.'

'What happened?' July asked. 'I can't imagine . . . I don't understand. Did you have a row? Is that what you're saying?'

'It was Mick,' Yaya said. 'I . . . I didn't like him, didn't like the way he talked to her. The way he spoke about himself and never asked Tony or me about ourselves. The way he'd give your mum these backhanded compliments, then laugh it off if I challenged him, saying he was joking.'

July recognised the person in the portrait her grandmother was painting then saw Mick lying on the floor of Mr Salter's kitchen. She blinked the memory away.

'And the way he looked at her sometimes,' Yaya went on, 'when he didn't know I was watching him – like he was . . . I don't know, like he was jealous of her. Then one day, the final straw . . . he called me up out of the blue, told me I'd upset her, that Peggy was fed up with my "attention-seeking behaviour", something about me embellishing stories I told about my past. He told me he was giving me a friendly "heads up".' Yaya laughed bitterly. 'He asked me not to mention it to her, but I made the mistake . . . Maybe I shouldn't have said anything. Oh God, why couldn't I have just stayed out of it? Left them alone?'

Yaya buried her face in her hands. July stared at her, dismayed. She'd always known her grandmother didn't like Mick, but she'd never known why.

After a few moments Yaya continued. 'I confronted her, about all of it – what she'd said about me, the fact that he'd called me, everything about him that wound me up. She wouldn't see it, wouldn't admit that he was anything other than perfect, wouldn't admit that she had changed, and so I lost it. I asked her, what did it say about her? That she was in love with such an arrogant tosser? Those words will haunt me forever. I was right, but I shouldn't have said it, and it cost me my daughter. Her life, July. It cost her life. I should have trusted her, she said. Let her make her own choices. She didn't speak to me for months afterwards.'

'I can't believe this happened,' July said. 'How could you fall out so badly when you had been so close?'

'You'll learn this,' Yaya said, sniffing. 'The worst arguments you'll have in your life will be with the people you love the most. They're the ones that can hurt you the most.'

Mick's face flashed through July's mind again, and she shook her head to make him disappear.

'There's . . . there's more,' Yaya said quietly.

July steeled herself, closing her eyes. *More?*

'Promise me one thing, Juju? Promise me that if someone ever tries to make up with you after an argument, you'll let them? Don't let pride stop you from healing your own misery.'

'But, I thought . . .' Confused, July tried to remember what Yaya had said minutes earlier. 'But you did make up. She was coming to stay with you.'

Yaya nodded. 'She came to me a couple of weeks before you were born, yes. I couldn't take it any more, being separated from her. We talked and talked, repaired things the best we could. Cried, a lot. But . . .'

'That's what's important, isn't it? You sorted things.'

'No. You . . . you don't understand. She had tried to make up twice before that. I was a stupid, stubborn cow. Mick had got between us, and I was so hurt, I couldn't handle it. I just . . . I thought I'd have more time. If I'd known what would happen, I would have let her in the very first time she came round to patch things up.' Yaya sobbed, wiping her face on her sleeve. 'God, I would even have gone to her myself! If I had, I would have realised what was going on. I would have been able to get her out of there sooner, away from Mick. I'm sorry, July. I'm so sorry.'

'You couldn't have done anything,' July said, wanting to believe it. 'You couldn't have changed him.'

'I could have helped her though. It was my fault that she died.' Yaya reached for July's hand. 'The day you were born, Peggy was packing some things and then she was going to leave. I was going to collect her. She was getting out. But when I came to get her, the police were there. I should have been there months earlier. It should never have happened like that.'

July considered what her grandmother had said. 'But it wasn't your fault. You said . . . Don't you remember, that day I came round to your house? You said it yourself – you blamed Mick. You said he could have prevented her death.'

'I blame him, I blame myself, I blame both of us,' Yaya said. 'I will never be able to prove it, but all that stress, the awful way he treated her, I just know . . . I know in my bones. That's what made her haemorrhage – that's what he . . .' She trailed off. 'But it was me, me!' She smacked her hand on her chest. 'I was the one who should have got her out of there. I was her mother.'

They sat like that together for a couple of minutes, silent apart from Yaya occasionally whispering 'Forgive me' and kissing July's hand. July went over all the new information in her mind, trying to picture her mother at Yaya's door, attempting to make friends. She was proud of her for this, but sad too. Had

314

her mother been desperate for help even then? Why didn't she just ask? Was Yaya right – could her mother's death have been avoided if the two women hadn't fallen out? For a moment she felt a surge of anger pulse through her, the first ill feeling she had ever experienced towards her grandmother. But it quickly passed as Yaya kissed her hand again and again. July knew the agony of feeling responsible for Maggie Hooper's death; she had experienced it too. She had spent days feeling like she was to blame, and still did. Yaya had lived for ten years with that burden – imagine! Ten whole years. July's entire life. And in her heart she suddenly felt her mother asking her to ease Yaya's pain. *I can't do it*, her mother was telling her. *But you can.*

So, finally, July returned Yaya's kiss, bringing her lips to the thin brown skin of her grandmother's palm. 'You did everything you could. There's nothing to forgive,' she said, before turning to look up at the folded shapes on the windowsill. 'Can I – I'd like to show you something,' she said. 'You said you didn't know anything about the notes she left me.' She stood up, pulling Yaya to her feet next to her.

Carefully, her grandmother picked each piece of origami up, turning it in her hands, bringing it to her nose to inhale whatever was left of July's mother. July did the same but could only smell the burned onions of Mr Salter's house.

'Where did you get these?' Yaya asked, her voice hoarse.

July turned the words 'my dad' over in her mouth like a boiled sweet, but they didn't taste right. 'Mr Salter.'

'These aren't notes. I meant what I said – I know nothing of any notes.'

'But you knew about these?'

'Yes. She was always folding paper, especially those last few times I saw her. In those last weeks. Making these for you. I thought Mick had kept them or they'd been lost.'

'Would you like to keep one?' July asked.

Yaya brought her fingers up to twist at the red silk scarf. 'I would love that. Are you sure?'

'You miss her too.'

Yaya nodded, pressing her lips together. 'Your mum used to slip her arm through mine when we walked down the street,' she said, staring out of the window. 'And it was the most ordinary thing, the most everyday thing, nothing special. But my arm aches sometimes, if I let myself think about it too much.' She rubbed the inside of her left elbow.

They stood for a few more silent minutes, looking at the different shapes. July knew that her grandmother was running her fingers across the paper like she was, imagining her mother doing the same thing more than ten years ago.

Eventually, Yaya picked up the butterfly. 'Can I have this one?'

July nodded.

'Why don't you bring these downstairs?' Yaya asked. The tears had stopped, and she was regaining her composure, returning to the version of Yaya that July was familiar with. 'Shelley says you haven't left your bedroom since yesterday.'

'I don't really feel like it.' July kicked at a pile of dirty clothes on the floor. She couldn't handle more questions. *Are you okay are you okay are you okay?*

'It's much cooler down there,' Yaya said, straightening her clothes and moving to inspect her face in July's mirror, wiping the smears of black from under her eyes. 'They've got the doors all open.'

'Maybe in a bit. You go down if you want.'

'I think I could do with a drink. I'll come straight back up, if you—'

'I'm fine, Yaya. I don't need a minder.'

After her grandmother had left the room, July scooped up the origami shapes and laid them out again on the carpet, in a large semicircle around her. She didn't dare unfold any of them in case she couldn't reconstruct them afterwards. She held each one up to the light of the window but couldn't see any writing inside. They weren't messages. These were all her mother had left her.

Miss Glover's words rang through her head: 'I'd like you to think about whether it's important to know where you come from, to work out who you are yourself.' July had spent her life desperate to understand her mother, to know everything about her, so that she could work out who she was and who she might become. But she was tired of chasing a ghost.

One by one, July kissed each of her mother's origami master-pieces and slipped them underneath her winter jumpers, at the bottom of a drawer along with the hand wrap she had stolen from Mick's bag. Standing up, she caught her reflection in the mirror on her chest of drawers. She lifted her T-shirt and ran a hand over the warm skin of her stomach, then closed her eyes. Breathing in, breathing out. She could no longer feel the air whistling – the hole in the middle of her tummy was gone. One day, many years from now, she would explain this sensation to someone after he told her he loved her: how she was sure the hole had not been darned or filled, that it had not been plastered over. It had simply closed up. Everything needed to fix it had already been part of her.

She pulled the pages of paper out of her wardrobe den, found herself a fresh sheet and started writing.

45

<u>Summer project 'Who are you?'</u>
<u>Ten things I have learned about July Hooper</u>
By July Hooper, aged ten years and two weeks

1. She isn't stupid.
2. She isn't clumsy.
3. She isn't useless.
4. She isn't a disgrace.
5. She is brave.
6. She can keep a secret.
7. She *is* like her mother.
8. But she isn't her mother. Or her father. Or the man she thought was her father.
9. July is herself and,
10. that is enough.

Author's note

Thank you for reading this book. I wanted to write about how easy it is for domestic abuse to take place unchecked – how even the best of us can see something troubling but not do anything about it. Perhaps we don't know the victim well or think we might have misunderstood a situation. Maybe we don't want to interfere or are embarrassed about doing so.

Domestic violence or abuse can happen to anyone. It includes physical, emotional and sexual abuse in couples or between family members. It can happen against anyone, and anyone can be an abuser. If you are the victim of domestic violence or worried about someone else, then please reach out for help.

- If you are under eighteen, call Childline on 0800 1111 – any time of the day or night. Whatever your worry, they are there for you. You can also visit www.childline.org.uk for more information or to send an online message.
- If you're worried about a child, contact the NSPCC. Visit www.nspcc.org.uk or call 0808 800 5000.
- Women can call the National Domestic Abuse Helpline run by Refuge on 0808 2000 247 for free at any time, day or night. Or visit www.nationaldahelpline.org.uk
- Men can call the Men's Advice Line on 0808 8010 327 or visit www.mensadviceline.org.uk

- If you identify as LGBT+ you can call Galop on 0800 999 5428 or visit www.galop.org.uk
- To talk about forced marriage or honour crimes, call Karma Nirvana on 0800 5999 247 or visit www.karmanirvana.org.uk
- You can also talk to a doctor, health visitor or midwife.
- For more advice on how to support someone you are concerned about, search online for 'domestic abuse help' for information from the NHS and charities such as Women's Aid.

Thank you

Acknowledgements

I remember the moment I realised how this story would be told.

It was April 2020. My family and I had just returned from our daily allowed exercise – a walk round the block, kicking through cherry blossom. I was reclining in a chair in a darkened room with my milk-drunk baby in my arms. As I drifted towards sleep, July showed up in my mind. *It's you*, I thought. *It's your story.* Immediately, I knew so much more about the novel – including the fact that it must be set in the 1990s.

So, you see, I have to (*grits teeth*) thank Covid. It gave me part of the magic of this novel. I would never have placed this plot so far into the past, had the present not been 'quicksand', as the author Val McDermid has so perfectly put it. I needed somewhere solid to set it; I needed the comfort of childhood memories to escape the horror of the unfolding pandemic. So thank you, Covid-19 (but also, very much, fuck you).

Thank you to the people who helped me to remember life in 1995. Susy Gibbs, I am honoured that you trusted me with your hilarious childhood diary entries. Thanks also to Kate Martin, Andrea Joughin and Sophie Riddell, as well as my old school friends: Linsey Cornwell, Charlotte Taylor, Helen Shepherd and Gemma Gibbs.

Thanks to the authors of my childhood, whose books I revisited: Sylvia Waugh, Jacqueline Wilson, Francine Pascal (and her ghostwriters), Anne Fine and, of course, Queen Judy Blume. Thank YOU if you were one of the people who answered one of my many questions on Facebook or Twitter about things like Flumps, pogs and Body Shop fragrances.

Next up: my gratitude to Victoria Medland, Penny Tate, John Long, Steve Mellen, Tom Aspinwall, Rachel Profit, Leah Edwards, John Downsborough, Alan Ryan and Carol Steel at Wembury Church and Kim Evans-Reid at Plymouth Central Library for all the invaluable help, in so many different ways.

Nikki Soden: thank you for inspiring the very first seed of an idea that became this plot.

Thank you to book bloggers, the Bookstagram community, reviewers and, of course, to all my readers. I cannot tell you how much your kind words and messages meant to me as I wrote this novel (keep them coming – you'll find me on Twitter, Facebook and Instagram!). And to the booksellers across the UK and beyond: I am in awe of the brilliant job you do. It's been a pleasure to get to know my local Bristol shops better over the last couple of years, and I am so grateful for your support, particularly Sam at Max Minerva's, Tom at Gloucester Road Books and Dan at Storysmith.

To Jen Faulkner, Lucy King and Sarah Yates: thank you for taking the time to read my early draft.

Mum and Dad: thank you for feeding my book habit back in the 90s. Sascha, Juliet, Farah, Mr P, Miss F and Mrs B, thank you for looking after and teaching my children while I have been getting these words down on paper.

I am lucky enough to have worked with three of the best editors in publishing on this novel. Jade Chandler, my earliest reader, thank you for pushing me. Thanks for your enthusiasm for this book and for looking after me, despite the incredibly difficult times we all faced. Liz Foley, your help in steering *What July Knew* to its current form was so intelligently and thoughtfully done, as always. And Katie Ellis-Brown, I've been stunned by how hard you have worked with me on this novel, and the passion you've put into it. Thanks also to the team at Harvill Secker and Vintage, particularly Dredheza Maloku, Sania Riaz, Kate Fogg, Anna Redman Aylward, Mia Quibell-Smith, Kate Neilan, Sara Adams, Mikaela Pedlow, Noor Sufi, Beth Coates, Polly Dorner, Sasha Cox, David Heathscott, Hannah Welsh and Dan Mogford. To my agent, Peter Straus, and your team at RCW: thank you for being my books' champions.

Gwen and Bobby, this wasn't supposed to be a book about sisters, but it became one – I can't think why? Thank you for sharing a bedroom so that I can have A Room of One's Own. And finally, Matt: you make all of this possible. Thank you.

Credits

Harvill Secker would like to thank everyone who worked on the publication of *What July Knew*

Agent
Peter Straus

Editor
Katie Ellis-Brown

Editorial
Jade Chandler
Elizabeth Foley
Sania Riaz
Kate Fogg

Copy-editor
Hugh Davis

Proofreader
Alex Milner

Managing Editorial
Rowena Skelton-Wallace
Rhiannon Roy
Sabeehah Saleq
Leah Boulton
Graeme Hall

Audio
Oliver Grant
Han Ismail
Laura Ingate

Contracts
Laura Forker
Gemma Avery
Ceri Cooper
Rebecca Smith

Toby Clyde
Anne Porter

Design
Suzanne Dean
Stephen Parker
Dan Mogford
Kris Potter
Matt Broughton
Rosie Palmer
Lily Richards
Ros Otoo

Digital
Anna Baggaley
Joel Burton
Claire Dolan

Finance
Ed Grande
Jerome Davies

Marketing
Chloe Healy
Kate Neilan
Helia Daryani

Production
Konrad Kirkham

Inventory
Georgia Sibbitt

Publicity
Bethan Jones

Anna Redman-Aylward
Zainab Mavani
Ivan Robirosa

Sales
Nathaniel Breakwell
Malissa Mistry
Caitlin Knight
Rohan Hope
Christina Usher
Neil Green
Jessica Paul
Amanda Dean
Amy Taylor
David Atkinson
David Devaney
Helen Evans
Martin Myers
Phoebe Edwards
Richard Screech
Justin Ward-Turner
Amy Carruthers
Charlotte Owens

Operations
Sophie Ramage

Rights
Jane Kirby
Lucy Beresford-Knox
Rachael Sharples
Beth Wood
Maddie Stephenson
Lucie Deacon
Agnes Watters

Thank you to our group companies and our sales
teams around the world

Emily Koch is an award-winning journalist and author of two previous novels, *If I Die Before I Wake* and *Keep Him Close*. Her debut was shortlisted for the Crime Writers' Association Ian Fleming Steel Dagger Award, won France's Prix du Bureau des Lecteurs Folio Policier, was longlisted for the Authors' Club Best First Novel Award and was selected as a Waterstones Thriller of the Month. She lives in Bristol.

LOVED *WHAT JULY KNEW* AND WANT MORE?

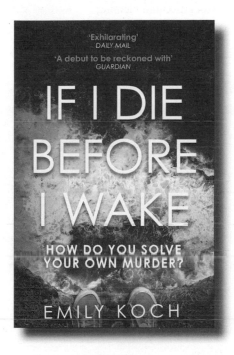

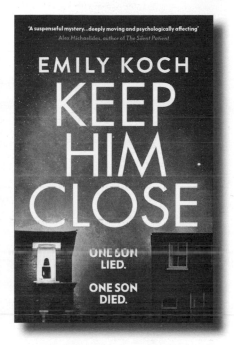

'Utterly compelling'

JO SPAIN, AUTHOR OF *THE CONFESSION*

'Heartbreaking suspense'

GYTHA LODGE, AUTHOR OF *SHE LIES IN WAIT*

OUT NOW IN PAPERBACK, EBOOK AND AUDIOBOOK

**Keep up to date with all things Emily Koch
and subscribe to the newsletter at emilykoch.co.uk**